The helicopters swooped close, heat and exhaust fumes a cyclone around Nickolas. Gabriel and another man holding on at an open door flashed past his eyes.

An arrow of thought pierced Nickolas's mind, trying to force him to the ground. Sheer stubborn willpower was all that pushed Gabriel out this time. Nick arrowed up, attempting to regain some of his lost altitude, but the helicopters forced him to arc over. He tucked his wings, rolling in the air while trying to dredge up some power to form a shield to keep Gabriel out.

Nothing.

He forced his tired wings back out into a glide and dropped closer to the treetops.

Nickolas, this is the end. There is a clearing behind us. You will land there.

NO! he shot back.

The pressure pushing at his mind increased and he lost precious air on a gasp of pain. He tried once again to gain some altitude.

The shots took him by surprise. Two bullets ripped through his wing membranes, causing his wings to falter.

Nickolas, land NOW!

Hissing in pain, he slowed drastically, his flight compromised from the stress of his tearing wing sail. They were slowly forcing him back to where they wanted him.

A careful wing beat, then two. He tried to minimize the ripping. He ducked under one of the metallic sheep dogs just as the sun crested the distant peaks and shot golden rays of light out across the land. The sun dazzle created one more obstacle for him to contend with.

FLIGHT

Sianna Wineland

Publisher's Note: This is a work of fiction. Names, characters, places, and incidents are a product of the author's imagination. Locales and public names are sometimes used for atmospheric purposes. Any resemblance to actual people, living or dead, or to businesses, companies, events, institutions, or locales is completely coincidental.

Flight/ Siana Wineland. -- 1st ed.
ISBN 978-0-9961331-3-5

Dedication

To my children. Who have put up with me mucking around with my stories. And now talk about their own.

Acknowledgments

I want to thank my wonderful editor Kelley Frodel. You helped make this book so much better. I really enjoyed the experience.

Chapter One

Explosions rocked the night. Nickolas Sinclair stretched his wings and raced across the sky, the moonlight turning the dark membrane of his wings pale as it rippled between the struts. The Facility, the place Nick had spent all but the first ten years of his life, blasted into rubble behind him while the sabotage Ian had triggered continued to cascade through the buildings, destroying all of the information Gabriel had sought. The joy of watching Gabriel dive for cover faded as the thought of his grandfather intruded. Cold December night air burned his cheeks and he pumped his wings. Grief needed to wait.

He angled his flight to the north. Away from the rendezvous.

I can't lead the hounds to the others. Lose myself in the foothills? Robin was north.

Jessica's brother had helped keep them out of Gabriel's trap before. His Flight would likely help Nick again.

Lead the hounds to the north. Away from Jessica, away from the rest of his clan.

A cross wind whipped the long, dark strands of his hair across his face, a biting cold that caused a new worry to intrude. There was nothing he could do to keep his people safe from the weather, but if he could ensure that was their only enemy for the journey....

The feel of Jessica's spark slowly pulsed in the back of his mind, and if he concentrated he could trace Christoff's energy as well. A result of the binding with Jessica and the blood bond with Chris, the new sensations unnerved him. He tried to ignore the invasive intimacy.

Chris will keep her safe.

He pushed harder. The longer his head start, the better.

Flight

Clouds scudded across the moon and the trees below turned dark. On a powerful down stroke, his flight muscles seized, clenching in a spasm. A groan escaped from him as he pushed through the pain, unable to maintain his speed. Tonight's hunt for Jessica, followed by the binding, had already tapped his strength. His body did not approve of this abuse.

He cursed his lost stamina, cursed Ian for grounding him.

His last sight of Ian suddenly flashed before him, and his anger translated into the powerful sweep of his wings. His breath caught and he pushed the painful memory aside.

Damn you, Ian.

The sound of Ian's vengeance faded as the miles sped by. He pushed himself faster, the pain a dull throb, his gaze fixed on the horizon. He shook his head then gave a vicious down sweep, refocusing his attention on listening for the sound of helicopters.

A piercing stab suddenly lanced fire through his brain, smoldering arms of invading energy trying to dig their way in. His vision dimmed and he lost altitude as he struggled for control. Gabriel. The more experienced Alpha's mind overwhelmed him. Recklessly, he yanked on his power to weave a crude psychic barrier, allowing him the time to tune his mental wall and hide his presence from the other Valkyrie. Mind finally clear, Nickolas skimmed the treetop, his silhouette racing like Peter Pan's shadow through the patches of moonlight.

A low chuckle whispered across Nick's outer mind. *Nickolas...I know you're out there.* Gabriel's voice sang softly. *You've managed to hide your power signature from me, but not before I got your heading. I have a lot of eyes, we will find you.*

The compulsion to respond to Gabriel gained strength, insidious as it wormed through and tried to control him. He angled up to regain his lost altitude and pushed on. Gabriel's failure in his first attempt to recover him wouldn't delay the helicopters, and the other Alpha was right. They would find him. There was only a short window of time to try and gain distance. He needed to make it to the foothills, where there were fewer roads for a ground pursuit. If he could lose them in the wilderness, he might be able to make it.

Under normal conditions he'd be able to make the flight in a couple of hours, but dodging pursuit and fighting total exhaustion? Suddenly the foothills seemed an awfully long way away.

He climbed higher and traded the safety of the low altitude shadows for a speed-increasing thermal up high.

But in the pressing silence of the night sky, Nick could not keep the memories at bay. His thoughts twisted as his feelings tangled with them. Clenching his fist, he felt the bandage wrapped about his wrist tighten.

Flashes of Ian.

Shaking his head, Nick flapped and rose another hundred feet.

Ian placing the gun to his temple. The familiar green eyes staring into his.

Growling, Nick pushed himself harder, picking up speed. But the exertion didn't do the trick this time. His hand shaking, he rubbed his eyes.

The sight of his grandfather's body slumped over the desk returned to haunt him.

"Damn it, Ian. Why?" he shouted into the night.

His breathing rasped between his lips, but he still pushed the pace, still tried to outrun the memories and the grief that threatened to crush him.

Nickolas ruthlessly stomped the feeling. He didn't have the time to deal with this. Forcing his mind along a different track, Nickolas realized he did have another fact to focus on. He knew Jessica was still alive, even if he didn't know her condition. Part of *her* sat quietly in the center of *him*.

The unnerving nature of the new sensations suddenly seemed like a good mental alternative to the hovering grief. He grasped the waiting distraction and delved into the new pathways through his mind.

The willingness to finally explore opened a mental vista inside him—a dreamscape that he could walk through lucidly—and he realized he'd been here before. He'd found it when he'd tried to use his talents to look for Chris and Donald in the Facility.

The deep well of water rippled with his breath. He studied the pulsing lines that plunged out of sight. Not yet knowing how to read them, this kept his attention for a while as he flew. He plucked at and then concentrated on the lines that *felt* like his brother, traced a mental finger through them. He could feel worry from Christoff, but nothing worse. Relieved, he turned his attention back to his surroundings.

After everything else that had happened tonight, they *had* to be ok.

He pushed the thoughts away.

Clouds covered the moon. The dark towering mass was pushing in from the north. The scent of wet filled his nostrils. Nickolas could feel the cold front flowing down and the warmer air he was riding pushing the cold mass under itself. He shivered a bit, even with all the exertion. Then the distant sound of the helicopters finally reached his ears. They would be on him in a matter of minutes. Scanning the ground far below, he looked for a place to drop down and hide.

Not a lot of cover given the season. Acres of open field spread before him. The forest land was still too distant to reach in time. He veered left, dropping altitude and quickening his pace. A dim light shone ahead and Nickolas arrowed toward it. The thump of the helicopters grew louder.

Flying close enough to the grass that he had to watch out for fences, he skimmed the contours of land into a farmyard then back-winged to a stop beside an old barn. The dim light that had led him here came from an upper story room in the farmhouse. The barn door stood ajar. Nick slid it open and slipped inside. It smelled of summer. Bales of dried grass filled the loft above him, and the cows lowed softly as they shifted nervously at the sudden appearance of a stranger. He pulled the door almost closed and peered through the crack out into the night.

Four helicopters appeared, spread out over the distant horizon. Two of them flew low and angled spotlights on the fields as they passed. In a matter of moments they were over the farmyard, circling around it. One set down in the grass behind the barn. The other three continued on in their search.

"Damn." Nick slid the door shut then spun to look at the interior of the barn. "By morning the whole countryside will know about me."

He scrambled up the ladder to the second floor and peered out the hayloft door, watching the team search the yard. Two of the men went to the door of the farmhouse and knocked while the other two continued to scan the area.

Should be a standard team of six, which means two still in the helicopter. Now what? I can't get into the air without one of them seeing me.

Lights came on in the house. Time was running out. He turned to search the interior of the barn.

Nowhere to hide from the recovery team.

His Sight flashed, graying out his vision. A cellar door. There was a cellar door somewhere in this barn. Leaping down from the loft, Nickolas slowly scanned the area. A faint tugging drew his attention into a back corner. Behind a couple of garbage cans used for grain, he found an old padlocked door. The top of it only came to his waist, the rest hidden beneath the floor. He ran his hand through his wind tangled hair before he realized the floor had a hinged section. He shifted the cans farther aside and lifted the trapdoor.

Descending a few steps, he grasped the padlock securing the door. Nick closed his eyes and felt his way through the device. It snapped open. The metal rasped as he unhooked it, then he pulled the door open, wincing at the slight scrape across the ground. He quickly turned and pulled the cans up to the edge of the steps so they looked more normal, then he entered the dark room and pulled the door shut.

Now, for the hard part.

The door opened out so there hadn't been a way for him to lower the floor section back down. Resting his forehead against the brittle wood, he concentrated on the trapdoor on the other side, though he hadn't had a lot of practice using this talent in the Facility. With a lot of strain, he slowly pulled the floor panel back into place with his mind. The cold and damp settled into him as his warm muscles cooled and he shivered. Then he started on the more difficult task of replacing the lock. Power poured out of him as he worked, a greater dexterity needed to thread the small lock back onto the hasp. He felt like a toddler trying to pick up beads.

After what felt like an eternity, he heard the lock settle on the hasp and he snapped it shut. The rush of power stopped and Nickolas slid to the ground. Fatigue settled like a blanket and he waited, listening.

A few minutes later, the outer barn door scraped on its track.

"Watch out. We know he isn't in the house, so if he's here, he'll be in the barn."

Nickolas heard the grounded whisper and shook his head. They never could understand how much Valkyrie hearing was improved compared to theirs. Footsteps scuffed across the floor. All four of the recovery searchers were in the barn.

Closing his eyes, Nickolas leaned his head against the door and tried to control the tremors invading his limbs as the fatigue and cold set in. In the blackness, the searchers' voices seemed extra loud.

"Nothing so far in the stalls except for cows. Disgusting creatures," one muttered.

The stern voice of the one Nickolas decided must be the leader snapped out, "They aren't the creature you need to worry about, Craig, so stay on your toes." More shuffling.

"I'm not finding anything in the loft."

"You've searched through the hay?"

"Yes, sir. As well as I can. I can't see how he could have gotten too far in by himself, sir. It's too tightly stacked and he wouldn't have had that long to be able to move it."

The leader growled in frustration.

Footsteps came nearer his hiding place and stopped. "Hey, there's a door here."

Nickolas tensed, holding his breath at the sound of the searchers moving swiftly to converge on the cellar door where he hid.

"Yeah, and it's padlocked. You think he locked himself in?" One of them scoffed.

Irritation laced the leader's voice. "Let's go. We need to move on. Gabriel wants us back in the air."

At the sound of the recovery team's departure, Nickolas dropped his head to his knees. His eyes started to mist and he fought the tears back. The events of the evening replayed in an endless loop of snapshots he could no longer push away.

Ian's death.

His parents alive.

His brother carrying Jessica away.

The rest of his Valkyries.

Ian's death. That was the center of the storm. The one solid reality out of all his worries. The one inescapable fact.

Ian was gone.

Wrenching his thoughts back to the present, Nick took stock of his situation. For the moment he was safe, but he couldn't stay here long. The hum of the helicopter filtered through the walls and he relaxed a little more. But every time he closed his eyes, he kept seeing Ian.

The man who had raised him and his brother.

He had never really been their grandfather except during their youngest days. He had been a surrogate parent after their parents died, then leader of their little band of Valkyries at the Facility. Memories of the strange life they had led sped past faster than he could grasp. It was much more of a dichotomy for him than it was for his brother. Chris didn't really remember their life before the Facility. Nick did. He remembered their parents and their grandparents. The house they had lived in. He remembered evening meals and holidays and playing with their dog, Shadow, in the front yard. But most of all, he remembered the pain of their parents' deaths. After all, he had been ten years old when his world had collapsed.

I can't believe you've kept this from us all these years, Ian. I don't know if I can believe you.

Nickolas lifted his head from his knees and let it fall back against the door. "They are not alive. They can't be," he whispered into the darkness. The damp earth of the root cellar had seeped into his muscles, stiffening them.

Flight

I need to get out of here before I seize up. And this is only the beginning.

With a sigh he pushed to his feet and stretched, then he concentrated on the door once more. It took a little longer to get out then it had to get in, but after a few minutes he heard the lock thump to the floor. He pushed the door open. After putting everything back how he found it, he climbed up to the loft where he could get warm in the hay. Tucking himself into a crevice between several bales, Nickolas curled up and pillowed his head on his arms.

Now that they've caught up to me I should let them get ahead before I continue on. I didn't realize just how much flight muscle I had lost during my confinement. I'm much more tired than I should be.

A little over an hour later, he pushed the hayloft doors wide and launched out into the night. Skimming over the fields, he worked his way toward the treed hillsides. He flew low, skirting the woodlands and taking a more circuitous route so he could keep cover nearby. As the hours passed, he found himself forced to the ground more and more frequently by the search. When the moon set, he dropped down to a road to give his wings a rest. The farther north he'd come, the more distance fell between farms and towns, but he was still in too populated a region. Still not far enough into the foothills, let alone the safety of the wilderness. Once into the Cascades proper, it would take a lot more effort for Gabriel to recover him. Lack of roads would help make a difference in evening up the odds.

Dawn was still a few hours off. Nickolas paused on the road to stretch his wings. Slowly extending them, he did a couple of exercises in preparation to take to the air once more. The crunch of gravel on pavement echoed through the trees and he froze. He cocked his head to listen for a second, then with a down sweep to lift him higher, he jumped the barbed wire fence bordering the road.

Scrambling through the thick layer of decaying leaves for several feet, Nickolas leapt again and caught the branch of a large maple. He swung himself up into a crook of the tree and hunkered down against the rough bark of the trunk to watch.

He had barely gotten settled when a line of jeeps running without lights drove past his hiding place. All were equipped with night goggles and scanned the sides of the road. His plan to occupy Gabriel's men seemed to be working better than he'd anticipated. The number of people out looking for him gave him hope that the others were free and clear, even if it did make things somewhat complicated for him now.

The last jeep drove slowly by and Nickolas relaxed against the support of the tree. But as soon as he closed his eyes, he saw Ian again. Swearing, he slammed his head into the bark of the trunk to try and knock the visual out of his mind. The memory of Gabriel's taunting laughter took its place, along with the feel of the other Alpha's mature power. He was a toddler up against a grown man. A snarl slipped past his lips and he leapt to the ground.

He reviewed the play-by-play of his confrontations with Gabriel as he worked his way farther from the road. The finesse and strength the older Valkyrie employed. Nick didn't have the luxury of twenty more years to gain the same level of skill, or more to the point, the ability to surpass him. A growl rumbled in his chest.

After a few minutes of trekking through the trees, he found a clearing large enough for him to get into the air. Once off the ground, he rose to the highest altitude he could maintain for an extended length of time. That would get him out of sight of the ground searchers, but the trade-off made him much more vulnerable to the helicopters. His only hope lay in getting into unpopulated terrain before daybreak.

He needed to reach the foothills of the Cascades.

The terrain skimmed by below. Christoff flew through the moonlight, his wing beats heavy. He pulled Jessica's unconscious body tight to his chest and continued to scan the houses, business districts, and countryside for trouble. A cold wind had kicked up and he tried to keep the emergency blanket he and his brother had wrapped up around her tucked in, but the foil resisted.

Flight

Each wing beat felt heavier than the last as the extra weight strained his flight muscles. *Thank you, Jays, for spotting that weak anchor muscle. If you hadn't insisted on those exercises...* He didn't want to imagine this flight otherwise.

He changed the focus of his search below. He needed a rest. A dark open space resolved itself into an unlit park. He landed in a flurry of wings. Knees buckling from the extra weight, he groaned and set Jessica down in the damp grass near a water spigot. Drained, he just sat for a moment, his arms lying loosely in his lap as the cramped muscles spasmed.

When he could move, he took a careful drink of the cold water out of the faucet. The water chilled him inside as the crisp December air stiffened his muscles from the outside, now that he wasn't keeping warm with exertion. He fished the map Nick had given him out of his pocket and oriented himself in relation to the rendezvous point. Ultimately, worry about Jessica getting chilled pushed him on sooner than his body was ready for. He struck out across the sky looking for the river he needed to follow.

After what seemed like hours, the derelict train trestle that served as the landmark for the rendezvous loomed up ahead, a dark shadow across the ribbon of water. Chris flew along the bank line looking for any sign of the rest of his clan. He landed on the beach where the sand and dirt had been churned up from numerous feet. They had clearly been here, and not that long ago from the wetness of the prints. He walked to the tree line and settled Jessica on a bed of fallen leaves, tucking the blanket around her again, then stretched his muscles.

Donald? Kieran? Hello? He skimmed his gaze over the area. Nothing but the normal sounds of night surrounded him, and Chris swore at how often he'd had to stop to rest. *Donald, where are you?*

He turned another circuit. *Will someone please answer me?*

Silence.

His shoulders dropped in defeat and he slumped down next to Jessica. Little tremors ran over her skin, so he pulled the foil tighter. Then he rubbed his eyes and yawned. *Damn, something must have spooked Donald. Now what?* His back crawled as the muscles ticked annoyingly. Stretching out on the ground, he took several deep breaths and forced his muscles to relax as he considered his options. The need to get back in the air pressed but his body screamed for a rest.

There wasn't sign of a mass recovery, so he didn't feel like the Facility had captured the whole clan, but the recovery teams couldn't be far behind if Donald had pushed them on before he and Nick had caught up.

He pulled his jacket tighter against the wet chill from the river and stared up at the dark tree canopy. *So where do we go? The map led here. Ian mentioned the wild Valkyries were in the mountains. Continue to follow the river?*

He waited until Jessica quit shivering then took her back into his aching arms. A path led to the top of the abandoned trestle and he walked out onto it. Once over the river, he spread his wings and took to the air by dropping off the side of the bridge. A much easier way with the extra weight he carried. He flew below treetop level, following the river's course.

The hours of night blurred together in a fog of fatigue. He would fly until his body rebelled at the added weight, then he'd drop down and rest until he could push on again. Periodically, he called out with his telepathy hoping Donald or Kieran would answer. He'd lost count of the repetitions. Darkness started to give way to twilight blue, and he began to look for an acceptable place to pass the day. His arms trembling, he spotted a huge maple just past the tree line of the river and banked toward it. With heavy wing beats he dropped to the ground and landed hard, smashing to his knees, just barely managing to keep Jess cradled to his chest. *Not much more to give tonight.*

It took a couple of tries until he managed to gain his feet. He stumbled through the trees to the base of the maple he'd aimed for. *Thank God.*

There was a hollow in the immense trunk like he'd hoped. He sank to his knees then bent to let his burden roll from his seized arms. With a groan he forced his arms straight. He looked up and blinked, taking a deep breath, then compelled himself upright. He lurched to the small opening. Darker blackness in the gloom of twilight. Now that he no longer had the drugs muddling his senses, the input from the world around him flooded channels more used to drought than monsoon. All six of his senses concurred that the hollow appeared safe enough. At least no large animals appeared to be using it as a den at the moment.

I hope she doesn't mind bugs, though.

He waved his arm through the opening. The dry, dead fronds of ferns, grasses, and weeds tangled with the fibrous tendrils of the tree. He brushed them to the side so he could inch in and compressed the brittle pile of leaves that had accumulated in the hollow.

His spirits buoyed by the natural warm bed that waited, he crawled out and managed to pick Jess up and get her safely tucked into the hollow. The leaves bundled up around her space-blanket-wrapped form. Backing out again, he used the tree to pull himself to his feet, then rubbed his eyes. On a yawn, he pulled an energy bar out of one of the cargo pockets on his pants and chewed it mechanically as he walked down to the river to get a drink.

The sun had just crested the peaks farther up the range. His mind dull with fatigue, he thought about Donald and worried that he got everyone safe undercover. He shook the water from his hand and remained crouched by the river to watch the pink streaks fade from the eastern sky, and finally faced the thoughts he'd shied away from all night.

Nickolas.

He wondered what had happened at the Facility.

As if thinking about Nickolas conjured him, Chris suddenly became aware of the mental bridge between him and his brother. Attention lit up the twisted strands of spider silk stretched between them in the unknown distance. He tentatively reached out a mental finger to brush the link— and suddenly he was with Nickolas.

He couldn't see what his brother was seeing, but he was aware of Nick's physical and mental state like he never had been before. Total concentration, absolute fatigue, and sorrow all resonated down the link. But the concentration was uppermost. Then a searing blast of pain shot down the link and Christoff reached out to steady himself on the boulders of the bank.

No! Nick! He screamed mentally. He couldn't get a clear idea what was wrong. Only that something serious had happened. He could feel Nick depleting fast. Going on instinct, Chris drew the last of his energy and shoved it into the strands, sending it to his brother. Total exhaustion descended on him.

Please let that be enough. He fell to his hands, his head bowed. He squeezed his eyes shut, a soft growl all that he could manage, knowing Nick fought something...and he couldn't help him.

Sunlight shot through the bare branches of the trees above him as the sun broke over the peaks. He got shakily to his feet and stumbled to the pile of leaves and to Jessica. He crawled into the fluffy bed and curled up next to her unresponsive body. He was asleep before he could finish sighing.

A tinge of pink and lavender had started to outline the clouds beyond the peaks of the mountains as color slowly seeped into the world. Donald's muscles ached from the unaccustomed exercise and extra weight of the net tethered to him. He had been leading all of the Facility Valkyries through the long night, following the river. He pulled his mind away from speculating on what had happened at home after they'd fled Gabriel's takeover. And the worry over his Flight leader and Alphas. The net twisted again, pulling Donald and his other three wingmates bearing it off balance. They flapped awkwardly and Donald barked, "Jays, just quit it already."

Muffled curses and threats drifted up from the suspended net and Donald cast a glance, equal parts sorrow and exasperation, to his younger cousin, Kieran. Neither one of them liked hearing their friend in pain like this.

Flight

His wings straining, Donald grunted when the whole group dropped ten feet from a particularly hard twist Jays managed to give them, and exasperation won out. Jerking the line back in retaliation, Donald snapped, "Jays, knock it off. This is hard enough as it is. You're starting to seriously piss me off."

Obviously the new fledgling couldn't care less because if anything, the struggling grew worse. After needing to slow their speed and drop more altitude, Donald had had enough. "That's it. I'm going to trank you. See if I won't."

"Don't you dare!" filtered up from the suspended net.

The net stilled and Donald grinned at Kieran. His cousin's wings flapped heavily and relief snaked through the younger man's hazel eyes. Donald glanced down at the other Wing in his Flight—the five of them skimmed closer to the surface of the water course they followed—and thought about picking a replacement for his Second. This night hadn't been easy for Kieran. His cousin was still in the middle of stage four of the change and his talent was empathy. *He must be receiving from everyone.* But if Jays cooperated for a few minutes, at least, they could relax and breathe a little easier. *That's better than nothing for now.*

The Wing he'd sent ahead to scout for a resting place large enough for the whole clan had yet to return. His worry grew as the light of dawn made the group visible to possible searchers from the Facility.

They'd fled their home in the Facility not long after darkness had fallen. The night had stretched for all of them. He'd thought they would be able to stay hidden at the rendezvous, but Gabriel tracking their trajectory when Donald had taken the last two Flights out of the Facility had changed that plan. Then the contact who was supposed to help them get to the free Valkyries hadn't answered the damn phone. *Dustin. It can't be a coincidence. That's not a common name. I haven't seen him or his twin, Zach, since before I changed. I suppose it shouldn't surprise me that their family would still have dealings with the Valkyries in some way. Both our families have been devastated by the onset of the change. Gods I miss Zach. I wonder if Kieran heard who our contact is.*

His mind wandered back to the present and he tried not to let regret swamp his thoughts over the need to leave the meet up without his Flight leader or Alphas. *They'll be ok. Nick is back to himself now. Between them they'll find Jessica and stay out of the Facility's hands.*

He hadn't wanted to leave the rendezvous without them. But as the third highest ranked Valkyrie in the clan he couldn't risk the safety of the five Flights, fifty people, under his protection. They'd met up at the river park in Monroe just long enough for Donald to get all ten Wings reorganized into five Flights for the exodus. He'd hoped his Alpha and Chris would show up with Jess, he'd even chanced delaying long enough for a couple of Hunters to sneak into town and get what food for Jays and David, the two fledglings with them, that they could. But then he'd hurried everyone into the air.

Jays had been difficult and restless for the entire night, which wasn't overly surprising from a fledge going into stage two, especially one who had spent all of his time on the other side of the scenario, overseeing the Hub with Ian for years.

A whistle pierced the wind of their passage and Donald saw the five Hunters from the Wing he'd sent ahead to scout fly into view.

They'd located a tree-shrouded grove away from the river that was large enough for them to shelter in for the day, free of choking undergrowth and plenty of soft grass. If everyone stayed out of the center of the clearing, they'd be safe from aerial searches.

His wings labored as he hovered with his three wingmates while they gently lowered Jays into the tattered mist on the ground. The rest of the Valkyries landed around them in the gloom and started to shrug out of their harnesses. Jays feebly clawed at the netting.

"Let me up. Out, I need out. I need to help Ian. Please, why won't you let me help Ian?" Tangling his hands in the net, Jays twisted around, rumpling the foil blankets and tangling the net. Dev rushed forward to hold him prone as Donald and his Wing touched down. They unclipped their tethers.

Jays fought, making a mess of the net, and Dev grunted in his effort. Their former medic was much stronger than his lithe body gave the impression it would be. "He didn't pass out during the flight?" The Flight leader for second Flight stated the obvious.

"We weren't that lucky." Donald helped hold a corner of the mesh. Jays's voice rose as he continued to try and rise from his prone position on the ground. "Jays, settle."

Under the direction of the Seconds, people started to shift the gear under the trees fire brigade style.

"Aidan," Dev barked. "Get that food over here." Then to Donald, "I bet he'll finally go under after he gets a full belly."

The teen, his blond head bobbing through the mist, came running up. "Sorry. I was getting David settled."

"We have to go back for Ian, Donald," Jays repeated.

"Not an option. He ordered us out."

"You don't know what you've left him to," Jays said brokenly.

Kieran started to unlash the net while he and Dev held it straight. "You need to eat, Jays. You'll feel better after you do, trust me."

"Trust you, Kieran? After you helped leave Ian behind too."

Aiden got the first of the cold cheeseburgers unwrapped from the paper.

"Kieran," Donald said, "make sure you eat a couple too."

Donald suppressed a chuckle at the glare his smaller cousin threw at him. *Just like old times. If only Zach were here. Kieran always did hate it when the two of us looked out for him.* Obviously reminding his Second of his fledgling state fell into that category.

Still grumbling Jays fell to the food like a starving man, bolting them down faster than Aidan could unwrap the cold fast food. Donald backed up with Dev and let the two Seconds deal with the fledgling.

Dev at his side they walked across the clearing waving at the other three Flight leaders to join them.

He settled against the trunk of a tree, a groan escaping. The other four flopped down, as tired as he.

Wisps of fog drifted around them through the forest.

"How'd your Wings hold up? Any problems?" Donald asked the Flight leaders.

"Everyone's tired," Van answered.

"My Second had to keep an eye on someone in his Wing who was struggling. Weak flight muscles it looks like. He had to redistribute her load, but she made it." Chelsea pillowed her head on her arms.

"This is the longest any of us have spent in the air," Dev added and ran his hands over his long face. "All things considered, I'm surprised there aren't more strained wing muscles."

"That would be why Ian and Jays got on our case all the time about our phys-ex tests, Dev," Donald added dryly. "We'll need to make sure that everyone has a thorough stretch before takeoff tonight, though. Dylan, I want you to get sentries set up. I also want someone assigned to Jays and David throughout the day, though I'm not worried about David. He's far enough into his change that he shouldn't be a problem. And remind everyone to take their pills."

"Do we know where we're going?" Van, the Flight leader for fifth, asked.

Donald rubbed his eyes with a finger and thumb. "No. I still haven't reached the contact in the phone Ian gave me. It just rings."

"We can't fly endlessly," Chelsea said.

"What are we going to do about food?" Dylan asked. "We have enough energy bars for a day or two, but that won't cut it for the fledges. They need meat and the fast food burgers are almost gone."

Kieran appeared out of the strengthening mist and sank down next to him. "Actually they are all gone. We got Jays and David moved out of the clearing. David's fine, but Jays is sluggish. Unlike when Jessica was exposed to the elements during the start of stage two, Jays doesn't have physical exertion to help his heightened metabolism keep him warm. I had to feed him all of the leftover burgers. He's finally passed out. But he's cold. Too cold."

Dev spoke up. "If we don't get him enough to eat, he isn't going to make it, you know that. And it wouldn't hurt David to have something to eat either. He's not in danger yet, but it's not going to do him any good to go without. Even if you get ahold of this Dustin right now, can they get us help fast enough?"

"I'm open to suggestions," Donald said.

"Deer? They're red meat, aren't they?" Dylan asked.

"Have you ever been deer hunting, buckwheat?" Chelsea snapped.

He glared at her and shook his head. "I don't hear any bright ideas coming from your way, buckweena."

"Knock it off. We're all tired and cold," Donald ordered. "We don't need to be wasting time arguing."

Kieran cleared his throat. Pain lines framed his cousin's eyes, and his fingers absently worried the Celtic knot medallion he always wore. Sure sign to Donald of how much trouble Kieran was still having with the last stage of the change. "I've been thinking about this problem during the flight. Remember that time when you came over for the summer, Donald, and Zach and you had that run-in with Sheriff Tony?"

Donald thought back and smiled a little remembering how much trouble he and his best friend had gotten into. Zach had just smiled and shrugged it off, cocky as usual. Donald's grandma hadn't been as forgiving as Zach's. "Trust a farm kid to think of the obvious. So, boys and girls. Who's up for a little cattle rustling?"

Excitement kindled in their tired eyes and he grinned, then he waved at Kieran to make the explanations.

"I saw several farms bordering the river. If we take a Wing back now, since it's just barely dawn, we should be able to down a steer and get it out of the field before anyone is up to notice us taking out some of their profit."

"How are we supposed to kill a huge cow without a gun?"

Kieran chuckled and it was the first time Donald had heard something so light come from his cousin since he and Chris had taken Kieran off the inhibitor a couple of weeks ago. "The old-fashioned way. We stun it. We don't have a sledge hammer, but we are stronger than before we changed. I think a rock between the eyes should do it. Then a knife to the throat and it's all over. If the entire Wing were to then attach ropes, it would only be one to two hundred pounds to lift, per person. We could then bring it back here and have enough meat not only for the fledglings for a couple of days, but we could all have a good meal as well."

The rising excitement drew the attention of the Hunters nearest them, and Donald saw some of the fatigue erased from their eyes at the prospect of a hunt.

"Ok. Dylan, get the rotations set up. Dev, you're in charge of the hunting party. Kieran, I'll kick your ass if you don't do what he says, got it?" Donald stared hard at his cousin until Kieran flushed and looked down. He could see Kieran still didn't like having a watchdog, but until he'd stabilized and completed the fourth stage of the change, he couldn't be allowed the responsibility of command. A smile touched the corners of Dev's lips at the empath's reaction, and Donald suppressed his own chuckle when he said to the lieutenant, "I needn't tell you to keep everyone out of sight. Be careful and get back quickly. I'll keep trying to call Dustin."

Donald watched Dev lead the Flight of Hunters and one Seer back into the rising mists of dawn before walking over to check on a sleeping Jays.

Chapter Two

Nickolas's breath rasped sharply in his lungs. His speed continued to drop and his wings trembled in fatigue. *Almost there. Those foothills should do.*

His gaze fixed on the pale outlines of his goal, he dredged up more energy from somewhere. The swelling whir of helicopter blades starting snapped his gaze down to the fields far below him. Swearing, he pushed on. The gray haze of dawn had just started to lighten the sky as Gabriel's hounds lifted up into the air. They were much too close for his comfort, especially since he didn't have the advantage of darkness anymore.

Give up, Nickolas. I can see your wings are barely supporting you. I want you alive, not splattered all over the countryside.

The soft persuasive voice flowed through Nick's mind, trying to bend his will. Fatigue was a heavy blanket, but he still managed to push Gabriel out of his mind. It cost him some altitude though.

He risked a glance down.

Finally, the start of true wilderness. He'd passed over the edge of inhabited lands. Every mile gained in flight took him farther away from where Gabriel would have easy ground access to come after him. *You'll have to work for every mile, bastard.*

The *whup* of displaced air popped his ears as the helicopters closed in. Now that he was clearly visible in the growing light, the giant metal machines swooped around him like a couple of demented crows to a hawk.

He swerved and met Gabriel's intense gaze in one of the doorways and wondered why the other Valkyrie didn't come out after him. Then the thought was driven out of his mind because he was diving again.

It didn't take him long to recognize their attempt to herd him. Down and back. Down and back.

The helicopters swooped close, heat and exhaust fumes a cyclone around him. Gabriel and another man holding on at an open door flashed past his eyes.

An arrow of thought pierced Nickolas's mind, trying to force him down. Sheer stubborn willpower was all that pushed Gabriel out this time. Nick arrowed up, attempting to regain some of his lost altitude, but the helicopters forced him to arc over. He tucked his wings, rolling in the air while trying to dredge up *some* power to form a shield to keep Gabriel out.

Nothing.

He forced his tired wings back out into a glide and dropped closer to the treetops.

Nickolas, this is the end. There is a clearing behind us. You will land there.

NO! he shot back.

The pressure pushing at his mind increased and he lost precious air on a gasp of pain. He tried once again to gain some altitude.

The shots took him by surprise. Two bullets ripped through his wing membranes, causing his wings to falter.

Nickolas, land NOW!

Hissing in pain, he slowed drastically, his flight compromised from the stress of his tearing wing sail. They were slowly forcing him back to where they wanted him.

A careful wing beat, then two. He tried to minimize the ripping. He ducked under one of the metallic sheep dogs just as the sun crested the distant peaks and shot golden rays of light out across the land. The sun dazzle created one more obstacle for him to contend with.

Damn it. He retracted his wings partially to help reinforce the weak points and dove through the gap between the two helicopters, erupting out the other side. *I'll be damned if I land where they want me to.*

Flight

He built speed by using a partial stoop and avoided flapping his wings as much as possible. He was still slowly angling down, but at least he was heading farther into the mountains again.

Fire brushed his nerves as the membrane tore a bit more. A gasp whipped away on the wind. *They're right, I have to land. My wings aren't going to support me much longer. I can't spiral down; I'll lose too much ground. I'll have to coast as long as I can before I need to break and drop down into the trees.*

The helicopters surged around him. He narrowed his eyes and concentrated on his wings. The struts vibrated from the force of the wind. Usually, the sail would take the strain and hold the whole structure stable, but with the weakness, he dare not extend them yet.

The smallest correction had Nickolas altering his course, dodging around his pursuers. *Not much longer...* He clenched his fists trying to hold his wings in position through sheer will.

A buffet of wind slammed him and he faltered and felt the membrane tear; pain ripped through his wing again. Fatigue slowed his reactions and he started to fall. A clumsy flail and he wobbled back into position.

Then a burst of energy poured into him and gave him a last push. He jerked and lost control for a second before he recognized the source as his brother. The thread of energy quickly waned down to a trickle then stopped. He had never been more grateful to Christoff in his life. That small burst of energy gave him just enough to keep going, along with the knowledge that Chris was still alive.

One of the helicopters surged in front of him and forced him to spread his wings to break. He yelled as the skin tore more. Gabriel stood in the doorway and met his gaze.

Nickolas felt time pause as he hung there in the air, wide open. He saw the door gunner take aim, but there was nothing he could do.

He was done.

The bullet took him in the shoulder with the force of a sledgehammer; the impact flung him head over heels. It was the last straw. His body finally gave out and plummeted down toward the thick evergreen trees. A scream ripped from his throat as he forced his wings in close to his body. He hoped beyond hope to save them from more damage as he broke through the canopy. He hit the thick evergreen branches with enough force to slam the air out of him, but they did break his fall as he tumbled from story to story. Breaking through the last level, there was a moment that seemed to last an eternity as he fell with no opposition. He crashed with enough force to send him into unconsciousness on the thickly fern-covered forest floor.

With dawn gilding the countryside, Gabriel gripped the doorframe of the helicopter and watched Nickolas crash through the tree canopy out of control. Roaring in outrage, he turned on the man next to him and grabbed him by the throat. He held the flailing man out the door; his gun spun lazily down out of sight. "Give me one good reason why I shouldn't drop you after him! I said the wings. Disable. Disable!"

He threw the man back into the helicopter in disgust and stared down into the lightly waving treetops after his quarry. He reached into his inner web to search for Nickolas's power signature.

There.

Faint, but unmistakable. The pulse of power continued long after he figured Nickolas should have crashed to earth. Now that he was reassured that the other Alpha had survived the fall, Gabriel called to him. *Nickolas? Hey, boy, I know you made it. You can't hope to get help way out here in the middle of nowhere.*

He paused, waiting for some flicker of response out of the downed Valkyrie then snorted in annoyance when he realized that Nickolas was unconscious.

"If you want something done right..." He grumbled as he stalked over to the radio, glaring at the man sprawled on the floor rubbing his throat. Gabriel picked up a headset and held one side to an ear. "This is Gabriel. The target is down. I'm going out after him, over."

"Negative. Negative, Gabriel. Command relays that you are to remain in position. Repeat, you are to remain. Over."

"Listen up, toad, Nickolas just crashed unconscious into thick timber. There's nowhere for the helicopter to land, and ground support is a couple hours hike out from his position. The only way to resolve this scenario quickly is for me to do it."

"The order stands, Gabriel. You are to stay in the helicopter. They are not willing to risk you. That's what you have subordinates for. You are *not* expendable. Base out."

Gabriel turned to glare out the window at the other helicopter. Obviously someone had already informed headquarters about what had occurred. He called up to the pilot and ordered him to circle around and look for anywhere that could possibly serve as a landing place then switched channels to call in ground support. "You heard me! Get the dogs out there, now! The pilot will relay the coordinates. Over."

He threw the headset into a seat. "God damn it, by the time they finally get there, he'll be gone. Can't they figure that out?"

He listened in frustration over the whump of the helicopter as the pilot relayed their coordinates. Gabriel shook his wings out in the confines of the cabin then reached back into his power.

The undefended pulsing of Nickolas's power signature beckoned. *Well, Nick, I know where you're trying to go. So even if we fail and don't bring you in, you'll at least serve the purpose of locating Marcus's stronghold finally. After which, maybe I'll have all of you. That could prove even better.* He considered that strategy for a while until his ruminations were cut short because status reports started to relay in.

Half the Facility was a shambles. Most of the fires had been contained or were out. They were only just starting to sift through the wreckage. The Valkyrie portion of the complex sustained the most damage, with the Hub completely destroyed, along with all of the medical facilities there. No sign yet of any of the resident Valkyries or of Ian and his staff.

Damn it, Ian. Where are you? You won't be able to last more than a week on your own, you know that. And I somehow think you don't want to die like that, or you would have left us for your son before now.

The team he'd sent after the group of Valkyries he'd seen leave the Facility reported that they'd found sign of a gathering of some size in the town of Monroe. *They must have been leaving all day; the Flight I saw wasn't big enough to be all of the control group. They'll be heading for Marcus, but they're too far south. If the whole contingent from the Facility is together, they won't be able to move fast.*

He ordered in reinforcements and directed the recovery group in Monroe to start tracking the fleeing Valkyries. "I don't care how much force you have to use to bring them down, with the two exceptions of Jessica and Nickolas's brother, Christoff. I want *them* alive and as unharmed as possible. And if you don't succeed in that, just ask my copilot what I think of failure."

He dropped into a seat and closed his eyes. Running his fingers through the knots the wind had put in his hair, he briefly thought about his bath at home then turned back to business. *If we can get Christoff, we'll have control of Nickolas. But if we lose all three, we have no leashes at all on Marcus. The rebels will be completely unfettered.*

A little niggling of warning worked its way through his system and Gabriel turned his attention to his web. Diving into it, he searched for Nickolas. When he found no trace, he surfaced. Ice froze all other concerns. He picked the headset up off of his lap. "Attention all searchers, he is on the move."

◆ ◆ ◆

Pain.

The be all and end all.

His whole world revolved around the sensation.

Then, after a while, individual sensations divided the whole and penetrated his awareness. A searing, burning heat. An uncomfortable amount of general stiffness and soreness. The tickling of warm stickiness as it ran down his skin. Throbbing. Always the throbbing.

A scream echoed off the tree canopy, startling birds into flight, when Nickolas rolled over onto his back. His eyes snapped open from the agony, and his awareness returned full force. Instantly alert, he breathed through the pain and looked up through the ferns to the tree canopy far above.

No sign of Gabriel descending after him.

He gave himself a moment to prepare before he gritted his teeth and tried to lever himself up. He collapsed back into the cold dirt when his left arm wouldn't work. Breathing hard, he forced himself into a sitting position and a new flood of warm wetness ran down his side.

He winced when he pulled the fabric away from the wound in his shoulder, too much blood to see anything useful. With his good arm, he slowly, laboriously made his way to his feet.

Groaning, he took stock of himself. It didn't feel like he had any broken bones. A miracle, all things considered.

He swallowed then shifted his wings; better than he had any right to expect. He still had complete movement; it hurt like hell to extend them, but he could do it. Slowly, he bent one, then the other, around in front of himself and examined them closely. The membrane of his right wing sail was torn beyond recognition. Flight was out of the question. He sighed as he slowly furled them onto his back. The rest of his body seemed in working order. Stiff and sore from overuse, but nothing worse.

That left his shoulder. The trauma to it had made it swell and stiffen up to the point that he couldn't move his arm.

A stream gurgled nearby. He stumbled through the ferns until he reached its bank and knelt to quench his ravenous thirst. With his good arm, he cupped his hand in the flow; the cold water slid down his parched throat. When he was done, he thrust his wet hand through his bangs and shoved his loose hair out of his face. He sat back on his haunches and unbuttoned his shirt before taking a deep breath then worked the wet sticky fabric away to expose the sluggishly bleeding wound in his shoulder.

He fished some gauze out of one of the cargo pockets in his pants and used a square, soaked in the frigid stream, to bathe the wound. He craned his neck to look at the ragged hole. Such a small wound to cause so much pain. Fresh blood welled as he gently wiped along the edges, trying to get the fabric out. After he got it as clean as he could, he used his teeth to tear off strips of tape then fumbled them and a wad of gauze over the hole, smoothing the tape down with his working hand. He struggled to pull what was left of his shirt and jacket back on then swayed where he sat from the shooting pain.

Closing his eyes, he took a deep breath before bending over to get another drink from the stream. After he finished, he climbed to his feet, fished out an energy bar from his pocket, and started out at a slow walk.

In a few minutes his body had warmed and loosened up, and he moved into a faster walk, then a trot, then into a ground-eating lope.

He pushed the pain into the back of his mind and concentrated on weaving his mental shield as tight as he could. *I wish I dared try to mind call. I'm not sure how to go about finding the wild Valkyries, but with Gabriel as close as he is, that's probably a mistake.*

As if the other man could hear that thought, Nickolas felt the other Alpha's mind reach out for his.

I can tell you're on the move, Nickolas. Why don't you stop and rest. I can be there any minute with med supplies to help with your injuries. Then you can come home. Your brother would like to see you, Nickolas. And I just got word on the radio that Ian is concerned about you. He wants you to stop and come in. When he heard you were shot, he got very upset. He wants you back where he can take proper care of your injuries.

Nickolas had paused in the underbrush when Gabriel had mentioned Chris, the chance that they caught his brother enough to confuse his thoughts, but at the mention of Ian, pain shot through his heart.

It scattered the fog that had started to form in his mind, and he realized the danger of the lie Gabriel spun. Just a means to control him, trick him into giving up. Ian wasn't waiting for him. He wove his shielding tighter and picked up his pace again. The insidiously compulsive voice slipped through his head anyway, and he did his best to ignore it as he trotted on through the thick undergrowth.

A few hours later, Nick paused to rest when he found another small stream. The rivulet rushed over a small rock wall, creating a soothing noise. He sat on the moss next to the stream and tenderly probed the blood soaked pad on his shoulder.

Heat. Infection. He closed his eyes.

Throughout the day, moving his shoulder even the littlest bit had caused a new leakage and the feel of inflamed tissue around the ragged puncture.

He stretched out to rest, not allowing himself to fall asleep.

Another motor echoed through the trees from above. Gabriel still had search planes flying. He checked the tree canopy anyway, just in case. Sun occasionally broke through the rushing clouds to send thin beams to the floor through the thick branches.

His eyes drifted shut.

The third time he jerked awake, he groaned and rolled to his side and levered himself upright. Stiff, he started the slow process of warming up his muscles again. He tried to ignore the fact that he felt a little like he was floating instead of having his feet planted on the cold earth.

That fact concerned him, but he started walking.

Soon the haze of fatigue and pain created a lens that overlaid his world. The signs of fever started to set hooks into his mind.

♦ ♦ ♦

The snuffling of a wet nose on his hand made Christoff crack his eyes open. The beady eyes of a raccoon stared back at him. The creature lifted its lips, exposing pointy teeth as it backed up a step, hissing. Christoff lifted his own lips and growled back, challenging the little beast to try something. It raised its hackles and advanced a step. Snarling, Christoff rose partially out of the pile of leaves and lunged at the tree opening. The raccoon's eyes widened at the behemoth that had lifted up out of the pile and it screeched, scampering into the forest.

Unreasoning fury shot through his system before he could gain control of it. Before he'd come off of the inhibitor this wouldn't have happened. The strength of their responses, whether emotional or physical, were so strong compared to an unchanged human and that kernel of truth was what the lies depended on and why they had believed them for so long.

He shook with the strength of the desire to give chase. The animalistic instinct overpowering. A growl rumbled in his chest. He closed his eyes and took a deep breath then lowered himself back to the bed of leaves. Their brittle crunching didn't stir his companion.

He brushed away some that had fallen across her pale face then worked his hand under the blanket.

At least she's toasty warm now.

She looked lifeless as she lay in the coma. The rest of the fury drained from his system. He reached out a trembling hand to gently touch her neck. The pulse was slow, but there, matching her breathing.

He crawled out of the small space, tucking the leaves in around her as he left, then he stood and stretched in the gray afternoon light.

There was no sign of the little beast. Not surprising really, but Chris growled anyway with a small return of his previous mood. He stalked down to the river to get a drink and figure out his next step. The silver bullets of fish darted around the rocks, and he stared into the calmly rippling surface. A low buzz intruded on his thoughts. His head snapped up and he scanned the sky.

Rising swiftly, he slid into the shadows of some evergreens near the water's edge. After a moment, a reconnaissance plane skated low over the river. *Damn. Why can't they just give up?*

Flight

The plane cruised slowly along. He moved deeper into the shadows. After the plane had passed and disappeared, he still waited, listening.

I knew I needed to wait until dark, but that sure put the point to it.

His stomach growled; another quick glance at the sky and he slipped down to the water once more, took a drink, then made his way back to the tree. He fished another energy bar out of his pocket to ease his hunger. *I hope I find someone soon. I spent a lot of energy yesterday carrying Jess.*

He leaned back against their tree and wolfed down the bar. His thoughts turned toward his brother and he absently traced the line between them. What he found drove him to his knees. The wrapper crumpled, forgotten in his hand, his eyes blind to the outside.

Pain.

Nick. He hurriedly sorted through the impressions. Hurt, but still running.

He slowed his breathing and centered himself then pushed as much energy as he could spare down the link to help his brother. He released the line reluctantly. *Keep moving, Nick, keep moving.*

He shook his head and opened his eyes. A ray of sun tried to peek through the lowering clouds, but it did nothing to cheer him. This experience of feeling Nick with this new psychic bond reminded him of the duty he still hadn't performed. *I wish I didn't have to do this while she's unconscious. She's probably not going to be too happy about me tying us together when she wakes. I trust Nick though. He felt that it was necessary for her to survive the coma. So I guess I'll survive her wrath. She didn't get her last meal and with how much exposure to the elements her body has gotten having a psychic link to keep an eye on her and hopefully help will be worth it.*

He wormed his way back into the small hollow and pulled the crumbling leaves away from her side so he could sit beside her. He brushed the coppery strands of her tangled hair away from her slack face and just stared for a moment. Then he firmed his resolve and fished her arm out of the foil blanket. He rubbed his thumb across the healed scab that

Nick's power had formed over the slice she'd gotten from the broken glass. Not seeing a better alternative, he pulled his knife and nicked a small segment of the scab, enough for the blood to well and start to slide down her wrist.

He steeled himself and captured the sliding trail with his tongue then sucked a mouthful in from the cut. The quicksilver threaded through him when he swallowed, shocking his system. As he tied her to him, he could feel how much trouble she was in.

The coma required all of her body's resources, unfortunately the link to Nickolas pulsed wide open. And his brother drank down everything she had to give like a desert in the sun.

Energy she couldn't afford to lose.

Damn. Sorry Jess. I'd hoped to at least give you half a choice. But I can only monitor you with a one sided link. I need to do more than passively watch.

No wonder her heart and breathing seemed so slow. He pressed his thumb to the bleeding cut while he fished out a bandage. After he took care of her wound, he slipped his arm under her shoulders and propped her up against his shoulder in a sitting position. Her limp body sagged in his grip, but he managed to nick the half-healed scab on his own wrist until he had a trail of blood that flowed. He let her head fall back and held his dripping wrist to her lips.

He stroked her throat and managed to get her to swallow a couple of good mouthfuls. He could feel a difference immediately. A small smile came and went and he got her tucked back into the blanket and leaves. Her breathing quickened, as did her heartbeat.

He doctored his wrist then burrowed in next to her, curling around her still form. He explored the newly formed link and felt the steady pull she exerted on him. Through her, he could see Nick's steady drain.

I won't be enough to counter that for long, he thought worriedly before falling asleep again.

He woke as darkness descended and then walked down to the river to get a drink, his stomach churning. *I need real food soon. I won't be able to sustain this level of energy output.* He watched the last of the daylight fade from the bank of the river, a cold wind ruffling his hair. The moon had yet to rise.

This'll be the best time to travel. Few, if any, search parties out right now.

He limbered up his muscles, preparing for flight. *I can't remember the last time I was this sore.* He groaned. Once he was warmed up, he uncovered Jessica and maneuvered her out of the hollow in the tree then wrapped her snug in the foil. Clutching her tight to his chest, he forced his resisting muscles to carry them into the air. He soared out, following the ribbon of water once again.

Donald? He waited a wing beat. **Kieran?** No answer.

He growled and studied the river bank as he flew, watching for any sign of his people. A few hours later, scuffing on the bank drew his eye. *It could just be a watering trail for deer. But, regardless, I need a rest.*

He landed in a flurry of wings, breathing hard. The marks were foot prints; he closed his eyes in thanks. Arms aching, he followed the tracks into the woods to a clearing. Underneath some thick evergreen boughs, he gently set Jessica down in the deepest shadows before he scouted around the clearing.

A faint lingering scent of wood smoke clung to the forest. He stretched his cramped arms and read the signs left behind. Dozens of people had walked around the area. *Ok, so Donald got everyone undercover. But a fire?* He crouched and fingered a bit of charcoal mixed into loose dirt. Then he sniffed again, stood, and made his way to the other side of the clearing. An animal had dug up shallowly buried entrails and started to drag them off. *Got it. Good thinking, Don, Jays has to have food. With all the excitement, I'd forgotten he'd started to fledge.*

A soft shushing set him on alert. He spun in the darkness, falling into a fighting crouch, scanning beneath the trees. Pieces of shadow detached themselves from different quadrants around the clearing. Christoff watched as four unknown Valkyries moved slowly and silently toward him.

They had entered the clearing in position to surround him. The starlight that filled the open space showed the feral movements of the wild Valkyries. He kept a slow rotation going to keep all of them in sight. His uninhibited senses recognized them all as Hunters. Each remained tense and ready to spring as they stalked him, forcing him to continue to turn, keeping him off balance.

A light-haired Hunter met his gaze. "What are you doing here?"

Chris continued to shift, trying to back out of their circle but having no luck. His dance partners countered each move. He raked his gaze over all of them. "Who wants to know?"

"There're four of us and only one of you. Answer our question," a bulky black-haired Hunter who had the invisible feel of being the leader replied.

"It would take more than four to bring me down," Chris snapped. The feel of a silent conversation passed around him and he flexed his wings.

"You seem too alone." The leader loosened his wings and continued to weave the circle to remain facing him. "I expected you to have grounded back up."

"What the fuck. We were sent out here because we were supposed to get help. What did you do with my people?"

The four froze and a silent exchange whipped by.

"James, call Kevin," one of the others said.

"Already done."

"Who are you?" the leader asked.

He growled at them and continued to rotate. "My name's Chris."

They perplexed him by reducing their aggression slightly. Wings beat the dark, then four shapes dropped feet first out of the sky through the small opening in the tree canopy at the center of the clearing.

His growl deepened and he dropped back into a fighting stance.

"Stand down. That's not Gabriel," the dominant newcomer said. Immediately all the Hunters surrounding him relaxed. He didn't follow suit but met the gaze of the new leader. He didn't feel like a Hunter.

"They thought I was Gabriel?"

The lithe sandy-haired stranger shrugged. "None of them have ever seen him, and you fit the description. Lone, blond, strong. Since we are out searching for all of you, it's not unreasonable to expect Gabriel following in their wake. However, why are you alone? Where's everyone else? I'm Kevin, Caster Prime of Aurora. I was there in Bellingham when you and Nick were set up."

The fighting happened so fast that he didn't recall the Caster. "I'm not alone, I have Jessica. And I wish to hell I knew where everyone was. I've been trying to catch up."

"Jessica? Where?"

"Over here." He led them to where he had laid her down. He crouched and brushed the hair away from her face.

"What happened?" Kevin asked.

"She's in the coma. But I think she's having trouble. She doesn't feel right; I haven't been off of the inhibitor for very long and don't know how to interpret these new senses."

"Come on. We need to get her to Beth. Dusty."

Kevin moved out into the clearing as the other Hunter stepped forward to pick up Jessica, and Chris reacted to the stranger instinctively. He growled and mantled his wings until the other Valkyrie backed up. He didn't want anyone else near her. The pack instinct took him by surprise. She was his to protect. His new Alpha. He'd gotten a taste of the stronger nature of the clan bonds when he and Nick met up with Robin's Flight outside of Bellingham, but that was nothing to what he experienced now. They had been aware of the instinct even in the Hub, but the pale, watered-down version resulting from the inhibitor hadn't prepared him for the full thing. The instinct stemmed from the need to establish the balance of hierarchy and dominance. Meeting up with someone outside of their own pack...clan, the need to establish status instinctively pushed them. Yet another kernel of truth used to support the lies they had been taught. The Hunter shook his head at Chris's lack of control.

Chris pulled her into his sore arms then followed the strangers into the center of the clearing where they had already laid out a net. Kevin and three others were buckling on harnesses.

He caught sight of amusement in Kevin's eyes. Obviously the other Hunter knew he didn't want to trust them with her.

"You carried her here all by yourself, Chris? How long were you in the air for?" the Flight leader asked.

Growling quietly, he knew Kevin was right, even if the other Hunter wasn't coming out and saying he shouldn't carry her by himself anymore.

"Come on, Chris. You'll be right there. Put her in the net," he coaxed.

He felt her weight drag at his arms. Getting her to help faster was more important than his desire to not let anyone else near her, and four carrying her would definitely be faster. Besides, if he was being truthful with himself, his body could really use the break.

But who wants the truth, anyway?

He forced himself to put Jessica down into the net and back away. Dusty quickly lashed it shut and they clipped on the tethers. Kevin nodded to him.

He shook out his wings and gave them a quick stretch, then he followed the Aurorans into the air through the break in the trees.

Above the treetops, Chris took his eyes off the swaying bundle that was Jessica and took in the big black clouds racing their way. *How far away are we going?* Chris sent to the silhouettes in front of him.

All the Valkyries shot looks over their shoulders at him, but Kevin was the one to answer. *About three hours northeast. And, Chris, unless you really need to talk to us...please don't use telepathy. Your sendings are too broad and erratic.* Apology laced the words Kevin sent.

His face warmed and he sighed. It wasn't like he hadn't been worried earlier that using his telepathy would be dangerous, but having it confirmed was a little irksome.

As they flew, the weather continued to grow colder. They dropped lower during the flight to stay below the freezing clouds. But his muscles burned. He no longer carried Jessica, but his body still rebelled. No amount of exercise could have prepared him for such lengthy strain.

They'd flown nonstop for a few hours, his eyes never straying far from the swaying bundle the strangers carried with ease. He suppressed a groan when they dropped altitude again, and his muscles protested the need to shift with each down sweep. *I'm gonna have to give in and let them know I need a rest. Before I fall out of the sky.*

But before he could get their attention, they dropped some more, and he noticed lights wavering through the trees up ahead. The descent continued until they skimmed the treetops. A tingle rippled over his skin. He shied to the side, expecting an attack, but Kevin and the others didn't pause in their wing beats.

Out of his element, he followed the Valkyries in front of him. The trees ended abruptly, and they burst out over a large mountain valley. Kevin led them lower still, and Chris saw cabins clustered underneath them, then they were over open grassland. Acres of grass.

About two thirds down the length of the valley, he saw another small grouping of buildings. The Flight angled that way. Lights spilled from the windows in two of them. Kevin led them to the flagstone courtyard the buildings shared, and he and his Flight back-winged to a landing, carefully setting Jessica on the stone just as the first big fat flakes of a slushy snow started to fall.

Chris was at the net and unlashing it before the wild Valkyries managed to get their tethers off. Too cold. The pull on his energy had waned during the flight. He opened his jacket before he picked her up, and her cheek created a spot of chill through his shirt. She hadn't had his body heat to help stabilize her temperature. He looked at Kevin.

The Caster gestured to one of the buildings then preceded him to hold the door open. "I called ahead. Beth will be here promptly."

He followed Kevin through a foyer and another set of double doors into an infirmary. At Kevin's direction, he laid Jessica on one of the tables and got a real blanket wrapped around her. Kevin seemed to know his way around the room; he started to get supplies of some sort laid out.

Chris stroked her cold face and hair. The flicker of her power still pulled on him if he looked close enough. And through both his links, he saw Nick struggling.

His stomach tried to chew through his backbone, and he clenched his fist on the bed next to her to stay upright. *Maybe I'm just too drained and tired. I don't have anything to give you, Nicky, I'm sorry.*

The doors behind him clicked open. "What have we got, Kevin?"

The voice shivered across Christoff's nerves and caused an unknown memory to play through his mind. Slowly, almost against his will, he turned his head. A lovely woman, who looked to be in her prime, with only a few streaks of gray marring her dark hair, strode into the room. The woman's mouth dropped open and her wings fell slack as she stared at him. Her hand slowly rose to her mouth.

"Christoff?" she whispered.

Confused by her reaction, Chris cocked his head, not sure what to do when he saw the tears gather in her eyes.

"You don't remember me? At all?"

The anguish in her whisper pulled at him, but he shook his head, not knowing what else to say.

The outer door opened again and he looked up, grateful for the interruption. But this time *he* stared in shock. The man who walked in stuttered in his step, but he covered it and continued into the room.

Chris felt his jaw slowly drop. He was looking into a mirror. The man standing in front of him, if he were twenty-five to thirty years younger, could have been him. Chris swiveled back to the woman. Now he recognized the strong resemblance to Nickolas. He sank down into the chair next to Jessica's table, shaking his head.

"No."

The man who looked too much like him put his arm around the woman's shoulders. "Christoff..."

Chris cut him off. "Who are you?"

"Christoff, it is us."

Shaking his head, he stammered out, "I don't believe...Ian said..."

"We know what your grandfather told you. There wasn't any choice."

Emotions ricocheted through him. He jerked out of the chair and his wings flared. He paced to the opposite wall and back. *No choice?*

"Bullshit! There's always a choice!" he snapped. The ramifications cascaded through his head. *They left us. Left us with the Facility. To be experimented on…. What if Gabriel had gotten….* He continued his prowl, adrenaline briefly countering his need for food and sleep. *Who else knew and kept this from us?* Then he thought of Nick. *Oh God, this is going to kill him.*

He scrubbed his face with his hands, trying to master the anger, the disbelief, then returned to Jessica. The link between them had flared at his reaction; he took a deep breath and picked up her hand, needing the contact, refusing to look at the two who had abandoned them to the Facility. "Look, I'm exhausted, and I haven't eaten in two days. I can't deal with this right now."

The room stayed silent for a moment before the two older Valkyries slowly approached the foot of the table. His mother cleared her throat. "You called us in, Kev? What's needed? Who's this?"

Kevin answered softly, "This is Jessica."

Her head snapped a look at the Caster, then zeroed back in on Jessica. All business now, she came around the side of the bed and shoved Chris out of the way as she started checking vitals and reactions. "What's happened to her? Is she in the coma? Or something else?"

A little nonplussed at how easily she'd been able to push him aside, he answered her, "Nick said it was the coma. But I don't really know, I guess."

"Ian said she should be getting close. Did she get her last meal?"

"Ian? How would you…never mind. I'll ask him that myself. I don't know, but I doubt she did."

Kevin wheeled a cart up. Marcus stood on the other side of the bed, holding his hand over Jessica's body, his eyes unfocused.

"How long has she been unconscious?" the man who claimed to be his father asked.

"Since the night before last, about six in the evening, I think."

"Right after they released that wave of energy, I'd say?" The deep rumble of his father's voice rolled over him. Unwantedly familiar.

Chris looked up at him. "How did you know about that?"

Marcus looked up, a smile hovering at the edges of his mouth. "I expect every Valkyrie west of the Cascades felt it that night."

He shivered and turned away as Marcus went back to whatever he was doing to Jessica. After a moment, he finally stammered out, "Yes...when...Nick landed with her, she was already out for the count."

"Where is your brother? And the rest of the control group?" Marcus asked as he shifted position down her body, his eyes still unfocused.

His mother, too, stared off into space, holding her hands over Jessica's head. Kevin cast him a sympathetic glance, which he ignored. "Control group?" No one answered him so he continued, "I don't know where Nick is. I was trying to catch up to Donald and the rest. Nick sent me ahead with Jess and went back to the Facility to make sure everyone got out."

"And you let him?"

He slowly raised his gaze to his father's, and after a moment he said, "You have no idea what you left behind."

Marcus blinked then turned back to his task with Jessica.

"I couldn't have stopped him. Not alone," he added into the silence that fell. After a moment, he rustled his wings but forced his body to remain where it stood and watched the two older Valkyries stare blankly. It reminded him of one of Nickolas's episodes.

Beth released a frustrated hiss and came back to herself. "Anything? What is going on? I don't get it."

Marcus shook his head and lowered his arms. "I don't know. Her energy isn't focused on finishing the coma."

He turned inward and did a split second trace; nothing different that he could see. Maybe they couldn't see it? "It's Nick."

Both swiveled and pinned him with a stare. Then his father said, "What?"

He stepped back up to Jessica's side and took her hand. Beth slid down for him. "She's supporting Nick. All her energy is draining down the link between them. Can't you see it?"

"No," Beth said and immediately fell back into trance, scanning Jessica.

"What do you mean, supporting Nickolas?" his father asked.

He shrugged. "I don't know what's happened to him. All I can tell from my link with him, and through the link I have with Jess, is that he's hurt and exhausted. I get the feeling that he's on the run."

"How badly is he hurt?"

"No idea. But knowing Nick's abilities and stamina, I'd have to guess, very."

"Damn, we need to get more people out there." Marcus ran his hand through his hair. "If he's running, then he's alone. We have two groups out there to find."

The outside doors of the building slammed. Chris twisted at the sound and the wave of strength that preceded and turned to defend his vulnerable Alpha. The inner doors crashed open and the Hunter he'd met leading the Flight in Bellingham rushed through. That Hunter may have helped them slip out of the trap Gabriel had set for Nick, but that didn't mean he trusted the stranger or his aggression.

His father leapt in front of him, blocking his defense. "Chris, stand down! There's no threat to you here."

Chris fought his instinct to respond to an obviously strong, aggressive newcomer and made himself step back. His gaze locked with his father's as the older male forced compliance with the strength of his will.

He fell back another step then almost broke free of Marcus's dominance when the Hunter strode to the other side of the table. Chris snarled and turned, and the other's eyes glowed in response to the challenge.

His mother stepped between them, Kevin right behind her.

"Robin," Marcus commanded.

"Marcus, she's my sister."

"Sister?" Chris snarled but was ignored.

"I know, Robin. But unless you want a fight to break out over the top of her, back off. He isn't in control of his instincts."

Robin growled but complied, slowly. His eyes locked on Jessica. "What's wrong with her? Beth, what's wrong with her?"

Chris's mother placed her hand in the middle of Robin's chest before she said, "She's in the coma."

Chris winced at the familiar gesture, a snake of jealousy inching through him.

"Robin, there's nothing you can do for her right now. We need to get her stabilized, and I need you out with the search teams." Marcus addressed Robin, but his focus had never left Chris.

Chris met Robin's eyes. *Looks like he wants to go for my throat about as much as I want his. Must be that sister thing.*

"I'm sorry, Robin," Marcus continued, "but I need you to get six more groups together. It looks like Nickolas is out there alone and likely injured. Kevin's team found sign of the rest of the Facility's Valkyries when they brought Chris and Jessica in. We don't want the trail to get colder, and with the weather starting to turn, there's going to be casualties if we don't get them in soon."

"Yes, sir," Robin said softly. Promise shown in the Hunter's eyes and Chris acknowledged it with a smile. The Hunter turned on his heel. "Kevin?" he called, walking out of the infirmary without looking back.

"I'll get him settled and on the way, Marcus," the Caster said and followed.

Once the doors shut, Chris slowly relaxed. Marcus gave a disapproving look as he moved back to check Jessica again.

I really don't care what you think, you know. Why should I trust any of you? Chris thought with some resentment. He silently watched the two Valkyries work on Jessica, his thoughts and feelings in turmoil.

Chapter Three

Sleet lanced down, soaking the group of Valkyries to the skin. They all could have done without the change in weather. Donald peered through the dark, down at the dim ribbon of river, looking for somewhere safe to land his group. He wiped the ice from his face again and suppressed a tremor.

Donald, he's starting to rouse. I can feel his confusion and pain. We have to get him warmer.

Kieran's mind voice radiated concern, and Donald glanced over at the silhouette of his cousin, who also shivered continuously in the driving sleet. *If we're this cold, Jays is in trouble. The space blanket won't be enough.*

As soon as there's a place to land, he sent back to Kieran.

A Hunter from Dev's Wing hove into view and gestured down. Donald scanned ahead then nodded to him.

A rocky stretch of beach grew in the distance. The rest of the Wings pressed forward, dropping to land amid the stones. The last to arrive, Donald and his team slowly lowered Jays into the waiting hands of the Hunters who unclipped the net from their tethers. By the time Donald was on the ground, they had Jays unlashed from the net. Two Hunters had their wings overlapped above the fledge, trying to deflect as much of the sleet as possible while Dylan struggled to untangle the sodden foil blanket then get him out of the soaked clothes. Dev ran up with drier clothes, and they got the trembling man into them.

"Here, Kieran."

Donald turned away from Jays. Aiden tugged at Kieran's soaked jacket with one hand; in the other he held a change for the empath. Kieran moved sluggishly but got himself into the drier garments, then he let them sit him on the ground and put Jays in his lap. Several blankets wrapped them.

Jays finally moaned softly as some heat started to penetrate the cold.

Dev walked up to him, shaking dark wet hair out of his eyes. "He doesn't look good. I brought the last of the meat for Jays and Kieran. I gave some to David, but he isn't anywhere near this bad, so we thought Jays should have most of it."

"Once Kieran gets him warmed up a little, we'll get it down him. Thanks for remembering Kieran. He's almost through the last stage, but obviously isn't quite done." He shook his wings. "We'll have to go hunting when we stop for the day. We're far enough into the mountains now that I haven't seen any more farms. Go pass the word I want all Flights to keep their eyes open for deer while we're flying. Maybe we can bring something down before we stop."

"Right. How long are we stopped for?"

"Until we get Jays warmed up."

"Ok. I'll pass the word."

Donald watched his long frame stride away as he pulled the phone out of his pocket. He called the number. Still no answer. With a soft growl, he shoved it back into his pocket then shook the water off again before he stepped over to where the two fledglings were huddled in the middle of the group on the ground. He hunkered down and combed Jays's wet hair out of his eyes then met Kieran's gaze. "Anything yet?"

His cousin shook his head.

Donald continued to comb Jays's hair; both of their shivering seemed to be a little less now that they were wrapped up. "Still no answer on the phone. I don't like this."

"Do you think..." Kieran cleared his throat, "do you think Zach's there?"

Donald's hand stilled. "I don't know. I've been wondering. He changed before either of us. I'd assumed he changed in the Hub like we did and had just been sent to the other facility like most of the fledglings. But now...Ian wanting us to contact Dustin, and Dustin is supposed to get us to the wild Valkyries? I'm still having trouble wrapping my mind around the wild Valkyries not being feral all of the time, even though I'm clear of the inhibitor. Too many years of believing a different truth. I'm worried that Dustin isn't answering. He must have been compromised."

"If that was the case, I'd expect someone to be answering the phone anyway, just so they could try and get us back. Instead we're dodging search planes."

Donald exhaled then shook his head. "Doesn't matter. And speculating doesn't change what we need to do. We have to keep trying to find the wild Valkyries. We shouldn't stay here too long. Everyone's getting cold in this rain. We need to get food into Jays and get back into the air."

Kieran tightened his arms around the fledge, rocking him slightly. "Come on, Jays, wake up."

The fledgling moaned again, then he opened his eyes.

Donald unwrapped the chunk of meat and sliced off a small piece with his knife. Jays's unfocused gaze wandered the area before he eventually met Donald's eyes.

Maintaining that look took strength. The once brilliant mind lay shattered behind those eyes. He hardened himself; even knowing the temporary nature of the situation didn't help.

This young man was second only to Ian in the Hub and had patched up or helped through the change a good portion of the Valkyries surrounding him. Donald held the meat up so he could see it. Jays licked his lips.

Donald fed the slice, and Jays bolted it. After a couple more, he managed to hack off a chunk for Kieran, then continued to hand feed Jays until the shivering subsided enough that he could hold it himself. The feral animal gaze turned wary. Water ran down Jays's face to drip off his nose.

As he polished off the last of the meat, the sleet started to turn into real snowflakes.

Jays licked his fingers and focused on the world briefly. "Thirsty."

Someone produced a container and brought water over. After he drank his fill, the new fledge stared around in bewilderment. "Ian? I need to speak to Ian. Where is he, Donald? What's going on? I don't feel well."

This was always one of the hardest parts, especially with someone he knew and respected. He blew out a breath as he studied the younger man. *Amnesia already.* He had a bad feeling about Ian. He didn't think the doctor had planned to walk away when he'd ordered him to evacuate Jays. *I hope I'm wrong. Please, let me be wrong.*

"Ian had us all leave the Facility, remember, Jays?"

Jays looked back at him. "Left? Where's Ian?"

"He's catching up. Gabriel got too close at the end of the evacuation so some of us are scattered. Without Ian, I have no idea where to lead us; you are Ian's Second. You have to know something."

"Dustin. Need to call Dustin."

Frustrated Donald held his temper. "I've been trying. No one answers. Where do we go, Jays?"

"Where are we?" The soggy fledge peered around from the safety of Kieran's arms.

"Ian had us gather in Monroe. I had to leave so we've been following the river ever since."

"Monroe? That's too far south."

"So, north?"

The fledge shrugged and burrowed into Kieran's warmth. "Aurora is on the western slopes of the Cascades and it takes a few hours to fly to Bellingham, I've been told."

Not much to go on. Donald looked at Kieran in exasperation. "Well at least we got a direction, sort of. Get the blankets wrapped around him securely and the net in place. As soon as you're ready, we'll take off. I want to get a few more hours flight before dawn."

Robin crossed his arms and watched his group of Hunters scout the clearing the Facility Valkyries had used yesterday. The sleet had washed away most traces, but they were still able to find some clues. He shook his head, sending water flying. The weather was miserable. The sleet had turned to snow and now the snow was starting to stick. At least the trees here were thick enough that they didn't have to contend with much accumulation yet. Though personally, he thought accumulation would be preferable to the snow that was melting on the evergreen boughs and then falling as an icy rain on the searchers.

After taking his Second's report, Robin waited for his lead Seer to give his insight. He wasn't sure where to go from here if Greg didn't See something. "I hope you or Noah have found something useful. Any physical traces that they left will soon be covered by snow. So it's up to you two now."

"I have a couple of ideas that I would like to try in flight to see if we can get a better bearing on them. At the moment, what I can tell you is that the Prime in charge is anxious about someone in his care and that he's still planning to continue following the river."

Robin shook out his wings. "Good enough, let's fly."

The snow continued to grow worse over the next few hours. Robin did a quick barrel roll to rid his wings of the accumulation. Everyone remained stoic. *We're going to be finding corpses at this rate.* He wiped his eyes and peered at his side of the bank. *They've never been out—how can they have hidden their tracks so well?*

He saw Greg's wing beats falter below him.

Robin, we got something. Both of us are fairly certain that they stopped up ahead.

Finally, Robin thought. He broadcast a call to everyone in his Flight. *Keep alert. The Seers think they stopped here. Let's find the trace, Hunters.* He dropped below the four Casters and two Seers in his Flight and led his group of six Hunters out into a low level reconnaissance.

They skimmed close to the river through the swirling snow, searching. Leslie, Robin's acting Second, yelled excitedly. *Here, Robin! I've got it!*

He called in the entire Flight as he landed on the slippery rocks of the beach, where Leslie stood waiting. The eddying snow and white blanket that softened the large rocks hid any sign, except at one small spot where the river lapped at the bank.

The water saturated the soil and reached a couple of feet up the bank. The wetness continually melted the falling snow, revealing the muddy skids of boot prints. Robin knelt down to examine the tracks. "The deer always do need to come and drink. What do you sense?" he asked Greg and Noah.

"Give us a few minutes."

Robin stood and shook out his dark wet hair, then gestured for the rest of the Flight to join him in the shelter of the trees up the bank to wait for the two Seers. Everyone sat down and made themselves as comfortable as they could. It wasn't long before the Seers joined them.

"They headed north, Prime."

"It's about bloody time. Finally, they're headed in the right direction. Any idea how long ago they were here?"

"An hour, two at most. It's almost dawn now, so they'll stop soon. We're flying faster than they are, so it shouldn't take us too much longer to catch up. And one of the two fledges is leaving a lot of psychic residue."

"Two?" Robin asked surprised. "I was under the impression that the Facility only had two fledglings in residence, and one of them is now in Aurora."

Greg shook his head. "There are definitely two of them."

Puzzled, Robin stood and stretched out his tired, cold muscles, the rest of his Flight following suit. "Well, there's only one way to find out. Everyone ready?"

They took to the air at the edge of the river then turned north and resumed their grueling pace to try and catch up with the Facility Valkyries.

The snow grew brighter as dawn approached, and Robin signaled his Flight to land at the first sign of the larger group.

"Ok, boys and girls, it looks like they've holed up in the copse of trees up ahead. I want the Seers and Casters to hold back, out of sight, and guard our flanks. Hunters, we go in cautiously. I don't know what to expect. They're searching for us, but that's no reason to be stupid. We don't know how they'll react, and they outnumber us, so spread out. I'll approach them first."

Robin waited for his Hunters to disperse silently into the shadows before he started to walk through the snow. Wet slush had filtered through the trees to partially cover the tracks. He kept his wings loose, his senses stretched to the limit. At the first moment he detected movement, he froze.

Two Hunters separated from the tree trunks and flowed to block his path. Robin eyed them. Aggression radiated, even through the inhibitor still muddling their senses, but Robin could sense uncertainty underlying. Interestingly enough, he recognized the young kid as the more dangerous of the two. His hackles rose, but he stood his ground and made them come to him, placing them in the subordinate position.

They fanned their wings and looked at one another before taking a couple of steps in his direction. Good so far.

"Who are you?" the older one asked.

"I'm Robin. We've been sent out from Aurora to search for you." He controlled the eye contact.

The Hunter flicked his gaze to the side and asked, "We?"

"I'll call the rest of my Flight in after I've talked to Ian and know that your sentries have been warned."

The two Hunters exchanged a glance.

"I'll take him, Dev," the young one said.

Robin nodded to the older Hunter and followed the kid. They walked through the snowy forest for a few minutes. "So how old are you?"

"I just turned sixteen."

Robin shot a surprised look at the Hunter's back. "That's young to have just turned."

The kid glanced over his shoulder at him before answering. "No. Young is fledging when you're thirteen."

Robin had to stop his jaw from dropping. To have survived the change at that age... "You've had your wings for three years?!"

"Yep."

"Crap."

"I have better words to call it than that."

I just bet you do. Robin shook his head. This was one to watch. They pushed through some thick underbrush, and when they came out on the other side, the trees were clear of undergrowth, giving the Facility people room to spread out.

The teenager wove through the trunks and around the exhausted people collapsing on the ground, taking Robin toward a group clustered around two nets.

"Donald," his escort called when they got near.

Robin craned his head, looking for Ian. A Hunter kneeling on the other side of one of the nets looked up when the kid called. But then the net pulled away from its contents and Robin gasped in shock. "Jays!"

His friend and contact from the Facility looked almost dead. He sprinted forward, falling to his knees next to Jays. "What's happened?"

The man across from him stared at him in surprise then glanced at his escort. "Aiden?"

"He came up to us in the woods. He said there're others."

The Hunter turned back to him and Robin could see wariness in his eyes, but also hope. "You're from the wild clan?"

"Yes. We've been searching for you. Christoff and Jess are already in the valley. Now, what has happened to Jays?" His temper simmered just under the surface, and he didn't care if the others knew.

"He entered stage two the day we evacuated the Facility. How do you know Jays?"

Another man pushed between him and finished stripping the net off of Jays then laid him gently on the ground. Robin suppressed a growl at the audacity. The stranger didn't outrank him from the feel of his strength so should know better, but Robin couldn't place his caste, either a Seer or Caster. That stayed his hand for the moment, not knowing where he fell in the hierarchy. He turned his attention back to Donald.

"My name is Robin. I'm Hunter Prime of Aurora. Jays was my best friend growing up. He's been my contact with the Facility for years now. He's not looking good."

"No, he doesn't." The Hunter scrubbed his face. "I'm Donald. The flight's been hard. We ran out of food for him earlier today. I was just about to send out a small hunting party, hoping to find some deer. Unless you..."

Flight

Robin shook his head. He hated to dash Donald's hopeful look. "Sorry, we don't have anything on us suitable. But my Hunters are more experienced at wilderness hunting. They'll come back with something faster. If I may bring my Flight in?"

"Please."

Robin cast his thoughts out and called his Flight in. The Hunters swept in then, the Wing of Casters and Seers behind them. He looked around at the muzzled Valkyries; they barely batted an eyelash as his Flight landed around him. His people eyed the larger group cautiously. He exchanged looks with Leslie. *Keep them leashed, Les.*

Yes, Prime.

He didn't know how long before the inevitable clash happened, but he didn't need his own people precipitating it. *Must be the inhibitor keeping them docile,* he mused.

He mentally singled out three of his Hunters and sent them a thought burst explaining the situation. They nodded and took flight again; the others stayed close and watched the Facility Valkyries, sending thoughts silently among themselves.

Robin ignored the mental chatter at first; his Wing didn't know what to make of the strange Valkyries either, but then Robin noticed Donald and a couple others glance up at his people.

Private! he snapped. *They're not all muzzled.*

Donald's gaze snapped to his. But at that moment, Jays started to stir, drawing their attention. His friend pawed feebly at the space blanket surrounding him before opening his eyes to look around, bewildered.

"Robin?" Jays struggled to sit up. "What are you doing here? I must be dreaming, that's it isn't it? The last few days would be so much better if they were a dream." He leaned forward and rested his head in his hands.

Robin squeezed his friend's shoulder and shook his head. "Oh, Jays. You always did have the worst timing, didn't you? Don't worry, you're going to be fine. I won't let anything happen to you. Remember, I promised. I'll get you to Beth, and she'll set matters straight."

"I'm so cold and hungry. I'm always hungry..." Shivering, Jays looked up into his eyes, the lost little boy that Robin remembered so well from childhood.

He brushed Jays's bangs out of his eyes. "We're working on getting you something to eat, but it might take a little time. Why don't you try to get some rest now that you're on the ground?" He pulled the space blankets up around the fledge's shoulders, tucking them in. "I need to talk to Donald, but I'll be back as soon as we have something for you to eat."

He turned and strode away with Donald, out of hearing of the new fledgling. The Hunter stopped on the other side of the cleared area, and his wings drooped with more than weariness.

"Where's Ian? I expected to be dealing with him." Outwardly, Robin forced himself to relax and leaned against a tree trunk to study the Hunter. Inside, he trusted his safety to his Flight to keep watch. The Facility Hunters weren't stupid after all. Donald had several people in position to take him down if necessary. Though, they were subtle about it.

"He wouldn't leave with us. I keep hoping that he left after we did...but I don't hold out much faith of that. The impression I got when he ordered us out was that he didn't plan to leave." The Hunter took a deep breath before his gaze returned to him. "So, what's a Hunter Prime?"

Robin leaned his head back against the rough bark of the tree, not sure what to think about the news about Ian. He really hoped it wasn't true for all of their sakes, but especially for his Alpha, Marcus. "I'm head of the Hunter caste in Aurora. All Hunters answer to me, and I answer to Marcus. I'm also lead Prime. Which means that I rank the other two caste Primes."

Curiosity lit Donald's eyes, and he brushed the snow out of his bangs. "How many are there?"

"Hunters? Or Valkyries?" Robin asked with a small smile.

"Both."

"There's about two hundred Hunters, a hundred Casters, and I think around fifty Seers."

Donald whistled softly. "Three hundred and fifty of you. Wow, I had no idea that many had succeeded in going feral.

There are fifty-two of us, counting the two fledglings. Then there are Nickolas, Christoff, and Jessica."

"Like I said, Chris and my sister were brought in earlier tonight. So you're only missing Nickolas now, and we have search parties out looking for him. As soon as Jays has eaten, we need to get everyone back into the air and headed toward the valley."

"But it's daylight."

"That won't be a problem. We have four Casters with us. They can hide our presence for the flight." Movement drew their attention back to Jays. The fledgling had tried to stand up, but he lost control and toppled over. Two people were trying to coax him back into his blankets, but he was arguing with them.

"I don't like his lack of coordination. I've mentored four new Valkyries over my fledged life, and it shouldn't be this bad. We need to get him into Beth's hands or he isn't going to make it. And that's not something I'm willing to accept."

"I agree. Jays is special to all of us. I'll pass the word that we'll be taking off again."

Inside Robin relaxed; Donald's ready acceptance of his authority made things easier. "Good. If we can get out of here soon enough, I'm hoping to make it back home before dusk."

"We still need to dig a pit to cook the meat in for Jays and David though, before we can leave."

"No. It'll be better for them as is. David is far enough along that he probably won't like it much, but steak tartar will help Jays tremendously." Donald shuddered and Robin grinned. "Trust me."

The snow grew thicker as the day progressed. Dusk now loomed and Robin glanced back over his shoulder through the swirling whiteness. He had gauged his rest stops based on the groups carrying the fledglings, but they were all tired. Robin's wing muscles burned with fatigue. He could only imagine how the control group was holding up.

That topic had engendered a constant hum of conversation during the flight, though he'd made it clear to keep their telepathy narrow and only use bond paths, since a few of the newcomers were no longer inhibited.

The new arrivals had certainly made an impression with their discipline and stamina.

Robin pushed the sixty-four Valkyries, hoping to get home before dark with the weather worsening. A tingle of awareness washed across his senses, letting him know they had passed through the shield protecting the land Aurora claimed.

He felt all those in his Flight exhale a mental breath, and he relaxed with them. A query buzzed at his mind and he answered the Seer in the tower. Truly only a formality, as it would be obvious to those on sentry duty who he was bringing in.

Twilight fell and lights winked on below in the trees. He led the group lower until they skimmed over the last of the treetops and shot out over the village in the south meadow. The upturned faces of his people flashed by as Robin led the refugees across the length of the valley.

In a flurry of wings, he landed with his Flight in the courtyard. They quickly moved out of the way so the Facility Wings had somewhere to land. Robin stepped back as all five Flights touched down in formation, taking up the majority of the courtyard.

As soon as Donald and his group landed with Jays, Robin stepped forward and started untying the webbing before they could get their tethers unclipped and remove their harnesses.

"How is he, Robin?" Donald asked as he unbuckled his harness.

"I don't know yet. He's not coming to this time." Robin pushed the net off of Jays then picked him up, soaking blankets and all.

"Kieran, with us; Dev, get David out and follow us; everyone else get unharnessed and stay put," Donald ordered.

The three of them headed toward the entrance to the infirmary. The doors opened before they reached them and Christoff walked out. Relief flowed across his face.

"Donald. It's about time."

"I can't tell you how glad I am to see you, Chris. I have never appreciated being Second so much until now." He grasped Chris's forearm. "This can all be your responsibility now. Thank God."

Shaking his head, Chris snorted. "That bad, huh?"

"You don't want to know."

Chris held the doors open for them and Robin heard Chris suck in a breath as he passed the Hunter with his burden.

"Jays? Donald, what happened?"

"Too cold, not enough food for the first day of the second stage? I don't know what else it could be. I've done my best, but I'm worried it wasn't good enough."

Robin pushed through the inner doors and made his way to the first available exam table, the other three Valkyries close behind him.

"Jays is tough, Donald. He'll pull through. We won't allow him any other choice."

Robin ignored their conversation and turned his attention to Beth.

Bethany started peeling the foil blankets away from the fledgling. "So what are we looking at?"

"Sixty hours into stage two, coupled with exposure. He's not coming around this time, Beth. He woke up at all the stops we made on the way here. But now, he's too limp. He doesn't feel right."

"We need to get these damp clothes off of him. Jillian, I need you over here."

Robin moved out of the way of the diminutive redhead. The two of them didn't waste any time cutting the clothing off, then getting him wrapped up in a warming blanket. Beth checked his pulse then lifted his eyelids. "Hopefully getting him warmed up will make him come around for a good meal," she said. "Jill, you stay with him. I'll check the other one."

Beth left Jays, and Robin looked up. He'd been so preoccupied that he'd missed when the other fledgling came in. His gaze strayed to the last exam table where his sister lay. Christoff sat by her side, watching him.

Staking his claim.

A snarl rumbled in his chest, which was cut short when Jillian elbowed him in the ribs.

"Not here, Hunter."

"Sorry, Jillie," he muttered. He turned his attention to Beth, who examined the other fledgling.

"So, young man, how are you doing?" she asked, brushing his wet bangs out of his eyes. He sat on the other cot.

"Cold and hungry, but otherwise I'm ok."

She urged him to lean forward so she could get a look at his wings. "How far along are you?"

"I've been at the Facility for about five or six weeks, I think. I was told I was brought in about a week after Jessica."

"Well you don't seem the worse for wear. We'll get you warmed up and fed. You can room with Amanda until we get her a mentor. Kevin and Robin just brought her in a couple of days ago, so she's still sleeping off the start of stage two." She patted David's shoulder then moved on to Jessica's bed. Robin followed her slowly. He wasn't willing to let the new Valkyries push him out, but he was making an effort to not draw attention.

Beth checked her vital signs and frowned. "There hasn't been any improvement, Chris. She's still extremely weak."

Robin's heart skipped a beat. He didn't like the sound of that. He inched closer then felt someone looking at him. He took his gaze away from his sister's face and met Kieran's eyes. He couldn't place the Beta's caste, and the power in his gaze...

Uncomfortable, Robin looked away. He would take Chris's straight forward animosity gladly. It was something he understood and shared.

Chris rested his hand on Jessica's hair and turned his attention on Donald and Kieran. "I want to try something. When I bound myself to her, I noticed an improvement in her pulse and breathing, I want Donald and Kieran to bind with her. I think it could make a difference in helping to get her stabilized."

Robin shot a look at Bethany. She didn't look too thrilled. The worry on her face ratcheted his up another notch. He would go with her judgment. Robin moved closer to the foot of Jessica's bed.

Beth pursed her lips in thought then shook her head. "No. When two fully fledged healthy people form a bond, it's extremely hard on them. I don't know what sort of complications a blood bond would have on a fledgling, let alone a one-sided bond. And she's already lost too much blood, along with the uncertainty of not having her last meal."

"It wouldn't be a one-sided bond."

"She can't ingest anything during the coma," Beth stated, shocked. "It's too dangerous a risk."

Robin couldn't agree more. His sister was unnaturally pale and lifeless. He had seen plenty of Valkyries make the transformation over the years, and none had looked like she did now. Unless they were dead. Fortunately for his peace of mind, he saw her chest rise and fall briefly.

His emotions spiked, then spiraled, and he clenched his fist to keep a check on his baser animalistic tendencies, then whispered, "No."

Chris's gaze flicked to his briefly before returning to Beth. "I can feel what is happening to her. Her energy, her power, is all draining to Nickolas. She isn't keeping enough for herself. I can feel her drawing on my energy. She needs more. It might be all that helps both of them through."

"No," Robin said louder. Christoff's gaze hardened and locked with his. "It's a nonconsensual bond first off, and second, Beth thinks it isn't good for her. She has more years' experience than anyone, other than Ian, in the change."

"Will neither of you listen to me?" Chris snapped. "It doesn't matter how many years of experience she's had. This is new territory, even for Ian. And believe me, I know just how happy not having a say in this will make her. But I know this is the right choice. I will do anything within my power to protect her."

"Then you'll have to go through me."

Challenge bored into him from Chris. "You have no say, Robin. And if you challenge me on this, I will take you down. Trust me on that."

"Stop it, both of you!" Beth snapped.

Neither of them paid any attention to her, and the tension between them rose. Donald and Kieran moved into position to intercept him if necessary and he growled.

"You can't stop us, Robin," Christoff snapped. "As long as Donald and Kieran consent, then they will be binding to her. None of you will be stopping us." Christoff raked Beth with a glare. "She and Jays both belong to us. Never forget it."

Robin loosened his wings in preparation for a fight.

Robin! The mind voice ripped into him.

No!

Robin! Stand down!

No, Marcus, she's my sister!

Robin heard the door slam open, but he didn't dare remove his gaze from Christoff. Donald and Kieran had come to stand between him and Chris, but they seemed to be blocking Chris as much as him, though he didn't doubt that they would help their Wing leader if it came to blows.

"I know she's your sister," Marcus said. "But she isn't one of us by her choice, Robin. Now, *stand down*. I repeat, Prime, stand down or meet me in the discipline circle."

Marcus stepped between him and his adversary. Having no choice, Robin broke eye contact with Christoff and furled his wings. He ground his teeth, but he bowed to Marcus and backed up to the wall. He was still too keyed up to sit though, so he paced the wall.

He felt Marcus study him for a moment before he joined his wife. Frustration welled as the new Valkyries warily surrounded Jessica, and he kept an untrusting eye on all of them.

Marcus cleared his throat. "Chris, can we please talk about this?"

"No." Christoff drew his knife and beckoned Donald closer. "I'm sorry it upsets Robin, but I really believe this is for the best. If she dies, so does Nickolas, and I won't lose either of them." Chris nicked the bottom edge of Donald's wrist. Robin saw blood drip onto the sheet pulled up around Jessica before the Hunter placed it to her lips.

He spun on his heel and stalked along the wall. It was all he could do not to launch himself at them. Marcus knew, because his Alpha turned to pin him with a stare. He growled back.

Donald withdrew his arm and Jillian slapped a bandage on it. Robin flinched when Chris sliced Jess's wrist. He couldn't stop the growl, Beth walked over to him, placing her hand on his arm.

"He may be right, Robin," she said softly. "Nothing else I've tried has made an improvement. I am concerned about the blood loss and how she'll adjust to the multiple bonds while in the coma, but maybe it'll be worth it."

Christoff caught Donald when the Hunter fell to his knees after the first taste. Robin took a step toward them, but Beth's hand held him back. Another moment passed before Chris took Jessica's hand from Donald and laid it on a towel at her side. Christoff's speed increased since Jessica's blood now flowed; he cut Kieran and repeated the whole ritual.

Robin studied the glassy-eyed look on Donald's face as the Hunter sank into a chair. Curious. He'd blood bonded to several people in his sept and in his Flight, and they hadn't had the ritual psychically overwhelm them like this.

Chris caught Kieran.

Beth let go of his arm and rushed to Jessica's side. She checked her vitals while Jillian dealt with her wrist. After a moment, Beth paused to take a deep breath then turned her head to look at him. She smiled.

Shaking from the adrenaline coursing through his system, Robin stepped up to the foot of his sister's table. Color flushed Jess's face as he watched, and her breathing grew stronger.

"It looks like your gamble worked, Christoff," Beth said. "She's improving."

Chris had his hand on Kieran's head. The Valkyrie sat in a chair, bent over his knees. Robin couldn't help but notice that his reaction exceeded Donald's.

"I'm hoping the three of us can keep her monitored and send enough energy to support her. I don't want to have to choose someone she's not familiar with to bond with her. She's going to be pissed enough with the three of us."

"Then I will," Robin said. "If she needs more."

Chris met his gaze and shook his head. "Not happening. If it's needed, it will be one of our own."

"She's my sister," he snarled.

"I don't care. I don't know you."

Robin's muscles all tensed to spring; he barely held himself in check. This just wasn't fair. He had only just got Jess back. Gazes locked. Neither one looked away.

The Hunter smiled, ready to oblige, then said softly, "I expect we'll find ourselves in the ring before too long."

"I look forward to it," Robin replied.

"If you two are done with the posturing and hierarchy testing, we have work to do," Marcus cut in. "There are ten Wings of Valkyries standing out in the snow. I expect they're cold and tired and would probably like to get out of the weather."

Chris brushed his hand over Kieran's hair once more then stood. "Kier, stay here and keep an eye on Jess and Jays. Donald, you're with me."

Robin turned away from Jessica's bed to join Marcus at the door. No expression crossed his Alpha's face. Uncertainty swamped him as he reached out to hold the door for everyone. He'd always known his place with Marcus, but now his true son had returned. Would Marcus even need him anymore?

A seething mess of frustration, anger, and anxiety, he followed the other three out into the snowy courtyard, the urge to hit something roiling.

Darkness had fallen during the time they had spent in the infirmary. The soft snow still drifted down lazily through the lights blazing in the courtyard. The five Flights of Valkyries shivered, waiting for the return of someone to tell them where to go.

"Chris, bring everyone this way. We can get them warmed up and fed while we decide what to do for tonight," Marcus said.

Flight

Robin held back and followed in the wake of the Facility Valkyries.

The wave of heat pressed against Marcus's skin as soon as he entered the cavernous room. The twin fireplaces positioned in the center of the two longer walls of the longhouse could pump out the heat when they were fully stoked. Apparently, tonight warranted such treatment.

He chose a table in the center of the room as all of the Facility Valkyries filed wearily in. Robin closed the door behind them. At first, he thought his Second was making sure there were no stragglers, but then Robin made no move to cross the room and join him.

Marcus waved Christoff and Donald to seats as he pondered his Second. *Robin?*

The young Hunter looked up.

Marcus had never seen him look so unsure before. *Are you ok?*

I think so.

Good. Then get your ass over here. Relief, quickly hidden, flashed through their mind connection. His Hunter Prime was clearly rattled.

Pulling out a chair, Marcus sat. There was nothing he could do for his Hunter at the moment, so he turned his attention to the new additions to their valley.

Primarily his youngest son and his Second. The two Valkyries examined everything warily.

He cleared his throat and the two younger men snapped their attention to him. Marcus could see the first hurdle was going to be a pain in the ass. How to channel their instinctive need to know where they fell in the hierarchy without a lot of fighting? Their unfettered gazes challenged him.

This would be much easier if my father were here already. He'd keep them in line.

Most of the Facility people could be kept separate for a few days. But the Flight and Wing leaders could pose a problem.

Robin hooked a chair with his foot and took his normal position next to Marcus, and Chris's gaze locked onto his Hunter Prime.

"Keep it leashed, Christoff," Marcus said. His son turned back to him, then both of the Facility Valkyries tensed. Raven Sept's Flight leader and his Second appeared in the doorway to the kitchen. He asked with a sigh, "Is this going to be a problem, Chris? Can you hold your people while the food is brought out? Or should I have Raven Sept leave?"

Donald answered as he threw a glance at his Flight leader. "It'll be fine. Most of us are still on the inhibitor. Those of us who aren't just need some time. It's a bit overwhelming."

"I can imagine," Marcus said softly but still kept his attention on Chris. "Let's get some stew into all of you, then if you don't object, you can all bed down in here tonight. Tomorrow we can show you the cabins."

"Object?" Chris snapped.

Marcus let his lips curve. "Well, it is a hard floor. And the cabins have beds. But we would be dividing you all up in the dark."

Donald snorted. "This is a whole lot better than where we *have* slept for the last two days."

"That was my thought, too." Marcus chuckled then sobered. "Chris, until we've had a chance to go over our laws and protocols and figure out what sort of classes we need to set up to teach all of you what the inhibitor kept from you, keep all of your people together and away from ours. Integrating this many new Valkyries will take careful handling."

Christoff and Donald exchanged looks, and Marcus got an uneasy feeling that he didn't have time to explore. Raven Sept moved carefully through the tense strangers, ladling out the thick stew and pouring mugs of hot tea.

Marcus thanked the Hunter who placed a bowl in front of him and watched the famished refugees dive in.

They reminded him of a pack of feral dogs, hunched over their bowls, hooded gazes keeping track of their surroundings.

He scraped up a spoonful of the rich gravy and looked at his son. Chris had grown strong. The photos and videos his father had supplied over the years didn't come close to the reality. The little boy from his memory had to still be in there somewhere. And Nick...

His thoughts shied away from his missing eldest son.

Marcus, should I have Wolf Sept bring bedding here?

He glanced out of the corner of his eye at his Hunter Prime. Robin subtly pointed his chin at the yawning group. Heat from the fireplaces and the warm meal had overcome their guardedness. Some were starting to fall asleep at the tables.

Yes. They won't last much longer.

The soft buzz of close telepathic communication whispered across his senses as Robin talked to Bruce, Wolf's Flight leader.

Donald sopped out the last of the gravy from his bowl with a piece of bread, his head propped on his fist as he chewed and asked Chris, "Where's Nick? What happened?"

Even though Donald was tired, Marcus could see the concern in his eyes. A quick glance at his son showed him there was reason to be concerned. He waited for Christoff's answer, curious to know, too.

"I don't know where he is. It didn't take us long to catch up to Jess; she hadn't gotten far, just on the other side of the slough. She was her usual cooperative self, no surprise there." Chris paused to take a drink. "Remember when we had to pull Nick out of her cell?"

"The glowing?"

"Yeah. As soon as we caught up to her, both of them went feral. Faster than I could believe. To get away from us, she dove out over the water."

Marcus blinked, not sure he heard right.

Donald's head slipped off his fist. "She flew?"

A small smile curled Chris's lips. "Oh yeah. Sent Nick over the edge."

He met Robin's raised eyes then turned back to the story.

Chris toyed with his mug. "She was willing to fly herself to the ground to keep from coming here. Between the two of us, we managed to subdue her in the air, but by that time they'd reached the point of no return."

Understanding dawned and Marcus said, "The wave of power?"

"Yes."

"Do you know if they exchanged blood?" Marcus asked.

"I don't know what they did, but it glowed like a goddamned sun during it. After he landed with her, his wrist was bleeding and he and I shared blood."

"A blood bond. That's what you've done with Jessica, and that's why you can feel Nick, though I'm surprised at the distance. I suspect the bonding between two Breeders is more intense. When did she go into the coma?"

"She was unconscious when he landed with her."

"So the power swell threw her in." His vision grew hazy as he looked inward in thought.

"She hasn't moved. The entire time I carried her." The anxiety in Christoff's whisper brought Marcus back, and his son rubbed between his eyes. "Nick sent me off with Jessica to meet up with you, Donald, at the rendezvous. He went back to the Facility to make sure everyone had gotten out ok. That's the last I saw him."

Chapter Four

Beads of sweat ran down Nickolas's face. The early morning sun turned the snow into a reflective glare. He stumbled to his knees, the pain of his wounds making him blind. He forced his injured arm to move and scooped up a double handful of snow, pressing his face into it. He could barely feel the chill through the fever.

Get up, Nickolas, you need to keep moving.

"Shut up, Ian," Nickolas groaned.

You're almost there. Not much longer now.

"Leave me alone, damn it." He shook the rapidly melting snow from his fingers then climbed to his feet to search through the blinding light of the sun's glare for the next patch of shadows. It was the only respite he had.

He stumbled forward, rubbing his eyes, the action wiping sweat into them and making them sting. The snow was easily a foot deep in the drifts he pushed through, hiding obstacles for him to trip over. He fell heavily against the trunk of a tree and concentrated on breathing through the nausea that had become one with the pain and his soul. He felt the chills starting again.

Nickolas slid down the rough surface at his back and clenched his arms to his chest in an effort to help keep the wracking shivers from tearing the bullet wound more. "You left me, Ian. I don't have to listen anymore." He mumbled through his chattering teeth. Pausing, he waited expectantly.

Silence.

"Ian?"

The nausea hit him hard and he lost the battle. He twisted to the side, expelling the only thing left in his stomach: water. Once the wracking heaves subsided, Nickolas curled up into a ball at the foot of the tree. His head was pounding and his body went through waves of tremors. He lay in the snow, waiting for it to pass, and watched as little puffs of snow dropped from branches above him to plop into the white blanket covering the ground. Power rose up within him, and Nickolas's vision started to gray out. He groaned and squeezed his eyes shut, praying the vision would leave him in peace.

No luck. He felt like he was watching a television screen. One in which he didn't control the remote. In the vision, Gabriel stepped out from behind a tree and crouched down to examine the ground. Nickolas recognized the place. It was where he had last paused to rest. There were blood hounds sniffing the ground beside the Hunter, their handlers standing back a respectful distance. The Valkyrie rose to his feet and called the rest of his team to his side.

A sharp pain pierced Nickolas's shoulder and brought him back to his surroundings. The vision evaporated like mist in the sun and he blinked his eyes. He wasn't sure what had aggravated his wound, but it felt like someone had pushed him in the shoulder. *I must have rolled on it*, he thought. *At least it stopped the vision.* He tried to sit up. After a couple of attempts, he succeeded, his head swimming. The whisper of Ian's voice drifted through his mind again. *Come on, Nicky, you must get up.*

He refused to respond to the hallucination. The infection from his wound was spreading; he was burning up from fever. He gripped the rough bark of the tree with his good hand and pulled himself to his feet. Sheer stubborn will forced him to place one foot in front of the other.

Go left, Nicky.

Nickolas veered to the left and gave in to his insanity. "Why did you have to do it, Ian?" He skirted around a clump of bushes then shook his matted hair out of his eyes. "Why am I even asking you that? You're just a figment of my imagination, a fever dream."

Get ready, here comes another one, Nicky.

Flight

Nickolas dropped to his knees in preparation and clenched his teeth. This time there was a flash of light behind his eyes before he was somewhere else.

Blood painted the walls. The metallic scent clogged his nose and coated his tongue. The echoes of screams still reverberated in his ears like they had off the walls, though the hall was now silent. As silent as the twisted body on the floor before him.

"On your knees, Gabriel." The command rang across the speakers, accompanied by the distant sound of booted feet.

Mist swirled and he faced a prune-mouthed older woman.

"You are not my son. You're a monster."

The searing pain through his heart woke Nickolas from the vision. He bowed his head and tried to focus on his hands resting in his lap. He needed to get up. The baying of the bloodhounds echoed through the wilderness, and he closed his eyes then slid over onto his side in the snow. "I can't do it anymore, Ian. I'm too tired." The cool of the snow felt so good. His body started to relax, and he imagined the light touch of someone brushing his hair back as his thoughts faded in and out. The shivers wracking his body subsided quickly; he still had enough mind left to realize this was a bad sign.

He didn't have long to consider the situation though. The soft shushing of several feet approached him through the woods. His run was over. Gabriel had finally caught up with him. He chuckled mirthlessly. No matter how tired or wounded he was, he just didn't have it in him to roll over and give up. Gabriel would have to work for every moment. He managed to climb to his feet to face the enemy.

Four Valkyries slipped out of the shadows under the trees to slowly surround him. Nickolas tried to clear the cobwebs from his mind.

Cautiously they circled him, and Nickolas flicked his eyes between the three Hunters he could see. The fourth had moved out of his peripheral vision. He didn't like that much.

"Nickolas?" one of the strangers asked.

Growling, Nick crouched down, twisting slightly, trying to catch sight of the one working his way behind him.

"Wait, we're here to help you," the one who had spoken before said.

Yeah right, I've heard that one before. Nickolas took a step to the side, trying to back out of the ring they were enclosing him in. "Tell Gabriel I'm not buying it."

The leader made a shushing gesture, trying to lull him. "We're not from Gabriel, Nickolas. We're rebels from Aurora. Remember me from Bellingham?" They were all slowly moving closer and Nickolas turned again, looking for the best way out. "Please, Gabriel is too close. We can get you to the valley faster if you'll cooperate."

Nick shook his head and inched back, but they had tightened the ring around him enough that they were able to block his attempt. He curled his lips and growled at them.

"What should I do now, Ian?" He turned slowly in the shrinking circle then shook his head, trying to make sense of the situation.

The dogs bayed, closer than before. Nickolas's thoughts jumped back to Gabriel and the hunt. "I won't be an easy acquisition. You're going to have to get your hands dirty, Gabriel." He feinted to one side of the circle to try and keep the Hunters back. They were squeezing him in tighter. He looked past them and called out, "Why aren't you showing your face, Gabriel?"

A frustrated snarl came from the lead Hunter, snapping Nickolas's attention back. Nick was surprised by the desperation he saw in the man's eyes and the concern emanating from his subordinates. Nick shook his head, trying to clear it. Sweat dripped down his forehead and he quickly wiped it on his good shoulder.

"Please, Nickolas, we are not from the Facility. Gabriel uses no other Valkyries. He doesn't trust them. We really are just trying to get you out of here before his search team gets here. And we don't have a lot more time if those dogs indicate anything."

Unsure, Nick relaxed slightly, wiping a trembling hand over his face. "Ian?"

The leader's voice had grown softer and more persuasive. "Ian isn't here, Nickolas. Please come with us."

But that wasn't right. "He has to be here." Completely lost for a moment, he straightened from his fighting crouch, forgetting to watch his surroundings. "He's been directing me the whole time."

Sudden movement from behind triggered his instincts and he tried to whirl around. But his body was sluggish, and he went down under the Hunter. Going with the momentum, Nickolas flipped the Hunter off his back. The other three Valkyries were only a step behind their teammate. He lashed out with his foot and caught the female Hunter in the thigh as he tried to regain his feet. The inflamed flesh around his wound tore with the exertion, and he suppressed a scream. Nickolas could feel the blood flowing again as he pushed up from the ground. Haze clouded his vision, and he responded solely on survival instinct, blocking and attacking as openings presented themselves.

The moment he gained a little space, he spread his wings in an attempt to fly, but he hesitated; something wasn't right.

One of the Hunters shouted at him, but the words were just meaningless babble in the heat and roaring. He shook his head, then a sudden weight slammed into his back and his wings collapsed.

"You can't fly, you idiot." The growl was whispered in his ear. "Your wings are shredded. Don't make them impossible to mend."

The Hunter tried to force him to his knees. Nickolas pushed back. Luck was on his side and he slammed them both into the trunk of a tree. The breath whooshed out of both of them, but the Hunter didn't let go.

Nickolas... The mind voice was soft, almost too soft for him to hear. Shaking his head, he slammed them into the tree again.

Nickolas...come to me.

The Hunter still hadn't let go. He had, in fact, gotten a better grip and was slowly forcing Nick to his knees.

Please...

Jessica? "Jessica!"

No reply. The faint sending was gone, as if it had taken all of her energy just to do that much. The Hunter holding him managed to get a foot up and pressed it into his knee. He dropped.

The Flight leader, blood dripping down his face, crouched in front of him and grabbed him by the chin, forcing Nick to meet his eyes. "We have Jessica in the valley, Nick. She's safe. So is Christoff. I brought them in myself. We can take you to them. They are both safe."

Nickolas's vision tunneled, centered on the other man. He could hardly dare to believe the leader's words. The fatigue and his injuries were finally too much for him. He sank under the fog that filled his mind.

♦ ♦ ♦

Kevin let go of Nickolas's chin as the Alpha passed out. "Richard, get the net out," he said quietly. "We need to get out of here." His impatience rode him hard. He wanted to grab Nick and run, but taking a moment now could save the injured man from greater damage caused by their ignorance. He looked around the surrounding woodland. Bergen laid the unconscious Valkyrie face down in the snow, and Kevin turned to help fold up what was left of his wings.

"This one is shredded pretty bad, Kev," Bergen said.

"This wing looks ok. So does his back, but there's blood all down his side. Let's get him turned into the net so we can triage the rest of his injuries." On the count of three, he and Bergen gently shifted the wounded man over onto the mesh while Dani and Richard pulled it snug underneath. Sitting back on his heels, Kevin wiped some of the blood from his face and took a breath. It was sore, and likely would be for days. It looked like the rest of his group fared about the same.

"Well that was more of a challenge than I had anticipated," he commented and ignored Bergen's snort. "What are we looking at, Dani?"

The Hunter peeled away Nickolas's shirt. Kevin could see that the source of the blood came from his shoulder. After she got the shirt free, she worked the caked gauze that Nickolas had tried to use to staunch the blood free. Kevin hissed when he got a good look at what lay underneath.

Dark blood leaked sluggishly from a red, inflamed wound. Puss and other signs of infection oozed.

"Gunshot wound, Kevin, and he's burning up. No wonder he was talking nonsense."

"It's still in there," Kevin growled. He stared at the damage to Nickolas's shoulder, swearing under his breath. "Get the net laced up. There's nothing we need to do to protect him from aggravating his injuries in the net. It's more important we get him back."

Everyone froze as the call of the dogs echoed through the forest. Kevin locked eyes with his Flight. "Come on, we need to move."

Slinging his harness on, Kevin quickly buckled up the straps, shivering his wings to settle it more comfortably. Richard finished lashing the net and they all clipped on their tethers.

"Ready? One, two, three." With a strong down sweep, they lumbered into the sunny morning air. As soon as he had gotten a couple of wing beats under him, Kevin reached into his well of power and started to weave a Sight shield around them all to hide their passage. A shadow drew his attention before he had completed his casting.

Gabriel prowled out from under the tree canopy, calmly following Kevin's Flight with his gaze. His heart lurching, Kevin made eye contact with the foreign Alpha before he finished his casting. *That was too close.* He directed his Flight to circle high above the trees while he tried to ignore how his insides quaked. He didn't want to contemplate how close the Facility had come to recovering Nickolas.

Kevin could feel Gabriel searching for them; the Alpha's mental probe speared into him as he tried to break through the shield. Kevin pumped more power into his casting, reinforcing it, then pulled his attention back to the group.

They were only a couple of minutes in the air when his Wing passed over Gabriel's recovery teams. Kevin could see that the grounded were exhausted as they hiked through the forest. The dogs stared up into the sky, whining at them, and he chuckled at the searchers' incomprehension as they hushed the beasts instead of trusting them. *Not that they could have done anything about us now*, he thought, and picking up speed, Kevin led his Flight home.

◆ ◆ ◆

Gabriel felt the feral Caster dim down his energy signature, but he wasn't able to completely mask it. He stared up through the tree canopy blindly as he set the direction in his mind and smiled. The first of the unit who stayed on his heels broke through the bushes, and Gabriel turned his attention to his leash. The exasperated look on the man's face told the story.

"Keep up, or get lost."

"Not an option. You know that, Gabriel."

The other five members of the team melted out of the bushes and Gabriel had to give them credit, they had almost managed to stay with him. And wonder of wonders, they were fairly quiet. For grounded that was.

"Your orders are perfectly clear."

Gabriel snorted. "Which set? Recover Nickolas at all costs? Or remain hamstrung?" He left the small clearing and started back toward the rest of his recovery team. His body guard fell in behind.

"The general doesn't want you taking risks."

"Kratz can go to hell, I even have a hand basket I can loan him. He can get it back to me when it's my turn."

"You're not replaceable," the leader of his guard said patiently.

He whirled around and stopped an inch from the grounded's face. "No, I'm not," he said softly. "That's why I'm here. No one else can do what I do. Clipping my wings and tethering me to the ground defeats the point of my being here."

The soldier held his ground, but Gabriel could see the fear deep in his eyes. He smiled and watched the grounded swallow. The nervous shuffling of the other members of the guard broke the tension, and Gabriel turned away, wishing he was home. Home, where he could take his frustrations out on this grounded if he felt like it. Though Kratz had made it clear that he preferred if Gabriel would content himself with the Valkyries in the holding pens.

With a shrug he moved on. A few minutes later, they converged with the main body of the recovery effort. Grateful for the rest, most of the men sank to the forest floor. His leash remained on his heels while he located the communications tech.

The young man pulled out a radio and handed it over so Gabriel could report in.

"We've lost him," he snapped into the receiver after he reached the base.

"Repeat that, Gabriel. You lost Nickolas's trail?"

"No, you dolt. The rebels pulled him out from under our noses. Like I told you would happen if you didn't let me go after him. But there's a chance I can still track after them if you let me go now."

"Hold," the disembodied voice said. After a minute it came back on. "Your orders are the same. You do not strike out on your own."

"Damn it. This is stupid. I can find them. Do you want them back or not?"

Silence. Then after another long pause the voice said, "It is still deemed too dangerous for you alone. But the general wants them, so take two teams with you. The rest can start the return hike."

"That still keeps me tied to the ground," he growled. "I can't move any faster."

"Two teams to back you up. That's the stipulation."

He tossed the radio back to the comm tech without bothering to answer and looked over his shoulder at his guard. "Get moving if you want to keep up."

He walked off into the forest, away from the bulk of Facility searchers, in the direction he'd felt that Caster's energy signature. As efficient as ever, his team fell in at his heels as a second team branched out around them.

It was a fast flight. As soon as they had passed through the Sight shield, Kevin sent a call out to Marcus. *We have him. We have Nickolas. We're landing in the courtyard now. He's in bad shape.*

I'm on my way. What do we need? Marcus's mind voice was strong and steady.

Everything. We just managed to slip him out from under Gabriel, but he saw us.

There was the slightest of pauses before Marcus clarified. *Where were you? Does Gabriel know where the valley is?*

We were an hour out. On the direct route we take to Dustin's.

Damn. Did you cover your tracks?

I think I got everyone's power signatures locked.

Ok, as Caster Prime I want you up at the tower first. Coordinate with Robin and Nathan and make sure the alert goes out, and that the scouts are aware to watch for an increase in Facility traffic. Then get your ass back over to medical and help us with Nick.

Yes, sir. Landing his Flight in the courtyard, Kevin hurried to get his tether unclipped and get Nickolas out of the net. The sound of feet rushing toward him didn't faze him until the scent of the foreign Valkyries washed across him and his instinct to protect the Alpha in his care roared to the surface. He had to grab after his control. He wasn't usually as volatile as some of the others, but something about this particular Alpha pushed his instincts. He clenched his fist, took a deep breath, and looked up at the two Facility Valkyries.

"Gah, Nick. What have you done to yourself now?" the taller, stockier one said softly.

"Crap, Donald, he looks really bad this time."

Kevin couldn't agree more. It was amazing that Nickolas, in this condition, had held the four of them off like he had. He finished removing the net.

"Let me take him," Donald said.

Kevin's first response was a snarl, but he held it in. Like two packs of wolves bristling over territory. He saw the effort the other two were making not to attack him. After all, *he* was crouched over *their* Alpha. They could all remain civilized here. He held his hand up, stilling his Flight, then backed up slowly and let Donald pick Nickolas up.

"The healers are all on their way," he told them.

Donald had just settled the broken Valkyrie in his arms when Marcus dropped to the ground. The Hunter only nodded to Marcus before striding into sick bay.

Kevin glanced at the other Facility Valkyrie before he turned his attention to his own Alpha. Marcus had gotten a good look at his son if his pale face said anything.

His Alpha's gaze tracked Donald into the building before he spoke. "Kevin, you have a job to do. Be quick. I think we'll need you sooner than I thought." Then he hurried after Donald.

Kevin sent his Flight off with a jerk of his head then turned to look at the Facility Valkyrie who stood silently watching him. The man was younger than he. Hazel eyes studied him from an almost delicate face. His brown hair touched his shoulders and was streaked with lighter strands. *Pretty boy. Though I bet his small frame is deceptive.* Kevin stripped the rest of his gear off while he returned the regard. He couldn't place his caste, which was strange.

"What caste?" he finally asked.

"Empath."

"Seer or Caster?"

"Both. At least that's what I've been told."

"Huh. Haven't seen that before. How long have you been clean?"

He shrugged. "Not long, a week and a half maybe. I'm Kieran."

"Kevin, Caster Prime of Aurora." He wadded up his harness and stuffed it into a bag with the net. The empath still watched him in a way that made him feel like a bug. At least the man seemed less like he wanted to attack than the Hunter who'd carried Nickolas away.

Kieran finally looked away for a moment then asked, "What's wrong? I can feel the turmoil, separate from Nickolas's trauma."

Surprised he was sensitive enough to differentiate, Kevin narrowed his eyes and studied the empath for a moment before answering. "Gabriel had caught up to Nickolas. He was close enough that he saw us take off with Nick, and we were too close to Aurora. To be on the safe side, Marcus wants me to alert the scouts."

A tickle of power quested out and Kevin realized it came from the empath. The power flared then was cut off. Stunned, he looked into Kieran's gold-flecked eyes. The brief glimpse of the depth of his power left Kevin shaken.

Kieran rubbed his forehead in pain. "Is it just precaution? Or is there a significant worry? Is there anything we can do to help?"

"I don't know. The Facility has been looking for us for years without success. As for help, I'm sure that will be arranged after you are all settled in, but I'll make sure to mention it to Marcus."

"Thank you. I should go help Donald with Chris. He's going to be upset over Nickolas."

Kevin watched the fledgling empath walk away, his power swirling around him in an unconscious sweep, and made a mental note to talk to Beth. That one was going to need help. That much undisciplined empathy could be dangerous. Receptive would be bad enough, causing the bearer difficulty, but projective was a whole other matter.

Still thinking of the possible dangers, Kevin launched into the sky and headed for the tower.

Kieran turned his attention away from the intriguingly square face of the Caster Prime. Even streaked with blood the man's strength was obvious. His wings shivered and he took a deep breath to focus on what awaited him in the infirmary. Even from outside the building, the emotions swirling around inside struck him with needled pricks. Stealing himself against the onslaught he would face, he opened the door and slipped inside.

Orchestrated chaos reigned. Nickolas had been laid on the center table and Beth worked at cutting the rest of his clothing off. Two strangers helped Marcus stretch Nick's wing out onto a table they'd attached to the side of the frame. Donald stood by Jessica's table, holding Chris back, a hand on his forearm. Quiet whispers urged Chris to stay and monitor Jessica. He could help his brother more by keeping her safe and staying out of the way.

The door burst open behind him and Kieran slid to the side as a tiny red-haired woman shoved past him. She raced up to the exam table then stopped abruptly. He thought he heard her say Nickolas's name. The emotions inundating him were so thick he had trouble sorting through them.

Beth stopped what she was doing to look at the woman with concern. "Will you be ok, Jill?"

Jill shook herself once then stepped up to the table. "Yes, sorry, Beth. It's the first time I've seen him since I left the Facility. It just surprised me. I know he didn't mean to attack me. I watched what the drugs did to him every day of his change."

Beth nodded and finished stripping Nickolas's clothes off, dropping them to the floor.

Another glance at Donald showed that he didn't need help with Chris, so Kieran gradually made his way to the foot of Nick's table. His Alpha's skin was caked in dried blood. Fresh blood oozed from a hole, high in his shoulder. Bruises covered his entire torso.

Beth dumped the scissors on a tray and picked up some gauze. "Jillian, see if he has any injuries that are more critical than his shoulder that we need to be aware of, then I want a detailed assessment on the shoulder wound."

"Right." The Seer held her hands out over Nickolas's body. She moved incredibly slowly, her face blank as she worked.

Overwhelmed by the sensory input, Kieran's head throbbed. He hunched his shoulders; so much pain, worry, and heartache permeated the atmosphere of the room. His heart contracted in his chest and his breathing accelerated in response. There was no way he could live his life like this and stay sane.

Shields. I need stronger shields. But then what? What good would my talent be then? Ian told me to use my imagination. Can I create a filter of some kind? Something that will let me know what's still going on around me without everyone shouting?

He turned his focus inward. In desperation, he strengthened the thin shield he'd managed to make on their flight. That gave him a sliver of breathing space from the flood.

He found his power well and started to spin and weave a sieve out of the energy. He sandwiched that with his shield. That stemmed the flood into a manageable seep.

Once he wove more energy into conduits, he could collect and categorize each individual, allowing him to *hear* the whisper each person projected.

Jillian's voice broke through his concentration, recapturing part of his attention.

"No other major body damage. Internal organs all intact. He has a few cracked ribs. The effects from fatigue and exposure are pronounced, but not life threatening at this time. There is a high fever from the infection. I think it likely the fever is responsible for preventing him from getting frost bite. He also has extensive bodily bruising." Slowly, she shifted position to hover just over the shoulder wound.

She flinched and Kieran felt the pain that caused it. He separated it and traced that line, labeling it and putting it into his mental map.

"His shoulder has extensive muscle tearing and tissue damage, full of infection. The bullet is still lodged within. We need Kevin to extract it." She flexed her fingers and blinked, bringing herself out of the trance, then stepped back.

Beth tossed a saline bottle at her so she could help flush out the wound. Nick didn't twitch a muscle as they started to clean him. But Kieran could feel pain radiate from him.

"Marcus, what have you found?" Beth asked without looking up from her task.

Marcus and his helpers had finished immobilizing Nick's wing on the table. "His left wing is intact. His right wing has fourth degree tears in the membrane. They're going to be tricky to hold together. The struts are still solid."

Marcus and one of his helpers took strips of adhesive that had eyelets attached and carefully secured them along the length of the torn skin. The second helper followed and loosely laced surgical threading through the loops. Then Marcus started the slow process of gently tightening the lacing to bring the edges of the tear flush so medicinal glue could be applied.

After all of the sail had been repaired, Marcus held his hand over the splinting. Kieran felt power shimmer through the Alpha as the Auroran called on his talent, filling the framework he had made to hold the membrane together with liquid light.

Kieran just barely managed to hold his mouth closed. The physical manifestation of Marcus's power was a little mind-blowing. He, Nick, and Jessica were the only Facility Valkyries so far who were more than Hunters.

Shock caused his mental muscles to relax, and like a restive horse, his talent took the inattention and reared out of his control. He grabbed after it with both mental hands as the tidal wave of emotion crashed upon him again. Wading upstream, he raced to tame the flow and only continued to watch the healing with a portion of his attention.

The rest of his attention was spent building layer upon layer of filters as he sifted through the onslaught of emotion. Identifying and categorizing, Kieran mentally pinned a label to each person in the room, until he got down to only one.

Nick.

The waves of pain rolling off of his Alpha seared through Kieran. He instinctively threw up a wall that damped down his reception of them to the point where he could read and understand what was happening to Nickolas but wasn't washed away with it. Once he had that distance established, Kieran recognized Nickolas's struggle as the healers worked on him.

Even unconscious, his pain mounted. Rousing him.

Something inside of Kieran reacted. The need to do something pushed against the inside of his head. His talent hurt him. This wasn't the pain of receiving other people's emotions. This was like the pressure of something inside of himself trying to break free.

He gasped and his sight turned gray. He braced his hand on the foot of the table and tried to take deep breaths. The pain in his head swelled and he felt something wet slide over his lip and tasted blood. He wiped it away with the back of his other hand. Nick's pain still pushed at him from outside.

He tried to reach his Alpha, but the pressure in his head grew until, with a pop, it released and he suddenly felt the unscreened surface of Nick's pain. This was not just the kind of emotion that everyone spread to the ether; his talent had changed from strictly passive reception to actively reaching out for the source.

His tongue of power flicked over the rubbery membrane surrounding Nickolas's mind. At least that was the visual his mind seemed to conjure to give him a frame of reference for what his talent was doing.

Nick's conscious was rising from the work they were doing to his body.

Kieran blinked his eyes and tried to get them to focus. "He's in too much pain," he said in a harsh whisper.

The others brushed him off with distracted comments as they worked. "He's unconscious, he doesn't know anything is happening, there's not a lot of choice."

There has to be some alternative. He ducked his head and smeared a trail of blood on his forearm as he tried to think. Kevin rushed into the room.

The new arrival slid to a stop next to Nickolas's shoulder. "So were we right, Jillian? Is the bullet still in there?"

"I'm afraid so, Kev. Be careful."

Face grim, Kevin nodded then went to work. Beth and Jillian had gotten most of the dirt and dried blood washed away from the wound and had started draining the puss before Kevin arrived. Now they waited patiently with cloths and antibiotics as Kevin used his telekinesis to lift the ragged chunk of metal out of Nickolas's shoulder.

Kieran suppressed a gasp as a sharp upsurge in Nickolas's pain washed over him. Nick's mind was too close to the surface. They would never be able to finish getting the bullet out before he woke up. Kieran wanted to scream but clenched his teeth on it. He forced his eyes to focus on the physical world and saw Nickolas flinch and his hand clench. The others had missed the movement.

Kevin eased the bullet higher, the blood started to flow red again, bubbling up out of the hole like an obscene fountain.

The membrane around Nickolas's mind pulsed under Kieran's mental hand. *You can't wake, Nick*, he thought frantically. *Stay down.* He pulled more power out of himself and tried to push his Alpha's consciousness back, but it was like trying to stop the tide. The waves just broke over him and pushed him back.

He poured more of himself into the effort, but it did nothing. The pain was waking Nick.

"Stop. He can't take anymore." Kieran's voice broke.

Everyone froze and turned to stare at him. Surprise and uncertainty washed across all faces but one.

A bead of sweat worked its way down Kevin's face, but he stared hard at Kieran. "What's happened?"

"He's waking up. The pain is too much."

"Can you stop it?"

Kieran struggled with the tide, still trying to use his untrained talent to hold it away from his Alpha. "I'm trying, but it isn't working. I don't know what to do."

Slowly, Nickolas's head shifted to the side and his breathing picked up. This time Beth saw the movement, and she looked at Kieran before addressing Kevin. "Stop it? Kevin?"

"Kieran is an empath, Beth. Receptive and *projective*."

The understanding flowed like quicksilver across her features, her gaze turned speculative. "You *can* block his pain—if you're strong enough. But you'll have to get uncomfortably close to him in the process."

Now that Kevin wasn't pulling on the bullet anymore, the pain had stopped surging quite so badly, giving Kieran a little bit of breathing space. "What do I do?"

"Without training, you're going to have to let instinct guide you. The first step you have to figure out is how to project your talent out, so you can get inside of Nickolas."

"I think I've got that," he whispered as part of his mind looked back inside where his mental hand rested on the pulsing membrane.

"Good," Beth said. "Now make sure you anchor yourself within your own body. Somewhere strong, and don't let go of that. Then you need to get through Nick's outer barriers if they are still up."

Using his imagination, he pretended to tie a rope around himself, then after it was tied off good and tight, he looked out into the mental void and leapt.

"Our outer barriers," Beth continued, "protect our mind, our emotions and thoughts, from leaking all over the place for the average person to pick up. Which is an essential life skill for people who use telepathy."

Kieran pressed into the rubber membrane surrounding Nick. He found a weak spot and forced his power through and started to open a hole when the whole balloon popped and he fell.

The moment he hit the sand, he gasped in agony. The pain he had felt up to this point had been a mere echo. His physical body stumbled into the exam table in response to its strength. His outer sight wavered briefly into focus as he leaned heavily on the table while he battled with the dark tide of Nickolas's pain.

"Once through his outer barriers, you need to find his core. The center of who he is. That is where you will find his inner barriers. You have to get through those. But that's where he will defend himself the most. No one wants to be that exposed and vulnerable to another."

Kieran pushed back the pain and rose to his feet. Jagged gray rocks, sharp as glass, towered over the gray sand he stood on. The susurrus of surf beat like a heart in his ears. As he watched, more shards poked through the sand and the waves grew louder.

Completely at a loss, he stared around the vision, panic on the edge of his thoughts. He shifted his sight and looked out on the real world. No one had moved. He searched out Beth's eyes.

"I...I don't know what to do. How do I find him?"

"I can help if you let me in." She set her things down on the tray then stopped next to him. She reached out and rested her hand on the back of his neck. The warmth increased, then he felt a scratching inside his head. Instinctively he wanted to push it away. She squeezed lightly and said under her breath, "Relax. You have to let me through your outer barriers."

He took a deep breath and did what she asked.

At some point he'd closed his eyes; when he opened them, she stood beside him on the sand. Her face had gone pale as she stared intently around.

Oh, no. She took a few steps and rested her hand carefully against one of the rocks. *We have to reach his core. I thought his physical injuries were all we had to contend with.*

What do you mean? He hurried after in her wake.

He has mental and emotional trauma that surpasses the physical. I don't have time to teach it to you right now, but I can read it in his dreamscape. The pain from his physical injuries is feeding back into the mental, increasing the intensity of his reaction.

They followed what appeared to be a faint path through the sand, and the sound of the surf grew harsh.

That in turn feeds a vicious cycle. His injuries blow his mental reactions out of all proportion, and in return his mental pain will hinder his physical healing.

The trail emptied out onto a beach. The water, the sky, the sand and rocks, all matched in their matte gray hue.

Be careful, don't cut yourself on the rocks. This is a dangerous dreamscape. She pulled him to a stop right at the edge of where the waves licked the sand. *He's out there. I can't get him. Only your talent can. But I can guide you once you have him. And we need to hurry. Time may move differently for us now, but that bullet needs to come out. Kevin can't hold it forever.*

Kieran took a deep breath. The water looked about as inviting as the rest of the landscape, he decided as he looked out over the churning sea. The bright flash of a butterfly danced over the waves.

Narrowing his eyes, Kieran studied the butterfly. It fluttered, exhausted, above the pounding surf. As he watched, one of the waves crested, swamping it, and Kieran felt Nick drowning in his own pain.

He responded without thinking. Pulling power out of his well, he fashioned a net out of the energy then started to wade out into the frigid water. Now Kieran was truly immersed in Nickolas's pain as he pushed his way through the waves to reach the butterfly that was Nickolas.

Every step ripped strips out of his mind and rubbed salt into the open wounds.

The butterfly floated on the water briefly before Kieran saw it lift its wings, struggling to regain the air. It managed to shake enough water from its wings to lift up from the surface only to be dashed back as the next wave loomed up.

Kieran pushed through the waves until he reached the struggling butterfly. Water lapped at his chest, whispering in his mind and weighing him down as it pulled at his clothes, trying to drag him under as well. Kieran blocked it and extended the net, scooping Nickolas from the water.

He pulled the net in close and quickly waded back to shore, thankful to be leaving that dark sea.

Good visualizing on your part. A butterfly is perfect, something small enough for you to overpower. Because as distasteful as it is, that's what you're going to have to do. If we don't lock him away from his own pain, he won't survive. You need a container to secure him in. After we have the bullet out, I will walk you through treating his mental trauma.

He sank to his knees in the sand, shivering not from the cold but the unfamiliar exertion of using so much power.

The roar of the sea grew as he gently extracted the struggling butterfly from the net. There wasn't time for him to prepare or even think about what he was doing. He carefully cupped the fragile representation in his hands, the shock of being this close to the core of Nickolas jolting through him.

There were no barriers. Nothing.

Nothing separated him from Nickolas, and the two of them twined together. Uncomfortable, unpleasant—both had been understatements. The butterfly went crazy in his hands.

Tossing his sweat-soaked bangs out of his eyes, he pulled more energy from his power well and a crystal box shimmered into existence on the sand next to him. Kieran gently slipped Nick's core manifestation into the box, securing the lid.

Good job, Kieran. That will buffer him from his pain briefly, as well as keep him safe from his own intentions. Monitor him while we get the bullet out.

She slipped from his mind. He rolled his shoulders then took a deep breath and turned part of his attention on the outside world. There was a moment's disorientation as he separated himself from Nickolas's pain as much as he could, then he pushed himself erect at the foot of the bed. He brushed his cheek against his shoulder to wipe the sweat away.

Beth was already in motion. "Get it out, Kevin," she said as she grabbed her supplies.

Without a word, Kevin resumed his extraction, slowly pulling the bullet out.

Kieran divided his attention between Nickolas's body and monitoring the box in the dreamscape. At first the butterfly rested quietly on the floor of the crystal, but after a moment its wings stirred, then it fluttered into the air to beat at the walls confining it.

Nick's physical body remained still, which reassured Kieran, even though on some level his Alpha was aware of the pain and that he couldn't react to it.

But then a jolt slammed into Kieran from a new source. He hissed and spun to look across the room. Both Donald and Chris had leapt for Jessica. All three had felt the surge through their bond with her. Chris held her face in his hands, staring into it. Donald gripped her hand tightly. Kieran switched his sight back to Nick's dreamscape. The butterfly slammed into the clear walls of the box, trying to free itself from Kieran's hold.

"Something's wrong with Jessica," Chris shouted.

"It's Nick," Kieran called back as he found the link between the two Breeders in Nick's mind. Energy spikes surged through it. "He's panicking and she's picked it up through their bond and is responding. Kevin?"

"I can't stop, Kieran. He'll bleed to death," the Caster replied. Kieran could hear the strain and frustration in his voice.

What little life force she had maintained during the coma was draining away like rain into sand as she tried to reach her mate.

Not bothering to respond, Kieran turned to his own link with Jessica and dove into it, hoping that what he'd learned in the last few minutes from Beth would be enough.

He sped along his bond with her, feeling himself stretching thinner and wondering how far, realistically, he'd be able to go. After a split second of eternity, Kieran touched the intimacy of Jessica's mind at her outer barriers and felt her recoil. It was dark in her mindscape. He floated around for a moment, getting his bearings.

Confusion. That was the strongest impression. Followed by the sensation of being trapped. That he understood. She had no control over her body at the moment, since it was still locked in the coma. Her mind should still be at rest as well, but Nickolas's need had roused her enough to start to wake her mind. Not sure where to start, he searched out her power well and didn't like what he found. It was a blacker hole within the black of her mindscape. The level was so low, Kieran could hardly make out the light at the base. There were lines leading into it that were still under construction and abandoned. Kieran worried that if she continued to regain consciousness, permanent damage would be done to her abilities.

Where is she? The core of Jessica was absent. Echoes and whispers were all around him, but he had yet to come across *her*. From inside her mind, he could feel her body weakening. He wouldn't be able to stop the energy bleed until he caught her.

Jessica? he called. He could feel the strain starting to take its toll on him. Maintaining a link simultaneously with Nick and Jessica, keeping Nickolas caged, and now needing to hunt her down as well...

Kieran gave himself a quick shake and ignored the drain. Pushing the panic to the side. He swept his mind out into

Jessica's and flooded her. The intrusion caused her to flinch, and he zeroed in on the movement. He kept his inner eyes focused as he chased down the spark that was Jessica's core and called out to Christoff and Donald at the same time to send everything they could down their link with her.

She was fast. Kieran chased her through her own dreamscape, gaining on her slowly. *Jessica, wait. It's Kieran. I'm here to help you. Please stop.* The spark hesitated for a moment in the darkness, pulsing in uncertainty, allowing him time to close the gap. Then realizing the mistake, it dodged to the side, evading him, but Kieran could see she was going slower now. This was not going to work, he thought. Neither one of them could afford to expend energy like this.

Kieran looked ahead into the dark, featureless plane. Narrowing his eyes, he conjured a wall in the distance and started to herd her toward his own destination.

She must have felt his intent, not surprising really, considering how closely linked they were, because she tried to dodge from the path he had them on. Another wall burst into being, channeling her toward the end. Kieran fell back and let Jessica take the lead, just blocking any attempts she made to deviate from his course.

Toward the end, she put on a burst of speed, shooting into the corral he had fashioned and diving into the hole in the wall he had set as a trap.

Floating to a stop in front of the wall, Kieran reached out his hand and fished into the depression. He scooped her up and pulled her out, gently holding the spark that was Jessica's core in his hands.

He was braced this time for the shock of intimate knowledge; he didn't flinch, just absorbed the information. Jessica's surprise, as she became aware of who he was, bore into him, and he tried to reassure her. Her panic was all too obvious as the little spark bounced off his hands, looking for a way to escape him. He pulled on his anchor to Nickolas to start reeling him back to Nick's mindscape.

Kieran? Jessica's voice whispered through his mind. After all the difficulties she had had during her change, and now in the coma, nothing had ever sounded as sweet, or reassured him more, than that brief contact..

That's right, Jess, it's me. Try to relax, I'm taking you to Nickolas now. Kieran could feel her mind waking more as her memories started to return to her. He needed to get her settled so she would hopefully drift back to sleep. Her body was not done with the coma yet. He tried to remain an unobtrusive observer while she sorted through her memories. The spark had slowed its panicky movements as she worked through things.

He stepped foot on sand as he crossed the border into Nickolas's dreamscape. The light touch of wings fluttered against his palms, and he lifted the lid to the box, then quickly slid Jessica in before Nick could escape.

The two butterflies danced wildly around the box before exhaustion took both of them and they landed together on the floor of the crystal box, their wings overlapping. Smiling tiredly, Kieran divided his awareness again and surfaced enough to look on the outside world.

"I have both of them in the box now, Beth."

"You," she cleared her throat, "you carried her core and placed it with Nick's in his dreamscape?"

A dull throb had started in the front of his head at some point. "Yes. Should I not have? She was bleeding out too much power, and that seemed to calm both of them."

"It's fine. Just fine," she rushed out.

He rubbed his forehead and wondered about the sideways looks he was getting then heard the clink of the bullet as Kevin dropped it into a pan.

"Ok, Beth, I'm out," Kevin said. "Your turn, Marcus."

Blood still flowed down Nickolas's side when Beth and Kevin backed away, giving Marcus room. The rebel leader held his hands out over the wound and closed his eyes.

Kieran could feel the heat through the link as he continued to monitor Nickolas. Nickolas's physical body remained still, but the pain as Marcus sealed the wound was still felt by his Alpha.

His head throbbed.

"What the hell happened to you?" Kieran heard Bethany ask Kevin.

Curious himself, he looked away from Nick to study Kevin's blood-caked face.

"He did," the Caster replied, nodding at Nick.

A beat of silence, then Beth said incredulously, "Are you telling me that Nickolas, in this condition, held off the four of you?"

"Yes, that's exactly what I'm saying," he snapped then shook his head. "Don't worry. I know how unbelievable it sounds. I don't *ever* want to go up against him when he is sane and at full power."

"I'll second that," Kieran said under his breath. Kevin heard him and met his eyes briefly. The look in the Caster's eyes left Kieran uncomfortable. He couldn't decide if it was interest or wariness or if the Auroran actually feared him.

I shouldn't try to judge anything at the moment. The strain of using so much of his power to hold both Nick and Jess was taking a toll. He felt like he was bleeding from a wound too. He had started to tremble from the continuous drain, so he locked his knees to keep himself upright and hoped he wouldn't pass out.

After a moment, Marcus pulled back. "Done. That's all I can do for the time being. We'll have to have another session tomorrow. I don't want to close the hole all at once and seal infection inside."

Bethany gently pushed Nick's filthy hair away from his forehead. "Hopefully his fever will break now that the wound has been tended properly. That's all the physical damage we can fix at the moment. You ready, Kieran?"

He took a deep breath and nodded. She stepped back around and laid her hand on the back of his neck again. When he opened his eyes in the dreamscape, he found her studying him with an intent gaze.

Can you do this? You have already expended far more energy than I would have bet on.

What choice do I have? I can't leave them locked in a box.

She snorted then knelt beside the box in question to look at the two still butterflies. *Of course not,* she replied absently. *I meant working with Nick afterward. Lancing his mental wounds won't be fun or easy. Start with getting Jessica back, then we'll go over what I need you to do.*

Kieran quietly lifted the lid to the crystal box. He captured Jessica and pulled her out of the box before either one of the trapped butterflies knew what was happening. Ignoring Nickolas, he sealed the enraged butterfly inside and left him flinging himself at the lid over and over. Kieran could hear his mind even through the barrier.

Sending calming thoughts to Jessica, he carried her to the edge of Nickolas's dreamscape and the start of hers. He released her core on the other side of the barrier. She paused briefly before trying to cross back over, but the spark had no luck crossing the boundary, she just bounced off. *Jessica, it's time for you to go home. I need to help Nickolas now. And you need to finish your own work without worrying about helping Nick, understand?*

Hovering, the spark considered him. Then he heard her voice, faint from disuse. *He is in a lot of pain, Kieran. I can't leave him like that.*

You don't have a choice, Jess. We will do what we can for him. I promise. The best way for you to help him is to finish your change. The sooner you wake, the quicker you can be there for him.

Kieran held his breath as he watched her making up her mind. Her spark pulsed slowly at him before dashing off back to her center.

He returned to Beth and the crystal box. The waves on Nickolas's sea of pain were still pronounced, and new jagged rocks had begun to appear in various places, pushing their way up out of the sand.

Beth took her gaze off of the frantic butterfly and looked at him. He swallowed hard.

I can't see the full depth of your power well, but it looks like you can still go on. We've treated his physical injuries, but now we need to treat the mental ones. The boil that has developed in Nick's psyche will hinder his physical healing. You are my tool to do this.

Me? Why don't you do it?

It's not in my talent. It is in yours, however. I haven't had access to someone with your talent in a few years. Thankfully we've had only a few cases where such an ability would have been necessary since we lost our projective empath.

What do you mean?

Well, in Nick's case, it's very likely that he would die, and we wouldn't be able to do anything to stop it without you.

Die, he squeaked.

She rubbed her hand over her eye. *Yes. The two types of trauma are twined together now. If we'd gotten to him sooner, maybe it wouldn't have happened. But until we know what he's fighting inside, there's no way to know. What's important at the moment is that he won't be able to heal from the physical wounds if he's battling his internal demons, and he won't get past them if he's too weak physically. We can only take the first step now. The pressure needs to be relieved. After you lance it, the puss can drain, but the infection will still be inside. Once we know what we're dealing with, we'll know the next step.*

Hesitantly he stepped closer to the box.

Are you ready? After you breach his inner barriers, you'll have to work fast.

Stealing himself for what was to come, he opened the lid to the box. The butterfly, waiting for its chance, tried to get past him, but Kieran was faster, snagging Nick in midflight.

Holding Nick imprisoned in his cupped hands, Kieran turned around to sit on the crystal box. The physical contact with Nickolas's core granted him access to all that Nick was.

His hopes, fears, dreams, and nightmares. Traumas both new and old. But right now the thing that concerned him most was current trauma. The festering wound that he sensed in his Alpha. Beth had that right. Now that he knew what he was looking at, he could see the signs all over the dreamscape. The poison it released into his system.

He rested his arms on his knees and bowed his head over his cupped hands, closing his eyes so he could concentrate on the task. Delicately, he slipped his power into Nickolas's mind. Nick's injured core tried to pull away and hide from what Kieran did, but he ignored Nick's struggles to read the extent of the mental and emotional damage his Alpha had, both new and old. He showed no mercy rooting out every detail.

Relentlessly Kieran laid the memories bare one by one; his own heart bled at what was revealed. He hated himself for putting Nickolas through this, but he nevertheless continued until there was nowhere left to hide and the butterfly that was Nickolas lay limp in the palm of his hand.

Kieran trembled in reaction and Beth's hand came up to stroke his hair.

We have to go. We don't have long. Her voice sounded hoarse. *I didn't...expect...*

What happens now?

The puss needs to drain. And with something like this, there's only one way I expect that to go.

He set Nick down on top of the crystal box and pulled out of his Alpha's mind. He swayed and nearly fell. He would have fallen if Chris hadn't been standing beside him to catch him.

"Strap him down." Beth's voice was rough.

Chapter Five

She suited actions to words and pushed past Kevin to start separating the Velcro at the side of the table.

Kieran staggered forward and started to secure Nick's ankle before the others snapped out of their stupefaction and got the rest of the straps across his body.

Marcus double-checked Nick's wing and made sure it was securely tied. They were just in time. Nickolas's breathing started to hitch and accelerate, then he moaned, opening fever-filled eyes that obviously didn't see the room. He pulled at the straps and tried to rise, fighting against the restraint.

Beth looked up at Kieran from the head of the table, their shared knowledge shining in the tears running down her cheeks. He stumbled back a step into Chris's chest and ran the back of a trembling hand across his eyes. His clan's Second gripped his shoulders firmly.

"Bethany?" Marcus said softly.

She bit off a sob and looked across the table at her husband.

Nick fought, twisting against the straps, shuddering from the pain the movement caused. Chris set Kieran to the side and joined Kevin and Donald to help add their strength to the restraints, hoping to stop him from aggravating his injuries.

Nickolas arched his back bowstring tight then suddenly collapsed. After a moment he opened his eyes and started to talk.

"Ian, it's me. Let me in! Open the damned door. This place is going to blow." His eyes looked around, seeing a different place, a different time. "Come on, we don't have much time."

Everyone else in the room froze. Kieran sought Beth's gaze again.

"I'm not leaving you, Ian. We can make it. I'll get you out. Please don't do this. No...Ian. Grandfather, no..." He screamed, then whispered brokenly, "No, oh God, please no."

Kieran felt the sob he tried to hold back break as he listened to Nickolas relive Ian's death moment by moment, the tears streaming down his cheeks. The wave of grief from the other's in the room added pressure to the grief he already carried. He was too exhausted to filter out the unwanted press from outside.

Nickolas circled back to the beginning, groping with the guilt; he repeated the memory over and over. Each run through, he added more details, changed his approach, tried to find some way, in hindsight, to save Ian.

Through his tears, Kieran looked up at Chris's frozen form and the stricken look he had as he listened to his brother describe their grandfather's suicide.

The stunned disbelief and horror held everyone in thrall. The only sound to break the unnerving silence was the sound of Nick's anguished voice. Wave after wave of grief from the listening Valkyries bombarded Kieran, but he had nothing left to give. He couldn't help them; they were on their own.

The words Nick's memory spewed forth were sharp knives slicing the listeners deeply. As the emotional puss of his wound drained, the intensity holding Nick faded. But the knowledge and memory of the storm would remain to haunt all those who had experienced it. Closing his eyes, Kieran tried to center himself, but he had nothing left. Instead he just sank down to sit on the ground, exhausted.

"Come on, Kieran. You need to rest," Beth said hoarsely.

He opened his eyes to her tearstained face.

"Jill, help me get him up. The rest of you stay with Nick. The worst of the storm has passed, but there will likely be more to drain."

The two of them hauled Kieran to his feet, and he stumbled between them. They led him out of the larger triage room and down a short hall that held a few smaller rooms. They took him through the first door on the right. Jays, still unconscious, occupied one of the two beds.

Jill pulled back the covers, and Beth lowered him down to the mattress.

"Jill, get him some milk, and there should still be breakfast left in the kitchen. After you eat get some sleep. We can't take the next step until Nick has regained true consciousness, and that likely won't be for a couple of days."

He blinked up at her. "What's the next step?"

She sighed and looked away from him. "We seal up his memories."

"Excuse me?" He inched up the headboard into a sitting position. "Does that mean what I think?"

She met his gaze without flinching. "Probably. But I'll lay it out. You will go into his dreamscape, through his inner barriers, and block all memories of Ian's death."

"I will do no such thing," he replied hotly.

Her gaze bored into his. "Yes, you will. Now that we know what the seed of his injury is, I have to make the judgment call. We won't be able to deal with the core of the problem until after his body has healed."

"He has a right to know," he snarled.

"Of course he does. And he will. But at what cost, Kieran? There's a high chance that the knowledge will hinder his full healing. It could mean the difference between him regaining flight or being crippled. If someone is brought into the emergency room, do you think the doctor sits down with the patient while they're bleeding to death and explains the pros and cons of the procedures? Or do they perform the necessary procedures to save the patient's life? Even with physical injuries, you triage and treat some while leaving others to wait. We are lucky to have the option of putting this injury on hold."

He jerked his gaze away.

"This will hurt him," he said softly.

"Of course it will. There's no help for that. He's nothing but pain right now, Kieran."

Jill came back in, and he took the tray she handed to him.

"Eat then get some sleep. I'll go over the procedure in more detail after you've had some rest."

He nodded but didn't look up at her, just toyed with the food on the plate. Jill clucked her tongue and pressed the glass of milk into his hand while Beth quietly shut the door behind her.

◆ ◆ ◆

Christoff stood in the hallway and watched the woman that he still couldn't quite believe was his mother shut the door to the room Kieran and Jays were in.

The sight of Jays's pale face before the door closed reminded him of that worry. This unnatural sleep couldn't be good. He stared at Bethany's tear-streaked face and thought about the conversation he'd just overheard.

"You'll really do that to Nick?"

She flipped her wings then settled them tighter on her back. "If it means he comes out whole, with no regrets."

"What if we say no? He's our Alpha."

"What would Ian have done?"

He growled and turned away. That pain was too fresh.

"You know as well as I that Ian would have done the same thing. At the moment the continuation of our species is dependent on Nickolas and Jessica. You can't let his relationship as your brother cloud that fact. If we have an option that will give him higher odds of a complete recovery, yet steps on his toes, I will take it. I am the lead medical here. Only Jays is my peer, Chris. You need to trust my judgment."

He stared at the toe of his boot and asked, "Is Kieran ok?"

She started to walk slowly down the hall. "He'll be fine. He just overextended his talents. Used more energy than he could spare in one sitting. So his body is demanding a rest. The fact that he could do what he did stuns me. His power well is deep."

He let the unfamiliar reference slip by and said hoarsely, "I hope I never have to go through anything like that again as long as I live. I can't believe he's gone."

He turned toward the entrance that led into the main treatment room, where Nickolas and Jessica rested. His thoughts circling a truth he couldn't yet bring himself to truly believe.

"Me either, Chris."

The catch in his mother's voice stopped him. "Are you ok?"

She straightened her shoulders then nodded. "Things haven't been easy for the last twenty years. We've gotten by, but we always had Ian's leadership behind us. Now we're free in a way that Valkyries have never been free before. But at a cost we never would have wanted to pay, given the choice."

"What do you mean? Free how? You've been out here, away from the Facility while the rest of us have been taught a bunch of lies and forced to live in fear of Gabriel. Under a lot of rules and regulations. Never allowed out of the Facility without permission and curfews. Our lives scheduled for us. Nothing but a series of tests and exhibitions. Watching our step around general Kratz, who oversaw the non-Valkyrie portion of the Facility."

Sadness crept over her face. "While it's true we've had a different kind of freedom than any of you in the Facility, we haven't been completely free. The same fear of Gabriel hovers over us. Many of our people over the years have disappeared into the camps at his hands.

"Your freedom came at the cost of your knowledge, Chris. We've been fighting a secret war. One that you were always a hostage of but are now involved in."

"Why didn't they use us to bring you in?"

She shrugged. "I have no idea what they think. Marcus and Ian both felt that the council was smart enough to realize they had more control over us this way. If they'd forced us back, that would have left someone else in charge of the clan. Someone they didn't have a hold on."

"Council? What's the council?"

"The Facility that you know is only one face of the Facility machine. I was never sure how many different groups vied for control. The council is the hydra head that is responsible for making all of the decisions that deal with us, the Valkyries. The original experiment started out with a tiny group of individual researchers, but they sold their souls to larger corporations for their research grants and then when the virus escaped, several factions of military got involved as well. Now the political jockeying within the group is a constant dance for who gets what they want."

"What do they want?"

She shrugged as they entered the main room. "Who knows? They all have different goals. None of them are our goals. Yet we are the cattle they build their farms on. So you see, we may now be free to do anything we want, but our safety has taken a serious down turn. Now that you and Nickolas are no longer in their control, and Ian is gone, the Facility will be going nuts trying to figure out what to do about us."

Off balance, Chris tucked that new information away to look at more closely later. The raw grief that burned in his heart and thoughts left little room. They approached Jessica's still form. He brushed his fingertips across her forehead. "She looks better. Do you think the healing done on Nick is responsible for it?"

"Anything is possible. Her breathing and heart rate are both improved." She held her hand out over Jessica's chest. "And she's back to work. All of her energy is focused as it should be, finally."

He sighed in relief. That matched with what he got through his own link with her.

"There's nothing else we can do for her but wait, Chris. Keep an eye on her through your link and hope that the energy the three of you can give her will counterbalance the lack of her last meal. Now it's Jays I'm concerned about. He should have woken by now. I wasn't worried last night. I figured he would wake some time before morning. But he's showing no signs of rousing. This isn't good."

"What can we do?"

"I'm not sure. I'm going to start with getting some tests done. But I'm betting Kieran will be our best hope here too. He has such a rare talent that couldn't have come at a better time." She turned away and walked over to where his father sat, sadly watching Nickolas.

The memory of Nickolas's words replayed in his ears, and he walked over to join Donald at Nick's side.

"I knew he didn't intend to leave, Chris. I could tell when he ordered us out. But I didn't really believe he'd be gone."

Chris squeezed his Second's shoulder. "We need to break the news to the others, Don."

"What about Jays?" he whispered.

"We'll have to cross that bridge when he wakes up."

They both watched Nickolas's restless movements. His brother whimpered in pain but continued to lightly fight the straps anyway.

"Marcus?" Kevin asked. "Is there still going to be a meeting this morning?"

Chris turned. Beth kissed his father's forehead then stepped away. Marcus scrubbed his hands over his face before he answered.

"Yes. And we need to get the Facility settled, so the Primes meeting will be short today."

"Ok, I'll go get washed up and let the other two know."

Marcus rose.

"There's nothing more any of you can do here right now," Beth said. "I'll let you know if there are any changes."

"You ready, Chris?" Marcus asked.

He looked at Donald then nodded.

They followed the Auroran Alpha out the doors. Once out in the cold morning air, Chris stretched his wings. A couple of his Hunters occupied themselves sweeping the snow off of the cobbles.

He gave a vigorous flap then settled his wings and followed his father across the courtyard.

Marcus held the door open then led them through the main longhouse and to a door in the side wall, waving them into an office.

"Have a seat. I have a meeting scheduled with my Primes, then we will take you on a tour and get you settled in."

Both of them took a chair in front of the desk, but before Marcus could get himself seated behind it, a brief rap sounded at the door, and Robin slipped inside. No emotion on his face, the Hunter took a place leaning negligently on the corner of Marcus's desk.

A comfortable pose. One that indicated Robin's frequency in this office.

Chris had to rein in his Hunter instincts. The two of them managed a civil nod to each other.

Robin looked at Marcus. "I'm sorry."

"Me too, Robin." He cleared his throat. "I had always thought I'd see him again."

After a brief moment, Robin asked, "Will Nickolas recover?"

"Maybe. It's still touch and go. We'll know more in the next couple of days. Where's Nathan?"

"He and his Second are setting up a new roster for the scouts. The Seers located Gabriel's recovery team where Kevin said they'd be. About an hour's flight northwest. Several hour's walk, so not too close, but close enough to keep an eye on. They have been closer a time or two over the years."

"So you're increasing the scouts?" Marcus leaned back in his seat. Another knock sounded on the door. "Come."

Kevin walked in looking somewhat haggard, but at least the blood was now cleaned up from his face.

Robin nodded at the new arrival. "We figured it was a good precaution. It doesn't look like the Facility is close, but why take chances. We have all these new people and the festival is coming up."

"Sensible." He turned to the Caster Prime. "Kev?"

"The imbuers have stepped up shifts making shields and those nifty exploding pinecones they came up with last."

"Good."

What are they talking about, Chris?

No clue.

All three of the other Valkyries' heads swiveled to look at them.

Marcus sighed. "Kev, you're in charge of organizing classes. They need to learn how to use their telepathy properly, as well as the talents, history, and protocol. Now to answer your question…." He turned to look at them.

Chris felt his face heat and he tried to suppress it. Donald's wings fidgeted next to him as Marcus continued.

"We need to discuss what the Castes and Talents are. I'm assuming Ian didn't go into much detail. Do you know what to look for in your people as they come off the inhibitor?"

"Ah..." Chris shifted in his seat. "Mostly we know that if their detox time is harder and longer that they aren't Hunters."

"Ok." Marcus sighed. "Percentage wise, Casters and Seers only make up less than a quarter of our population. Of those individuals, each will have to be graded to determine their talents and the depth of their power well, their strength. If more than one talent is present, there can be up to three, then it's the major talent that determines Caste. A major talent has a strength of four to five on the scale, any talent below that is a minor talent.

"The talents themselves are divided up into Casters and Seers. How a talent manifests determines caste. If it takes place within the users mind, like the precognitive abilities such as clairvoyance or dreams, then it is a Seer talent. But if it manifests outside of the user," Marcus held out his hand palm facing up and suddenly a pillar of light lifted out of his hand. The sunlight-like beam shimmered and morphed into what looked like a plucked flower suspended over his gently moving fingers. "Then it is a Caster talent."

His father closed his fist over the creation and the light vanished. Chris felt Donald shiver next to him and understood the feeling.

"So for the question that started this, an imbuer is a Caster. Their talent allows them to act as a conduit for someone else's talent and imbue that ability into an object. For example, an imbuer who is working with a shield builder can take that ability and place it into a piece of clay that would temporarily allow someone without that ability, like a Hunter, to invoke the shield held within it. It just takes a touch of telepathy to trigger it. The imbuers have become our weapon experts, and in general, inventors as they come up with more and more ideas of how to utilize their talents."

"So is that what they were throwing during the fight in Bellingham?" Chris asked.

"Yes," Kevin answered. "I had some experimental globes filled with lightning from an electrokinetic with me. Several of the Hunters were using shield amulets. That is the sort of thing the imbuers do for us."

"How many of you are clear of the inhibitor, Chris?" Marcus asked.

"Not many. Nine of us. That includes Nick and Jess. Kieran is the only one so far to show talents. Not including the Breeders of course. We are taking them off in lots of five or so. That way we aren't overwhelmed by aggression."

"Talk to your mother, she might be able to help with that, but otherwise that sounds like a good plan."

"We had set it up with Ian and Jays."

Marcus nodded, sadness passed across his face.

"Marcus, any idea how many we can expect to enter the castes? Nathan was asking me too," Kevin asked.

"Until they are all off of the inhibitor, we won't know."

"But a rough guess would be ten to fifteen of the Facility Valkyries will turn out to be in the castes, right?" Robin said.

"For an estimate that's as good a guess as any. But it really won't answer your question, Kev. There's no way to guess how many of those will be in which caste, so Nathan will just have to be patient like the rest of us to find out how many new Seers will join his ranks. The best we can do is get them divided into the septs and let them get used to life outside of the Facility, and once they are all through stage four, they can tackle the new challenges a different caste brings."

"Hold on. Divided?" He met Donald's eyes and could see the agreement in them. "No one is dividing us up."

"Settle down, Chris. I'm not talking about it happening today. We'll get you guys settled, let you get comfortable outside of the Facility. Teach you the basics of what you need to know."

He stood, his wings shivering with the need to snap them open. He paced behind his chair. "That's all fine. I don't argue the need for any of that. But when you start talking about dividing up my Flights, then I have a problem. Until *my* Alpha, until Nickolas is awake, they are mine to lead. I will work with you, and we want to learn how you do things, but we are not yours."

Both Marcus and Kevin looked stunned, but Robin didn't look surprised in the least.

"I see," Marcus said warily.

A tickle in Chris's head let him know the three spoke. Donald met his gaze then rose to stand with him.

"Ian sent you here to me," Marcus tried again.

"Ian evacuated the Facility because he had no choice."

Another buzz of conversation, then Marcus continued, "Sit back down. Please. We will take this slower. Maybe once you've settled in, you can learn to trust us."

"Where do you think all of you are going to go?" Robin asked on top of Marcus. "None of you have been in the out world since you've fledged."

Chris glared at the other Hunter, ignoring Marcus. "I have no idea. We don't know our options yet. But obviously you all survived on your own."

"You're so ready to put your Flights to that kind of hardship," Robin sneered. "For what? Because you don't want to follow someone else's rules?"

"Rules? You have no idea what kind of rules we've lived under."

"Really? We got our orders from Ian. You have no understanding of what we know."

"Of course not! We've been lied to forever."

"Enough!" Marcus barked. "Robin, stand down. Christoff, sit your ass in that chair."

His father's green gaze pinned his. He tried to hold out, but he felt his own gaze drop and his body followed suit even though he had no desire to sit still. A growl rumbled in his chest. Donald slunk into the chair next to him.

"We will handle the future in the future. For now we need to get your people settled. We've cleared a section of cabins in the south end of the valley so you all can stay together."

Chris couldn't help but hear an unspoken "for now" on that sentence. He glanced up from under his lashes and met the heat in Robin's eyes. This wasn't over.

Marcus continued. "They aren't large and you will have to do some doubling up. But they are separated from us somewhat. Hopefully that will make you all more comfortable. Let's walk out there and show you what you've got to work with."

Chris rose and caught his Second's gaze then walked out of the room. Out in the courtyard, he put on the coat Donald tossed him then stretched his wings, his equilibrium shot.

The fear that he was out of control because he hadn't been free of the inhibitor for very long reinforced the lie that had been instilled in all of the Facility Valkyries that they were just animals. He didn't like the picture that made in his mind.

Robin paced the cobbles in a slow stalk, his gaze steady. Tensing, Chris watched.

"Robin," Marcus snapped. There was mental static, and Robin shot a look at Marcus then lazily stretched his wings. Marcus studied him for a moment then turned his attention to Chris and gestured at the different buildings bordering the courtyard. "You already know the medical building and the longhouse. This large building we use for a gym. The weather here can get harsh, so an indoor workout space is necessary. The fenced in area over there is the vegetable garden."

Marcus led them along a path that followed the north side of the longhouse and then connected with another that paralleled the creek. They walked slowly through the packed snow while Marcus pointed out different landmarks.

"That large field on the right takes up the center of the valley; we primarily use it for grazing livestock. The woods on the other side of the field are where most of us have made our homes. The cabins I'm taking you to were our first dwellings after the longhouse."

He pointed across the snow-laced creek. "Over there is our outside practice grounds. And the fields on either side are used for grazing as well, but we also cut hay from them during the summer."

Chris listened to Marcus talk about the valley and their customs and took a deep breath of the crisp air, trying to center his emotions. The beauty of the natural scene succeeded in breaking through and Marcus's voice turned into a drone as Chris stared in wonder around him. Delicate ice sculptures edged the creek where the water had splashed and frozen on rocks and twigs. The sunlight glinted through them, casting rainbows, and the sound of the unfrozen water underneath the ice burbled.

His senses soared. No longer inhibited and no longer locked up in the Facility, Chris wondered what he had missed. All of the other Valkyries had memories of life in the "out world," as Robin put it, from before they changed. Even Nick.

But for him, he'd spent his entire life in the Facility. With Ian as his father. The clutch to his heart came swift, and he pushed it aside. With a shake of his head, he focused back on what Marcus had to tell them.

"The barns and several other important buildings are tucked up against the back cliff wall on the far side of the creek. And up above, at the top of the cliff, is what we call the control tower. It's our lookout station and our center of defense. We've just finished installing a couple of water turbines in the falls that feed the creek. So this year our electricity situation should pose no problems."

They crossed over a small wooden foot bridge into a miniature neighborhood of about thirty cabins. The little houses had been built in a grid, each with its own tiny yard. Wide paths, that were likely grass under the snow, reminded him of where roads would be placed in a normal neighborhood and separated the blocks.

"You've built all of this? In the last twenty years? How?"

Marcus mounted the steps to the nearest house and opened the door. "When we first escaped the Facility, some of us were able to clear out our bank accounts before they were shut down. So we had some starting capital. At first we all lived in the longhouse. But we've been steadily expanding ever since. Bringing in new improvements and technology. With some help, we've been able to set up fronts and invest our money, and Ian's worked to free our assets when he could."

Chris wandered through the little house. It only had two rooms, a sparsely furnished living space with bright airy windows, a small wood burning stove, and through a door on the back wall he found a smaller bedroom and a closet.

"Most of the cabins are one or two bedrooms. Just like this one. I'm afraid private plumbing is an issue. There are communal bath houses close by. Not so bad in the summer, not as much fun on a snowy night in the winter. Everyone takes their turn chopping wood, which will need to be a first priority for you. Kevin can get you acquainted with that."

He followed Marcus back outside.

Donald talked with Kevin on the steps, but Robin caught his eye. The banked fire in his gut started to flare. The Hunter had been quiet for the whole tour.

Without turning away, he asked Marcus, "We are used to working out regularly. Can we use the practice grounds to work out on?" Chris smiled at the answering excitement that entered Robin's eyes.

"You are free to make use of the grounds, but only with your own people. Until I give the go ahead, there's to be no fights between my Valkyries and yours."

His head swiveled to meet gazes with Marcus. He suppressed a growl of frustration when he realized that Marcus was aware of his and Robin's desire to butt heads. A soft snarl let him know he wasn't the only one annoyed at being thwarted.

Marcus's stony eyes bore into his. "You will abide by that."

Chris held the look for as long as he could but finally dropped his gaze to the ground.

The Alpha's voice gentled. "Get your people sorted, then come back over to the longhouse for lunch."

With a nod of acknowledgement, Chris gathered up Donald and flew over to bring his people to their new homes.

A few hours later, Chris lifted off into the air. He and the rest of the lieutenants had worked out the housing assignments, gotten what little personal possessions they'd managed to bring moved in, along with everything Ian sent with them. He knew Marcus was going to want that stuff, but until Nick and Jays could both weigh in on that decision, he'd decided to keep possession of it.

Flight

Instead of dragging everyone back to the longhouse for lunch, he sent some of the Wing leaders to bring enough back for the whole clan. That allowed them all time to get over the first spate of grief together, though it was a tight fit squeezing that many Valkyries into his new house. He'd taken one with two bedrooms, using the second as a storeroom for the evacuated materials.

The early afternoon sunshine felt good on his wing membrane, and he wished he had time for an extended flight, but Beth had called him back to the infirmary. He dropped down into the courtyard.

He walked through the doors to find Kieran alone, watching Nick. He pulled up a chair and sat down next to the Beta.

Nick remained strapped to the table, pale and still. A glance across the room showed Jessica hadn't changed position from the last time he'd seen her. Chris stretched his legs out. "Beth called me back. Where is she?"

Kieran fidgeted in the chair next to him. "She's in the lab getting some test results she did on Jays."

"I had hoped I was being called back because he'd woken up."

"No luck. Sorry."

They fell silent watching his brother breathe slowly.

Kieran broke the silence. "He's been cycling through purges all day. Not all on the same subject. He's in a quiet spell at the moment. But I don't think it's going to last much longer. His fever still hasn't broken."

"How are you doing?"

"All right, I suppose. I don't like causing pain like this."

Snorting, Chris turned a glare on Kieran and his self-pity. "I should take you out to the field and run you around. That would get your mind back on reality." He sighed. "Look, Kieran, try and think logically, think past the emotion. You didn't cause the pain. You know that. It was already there. Yes, what you and Beth did was hard on him. Hell, it was hard on all of us, but wounds need to be cleaned out. And that doesn't feel good. Also try to remember that you haven't finished the fourth stage yet. You are only coming into your talent."

Kieran scrubbed his face. "That's a little hard to forget with everyone shoving their feelings up my nose."

They were quiet for a few minutes, watching Nickolas.

"Do you know what Beth wants me to do?" Kieran asked quietly.

"Yes."

"I don't know if I can, Chris."

"She's right." Chris paused for a moment. "She brought up a good point. What would Ian have done?"

Kieran growled and stood up. He flexed his wings in the open part of the room. "Damn it."

"I agree. I don't like it much either. She also reminded me of a fact we shouldn't have forgotten. What caste he is in. His survival is important. If it helps, you need to hold the thought of Nick never flying again in the uppermost part of your mind. Try not to think about this hurting him. The knowledge is going to hurt him, one way or another. Let him deal with healing his body before he has to concentrate on healing his mind."

Kieran kept his back to Chris but hunched up as he wrapped his arms around himself. "What if he hates me for hiding this? For lying to him?"

Chris sat forward in the chair, leaning his arms on his knees. "That's possible. At least at first. You know that. But do you really think he'll hold that forever? We are all behind you, Kieran."

"All right," he whispered.

"Come on." Chris stood. "I want to see Jessica before Beth comes back."

Kieran joined him by Jessica's side, and he ran a quick scan along his link to her. A fluttery feel accompanied his check. He mentally backed out to stare at her in confusion. "I'm not sure, but I think Jessica might be coming around. I just did a quick scan down my link, and I got a response. I have no idea what it should feel like when she's awake though."

Kieran nodded and touched her hand. "In the dreamscape, I talked to her. I had to convince her to return to her own body. I had a feeling that she would finish up quickly and wake to help Nickolas."

"This is too soon. I hope she's all right."

"I know it's faster than we're used to, but we aren't in the Facility, so she's not on drugs or being tested and studied. Add in the differences in her change because she's a Breeder..." He shrugged. "I spent a lot of time with her in the Hub. So I'm not completely surprised. I think she'll be fine."

He brushed his hand over her hair.

"To add to things," Kieran said, "David is having his Last Meal right now."

Chris looked up at him then said, "I'll let everyone know. I want one of us to stay here at all times to keep an eye on our people."

Kieran cocked his head and studied Chris's face. "Any reason why?"

Chris blew out his breath. "I don't know. We should trust everyone here, right? Ian did. He sent us here. And it's my parents.... But we aren't them. We're refugees. I don't think they understand how different we are. It's not like we're fledglings, you know? Marcus wants to assimilate us."

"But we have our own Alphas," Kieran added.

"Exactly. I don't think he grasps that."

"Nick will have problems with this."

"Tell me about it."

Kieran blinked then turned back to look down at Jessica as footsteps came down the hall.

"Good, you're here already," Beth said. "If we don't get Jays to wake up and eat, then we will lose him. The trip here was hard on the healthiest of you. For a second stage fledge in the first couple of days...I'm actually surprised he made it this far."

"Did you find out what is wrong with him?"

She shook her head. "All of my tests have come back fine. He should be awake. The question is why isn't he? And my only guess is that it's got to be the same thing that's going on with Nick."

"Huh?"

Kieran's wings rustled, and Chris turned to him. His face looked pinched.

"Both Nick and Jays had strong bonds with Ian," she said softly.

"Well, yes. But Jays doesn't know Ian's gone. He's been unconscious since before we found out."

"You didn't see him during the flight, Chris." Kieran looked sick. "He knows."

"How?"

The empath shrugged.

"The only thing keeping him from waking is his own mind," Beth said. "And Kieran is the only mind healer we have."

Kieran's head still throbbed lightly, even after four hours of sleep. He felt bruised inside. He evaded Chris's searching gaze.

"I've done everything I know," Beth said. "Now it would just be a matter of waiting, most likely for him to fade away, hoping he would wake in time. But Kieran's talent could change that."

She turned and started walking down the hall. With a sigh, he joined Christoff in her wake. The memory of Nickolas's pain still licked at Kieran's nerves.

She pushed the wardroom door open. Robin sat at the head of Jays's bed. Kieran felt the sweep of emotion from Chris as his body tensed and the return volley from the Hunter in the room.

Those two aren't going to hold off much longer.

Beth snapped a look at Robin as she moved to Jays's bedside. She checked the fledgling's vitals then brushed his limp hair with her hand.

"Kieran, this will be similar to what you did with Nickolas this morning. I don't know what sort of barriers he will have yet, since he's only started to fledge. We go in, find his core, then take it from there. Until you get me into his dreamscape, I can't assess the sort of damage we're looking at."

He nodded.

She pulled two chairs up next to Jays's bedside then sat in one. "Place your hand on his chest. The physical contact, skin to skin, will give you easier access."

He folded his wings tighter and sank down into the chair. Hesitantly, he placed his hand on Jays's bare chest. "I didn't do that this morning."

"No. You didn't. You are surprisingly strong. But you are inexperienced. And I bet your head still hurts, doesn't it?"

He sucked in a breath, and she chuckled.

"As you found this morning, you don't necessarily require physical contact, but that doesn't mean it won't make it easier. And you wore yourself out earlier. Now, relax and drop into a trance. Don't forget your anchor."

Kieran closed his eyes. Her hand wrapped around the back of his neck again, and he dove out. Freefall straight into Jays's mind.

She was right; the contact created a conduit. When he opened his eyes, he stood among the round river rocks lining the beach of the river they'd rendezvoused at. The dying sun sank before him.

Is this a real place? Or created, like Nick's? Beth asked beside him.

This is where the Flights rendezvoused when we left the Facility. He squinted through the red-gold haze.

So, he's stuck.

The sun continued to sink.

He stared at it a moment. *Why is the sun important?* He looked around at the lengthening shadows, trying to decipher the clues his talent screamed at him.

There's something about the sun...

Beth's gaze shot to his, then she looked intently around. She raised her arm, her hand palm out, and slowly turned a circle.

She clenched her fist and dropped her arm with a growl. *We need to hurry. The sun is a representation, a ticking time bomb. If we don't get him out before it sets, we've lost him.*

He started to scramble over the large rocks, Beth right behind. They hurried around a bend and found Jays, sitting in the shadows of a thick hedge on a boulder, pitching rocks into the river. Beth pulled Kieran to a halt.

Wait. She held her hand out again as she stared intently at Jays. He sat skipping stones into the water. *I'm a diagnostic talent. I can read his dreamscape, but it's your talent that can affect it. With training you will be able to read it better than I can. Until then I can tell you that he's fighting himself. Definitely in denial about what has happened. Not only to Ian but his changing self.* She turned to look at him. *He didn't know he was changing, did he?*

No. He entered stage two as the evacuation started. He hadn't even gotten to the passing out point, where they are normally recovered, before we hauled him out of the Facility. Ian broke the news to him right when Donald took him away.

Right. She turned back to watch the fledgling. *Looks like you get to practice. Basically he has the same issue Nick does, but for different reasons. Two competing conditions acting like flaming oil on water. For him to make it through the change, he needs to wake up and not remember what is keeping him locked up inside of himself.*

How do I do that?

I have no idea. I don't have your talent. You'll discover that a lot of using our abilities is doing just that. Using it. Some skills are the same from person to person and talent to talent. And that can be taught. But each person is different, and how an individual talent manifests is also unique, so there is trial and error involved in learning the full range and usage of our abilities. So I can lead you here, direct you in the end goal, but how you accomplish that depends on you. But whatever we do, it needs to be now.

The sun was a great flaming ball near the horizon line.

Staying in the light of the setting sun, Kieran left Beth's side and sat down next to Jays, his mind racing. He took a deep breath and tried to relax. While Jays skipped stones, Kieran released little tendrils of his power, tasting the currents around him. The fledgling hadn't had any outer barriers to breach, but his inner barriers were solid steel from the feel of them.

So, Jays, what's up?

The fledge picked out just the right stone then skipped it. *Waiting.*

For what?

Just waiting.

Do you know who I am, Jays?

Pale blue eyes looked up at him as if he were stupid then went back to the stones. *Of course I know who you are, Kieran.*

He couldn't get close enough from outside of Jays's core. He released a little more of his power and let it brush across the barrier; he flinched like he'd been struck.

Stop! Jays scrabbled back on the rock, farther into the shadows.

Damn it. He had to get through Jays's barriers to deal with the memories causing this problem in the first place. Nick's inner barriers had been almost nonexistent because of the tremendous pain level he had. Not so with Jays.

Do you know where you are, Jays?

What do you want, Kieran? Jays asked quietly, inching back even farther.

Kieran sighed, knowing he was going to have to go into those shadows, just like Nick's sea.

We want you to wake up. He stood and started to stalk Jays through his shadows. The light began to fade. *Do you know where you are?*

It doesn't matter, Kieran, just go away. Jays continued to retreat until he'd backed to the tree line and bushes beyond the beach, then he skirted along their obstruction.

It does matter. We want you to come home. Will you let me in? I can help you.

No. Don't touch me.

What are you hiding from?

Go away, Kieran.

Still following his retreat through the shadows, Kieran brushed across his friend's mind again, wearing away at it. *I know you don't want to remember. But if you won't let me in to help, I have to keep pushing you. Where are you?*

Don't, Kieran. Please, Jays whispered.

You have to remember.

NO!

Trying to protect himself, Jays sought the darkest shadows. Using his mind, Kieran started uprooting the trees, letting the light through. Jays shrieked and shied to the side, avoiding the light, then tried to bolt. Finally close enough, Kieran grabbed Jays by the shoulders. The shock of sudden contact slammed into both of them.

Where. Are. You? Implacably, Kieran repeated his question, forcing Jays to remember.

At the rendezvous! His eyes widening in shock, he sank to his knees, pulling out of Kieran's grip. *At the rendezvous. No...* Then he jumped up and spun around frantically, looking. *We can't leave him. You don't know what they'll do to him.*

His inner barriers collapsed, and Jays dropped to the ground.

No. How could you! he cried. *You made me leave him!* You made me leave him!*

Kieran dropped to his knees and pulled the sobbing man into his arms. He immediately sank his mind into Jays's and went to work. Using the river and stone of their surroundings, he created the cage to hold the memories at bay. The respite his friend needed to survive the change.

Shivering in reaction, Jays finally calmed in his arms. As Kieran placed the last stone, the fledgling arched in his arms with a scream, his mind torn in two.

Holding back his own grief, Kieran gently laid his friend on the sand. He rose, and Beth squeezed his shoulder.

Kieran slid out of Jays's mind and became aware of his physical surroundings. Beth brushed her fingertips against the back of his neck. He opened his eyes. Jays's chest rose underneath his palm as color flooded through his skin, chasing the gray pallor away.

With a gasp that lightly arched his back, Jays's eyes snapped open. Robin leaned forward and grabbed the fledgling's hand.

Beth held her hand above him for a moment. "You did it, Kieran. His body is coming back into balance and starting to get to work."

Jays's gaze darted around the room, glazed. "Robin?" he said, confused, then he turned his head and met Kieran's look. "Where are we, Kieran?"

"What do you remember?" Kieran asked softly.

"I..." He shook his head then looked at everyone, one by one. "Chris?"

"Sorry, Jays, answer Kieran's question."

He squinted his eyes. "I can't think. My head feels thick. What's going on?"

Kieran pulled his hand slowly away. "You've started the change. Do you remember that?"

Jays's breath froze, and he jerked his head once in disbelief.

"Chris," Beth said softly. "Please go to the kitchens and ask them for slivered beef broth."

Jays twisted to look at Beth then back to look at Robin. "Where are we?" he whispered. "Ian. I need to talk to him."

"He's..." Kieran had to swallow before he could continue. "Busy at the moment. He has us looking after you for now. You've been out for a while. You need to eat. After that maybe you'll remember more."

Jays exhaled then relaxed into the bed, keeping his gaze pinned to Kieran's. "Ok."

Beth squeezed his shoulder as she rose. "Get him to eat. I'm going to go check on Jessica and Nick."

Kieran broke away from Jays's gaze and watched her abandon him with what he'd done.

There would likely be hell to pay when he returned to his watchdogs. That didn't stop Gabriel's grin. *Let them try something.*

The silence of the forest surrounded him. The faint trace of the Caster who'd picked up Nickolas that morning had led this way. He slipped between the trees, his steps cautious.

The uninhibited power signatures of two Valkyries blazed like a beacon in his thoughts. The two moved as silently as only Hunters could, patrolling a section of the forest. He flattened against a tree trunk.

After they passed, he continued through their line and kept his own power signature damped down. *They're good.... Then again, they've never needed to guard against one of their own before.* He slipped over a soggy fallen log, careful not to disturb the patchy snow, then froze.

A tingle, like the invisible buzz you'd feel walking underneath a giant electrical tower, shimmered in front of his nose. Another step and he'd have blundered through. He backed away and pressed against the log.

The urge to turn aside and head in a different direction insinuated itself. He paused, his senses reaching.

A perimeter warning? A sight shield to keep wanderers away? *That would account for why we haven't been able to locate them from the air. What the council wouldn't give to know about this.* Depending on which faction of the council took control, this package of information could be used in a number of ways.

How did they manage a shield like this on such a large scale? Through his senses, he felt the shimmer of power stretch in a line through the forest. Careful not to touch the barrier, he paced along the perimeter. Silent.

The last of the sunlight filtered through the needles, turning the snow that had managed to fall to the forest floor into sparkles. A whisper of warning shivered across his senses, and he crouched. A sentry appeared through the ferns and from between the tree trunks then stopped to lean against one, staring toward the energy line. A moment later another Hunter walked out of the trees, and the first pushed away from his trunk.

The two chatted quietly, and Gabriel inched his way to the energy line. He strained his mental ears and listened.

With a sigh, the man clapped his relief on the shoulder and started to walk home. The moment the Hunter crossed the energy line, Gabriel rolled to the side, allowing the energy to wash across his skin as he crossed the barrier in tandem.

He stayed flat to the ground as he listened to the Hunters walk their separate ways. Gabriel gave both scouts time to move before he slowly rose through the ferns. He stretched his wings to shake the snow and soggy forest debris from them then tracked off after the retreating Hunter.

Tailing him was child's play. Gabriel snorted. *Too complacent. They depend on their barrier to keep everything away, with their scouts as a failsafe. They never expected me to come in alone. Though to give them their due, none of the Facility could come upon them without their knowing it. At least before now.*

The trees thinned then ended, and he stepped out onto the rocky cliffs overlooking a valley. He shielded his eyes from the setting sun and stared down into a surprise.

A couple hundred feet below, at the base of the cliff, a snow-covered field stretched out. Smoke curled from chimney pipes on several dozen cabins farther in the distance on his left. More buildings and what looked like animals speckled the opposite northern end of the valley.

The hustle and bustle of people, some on the wing, others on the ground, filled the valley with life. A large valley. One they should have found long before now. He turned his gaze to the open sky above then back to the well-developed settlement. He wondered which faction of the council he could sell this to. Maybe he could get out from under Kratz's thumb.

The sun dropped below the tips of the trees on the far side of the valley, and Gabriel left the edge to return to the cover of the trees. With a quickened pace, he worked his way back to the boundary. He damped his energy signature then crossed the line, the energy tingling across his skin. He bounded away to gain distance from his crossing place then slid under a large nurse log, the muck and rotted leaves covering him.

He felt the telepathic sending close by, and he opened himself just enough to eavesdrop on the broad send.

I'm not finding anything, tower. Another deer most likely. They have been heavy near Aurora this year.

All right. But keep your eyes open. The Seer on duty is twitchy.

Got it.

The Hunter moved on, and Gabriel let his breath out. When he was sure he was alone again, he crawled out and shook off. He scanned the canopy for an opening big enough to get into the air and started to move. *I have to get to my watchdogs and stop them before they prove that Seer's feeling right. They won't be able to stay out of the scouts' sights. And then they'll start wondering about unexplained deer crossings.*

Still silent, he leapt obstacles and worked his way farther away from the rebels.

◆ ◆ ◆

Chris opened his eyes and looked around the unfamiliar room in the grey light of early morning. He reached his senses out, looking for what had woken him. Then he felt the pulse surge down the link he had with Jessica, and he sat bolt upright.

After a brief pause, he flung the covers back and quickly pulled on his clothes, shivering in the chill air. Still buckling his belt, he walked into the living room and opened the stove to see that the fire had gone out. That accounted for the chill. Slamming the door shut, he threw on his coat before heading out the door.

Donald?

I felt it too. Kieran said to hurry.

He hopped down the steps from his porch, spread his wings, and jumped into the air. Donald's shadow skimmed over the bridge and field up ahead of him.

They landed in the courtyard seconds apart then walked into the medical building together. Chris tucked his wings in tighter and looked around in the dim light.

"Here." Kieran stepped away from Jessica's bed and turned the dimmer switch. The lights brightened slowly as the empath nodded over to Jessica. "She's definitely coming around. I can feel her even without the link."

Jessica stirred.

Her legs slid under the sheet, then her arm twitched, fingers tapping as the muscles contracted. Flickers of muscle movement skittered under her exposed skin. After several larger reflex movements, her whole body jerked, then she groaned, and her trembling arm rose to cover her eyes.

She tried to roll to her side but got tangled in her wings; all three of them grabbed her before she fell off the bed.

She opened her eyes then slammed them shut with a hiss, rubbing her temples.

"Where am I? What's happened?" she said, her voice low and gravelly from disuse.

When she tried to sit up again, Chris helped her swing her legs to the side while Kieran adjusted her wings to the new position.

"Congratulations. You're a Valkyrie now, Jess."

"What..." She coughed, her throat dry. "What are you talking about? That kind of happened the day you broke into my house, dickhead."

"Language, language." Chris laughed. "What I mean is that you lived through stage three. You're now fully fledged."

"Stage three?"

She accepted the glass of water Donald handed her and started to gulp it, but Chris grabbed her wrist. "Sips. You haven't had anything to eat or drink in several days."

She squinted at him but complied, taking a small sip. "Stage three?" she asked again.

Kieran answered, and she bowed her head as he rubbed the back of her neck. "Each fledge drops into a coma so their systems can reboot, basically. It's the most dangerous time. Not everyone survives it. That's why Aiden and I tried to stop you from leaving during the evacuation."

She sighed then tilted her head so she could look at Kieran out of the corner of her eye. "And you couldn't have just said that?"

"No," Chris said. "Besides, would knowing have stopped you?" He caught her brief grin and chuckled.

"God, my head is killing me."

"Keep taking sips. The headache is normal."

"I think my head didn't stop hurting for about two days," Kieran added.

"Thanks, Kieran, that makes me feel loads better."

"Glad to help."

"Want to help? Don't stop rubbing."

Smiling, Chris exchanged a look with Donald while they listened to Kieran banter with Jessica.

"You still haven't answered my question. Where are we? This isn't the Hub." She looked around and took a couple of deep breaths. "Where's Ian and Jays? Why are you guys here?"

"It might take some time for the fog to lift. A lot of your memories of your isolation will be lost."

Her empty hand squeezed her eyes, then she froze, and power whipped around Chris. She raised her face, her gaze locking onto his. "Where's Nick?"

He shivered at what he saw in her eyes, and his wings clamped tight to his back. He tried to drop his gaze but couldn't.

Kieran squeezed her neck, and she hissed, releasing Chris's gaze so she could whip a look over her shoulder at the empath.

"Knock it off, Jess."

"Then stop pussyfooting around and give me some answers."

The door to the outside opened and preempted what Kieran had been about to say. Robin walked in then froze.

Jessica's head snapped up. They stared at one another.

"I'm in Aurora."

Chapter Six

Chris felt the mental static of close telepathy, then Robin started to walk toward them. Kieran growled and lunged around the foot of the bed, snapping his wings wide, halting Robin in his tracks. Chris cocked his head at the empath before he realized Kieran was reacting to Jessica's feelings.

Jess pushed to her feet, and Chris had to catch her as she fell. He steadied her. "You haven't used any of your muscles in days; they aren't going to respond right away. Take it slow."

Shivering, she nodded. He held her in his arms as her quivering muscles firmed.

"Jessica?" her brother asked tentatively.

"Robin," she mimicked.

The Hunter Prime tried to circle around the blocking empath, but Kieran growled and Donald stepped up to back him.

Chris brushed his chin across the top of her hair and watched Robin's cautious movements across the floor. Jess leaned into him, turning her face into his chest. He wrapped his wings around them both, offering comfort.

He kept his gaze fixed on the pacing Hunter. Robin ran his hand through his hair, looking for a way through the three of them. Their gazes clashed, and Chris grinned.

The Prime suppressed his snarl. Chris had to give him credit for that.

"It's good to see you. I've missed you," Robin finally tried.

"Really? Now why don't I believe that?" Her voice was already firming, and she mostly supported her own weight now. She pushed against Chris, and he let her venture out of his support. Her first steps shuffled along the edge of the bed, hands pressed into the mattress. "Oh, I know. Maybe it has something to do with the fact that I haven't seen you in almost ten years. That must be it."

"I tried. You wouldn't see me, remember?"

"Once," she snapped with almost the same vigor she used to show. "You tried once, right after you left me. How did you think I would feel after you left me all alone? Give me a break. You knew how I felt about Marcus. And you didn't even try again."

"Yes, I knew how you felt about Marcus. That, combined with Mom and Dad's wishes, is why I didn't insist on bringing you here. And I didn't leave you all alone; you had May. Who, by the way, has always stayed in touch with us. We received regular reports on how you were doing."

Jessica stiffened, and Chris laid a reassuring hand on her shoulder. She grabbed it. "I see. So you could be bothered to have someone spy on me, but you couldn't make the time to try and see me."

"Jessica, please, be reasonable. The Facility had you under constant surveillance after I slipped through their fingers. But as long as you were protected by May and hadn't started to change yourself, they couldn't do anything to you. But that didn't stop them from hoping to catch me or any of the other rebel Valkyries."

"Full circle, I guess. We're back to what Marcus wanted. It's always come down to that, hasn't it?" She turned her back on him and closed her eyes then slowly extended her wings out in a stretch. Chris backed up to give her room.

Agitated, Robin flexed his own wings, growling at Kieran and Donald.

"Chris, I still need to know what's going on. Where's Nick?" Jess asked, ignoring her brother.

He pulled the chair at the head of her bed forward. "Here, sit. Don't overdo it. Your strength will return fairly quickly, but it'll still take some time."

She wobbled over to the seat without the support of the bed and sank down with a sigh. Chris stared over her head, meeting Robin's eyes. Tension thrummed off of the Hunter Prime.

"Give it a little time, Jess. You only just woke up. You'll get all the details you want. As for Nick...he..."

She turned her head to look up at him when he paused, and he looked across the room to the bed Nick occupied. A stifled gasp left her, and she shoved to her feet. She slapped his hand away and swayed across the distance with all three of them flanking her. Robin skirted as close as he could.

Her steps already strengthening, she reached Nick's side and held out her hand. It trembled slightly. Chris couldn't tell if it was from weakness or emotion, but Kieran kept shooting glances at her. She finally settled for resting her fingers in Nick's hand.

"What happened?" she growled.

Chris shifted position and walked around the bed so he could look across his brother into Jessica's face. He sent a little energy pulse down the link he had with her, and her eyes widened and shot up to lock gazes with him.

"What...is...that?"

"One of many things we need to discuss. But I figured it should be acknowledged right away. As for Nick, after we found you, he went back to the Facility to make sure everyone had made it out."

"Did they?"

He dropped his gaze from hers and stared into Nick's face. He swallowed before he answered. "No. Ian didn't."

"Jays?" she asked softly.

"He made it, but he isn't in great shape. He entered stage two during the evacuation."

She flexed her wings. The door to the outside opened, and her head shot up like a deer's.

Marcus and Bethany stepped through. They didn't look surprised to see Jessica up, so that confirmed his guess on the telepathy he'd felt earlier.

They paced themselves as they cautiously approached Nick's bed. Robin fell in behind them.

"Hello, Jessica," Marcus said. "It's been a long time."

"Not long enough," she rumbled. Chris placed a restraining hand on her arm.

Marcus shrugged and turned his attention to Nickolas. "Be that as it may, you're my daughter-in-law now. And I'm very glad you made it out of the Facility. For Nick's sake and your own."

"Wha...excuse me? Wait a minute. Nick said his parents were dead."

Chris felt her shock course down their link.

"He didn't know. Both of my sons were told we had died."

"Well, doesn't this just take the cake?" Jessica laughed without humor.

"I wouldn't worry about it, Jess. I expect Nick is going to have similar feelings about the situation as you do."

Marcus shot a steely look at Chris, and he shrugged. There wasn't much he could do to change that reality.

The Alpha turned his regard back on Jessica, and he pulled a chair over. "Sit."

Chris felt her hackles rise, so he steered her to the chair and pushed her into it. She growled at him, and he smiled. At least he took her mind off of Marcus for a moment. Donald and Kieran both crowded in as well. A loud sigh from Beth filled the room. He met his mother's half-amused gaze.

"I do need to get near her, boys. You know that?" She folded her arms and stared at the three of them.

With a look, he ordered his Second and Kieran to back off, but he stayed, clutching the back of Jess's chair.

Power flashed in Marcus's eyes, a soft rumble of a growl accompanying it. Tense, Chris waited while the two Aurorans checked Jessica over.

"Hello, Jess."

"Hi, Beth," she answered, rubbing her temple. "How is he doing?"

Beth looked up at Nickolas. "We managed to get him stabilized. So far. Now, how are you doing?"

"My head hurts, and I have no idea what's happened. Everything is fuzzy. I feel like I've just woken up from a dream."

"That's pretty normal. A lot of your memories from your isolation will probably fade or just not return from your time in the coma." Beth grabbed equipment from a cart that

Marcus had pushed up near her. "I'm sorry to say, though, there isn't anything we've been able to find to help with the headache."

Robin dared to inch closer, and Chris started to growl, his fists squeezed the rail on the chair. Marcus caught his gaze and stared him down. Beth finished with her equipment then held her hands out over Jess.

"So far, everything checks out. All your vitals are back within normal ranges. Today you're to stay close to the infirmary and only take gentle walks to get your balance back. And no flying."

"Don't worry, Beth," Kieran answered her. "Jessica isn't stupid. She wouldn't do anything that would risk her health and safety, now would she?"

Chris held back a laugh when Jess turned a lethal glare on Kieran, who just returned her stare steadily.

A twinkle in her eye, Beth turned away and pushed the cart toward the head of Nickolas's bed.

"His wing's looking good, Beth," Marcus said. "I should be able to give it a little more healing after we're done."

She folded the sheet down, exposing his brother's wound. Marcus joined her as she probed it. "The swelling is down, and his delirium has abated, though his fever still hasn't broken. Still, it should be safe to remove it now. Then do a second general healing."

"Good, I'll get the tray. Robin, we could use your assistance," Marcus said.

Chris's father moved off to one of the supply cabinets while Robin eyed them carefully, approaching Nickolas from the other side.

Confused, Chris asked, "I thought they got the bullet out yesterday? Was there more than one?"

Checking the straps holding Nickolas down, Robin tightened one. "No, they're removing a microchip. Its location was too close to the infected wound for safe removal."

Thunderstruck, Christoff watched as Marcus set down a surgical tray and Bethany chose a scalpel then started to incise a line close to his wound. As the blood flowed down Nickolas's shoulder, the only thing that stopped Chris from leaping across the table and spilling someone else's blood was the death grip Kieran had on him, and the fact that the empath must be redirecting his emotions somehow.

"What have you done to him?" he could barely whisper.

Beth and Marcus were too focused on what they were doing, so Robin answered from where he held Nickolas's right shoulder immobile. "When Nickolas first fledged and went into his coma, Ian implanted a microchip. We have used it to pass information between us and the Facility ever since. Now that the need is no longer there, Marcus has decided to remove it completely to retrieve Ian's last message."

Shocked, he barely felt Jessica's hand reach up and encircle his wrist. "Do I have one?"

"No. Only Nickolas," Robin replied.

Chris met Robin's gaze. The other Hunter's eyes just shy of feral in response to his own descent.

Vibrating, Christoff watched Bethany pull a small capsule out of the incision. Rinsing it off, she set it into a dish and turned to finish. Marcus handed her a threaded needle then held his hand out over the wound as she quickly set some stitches. Gentle light flowed out from his hand, bathing Nickolas's entire shoulder.

She stepped back when done to let Marcus finish using his talent to help speed up the healing. After a minute, Marcus moved to the staked-out wing and repeated the procedure. The light faded, and Marcus took a deep breath before he picked up the capsule to look at it.

"That's all I can do for now, Beth. Call me if you need to. I'll be in my office." Closing his fist on the capsule, he left without another word.

Chris's gaze tracked the Alpha out the door. After Marcus was gone, he felt Jess's hands still on his wrists, and Donald clamped to one arm while Kieran leaned on the other.

"Chris, I'll stay with Jess," Kieran said. "You need to leave. Go, fly or work out, or something, but you need to do something to get yourself under control."

It took him a moment before he could nod and get his hands to let go of the chair. He walked out, not seeing anything. The early morning sunlight filled his eyes when he reached the courtyard, and he stopped.

He didn't turn when he heard the door open behind him, but he smiled. The same sort of violence that swirled through him now approached. Chris watched the Hunter pace around him, assessing him.

"So, you've known about this chip," Chris stated.

"Of course. I set up all of the retrievals for the last eight years. It was the most secure method devised to allow Ian to communicate with us without the council finding out about it. It's been driving Gabriel nuts trying to figure out how Ian has been passing the information."

Chris flared his wings then started circling Robin, matching the other Hunter move for move. "Did you know that Nick didn't know about it?"

"Yes."

"And you didn't find this the least bit betraying?"

"Whether or not you realize it, we are at war, Christoff. A silent one to be sure, but it's war just the same for us. Now that you're out here, maybe you will start to understand, but we need to survive. And if that means we do things that not everyone likes, but helps keep everyone safe, then so be it. Nick will have to cope." Smiling viciously, Robin waved his hand toward the other side of the creek. "Shall we take this somewhere more appropriate?"

"Gladly." Spreading their wings, they both took off, heading for the practice grounds.

They circled the empty grounds once then landed in the slush in the center, facing one another. Chris settled his wings and cocked a brow at Robin. "So, any rules you guys like to follow?"

Smiling in anticipation, Robin shrugged. "Sure, lots. But in this case, let's just keep it simple. No death blows, and try not to permanently maim."

Smiling as well, Chris flexed his knees, bouncing lightly. "Works for me. Shall we begin?"

They slowly circled one another to take each other's measure. Robin lunged a feint and Chris stepped into it, striking the first blow. Ready for it, the other Hunter blocked and scored with his own kick then both bounced out of range, having gotten a taste.

The pause was brief. Coming together at full speed this time like two battling rams, they crashed into each other. Blow after blow, kicks, punches, the tension between them built as their focus narrowed. Spiraling to drive rational thoughts out of their minds. Left with only instinct and the need to release their pain and frustration in the only way they could, they fought. Time became meaningless. Just the move and stretch of their bodies, the pain of the blows.

Striking a backhand, Chris connected with Robin's already bloody face while blocking the roundhouse thrown his way. But he missed his next block, and Robin lashed him in the lower jaw. He saw stars, and it flung him back. Rolling out of the way, Chris took a wing beat into the air as the other Hunter landed where he would have been.

Breathing hard, he dropped down behind Robin and managed a solid kick to his midsection before Robin spun away, cursing.

The only partner that had ever pushed him like this was Nickolas. He grinned and pushed the offensive. The other Hunter was quick and turned the tables on him.

Wiping sweat out of his eyes, Chris dodged Robin's next two attacks, then fanning his wings, he launched skyward, Robin on his heels. They spiraled around each other then hit midair like two rams, arms squeezed as they grappled, trying to gain control. He just missed getting Robin in a strangle hold when the Hunter slipped through his grasp and dropped to skim low over the grounds.

Chris stooped like a hawk and dropped after Robin, intending to land on him, but at the last minute Robin turned upward, causing Chris to back-wing rapidly or crash to the dirt. The tables turned, Chris hit the ground hard under Robin's weight. Bucking him off before Robin could pin his wings, Chris launched at the prone Hunter and managed to grab his foot. Then twisting, he tried to pull Robin off balance and toward him but only succeeded in getting the other foot in his face.

Trading blow after blow, the two Hunters were much too focused to notice the crowd that had begun to gather around the edges of the practice field. Word spreading, more flew in to land until nearly the entire population of the valley avidly watched the two strongest fighters they had ever seen beat the crap out of each other.

Marcus sat at his desk and typed in the last command to access the information loaded on the microchip. Feeling the grief start to well up again, he waited for his father to appear then closed his eyes briefly at the tired, resigned look that met his when he did.

"Marcus, if you are seeing this recording then I am glad to know that Nickolas made it to you safe and well. You probably also know by now what has happened to the Facility. I've done my best to destroy and disrupt their operation. I regret that I won't be able to do more. I've tried to work out a way to overcome the hold they have on me to no avail, so this will be the last communication I'll be able to make. I wish I could have seen you and Beth one more time. It's been so long."

Pausing, his father looked at the ground, clearing his throat.

"I have attached individual messages for Nickolas and Christoff as well, but please try to make them understand. They have been two of the three things that has made captivity here bearable. If there had been any way for me to have told them the truth, I would have. I just wish I could explain it to them in person.

"Take care of Jays for me. He's the third reason. I know you have never known him in person, but he's your little brother in everything except blood. He wasn't very happy with me when I made him leave. Tell him I'm deeply sorry. I recorded a message for him a while ago; it's with the computer disk I gave him when Donald took him away. Make sure he finds it please.

"I have also attached another recording. One I made for this eventuality. My good-bye to my clan. Once you have them settled, show it to them.

"The rest of the data on this disk is the last research Jays and I completed, along with several coded messages that we had not yet deciphered. When he is up to it, I would recommend getting Jays's assistance with them. He has had an uncanny knack for figuring them out. I have also included some research I had started concerning Jays. We haven't had a lot of opportunity to study an individual during stage one. As soon as I recognized his state, I started tests on him. The results have been intriguing.

"I want you to know, and to tell everyone who needs this as well, that I don't regret what is about to happen. I wish it were different, of course, but unlike the rest of you, I have always been stuck between two worlds. I'm tired, Mark, and I'm ready for it to be over. I have kept fighting as long as I could, but I can't fall under Gabriel's control. You know how much that would compromise.

"I love you, son, and I am proud of everything you have accomplished in your life. Take care of my Valkyries and keep fighting for all of your freedom. Good luck, clear skies."

The screen went blank.

Marcus stared at it, his mind as blank as the screen. Then slowly, the noise out in the common room started to penetrate the thick fog of grief shrouding his mind. Puzzled, he started to rise to find out what all of the ruckus was about when Beth sent to him frantically.

Marcus! Where are you? You've been so tightly shielded I couldn't reach you.

I'm in my office, what's wrong?

Chris and Robin. They're going at it. And I don't think there is anyone else here who can stop them.

Where?

Out at the practice grounds.

I'm on my way.

Rising, Marcus opened a cabinet door beside his desk. Grabbing something off of a shelf in the back, he pocketed it, then left his office. The cafeteria that had been so noisy previously was now deserted. Suspecting he now knew where they all were, he left the building quickly, his own temper rising. He took wing as soon as he was clear of the door and flew across the valley.

From the air, he could see both his surrogate son and his blood son clashing. The population of the valley surrounded the grounds. Then he noticed the knot of Facility Valkyries to one side, and Marcus hoped they would keep themselves under control. That was all he needed, all of them engaging in an attempt to help or defend Chris.

Winging in, he landed in a flurry about ten feet from the combatants. Roaring, he called for them to stop. "Robin! Christoff! Stand down! Stop!"

Either they didn't hear him, or more likely, they just weren't listening, because the two bloody and battered Hunters continued to engage. "I said STOP!"

The two of them starting to take their battle aerial sent Marcus over the edge. His temper slipping the leash; he formed two bullwhips with his power, and when each had only gotten about ten feet off the ground, he snapped the whips out, coiling one around each of their ankles. With a jerk, he yanked both out of the air.

The Hunters landed with a painful thud. But they still tried to get up, not taking the hint that he was serious. Quicker than they could move, Marcus extended his whips into ropes and twisted them around their legs, then lashed their wings down and bound their arms behind their backs.

He pulled them into a kneeling position and came to stand in front of them. He stared at them. The shock of their sudden change in position broke through their feral mindset. His wings mantled, he folded his arms across his chest and stared at the two of them silently.

Letting the magnitude of the situation settle around them, he attempted to contain his own temper, succeeding only partially. As their eyes cleared of the battle haze, he saw fear start to replace it as they tested their bonds and found they couldn't move. Robin's eyes finally focused and looked past him; his face paled as he saw everyone gathered watching, and his gaze snapped back. Chris's eyes were just wary, with fear lying underneath. Unlike Robin, he hadn't a clue what to expect. Smiling grimly, Marcus let the silence of the crowd build the tension before he addressed them.

"I distinctly remember ordering that there was to be no fighting until I authorized it." He spoke softly, but the silence of the crowd still allowed all assembled to hear him. He studied their bloody faces and could tell the cold was starting to stiffen up their overheated bodies. He expected they were about to become very uncomfortable from their injuries. *Too bad. They're young, they can cope.*

"Well, we have just about all of the elements of a discipline battle it would seem. We have the offenders." He waved at them, then waved at the audience. "We have the witnesses. We have the judge." He smiled wickedly at them. "And then there was the battle. The two of you seem to be fairly evenly matched, at least the state of your injuries lend that credence. Now, normally the battle is the punishment, but since the battle is the offence, I have something else in mind."

He reached into his pocket and pulled out the object he'd taken from the cupboard in his office. Then stepping forward, he let the boys get a good look at what he was holding. Smiling in satisfaction at the dawning expressions of fear and resignation that crossed their faces, he continued. "Since the two of you can't seem to get along, you will stay together until you sort it out. To help promote that end, the two of you are assigned, until I say otherwise, to the task of chopping the firewood. You will have to cooperate to succeed."

His mind twisted the rope of energy, extending Chris's right arm and Robin's left, thus allowing Marcus to snap on the pair of handcuffs, securing the two Hunters together.

He stepped back and watched as the two of them bowed their heads. "I'm very disappointed in both of you. Yes, there has been a lot of stress, and I know it's hard, especially for two unfamiliar Hunters, but both of you are leaders; you have more discipline than this. And while I can't completely relieve either of you of duty, and trust me, I would if I didn't think it was a bad idea with the uncertainty of so many new people to settle, you will turn most of the day-to-day decisions over to your Seconds until you are reinstated. Do I make myself perfectly clear this time?"

Both of the Hunters nodded their bowed heads.

"What was that?" Marcus demanded.

They lifted their heads, and Marcus could tell that they were both bent but not broken. Fire lit the depths of their eyes; they both answered quietly, "Yes, sir."

"Good. Robin, you know the drill. Since you didn't sit in the penitition circle, your time starts now. You can explain it to Chris. Someone will come to release you." He removed his light ropes and the two Hunters sagged from the sudden lack of support. Then, turning his back on them, Marcus launched into the sky, heading back to the longhouse.

Jessica spooned up another mouthful of rich broth. Her stomach grumbled, but it was stuck with broth for the day, she'd been informed. She sat on the bed and looked across the tray at Kieran. Thankfully, Beth had sent her brother away right after Chris left. He was more than she was up for. *Why couldn't I have been important enough to come back for?*

She pushed the memories away and spooned up more soup.

"You were saying?" she prompted.

"He and Robin have been rubbing each other wrong since we arrived. What's happening is inevitable," Kieran replied.

"You couldn't have stopped it?"

"Are you kidding? That's a train wreck waiting to happen. I'm not jumping in front of it."

They were alone in the room for all intents and purposes. A few minutes ago, Beth had come running in with Jess's food, thrust it at Kieran, and told him to hold down the fort. There was an emergency at the practice field. Kieran snorted, knowing exactly what was happening.

Flashes of the last few months were hitting her hard and fast, leaving her somewhat dizzy. She ate more soup and tried to sort through it. Most of her memories were a jumble, but several of the clear pictures featured Kieran.

A snapshot of him in her cell. Bringing her food. Comforting her. Playing his drum. Blood running down his forearm. "How many times did I hurt you, Kieran? What the hell happened to me? Did I really come at you with a knife? Why are you even here now?"

"Don't. You were a trapped animal. They will either bite you or gnaw their own leg off. Of course you responded."

She sighed and scraped the last of the broth out. "So, tell me what Chris didn't get around to."

"Well..."

She almost dropped the bowl when a burst of energy broke across her internal mindscape. Her head snapped up, and she stared into Kieran's eyes. "First Chris, and now you?"

"Donald too."

She growled and would have shoved the tray off if he hadn't grabbed it first. She stood up. Her muscles still felt weak, but she could support herself now with a minimum of tremors.

"We didn't have a lot of choice, Jess. Your tie to Nick probably helped save his life, but it almost cost yours."

She laboriously paced the length of the room. Her wings fanned repeatedly. The map of her internal mindscape occupied her thoughts as she traced the lines. Now that she was aware of it, she could feel Chris's internal turmoil if she focused on the line that led to him. She switched to the line marked Kieran and felt a familiar spark filled with caution.

"You were dying. Chris had us blood bond to you so all three of us could send you enough energy to get you through the coma. If you had been on the other side of the coin, if it had been me in that bed dying, would you have done it? Would you have taken my choice away and bonded us together?"

She growled then turned and stalked back down the room to stop in front of him. "Damn it. That's not fair."

His lips curved up in a smile, and she wanted to punch him. Then she brightened because she realized soon she'd get to. Once she was strong enough to take to the ring.

He laughed as if he knew what she'd just figured out. *Jerk, he probably does.* Then she realized she'd come closer to the truth with that thought than she should have. She looked closer at that link. "You aren't a Hunter."

"Nope."

"What are you then? I can't tell whether you're a Caster or Seer."

"Both, I guess. I'm an empath."

She narrowed her eyes. And realized how screwed she was with him. That really made him start to laugh. "Just watch it, Kieran. You'll be in the ring with me, someday."

"I've been threatened with that before."

He put his arm around her shoulder, and together they walked over to Nick's bedside. She let the smile turn up her lips, but it faded quickly. Her mate lay still. Only the shallow rise of his chest let her know he lived, and the reassuring pulse down their link. The sheet had been turned down, and she got a good view of the bandage on his shoulder and the storm clouds that covered his chest.

She brushed Nick's hair back, her fingers trailing through the strands.

"What happened to him?"

"We don't have all the details. The binding threw you into the coma. Nick put you into Chris's safekeeping and sent him to catch up with us. But we had to leave the rendezvous because Gabriel had seen our direction. Nick went back to the Facility to make sure everyone had gotten out. Ian was the only one left at that point." He brushed his fingers along the injured man's bruised ribs. "He saw Ian die."

She felt Kieran's pain flow down their link.

"He was out longer than any of us. He must have tried to lead them away from the rendezvous, because he was way in the north when the search party found him. Shot and bleeding, but still fighting. They got him out from under Gabriel's nose."

She continued to run her fingers through Nick's hair, the slow pulse of the link between them like a second heartbeat. Memories of Nick's power surrounded her, a bright light, and the want and need almost swamped her. Her throbbing head couldn't take much more.

"Let it go for now. Come on, I bet you're dying for a shower."

She let him lead her away, but her mind continued to circle around the dream-like memories of the last few months.

◆ ◆ ◆

Chris knelt on the cold ground and shivered again. The crowd had dissipated a while ago, and he still hadn't a clue what exactly was going on. He shook his bound wrist in disgust then looked over at Robin. The Hunter sat with his eyes closed, relaxed and still. "So what exactly are we doing?"

Not opening his eyes, Robin responded, "We're meditating."

"Meditating. Right. Why?"

"Part of the discipline is meditating on what you did. Why did you do it? What are the consequences? Was it worth it? That sort of thing."

"Uh huh." Chris sat for a moment, looking around at the slushy ground and the clouds coming in that had started to obscure the sun. "What do you think?"

Robin sighed. "I think it's supposed to be quiet."

"Uh huh. So, how long are we supposed to stay here?"

Opening his eyes, Robin cast a quick glare at him before regaining his pose. "As long as Marcus wants us to."

"And that would be?"

Expelling a quick breath, Robin opened his eyes again. "I haven't a clue. It depends on how mad he is, I suppose. Usually it's an hour or two. For really bad offenses, I've seen a couple that went all day." Shrugging, he stretched his wings, wincing as he did so. "We are supposed to stay in a kneeling position and meditate quietly for however long the judge deems the penance period should last. After which, normally, would come the fight. How they comport themselves during the fight has a lot of bearing on the final outcome. It can be a complicated dance based on hierarchy. Those of you from the Facility have all been in an artificial environment. You'll discover that how you used to do things may not work as well anymore." Closing his eyes, Robin settled his wings. "You should at least try to meditate."

Chris thought about what Robin said and closed his eyes, but after a short time, he opened them again. He couldn't take the silence behind his eyes. His world was rocked. He needed Nick to wake up. He wanted Ian back; he tried not to think about that one.

Sitting here without the outlet of movement brought all of the uncertainty of the last several days home. Right where he didn't want to think about it. He restrained the urge to jump up and looked back at Robin's still form. A trail of dried blood traced his cheek, his eyes closed as he meditated. Chris asked, "So, was it worth it?"

A smile stretched Robin's face.

With a smile of his own, Chris turned to watch the lowering clouds and contemplated whether they meant more snow when he heard wings. He felt Robin tense next to him and he looked over the Hunter's shoulder to see Marcus swoop in for a landing.

Everything that he was centered within himself as he waited for his father. Robin opened his eyes next to him then bowed his head, waiting. Chris couldn't seem to manage that. Partly out of defiance, but also somewhat out of fear because he didn't know who this man was or what he was capable of. He'd always known his place in the world, who he could best, who could best him, not that there had been a lot of those.

But to be yanked out of the sky like that, by something he hadn't seen and didn't know how to counter? Warily, he watched Marcus's face. The glint of amusement in the Alpha's eyes had the strange effect of causing relief while at the same time making him worry all the more.

The older Valkyrie stopped in front of them, contemplating them for a while. Chris wished he could manage to hold as completely still as Robin, but he did his best.

"I'm still really annoyed with the two of you. You interrupted the last message I will ever receive from my father with your fight."

Next to him, Robin winced, and he closed his eyes briefly before looking back at his father's face.

"But even so, I figure an hour and a half of kneeling in the slush in this cold..." a cruel smile flirted at the corners of Marcus's mouth, "with the extent of the injuries I suspect you have, is enough."

Finally raising his head, Robin looked up at Marcus. "I'm sorry we interrupted the message from Ian, Marcus. Truly."

He stared at them then nodded. "Get up, if you can, and let's go. There's a lot of wood for you to chop."

It took both of them a few minutes to manage to rise, between stiffened muscles and handcuffed hands. Chris tried to ignore his father's amusement and stretched his wings with a groan. Then the two of them fell in at Marcus's heels for the long walk across the valley to the main firewood shed.

He sighed in resignation when he saw the pile of wood that waited.

"Now, the two of you are going to be spending a lot of time in each other's company. At least two or three days. And if you haven't learned to cooperate by then, it will be longer. You will eat together, sleep together, you will even visit the privy together. Robin, now that Kelley is reinstated as your Second, I'll send for her so you can give her orders for the next few days. Who is your Second, Christoff?"

"Donald."

"Then I'll send him over as well. Do either of you have injuries that need attention immediately?" Both shook their heads, so Marcus continued. "Check in at the infirmary before lunch then, so Beth can check you both out. That should give you a few hours to get a good start on the wood." He shook his head at both of them and took his leave.

Chris stared at the pile of wood and wondered how to even begin. "You know, Robin, I've never chopped firewood before."

"Doesn't surprise me. It's not like they have much need of that where you were. Here, this is called a splitting maul. It's designed to wedge itself into a block of wood. That's why it's thick, unlike an axe. Marcus is right, this is definitely going to take team work to accomplish. This task is best with two hands." He pulled Chris over to a wood round. "If we both lift together, we can get it onto the splitting block."

They fumbled with the wood until the two of them worked out the best way for three hands to accomplish the task. Once they got the round up onto the block, Robin showed Chris how to handle the maul. Eventually, they managed to get the round split in half together. They took turns with the maul, and sweat started to run down their faces as the split pile grew.

Robin called a break, and they both sat on the splitting block, using their unbound hands to wipe their faces. Sweat and blood streaked across both of them like war paint. Looking at the cuffs, Chris shook them lightly. "You know, I'm too old for time out."

"Apparently not."

"We could get these off, you know." The shocked expression on Robin's face made him pause. "Why do you obey?" he asked.

"Because he's Alpha. You saw what he did. He pulled both of us out of the air in full battle. Are you willing to find out what else he can do?"

"No, I suppose not." Chris ran his free hand through his damp hair and thought, with a touch of fear, about how the fight had ended. His *father* had done it, he thought reluctantly. "What was that he did, anyway? The only experience I've had with anything psychic has been with Nick. And he couldn't pull us out of the air like that, I don't think."

"No, he wouldn't be able to; Nick's talents don't lie there. Marcus is a Caster, a light weaver. He can take energy and turn it into physical light. It's versatile, as you can see."

Uncertain how to ask, Chris looked at Robin on the stump next to him. Just a couple of hours before, the two of them were at each other's throats, literally. Now they were being forced to think and respond to one another instead of react. Looking back out over the grounds, he cleared his throat. "What is he like?" Catching a sympathetic look out of the corner of his eye, Chris growled lightly. "I don't know what to think. A couple of days ago he was *dead*. Now? I don't like feeling uncertain like this."

The two of them stared out across the snow toward the longhouse. After a while Robin replied, "He is good. He can be strict, but he's fair and caring."

Robin tossed another look Chris's way, leaving him uncomfortable with the knowledge displayed.

"I know you lost him as a father, Christoff, but I gained one. After my parents died, he was there. He helped me through my change and taught me what it was to be a Valkyrie." Robin picked up a piece of bark and started shredding it, pulling on the cuffs in the process. "Something to keep in mind, though. You might know him better than you think. You were raised by the man who raised him."

"I don't feel like I know anyone at the moment, Robin, except Nick and the rest of my clan." Chris clenched his fists, and it took all of his willpower not to jump up and fly. Like he could, tethered to Robin the way he was. He took a deep breath and continued. "All the lies and secrets." He shook his head. "It's easy for you to say how they were necessary, how they benefited the majority. But you were on this side of them. As each secret is revealed, there is always another one behind it. Who do we believe? *When* do we believe, Robin? I start to think maybe we've reached the end, then we find out another lie. How do we learn to trust?"

Robin tossed his bark aside and shook his head. "I don't have an answer for you."

"Yeah, I know." Chris gave himself a shake. "I would prefer just fighting you. It's much more straightforward."

"I know what you mean. I like the action; it drives all of the pain and uncertainty away. Like you, I prefer physical pain to emotional any day."

"Jessica?"

He nodded. "And Jays."

"Jessica I understand. She's made it clear she's not happy with being here. But how do you know Jays?"

Robin turned a glare on him and bared his teeth briefly. "You know you don't have to defend her from me. It's not like I'm going to hurt her or anything. She's my sister. How would you feel being kept from Nickolas?"

Chris pursed his lips thoughtfully. "I don't know your background...or hers. All I have to go on is how Jessica responds and what I receive through my link with her. She was distressed. And we're in a situation that none of us are too sure of. So I think you would agree that it is only natural for us to band together until we're comfortable. I'll make an effort not to block you. But I think you're going to have a lot to straighten out with her before she quits blocking you herself. But keep in mind, she is ours. That's something none of us will allow to change."

A growl issued from Robin. Their gazes clashed, and neither of them were willing to back down. The wind kicked up, blowing snow around them, breaking the contest of wills. Chris shook the fluff out of his face then looked back out across the field, watching the promised snow start to fall from the clouds. He cleared his throat then prompted, "You were going to tell me about Jays?"

Willing to go with the truce, Robin used a little of the snow to rub off some of the blood on his hand. "Before I came to the valley permanently, when I started my change, Jess and I used to live with our guardian, May. I don't know how or why our parents managed to maintain an outside residence. None of the others had. I think it had something to do with the fact that my mother hadn't changed before Marcus led the evacuation. And, likely, May somehow....

"Anyway, they never explained why they didn't want us to live in Aurora. But Mom was a powerful Seer, so there had to be a reason. Jays was my best friend. He was a year younger than me and lived a couple of doors down. He and I spent a lot of time together.

"Then one day, he disappeared. I was worried sick. This was before Mom and Dad were gone; they said they'd look into it. I don't know what they could do. They were both fledged at that point, so their movements were restricted and they tended to hide their wings. Eventually they told me that they found out that Jays was fine and there wasn't anything for me to worry about. And they left it at that. I was about thirteen at the time, I think. I was devastated. A couple of years later, my parents went on a mission and were killed, and then I had to take care of Jessica. When I was eighteen, I started the change. That's when I found out that the Facility had been keeping tabs on us; it was only because May got a message to Marcus that I didn't end up in the Hub. Marcus barely got me out before the Facility recovery team. It was close. But they managed it, so I changed in Aurora.

"Not long after I was fully fledged, Marcus started sending me out on the supply runs. Imagine my surprise when on my first mission I found Jays. Several years older of course, but we recognized each other immediately. My Wing leader at the time nearly trounced me for my reaction. It turned out that Jays's mom had gotten a position in the Facility. He'd gotten to know Ian and had become his protégé. He'd gone to school and was now a doctor and Ian's Second, for all intents and purposes.

"Jays has been my contact with the Facility ever since. I've actually been surprised he hasn't changed before now, considering how long he's been in contact with a large population of Valkyries. It used to be one of my worst nightmares, that he would change and Gabriel would take him to the camp. I promised him I wouldn't let that happen if I could."

Seeing a new side to Jays, Chris wondered what else had been going on under their noses at the Facility. He took a deep breath, then they both stood, shaking out their wings, and got ready to continue chopping.

"If we use the wedges, Chris, we would have better luck splitting these things. We can get another couple of hours in before we need to head over to the infirmary before lunch."

Chapter Seven

They set aside the maul and wedges, then the two Hunters stretched their wings, groaning. "You know, Robin, I've decided that I really don't like splitting wood."

"Be happy. Marcus was being merciful. He put us in front of the pile of fir. If he'd really wanted us to die, he would have made us split the maple." They headed toward the infirmary, walking at a snail's pace. "It's not so bad actually, when you can split properly. It can be kind of peaceful. I've done it a lot as an outlet for my temper when I can't get a good sparring partner. But I don't think that will be an issue anymore, as long as you're here."

Chris joined Robin's grin. "Yeah, it was fun. I'd like to finish what we started. I hate quitting before I've won."

Robin snorted indignantly. "You weren't winning, I was."

"You wish."

They shoved each other like a couple of boys as they entered the medical building then grew serious as all eyes turned to them. They walked up to where Bethany stood, holding an open medical folder.

A cough that sounded suspiciously like a chuckle came from Jessica, and Chris looked over his shoulder at her, glaring. He returned his attention to his mother and saw her suppress a smile as well.

Sighing, Robin spoke. "Marcus wanted us to come in and have you check us out to make sure we didn't damage ourselves too badly."

The doctor waved them to a seat on the only unoccupied bed then went to grab a few supplies. They tried to settle their wings as they sat and Chris gave Kieran a cold look when the

Beta approached. He sighed to himself at the smiling, undaunted look the empath wore.

"I missed the fight, but I hear it was a doozy. It looks like it too. You don't usually get marked quite so much unless you're facing your brother," he commented, waving at their blood-spattered faces. "Wait until Nick hears about it."

A groan escaped as Chris looked over at his brother. Nickolas seemed like he might be resting easier. "How's he doing?"

"His fever just broke. Beth thinks he might wake soon. And I agree. I've done a couple of quick scans and his dreamscape shows that he's strengthening. What does your link tell you?"

Chris turned inward as his mother returned and started examining Robin. He followed his line to Nickolas and let his strength flow into his brother while he mentally assessed the other's condition. With his eyes closed, he reported to Kieran. "He is much calmer. I feel less pain pouring through the link." *Nick can you hear me? You're safe now. Please wake up.* Mentally cocking his head, Christoff listened. A faint feeling of a breeze washed through him but not Nickolas's voice.

Chris opened his eyes to look at the others. "I tried talking to him. He didn't exactly answer, but I did get a response. So I think you're right. He's finally rising."

He rubbed his wrist where the cuff rested as he looked over at his brother, hope rising. Robin hissed next to him and brought his attention back. The blood and dirt had been washed off of Robin's face, revealing a good black eye developing, along with a split lip. Beth turned to him next and his mother started to wash his wounds while telling them the extent of their injuries.

"You're lucky. There's nothing too serious. You both have some excellent bruises, several of which are likely to impair your movement painfully for a while. Robin, as you've already noticed, be easy with your left wrist. At the moment it's only sprained, but it won't take much to break it. I don't think either of you has cracked ribs, but it will feel like it from the bruises. That's it."

Both of them ducked their heads sheepishly at her stern look as they slid off the bed.

"Come on, Robin, I'm starving. Let's get some lunch." In an effort to redirect the painfully wistful look Robin cast at Jessica, Chris pulled him out of the hospital. "Look, now's not the time. Give her some space. She has a lot to adjust to."

Robin nodded, and they both walked across the courtyard, hunching their shoulders against the swirling snow as they made their way to the longhouse for lunch.

The low moan of the wind outside filled the night air. Opening his eyes, Nickolas looked around the dim room in confusion. His head pounding, he tried to raise his hand to his eyes but couldn't. He twisted, wanting to roll over, and moaned as his shoulder caught fire. He still couldn't move.

Beginning to struggle against the restraint, his breathing accelerated and his head spun. Not sure where he was or what was happening, Nickolas tried to force his mind to focus. He stared at the strap on his right wrist and tried to make it move. He started to shake, so he let his head drop back down onto the bed. Feeling the panic rise, he tried again. He gazed at the strap intently and visualized it opening. He pulled mentally for all he was worth, and the strap started to slowly separate. Gritting his teeth at the pain, he continued.

The soft rush of footsteps followed by a quiet "Nickolas, stop" made him look up, squinting in pain as he lost his hold on the strap. He met Kieran's eyes and jerked both of his arms.

"Let me go," he rasped out, hardly recognizing his own voice.

The younger Valkyrie smoothed down the strap Nick had managed to get half undone and shook his head. "Wait, you can't get up yet. You have injuries."

Nick pulled again and growled. "I don't care, get these off me." The straps and the dim lighting both contributed to making him feel like the walls were closing in. His breath sawed, and he jerked them harder. "Let me up NOW!"

Kieran grabbed his face and forced Nick to meet his eyes. "Nick, calm down. You can breathe. Take a deep breath. You are not in a small space but a big room. Now listen. Your wing has been damaged; it is immobilized, and I don't know if it can be moved yet."

He stared into Kieran's gold-flecked eyes and tried to make sense out of what he was being told. A soft buzzing in his head, just under the pounding, started. He focused on it and heard Kieran's mind call someone.

Beth, Nick's awake! He's struggling against the straps. I'm not going to be able to hold him for long; he's already tried to use telekinesis on them. Do I do it now?

Not alone. Try to hold him. We're on our way.

"Let me up, Kieran. Who're you talking to? Where are we?" His voice flat, he tried to jerk his head away from Kieran's grip, but he was too weak. Stuck staring into Kieran's eyes, he could feel the empath's energy brush against him, and he mentally recoiled.

Donald, I need you, Kieran yelled.

Kieran? Donald replied.

"Get out of my head," Nick gasped. He pulled against the restraints, and his mind surged out, weaker than it should be, but he managed to push Kieran back a couple of feet. He stared at the strap and ripped, but Kieran clamped it back down and grabbed his face again, jerking his gaze away. Determination stared at him. "What has happened, Kieran?"

"Nickolas, focus on me."

"Let me go."

"I can't. You're hurt."

"What happened?" His breathing grew shallow, and something in the back of his mind started to break free.

The slam of something large hitting a door ricocheted in the room. His head jerked, but Kieran kept it clamped between his hands so he couldn't look at whatever entered. It took all his willpower to get his gaze to slide away from Kieran's and turn his eyes to look. His lungs and heart seized.

The anguished, mournful scream of the ten year old he had been filled his head. The grief that had left him devastated when his world had collapsed returned as he looked into the eyes of his mother.

The dam broke and the memories flooded his mind.

"Ian!" he gasped, then his body seized.

"Donald! Help hold him," a familiar male voice called. "The convulsions will tear his shoulder open and pull apart his sail."

"Now, Kieran. Get me in there."

Hands like branding irons pressed into his chest. He screamed again, then the knife of a presence sliced through the barrier he had made around himself, forcing its way through. He felt the tattered remnants of his power gather. He would use anything to push them out.

He's going for lethal. Disrupt his power flow.

Rocks rolled into his path, breaking up the momentum of his power. He tried to pull it all back together and got a weak current that he pushed out with his mind. He didn't care what it did as long as it got them to leave him alone. He heard someone grunt, and then his energy drained through sand.

On his knees, he dug through the sand with his hands. Chasing after the liquid he needed. He felt like he was torn in two. The contracted muscles of his body were on fire, countering the focused determination to dig back to his draining power as his mind splintered around him. *IAN!*

The memories exploded.

Soft voices disturbed him. The inside of his head felt pulpy, like an overripe melon. He groaned and tried to lift his hands to his eyes. They jerked to a stop. He pulled harder and realized he could only move an inch. Then he felt the straps holding the rest of his body. *Where am I?*

His breath caught. Memories of his isolation and being strapped down swam through his mind, and he started to struggle. The dim room shrank. He didn't care that his shoulder felt like it had been dipped in acid.

"Ian," he groaned. "Why are you doing this? I finished my change, remember? Let me up. Jays?"

The voices stopped, and he quickly had Kieran and Donald hovering over him, their expressions pinched. He jerked his wrists. "Let me up. What's going on? Why is Ian doing this?"

"What's the last thing you remember?" Kieran asked.

Nickolas pulled his tethered feet then his wrists. "I..." He tried to think. Everything seemed hazy. "I'm not sure. Why am I like this?"

"You're hurt. Do you remember anything about that?"

He pummeled his brain. A few pieces broke free. "I remember...Chris and I chased Jessica down. I caught her." He trailed off. "We did something that tied our power." He looked at Kieran in shock.

"That's the last memory you have?"

He shook his head in bewilderment. "Where's Jess? Is she all right?"

Kieran's hand reached down, brushed the hair off of his face, and said gently, "She's fine. She's asleep at the moment, since it's the middle of the night."

Nick turned his head and looked around the unfamiliar dim room. "Where are we? What's going on?"

"We evacuated the Facility," Donald said. "You were hurt during it."

"How bad?" He pulled lightly at the straps; he couldn't help it. It was taking all of his willpower to keep from hyperventilating. "I need these off, Kieran. Ian knows that. Where's Chris? Why isn't he here? Get these off."

"You don't remember waking up a few hours ago?"

"No..."

"Listen, it's not up to me if you are freed yet. Your wing sail has fourth degree tears in it, and you've been shot in the shoulder."

"Shot!" He started losing the battle to keep his calm at the restraints.

"Yes. Relax. Take deep breaths."

"Ian! Get these damn things off me!"

"Nick," Donald snapped. His gaze shot to the Hunter's. "It's not Ian's call."

That's when Nickolas realized that there were two more people watching from the shadows. They stepped toward him and into the light.

"N-no. No." He shook his head. "You're dead. He told us you were dead."

His mother brushed his hair back like Kieran had while his father looked down on him in concern. Nick couldn't stop the tear that forced its way out, but he managed to keep more from following.

"Beth," Kieran said softly, "we can't keep him down. His claustrophobia won't let us. If he's not ready to get up, you'll need to sedate him."

Nick's gaze shot to Kieran's then back to his mother's. She turned to look at his father. "How's his wing? That's the only thing holding us back from giving him movement."

Nick turned his head to the right and saw his wing stretched out for the first time. His father examined the tears closely. There were two large jagged rips in the membrane, held together with splinting.

His father pushed and prodded at the tears, murmuring to his mother as he did so. She nodded her head, and Marcus then held his hands out over the sail. A soft light glowed, falling to fill the seam in a gentle warmth.

When he was done, he backed up and shook his hands out then looked up into Nick's eyes. "I've stabilized it as much as possible. You can move it but only carefully. I can't guarantee that I can make it flight worthy again if you open the tears."

"How long?"

The Alpha started to carefully unlash Nick's wing from the board and shook his head. "I don't know. You heal unusually fast on your own, and coupled with the extra healing energy.... We'll just have to check it every day to judge its progress."

"How do you know I heal quickly?" Nick sought both of their gazes and saw what he didn't want to. "He knew? This whole time he knew? Why? Why did Ian hide this?"

"That is too much to go into right now, son."

"Don't call me that. Don't ever call me that. You lost the right to that twenty years ago," Nick said viciously. The rest of the straps were removed, then Kieran and Donald supported him into a sitting position. His wing was manually furled onto his back.

Bracing himself, he slid to his feet and nearly collapsed. Donald had placed himself strategically, both catching him and allowing him the illusion that he held on himself. He had to carefully breathe through the pain. The primary source was his shoulder, but the rest of the bruising across his body wasn't anything to laugh at.

"What happened to me?" He toddled a step away from Donald, keeping his hand braced on the high pad of the table he'd been on. "Where are we?"

His father cleared his throat. "We are in our infirmary in Aurora, our village up in the Cascades."

He didn't acknowledge his father and looked to Kieran.

"They brought you in over to two days ago. Before that, you spent three days fleeing Gabriel and were injured pretty badly. Massive bruising, exposure, and infection. You were shot in the shoulder, and your right wing sail was shredded," Kieran replied.

"I don't remember anything," Nick whispered.

He noticed a look pass between Kieran and his mother before Kieran said, "That's not surprising considering the massive trauma you've been through. Try not to worry too much about that. Just let yourself rest and your body recover. I bet once you're healthy enough, you'll remember."

He continued to use the support of the bed to walk around it, though his muscles started to firm up fairly rapidly. He was still wobbly, but it didn't take long before he stood weakly on his own.

His mother walked to the door and opened it for someone she seemed to be expecting. She took a tray from them and placed it at a table on the other side of the room. The smell hit his nose, and his stomach cramped enough that he groaned. Donald was at his side with a supporting hand so he didn't fall.

His mother looked at him, challenge in her eyes. "You haven't eaten in days. If you want to eat, get over here. By yourself."

He growled, though it was a pale shadow of his normal ferocity. He took a wobbly step away from Donald. She watched him make each move with the same assessing gaze that Ian had always given him. Each limping step came at the cost of pain, and he was grateful to sink into the chair at the table. The rich broth made his mouth water.

"Take it slow," she said softly. "Or you might not keep it down. Think of it like when you came out of the coma."

He averted his gaze from his parents and looked at Donald and Kieran. "Where is Ian and Jays? Why isn't Chris here? You said I was alone when I was hurt? Why?"

Donald pulled out the chair opposite from him. "Slow down, Nick. A lot has happened this week, and you only just woke up. Start with eating. You don't need to have all the answers instantly."

He reached out for Chris, intending to call him, but he had no strength to get past the gravity of his own mind. His spoon clattered into his bowl with a splash, and his mother rushed forward, but it was Kieran's eyes that stared into his.

"I can't call him," he whispered. "What's wrong with me?"

"Wait. Who?" Kieran cupped Nick's chin to hold him steady as he peered into his eyes. "What did you do?"

"I can't call Chris. I can't even talk to you. I'm trying." He could feel his breath getting shorter again, and he tried to slow it down.

"Stop. Don't try to do anything with your mind. Not right now. We'll get Chris. Just relax." Kieran threw a look at his cousin then turned back to Nick. "Your job right now is to eat then rest. You need to recover. I'm sure that as soon as your body has healed, your mind won't be far behind."

Shaking lightly, Nick picked up the spoon and started to eat again. But he was exhausted.

"Chris is on his way," Donald said.

Kieran pulled out another chair and answered his unspoken questions. "He got himself into trouble with Marcus. He and Robin got into a fight; a big one. It was quite a spectacle, I'm told. I missed it since I was here. I'm afraid the fight was inevitable though. The two of them had been dancing around one another since we arrived."

With a rush, two Valkyries came running through the door. Chris, followed by another Nick quickly recognized as Robin. The joy in his brother's face was plain to see, and so were the handcuffs tying the two Hunters together. Sitting up straight, Nickolas snarled, "God damn it, Christoff, what the hell?"

Looking sheepish, Chris glanced down at the cuffs. "Well, you see.... Um..."

Nickolas checked his brother out closely and was relieved to see that all of the damage was superficial. There was stiffened movement from bruising, and a spectacular purple black bruise covered one side of his jaw. Robin fared the same, but with a black eye instead. "You couldn't wait for me to wake up first, Chris?"

Chris's face blanched as he and Robin sat on two chairs that Kieran fetched. "Nick, we didn't even know if you would wake up."

"I didn't realize it was that bad...." Nick mumbled.

"You nearly died twice," his mother said softly.

He took another bite, trying to come to terms with that; instead he glanced down at the two Hunters' bound wrists. "So, Chris, it's the middle of the night. Care to explain why you and Robin are handcuffed together?"

All of the Valkyries except Chris and Robin burst into laughter. They cast sour glances around, and Chris said, "This was Marcus's idea of punishment. We're stuck like this for a couple of days until he thinks we've learned to work together instead of butt heads."

"Well, that's inventive. Reminds me of the time Ian..." Nick trailed off. A sick pit had opened up in his stomach, and he felt like his food wanted to revisit. He set the spoon down. "Maybe I did eat a bit too fast after all."

His mother and Kieran shared a look, then she said, "I think it's time for you to get some rest."

Not up for arguing, he forced his stiff body to its feet. They let him sway on his own until he got his balance, then he slowly made his way back to his bed. It took two of them to help him lie down so his wing wasn't damaged. He stiffened when his mom brushed his hair back, so she pulled away.

His eyes drifted shut to the sound of soft voices on the other side of the room. Jumbled images of incessant flying and ghost pain in his wings flashed through him. The sight of the tree canopy rushing up to him swirled in his mind as he fell asleep.

♦ ♦ ♦

Kieran sat back down at the table. Nick kept his back to the rest of the room, but Kieran could feel his Alpha's emotional state as it fluxed. It didn't take him long to fall asleep, thankfully.

Beth squeezed his shoulder. "That went better than I could have hoped. The block seemed to hold, and his talent is locked down. I was able to evaluate his physical state when I got him to walk across the room. Ian was right. He really does heal fast."

"He always has."

"Come on, Beth." Marcus took her elbow. "We need to get more sleep. Morning is much too close, and it's a busy day today."

"Call me if anything else happens," Beth said.

"So we have more wood chopping tomorrow, I guess?" Chris said quietly as the older Valkyries left.

Sighing, Robin answered. Kieran could feel his wistfulness. "Yeah, which is too bad because tomorrow is the day we cut the valley Christmas tree."

Chris shook his wrist, rattling the handcuffs. "And we're stuck like this."

"Yep," Robin said gloomily. "My sept is going to be pissed; they don't stand a chance of winning now."

Chris looked off across the room at his sleeping brother, and Kieran could feel his worry. "So, you did it, Kieran."

He sighed. There was no need to answer.

Chris turned back to look at him. "How long will he not remember?"

"Beth is hoping to keep him out of the loop until his physical injuries have healed enough. Ideally she'd like a full month so she could see him back in the air first. But I doubt we'll get that long. Word is already going around to not mention that Ian's gone near Nick or Jays, but there's still a lot of people here."

"I'll spread the word too," Robin said as he rose from his chair.

Chris followed. "Are you staying for a bit, Donald?"

"Yeah, I thought I'd keep Kier company. Just in case Nick wakes again."

"Good. I'll check in first thing in the morning, Kieran."

He nodded and watched the two Hunters walk out the door.

Sitting at his desk drinking his morning coffee, Marcus listened to the excited sounds coming from the common room. Everyone who wished to participate in the annual tree hunt was gathering, waiting for the instructions that would start the hunt. The low undertone of grumbling coming from Puma Sept made him grin; it was good for the rest of the septs to know they now had a chance to win with Robin out of the competition this year. The happiness was a sharp contrast to the way he felt.

On one hand, he was happy to see and so very proud of his sons. But on the other, their anger, while understandable, was depressing. Holding his wife last night in bed while she wept caused his heart to weep as well. And wishing there had been some way, any way, to have changed the past certainly didn't help.

Regrets overwhelmed him. Holding Nickolas after he was born, a small squalling little thing, afraid he would break with a wrong move. Teaching him to walk and to talk. *I should have been there to teach him to fly as well.* He set his coffee cup down and rubbed at his eyes.

He glanced up at the wall to look at the photos he had of both of his sons. Ian had sent regular reports on their progress and activities along with the photographs. Whether or not either of them wished to believe it, their parents had been deeply concerned over their welfare. *It will probably come as a shock for them to discover that we know pretty much everything that happened to them for their entire lives.*

An echo of the memory of Nickolas's cry for Ian shuddered through him. Not ready to contemplate that his father was truly gone, he pushed it out of his mind. *I'm hardly the only one grieving for him.* He berated himself and turned his thoughts to the reports on his desk.

Loud laughing and applause broke his concentration again, and he glanced out his open door. Beth stood up in front of one of the fireplaces and held her hands in the air, smiling. It was nice to see her looking happy, even if he could feel her sorrow in his mind.

From the laughter, he guessed she must have said something about Robin in the middle of announcing the first clue. As the septs all went running, he picked up the first report and scanned through it. So far their extra patrols had turned up nothing. No increase in traffic and no sign of Gabriel. The precog's were still twitchy though. That worried him, but without more to go on there wasn't a lot they could do other than keep the extra scouts out.

He set the Seer's report aside to pick up the Caster's. Kevin was concerned about running the imbuers ragged. Even though there hadn't been any supporting sign of the enemy, the imbuer's were working overtime strengthening the defensive shields, as well as working to stockpile new devices in between renewing old charms.

Just in case.

Both reports should have left him feeling reassured, but he still felt restless over the safety of his people today. They would be scattered throughout the forest. He growled. Worry without proof was not enough to call off an event that several hundred people had their hearts set on.

I'm just keyed up from Nicky. But to ease my mind, I can at least send in Robin.

Berating himself over foolish worry, he reached his thoughts out. *Robin, report to my office.*

Yes, sir.

Appeased by the hesitation in Robin's mind voice, he waited for the two Hunters to arrive. He turned his chair to stare out the window into the snow. The rustle of wings announced their arrival.

He swiveled back around and suppressed a smile at the looks on their faces. Faint hope mingled with dread. Good. The two of them needed to know the hierarchy. Robin had gotten too complacent.

He let their tension build for a few moments as he watched them stand before his desk, then he broke the silence. "Robin, I want you up in the tower today. Coordinate with Kelley. Nothing has come up, but I'll have an easier mind, with all of the septs running around today, if you are monitoring everything."

"The tower?"

He didn't hide his smile at the disgust evident in Robin's voice. "It's definitely too dangerous for you to be in the field when neither of you can fly effectively. And no, I'm not removing the handcuffs. This is a perfect opportunity for you to show Chris the ropes." He leaned back in his chair and smiled even wider. "Kelley will take your place in the field."

"Marcus, how are we supposed to get up to the top of the cliff to the control tower?"

"I guess that will be an exercise in cooperation, won't it?" Laughing at the annoyance and uncertainty on Robin's face, and the incomprehension on Chris's, Marcus continued. "I want you to check on the imbuers while you're there. Show Chris what they can do so he'll know what to look for in the Facility people. If any of them turn out to be imbuers, that would be great, but even talents would be helpful to work with our imbuers. They are stockpiling as a precaution, and Kevin is concerned they are overworking."

Robin nodded and looked down at the handcuffs then over at Chris. "Marcus, may I ask?"

He stared into Robin's eyes, letting the Hunter squirm for a moment. His subdued tone when asking indicated his uncertainty. Marcus thought about the punishment before he replied, "You two have shown remarkable restraint together, but a punishment doesn't just end because you're ready for it to. There's more to a lesson than the obvious sometimes. I'll think about removing them tomorrow."

For the first time, Christoff raised his voice. "I'm worried about Nick. He was unhappy when he saw us last night."

"Regardless of how Nickolas feels, the punishment stands. If it's a problem, I suggest you try to avoid him until it's done."

Christoff's eyes blanked, but he nodded his head, and his wings flinched. Noting the signs of agitation, Marcus waved them out. "You're dismissed. You should start figuring out how you're getting up to the tower."

The two Hunters stalked out, and Marcus breathed a sigh of relief. Sometimes walking the tight rope of command over so many strong personalities was more than he had ever bargained for.

The door to Jessica's room opened behind her, but she continued to stare out into the soft snowy field. Her head throbbed hard enough that she felt sick to her stomach, and she wasn't looking forward to forcing more broth into it for breakfast.

The door clicked shut.

She closed her eyes.

"I felt you wake," Kieran finally broke the silence. He moved into the room and she heard his wings rustle as he sat down on one of the beds.

She looked out onto the snow again.

"Do you want to talk about it?"

"What's there to talk about? You already know I don't want to be here."

"Truth. Yet not true," he said.

She turned a glare over her shoulder. He just stared back at her.

"I spent more time with you in the Hub than anyone, even Nickolas. Besides, I can feel your turmoil."

She turned back to the window and wrapped her arms across her chest, but he was stubborn and just waited her out. "It's stupid and petty and I don't like it, but I can't seem to not feel it. I wish I could rise above it."

He continued to wait, and she ground her teeth in frustration.

"The last time I was here, my parents had just died. I was already mad at Marcus because he always seemed to make my parents leave me to do things he needed, and then the last time they never came home. Intellectually, I know Mom didn't tell him about her vision, but..." She rubbed her arms as she paused for a moment. "And then later, Robin started to change, and he took off for Marcus just like Mom and Dad always did. Why wouldn't he come back, Kieran? Why am I never important enough for anyone to ever come back for?"

The bed creaked as he rose. His hands slid up her shoulders then firmed to turn her toward him. She settled against his chest, his heartbeat in her ear.

"And this is just stupid. I should be glad because I'm not locked up in the Hub in a little room anymore, getting shot up with all kinds of drugs against my will. But I'm still as much a prisoner now as I was in the Facility, Kieran. The cage may be larger, but it's still a cage."

"Nothing says we have to stay here forever, Jess. I very much doubt that Nick will ever be comfortable staying here for a long period of time. Besides, you shouldn't be so hard on yourself about feeling bad. You've only been awake from the coma for twenty-four hours. You still have the post-coma headache and haven't even graduated to full solid food yet. Pain and hunger will amplify any emotion, but especially negative ones. It doesn't surprise me that your mind shies away from the bigger issues to focus on old hurts that are comfortable."

His hand skimmed down her hair before he raised her face to look at him.

"Besides, you are important enough to come back for. Look at all the trouble Nickolas went to when they caught you the first time. And when we had to hunt you down in the Facility, not once but twice. And don't forget when you took down Aiden and me." He chuckled at her response to his reminder.

"You're never going to let me forget that are you?" She pulled away to look up at him.

"No, probably not. It's likely to be the only revenge I get." He paused. "I think, Jess, that you just need to give yourself time to find who you are now. And try to talk to Robin. The pain he feels about you is a match for yours. He needed you just as badly as you needed him."

Not yet ready to give in to that, she snorted softly, which made Kieran chuckle again.

"Now," he said. "When I felt you wake, I actually came in here for a reason."

She cocked her head.

"Nickolas woke last night."

"What!" She balled her fists but then pressed one to her temple to ease the exacerbated throbbing. "Why didn't I feel it? Why didn't you wake me?"

"We were too busy handling Nick the first time he woke. After that, you needed your own sleep. I'm sure the reason you didn't feel it is because of the pain you are in right now. Besides, you're at the beginning of stage four. So your power and talents aren't reliable and are only starting to expand."

He gently lowered her fist from her temple and gave it a squeeze before he turned away and walked toward her door. "He's awake now. I thought I might go and check on Jays for a while."

She stared at the hallway revealed through the opening. Trepidation washed through her. She shifted from foot to foot. Then with a sigh, she slipped out of the room. She padded down the hall on bare feet. In the larger triage room, she paused. Nick sat with his back to her on the middle bed in the main part of the room. His wings hung limp, and he seemed to hold himself still. He slowly turned his head to look at her over his shoulder, just as she got up the courage to continue crossing the room.

She met his gaze and could read the physical pain in them. Neither of them spoke. She came to a halt in front of him.

"I was worried they were lying to me when they wouldn't let me see you last night," he said softly.

She reached a fingertip out and brushed it across the fabric covering his knee then pulled her hand back. "Kieran just told me you woke up. Or I would have been out here sooner."

"Do you have any info? No one will tell me what's happened."

She remembered the lecture Beth gave her about not telling him about Ian. "Probably not much more than you. I only woke up from the coma yesterday."

"You've completed stage three?" he asked, surprised.

"I have the headache to prove it."

He smiled slightly. "Well, I'm glad to know that's behind you. Now I don't have to worry about it."

She chewed on her lip and hugged her arms. "So...what do you remember?"

"I remember catching you. I remember you and me in the air."

Her gaze shot to his.

"I remember power, pulsing heat, light so bright I could only feel." He lifted his arm slowly and traced her cheekbone. "I remember feeling the heart of you inside of me."

"I do too," she whispered.

His hand dropped with a slight tremor. She stepped closer. "What does it mean?"

He carefully shook his head. "I don't know."

She traced the cloud of bruises visible outside of the bandage on his shoulder. "Do you know what happened after you left me with Chris?"

"I left you?"

"That's what I'm told. I was in the coma by then."

"Nothing. I remember us in the air, then waking up here."

Her hand curled into a fist, and she turned away to pace. "Same for me. I really didn't want to come here. That's why I ran."

Nickolas slid to his feet. She watched him wince, but then he stretched lightly. He took slow careful steps out into the room. In the open, he unfurled his wings in a controlled motion then resettled them just as slowly. "I understand the sentiment," he said to the room at large.

She twitched her wings and paced around so she could look at his face again.

"You didn't know."

"That they were alive? No."

"It's funny. We both don't want to be here for the same reasons. Because of your parents. They took both of our families, in a way." She paced a bit. "I guess you're the lucky one, though. At least you have a chance again. Mine really are dead."

"There's your brother."

"He made his choice."

Nick's steps strengthened as he worked his body. He cut her off and stopped in front of her. His hand brushed over her hair. "At least we have each other."

"Do we? Here? Do you think that's possible?"

He shook his head. "I don't plan to stay. Do you?"

"Not on your life."

The doors to the entry foyer opened, and a Hunter came in carrying a tray with food for them. He set it on the table then left.

Nick looked at her. "Then let's sit and figure out what we want while we eat."

Donald stepped out of the house he was supposed to be sharing with Kieran and into the early twilight. He finished buttoning his coat then launched into the air to make a quick circle around the houses the Facility Valkyries were using. It looked like everyone had gone.

Tonight was a special occasion, they'd been informed. Dinner and a tree decorating party. Memories of his whole extended family meeting up at his grandma's farmhouse for something similar gave him a pang of homesickness. Which made him think of his best friend, Zach, and Zach's twin brother, Dustin. *It's just too coincidental for a different Dustin to be involved. It has to be Zach's brother. They live too close to*

Grandma. And if it hadn't been for Dustin getting Kieran out of the fair when he started to change…. They're too familiar with Valkyries.

With lazy flaps, he flew on to the longhouse. He settled down onto the freshly swept courtyard and briskly folded his wings, then he walked into the building. The welcoming noise battered his ears. A quick scan of the faces located his own people.

The Facility Valkyries congregated together near the opposite fireplace. He wove through the crowd, eyeing the huge tree. It was at least fourteen feet tall. He shook his head. *How did they get that thing in here?*

He crossed the invisible border marking the edge of his clan's space. It wasn't that the Aurorans didn't try to include them, but they'd all learned from Chris's example. And none were willing to get into a situation that could precipitate a fight.

At the grouping of tables they claimed, he joined the other Flight leaders and met Dev's gaze over Dylan's head right before he tipped Dylan out of his chair. The other Hunter landed on his rear with an exclamation as Donald settled into the seat.

"Care for my seat, Donald?" Dylan groused.

The table erupted into laughter as the Hunter picked himself up off the floor. Donald grinned. "Kind of you to offer, thanks."

He caught a roll Dev tossed at him then slathered some butter on it. "Looks like everyone is here."

"Not quite. When do we get to see Nick and everyone else in the Hub, or whatever they call it here?" Buttering his own roll, Dev moved over, giving Dylan a place to sit.

"Hopefully soon. Tonight, I think. Ah, our prodigal leader returns." Spotting Chris and Robin crossing the space, he slid over while someone else pulled up two chairs for them.

The two Hunters sat, and Chris reached forward with his left hand, grabbing a roll. Then using his bound hand, he buttered it, handing it to Robin to eat while he made one for himself. "How's everything going, Donald?"

"Decently. We haven't had too many problems. There's been a bit of shuffling in the housing department, but nothing major. You do realize, though, that you're the one who's supposed to be dealing with this, right? I gave command back to you."

Chris grinned and took another bite of his roll. "I expect you'll cope. Have you gotten everyone out to spar yet?"

"No, not yet."

"I want everyone out first thing in the morning. They've had enough of a rest."

"Sure thing." Buttering another roll, he watched as Dev passed out the soup bowls. "Anything in specific you want me to work on?"

"No, just run everyone through a simple workout and sparring session. Our basic phys-ex test stuff. There's a lot to get used to here, and something familiar will be comforting."

Nodding his head, Donald ladled out some soup for Robin and Chris and himself. An audible *umph* coming from Robin had Donald glancing in his direction. A blonde female Valkyrie sat down on the table next to Robin, who was glaring at her and rolling his shoulder.

"Well, we lost, not that that's a big surprise. Wolf Sept found the tree. You know, I had big plans for tonight. This is the first time since I was reinstated that we had a date that I could participate in. I'm extremely unhappy with you. I will most certainly find a way to make you pay, Robin. Trust me."

"Oh, come on, Kel. I'll be paying enough already, missing tonight."

Smiling, she walked off, leaving Robin to glare at Chris.

"What?"

"I'll have you know I haven't danced with her in two months, and now I'm not tonight either." Shaking the handcuffs, Robin growled.

Christoff laughed and spooned up some soup. "Poor baby. Don't let me stop you from joining her."

"You know, we still haven't finished our fight," Robin snapped.

Donald smiled and dipped his bread into his soup when a hush rolled across the common room. All attention turned to the door where Nickolas and Jessica had paused, looking around. Fire lit Christoff's eyes, and Donald could feel all of the Facility Valkyries tense.

Robin jerked the cuffs, grabbing Chris's attention. "Settle, Chris. Nothing's going to happen. All of you get yourselves under control. Now."

Chris bowed his head once in acknowledgement of Robin's rebuke and swept his gaze over all of his people.

The two Alphas stepped in to allow Kieran's and Jays's entrance. The four made their way at a snail's pace through the crowded hall.

Donald's heart clenched looking at Nickolas. He hadn't thought Nick could ever look worse than he had a few weeks ago, when he was finishing his change.

He had been wrong.

Nickolas moved like an old man. It went beyond the physical injuries he sported. The haunted, fey look that clung to him accented the pain in his eyes. Donald pushed his own recollection of Nickolas's storm from his mind.

The mental fragility that he could sense from his Alpha was enough to make him want to cry. Jessica, in contrast, was starting to come into her own now that she was awake and fully fledged. Her position beside her mate stated clearly that nobody had better mess with Nickolas—or they would be answering to her.

The Facility Valkyries shifted to make space for their Alpha pair and Jays near the fire. Bowls of soup and bread appeared before them. The clan subtly closed ranks around the three vulnerable members as Donald watched. A steady tide of individuals shifted around the two Alphas as all members of the clan took a turn to connect with them.

Kieran kept a close eye on all three of them.

The noise level returned to normal as people finished eating and started decorating the huge tree with ornaments pulled from boxes lined up against the wall. Donald elbowed Chris and pointed across the room to where his parents stood. They watched Nickolas eat with a combination of pain and wistfulness in their eyes.

Christoff's hand tightened on his spoon before he nodded. "Seeing them again has been particularly hard for Nick. He was much older than me when they...well, when they went away. I have some memories, but I was only five. He can remember them quite clearly. I don't know exactly how I feel. I can see both sides, you know. I'm sorry for their pain."

"Marcus talked about you all the time, he was so proud of what the both of you could do." Robin didn't look at either of them, just continued to eat.

They ate the rest of their food in silence.

As more and more people got up to place ornaments on the tree, Robin encouraged the Facility Valkyries to help.

The comforting aroma of baking cookies and hot apple cider filled the air, along with the smell of the logs burning on the fires in both of the hearths. People laughed and sang, erasing the fear that had been present in the hearts of all of the refugees for at least a little while.

Donald smiled at the friendship that had developed between Chris and Robin. The two Hunters hung ornaments while ribbing each other mercilessly. He grabbed a couple of the Christmas cookies as they went by and caught Nickolas and Jess looking at him, so he stood and walked over to join the pair. Pulling out a seat, he smiled at them.

"It's really good to see the two of you out."

Nick raised his eyebrow and smiled slightly. "That seems to be a popular sentiment. You were one of the few who hadn't come by yet. Everyone seems to be settling in nicely."

Donald recognized the uncertainty in his voice and replied, "To a certain extent they are, but we're not truly comfortable here. Maybe it'll just take time, but I'm not so sure of that. We're different than they are. The experiences we've had living at the Facility is...different, I think, than when they were at the Facility. Then add in the years of being on their own. We've both developed strong cultures. I think there is value in learning each other's ways, but ultimately, we need to adapt what will work for us."

Jessica and Nick looked at each other. "We've been discussing this very topic, Donald. Nick and I wish to found a new settlement. Neither of us is comfortable staying here permanently; any who wish to join us are welcome. We obviously can't leave until all of our people are healed."

She gave a stern look at Nickolas, leaving Donald to suppose that Nickolas was in favor of just up and going. "And I think we need to spend some time here, learning what we can so we can avoid some mistakes. But we wish to leave. It's not like all Valkyries will be able to live in one place forever, after all."

"So where are we going to go?" He grinned at their surprised looks. "What? You're not going without me. And I expect most, if not all, of the Facility Valkyries will agree with me."

"We were thinking about the Olympic Mountains. We could stay in contact with Aurora, but we would like some distance."

"If we stay here for a few months, learning what we can, we could plan the move for the spring when we have all of the rest of the nice time of the year to get settled."

"That was our thought as well."

He grabbed another cookie as a plate went by and watched the festivities around them. Drawing Jessica's and Nick's attention, he pointed out Jays. Dev, Kieran, Dylan, Chris, and Robin were lifting him up into the air while he laughingly cursed at them. They were forcing him to be the one to put the tree topper on while everyone watched, laughing at their antics.

Nick started to smile then placed his hand over his eyes while he clenched his other into a fist. Kieran swiveled to stare across the room at Nickolas. The empath said something to Chris then left them, heading over for Nickolas. Watching, Donald waited for Kieran.

"You ok, Nick?"

"I...don't know. For a second..." He shook his head then took a deep breath. "My head hurts, that's all."

Kieran pulled out a chair. "You've been up for less than a day. Take it easy." He grabbed a cookie then raised his booted feet to rest on the chair next to him. "How's everything going,

Donald? I've spent so much time in sick bay that this is the most I've seen my Flight since we arrived."

"We're settling in. Chris has ordered everyone to the practice grounds tomorrow. Unless you're needed in the infirmary, I expect to see you there."

Making a face, Kieran nodded.

"Can I come?" Jessica asked hesitantly.

He glanced at Kieran, who nodded slightly, before he answered her. "If you're ready to join us, then by all means, please come." He stood and shook out his wings. "Well, I'm tired. I think I'll head off to bed."

"I think that is an excellent idea, Donald," Kieran added.

He recognized the steely look in Kieran's eyes and laughed, very glad it wasn't aimed at him.

A soft snarl escaped Nickolas. "I'm not an invalid."

"Of course not. But you're not at your peak now, are you? Look, Nick, you need to give yourself time."

Nickolas rose, his eyes full of a tempest, but he started to walk out without comment. Kieran raised his hand, signaling Chris, and they walked over with Jays then caught up with Nick and Jess at the door.

Nickolas shuffled across the courtyard. Someone hung colorful lights from the eves that cast cheerful splotches on the snow lining the sides. Donald paused in the center of the courtyard and made his farewells as the others headed off to the infirmary, then he took off in the crisp night air to fly home.

◆ ◆ ◆

Soft skin slid under Gabriel's hand. Pet's warm breath tickled his chest as she slept curled against his side. The gauze curtains around the bed diffused the morning light. His hand dipped into her waist then moved to circle absently over her hip.

The orders still stung. His thoughts wandered over yesterday.

He hadn't been able to use the information he'd learned about the rebels to his advantage after all. And now, not only were they delaying the operation to retrieve both the Facility and rebel Valkyries, but he'd lost control of the Facility too.

Kratz, the stupid pig, had moved while he'd been occupied with Nickolas. The general had convinced those above them to turn the entirety of the Facility over to him since Gabriel had allowed Ian to destroy the Hub and let Nickolas get away.

That effectively kept him under General Kratz's thumb.

Completely disregarding who was actually sitting in the Facility at the time Ian evacuated everyone and set it to blow.

Pet stirred at his side. He pulled her tighter and dropped his nose to her hair. The sweet scent soothed him. *Stupid politics. Anything could happen between now and the next few weeks before the council gets its shit together and finally decides to go after Marcus.*

The majority opinion was that since the rebels didn't know they had been located, the Facility had time to get itself under control and ready to handle that many recovered fully fledged Valkyries. Most would come to the compound here, but the presence of the control group in town was too valuable. How many could return to the Facility wouldn't be known until they had them in custody though.

Gabriel snorted. *Like any of them will be willing to do what's necessary to stay in that cage. Not now that they've tasted freedom.*

Pet sighed, and he rubbed his lips against the crown of her head. "Come on, sweet. Time to wake up."

She stretched and yawned. He pulled her over his chest and ran his hands down the folded suede of her wings, along her spine. Then he gripped her ass and kissed her sleepy mouth.

"How would you like company?" he asked.

She pulled her face a couple of inches away and blinked cloudy eyes. He chuckled at the fear and uncertainty she tried to bury.

He rolled her under him and she gasped at the sudden movement. His weight pinned her to the mattress as his wings spread around them. His tongue licked across her lip before he continued. "I have to go to the lab this morning.

And if everything works the way I plan, I'll be bringing a new addition to our little family home for breakfast."

"Who?" she asked softly.

He smiled then took her mouth in a heated kiss. With a sigh he pulled away. "No more time now. Come on."

He grasped her hand and helped her to her feet then tugged her across the room to the cage he'd had set up. He punched in the code and unlocked the door. She settled to the floor with a frown amid all the colorful cushions.

He laughed. "Don't look so disgruntled. I'll be back soon, and I've been over this before. This is to keep you safe. I don't want anyone coming in here and removing you. It'll be a lot harder for them to break into the cage than to cut a chain."

He left her and went to his closet to pull on some clothes. He spread his wings to settle them, then on the way out of the room, he ran his fingers along the bars as he passed her cage, his thoughts already turning ahead.

The halls were quiet in the early morning hours. He pushed through the door into the observatory balcony. The guard on duty looked up at his entrance.

"A lot of activity this morning, sir." The guard handed Gabriel a clipboard.

"Really?" He flipped through the notes then stopped to read a section in greater detail.

"Really?" he said again under his breath. He handed the board back to the guard and turned to the stairs. "No one enters until I say so."

The door hissed shut behind him, and he clattered down the metal stairs. The large room was empty, so he made his way to the office and smaller observatory.

There he found Fredrick writing quickly at a table.

"Ah, Gabriel. I was about to send for you." He finished his notes then closed the folder with evident satisfaction. "We had a breakthrough today. I've got two Hunters who survived the latest generation."

"I just saw that in the notes." Gabriel prowled the room.

Fredrick leaned back in his chair. "Thanks to what we've learned from B five, I was able to adjust the drug. Both Hunters show promise."

"What about Zach?"

The doctor cocked his head, his brow furrowing. "Who? Oh right, B five. I'm breaking his resistance slowly. The last tests you ran were spectacular. But only you have been able to achieve those. The rest of us can't go into his mind the way you do."

The doctor rose and went over to a bank of screens. He typed on the keyboard, and one of the screens lit. Zachary stumbled around the miniscule room, his hands pressed to his ears, his mouth open and obviously screaming.

"Breaking down his mental barriers is taking more than I thought it would. He's strong. The physical pain and stress of the piercing noise is taking its toll, finally." Fredrick studied the subject.

Gabriel clenched his fist, and he released a controlled breath through his nose. "Now that you have two new subjects, I've got a new direction to take with Zach."

Fredrick turned to look at him in surprise.

"I'm removing him from the lab."

"What? You can't just walk out of here with him! We don't have control of him, Gabriel. I'm still using him to fine-tune the latest gen of the drug..."

"Stop," Gabriel said softly and turned to pin the doctor with his gaze. "As you've pointed out, I can go into his mind. I have control. He will still be supplying data on the drug. This is a new step. You haven't succeeded in breaking him yet, and I have some ideas. You can focus on the new Hunters."

"I don't like this."

"Noted. Now, stop the audible." He gestured at Zach's screen.

Grumbling, the doctor typed on the keyboard. The man in the room collapsed to the floor in a fetal position, his wings lax. Gabriel walked out of the office and down the hall to the proper door. After punching in his code, the door released, and he stepped across the threshold. Hoarse sobbing reached him.

He knelt at the man's head and gently brushed the stringy brown hair. Zach tensed under Gabriel's hand, and the sound cut off. His mental barriers were thin and erratic when Gabriel probed them.

Zachary, Gabriel sent, figuring Zach's physical hearing still rang. *Come with me.*

The Seer started to tremble and tried to inch away on the floor. Gabriel clenched his hand, gripping a fist of hair, and pulled Zach's head up. He was shoring up his mental defenses faster than Gabriel could believe. Gabriel smiled and sent a little push, scattering the attempt like clouds in the wind.

Or I could just let Fredrick start the noise again.

Kill me, he begged. *Why are you doing this? Just kill me.*

That would be a huge waste of potential. If you don't want to stay here with the noise, then get up and come with me.

How is that better? he muttered softly, and Gabriel chuckled at it.

He helped the Seer to his feet then clamped his hand around the back of Zach's neck as they walked to the door. His mind arrowed in, and Zach gasped at the suddenness of the intrusion.

He leaned in, his lips brushing the Seer's ear. "No sudden moves. Walk calmly with me and don't speak."

Gabriel felt the shiver that rippled through Zach's wings where they were pressed to his chest. He prodded the younger man out into the hallway. Fredrick waited, his arms crossed.

"I still do not think this is a good idea, Gabriel."

"I didn't expect your opinion to change in the last five minutes." He kept Zach moving, and the doctor fell in beside them.

Fredrick fished in his pocket. "Here. This is his next dose. He should receive it at five tonight."

Gabriel took it.

"I want written reports. Detailed. Especially since we will no longer have his reactions on tape."

"Fredrick, go play with your new toys."

He left the sputtering doctor and led Zachary up the metal steps out of the labs. The wide-eyed guard behind the desk started to rise.

"Don't bother," Gabriel purred. The guard gulped and sank back to his seat. "I have what I came for. You know nothing if anyone asks."

He smiled at the man's frantic nod.

"Good. I would hate to have to make an example out of you if I found out gossip was spreading about my business."

"No. No, sir."

Zachary's body was stiff, but he still walked at a steady pace, so the command was holding. Gabriel herded the Seer out of the observatory office. Out in the hall, he let his breath out. This would take some careful balancing. The Seer was not like Petra, who he could just take out of the hold. Removing someone from the labs was another matter.

"I think we'll start in the arena. Let's see how out of shape you are."

Chapter Eight

The next morning, Jessica woke excited. Impatient to get moving, she pushed Kieran out the door. Laughing at her, he shook his wings out, and she frowned at him. "Come on, Kieran. If you don't pick it up, I'm leaving without you."

"Relax, Jess. They'll be there practicing all morning."

Marching off, she said over her shoulder, "You haven't been cooped up for over two months; I can't wait to move." She stopped when he didn't follow and looked back at him. He was grinning from ear to ear.

"Then I suggest you follow me, since you're heading in the wrong direction."

Hissing, she turned around and followed him down the path around the longhouse. "I haven't been here in a long time. They used to practice over there. How far away is it? Could we fly?"

He slowed so they would walk side by side and looked at her. "Sorry. Chris or Donald need to check you out first before you make your maiden flight. Normally Nickolas could as well, but he's not really up for it at the moment."

She flipped her wings lightly and snorted. "I've already flown, Kieran."

He laughed then stopped, looking at her in disbelief. "No you haven't." Then he looked at her more closely. "When?"

"The night I escaped you and Aiden. Nick and Chris stalked me in a yard, and my only escape route was out over the river. So I took it."

"You flew before the coma? Well that's a stupid question; when else would it have been?" he mumbled. "Wow, I don't know if anyone else has done that."

They reached the bridge, and Jessica looked out across the snow-covered field to the practice grounds on the other side.

"I would still feel better if you would wait, Jess. Otherwise, how are you feeling today? You've only been awake for two days, and since you're in a higher caste, you aren't technically finished with the change yet. You still have your talents coming in."

She paused on the bridge to admire the icy water rushing by underneath them and thought about Kieran's question, taking stock internally. "I'm excited, Kier. I can feel something deep inside, something warm, like molten honey. It's filling up an empty space I never knew I had before. I think that's where I drew the ability I used to tie you up from."

They continued walking, and she listened to the sound of their feet echo hollowly on the wood before they stepped off, crunching through the snow on the pathway again. "Physically though, I'm tired. It's real easy to get out of shape locked up in a box for months."

"Yeah, I remember."

Halfway across the field, Jessica paused; all the Facility Valkyries were scattered across the level ground of the practice arena, working out in pairs or small groups. She felt a smile stretch across her cheeks then picked up her pace. Kieran chuckled behind her.

When they arrived at the edge of the arena, she stopped. With Kieran next to her, she watched the Valkyries work—for the first time as one of them. What had seemed scary as a kid, was now simply breathtaking. The fluid grace with which they all moved, predatory and lethal. They fought on the ground and in the air. Their wings worked seamlessly into their moves, to defend or attack.

Intent on watching them, she missed when Donald stopped next to her. The pulse of energy down her link caught her attention though, and dragging her eyes away, she met his assessing ones. He slowly paced a circle around her, examining her like he had never seen her before. He pursed his lips.

"Kieran, I'm going to have you run her around a little. We need to see how she moves so I can see what style of fighting will best suit her."

"Donald, I'm not inexperienced. I..." Jess began.

Donald cut her off. "A lot of new fledglings say that, Jess. Now I want you to just try and defend yourself. Kieran, don't go too hard on her."

Irritated, she started to open her mouth again when a thunder of wings announced the arrival of another Valkyrie behind her. As she started to turn, she caught a vicious grin from Donald.

"Well, Chris, I see you're half the man you were yesterday," Donald quipped

Settling his wings, Christoff gave him a cheerful smirk. "Definitely the better half." Then he switched his attention to her and eyed her from top to bottom, much the same way Donald had, setting her temper to simmer again. "I'll take over her evaluation, Donald."

"As I was trying to tell Donald, Chris, I'm not inexperienced in fighting..."

His eyes flared with amusement. "Your body is different now, Jess. Your instincts and reflexes will react in an altered way. Regardless of whatever self-defense courses you took before the change. It's usually a little overwhelming for the new fledges to have such strong instincts pushing them. Part of the training will be in how to control your natural desire to lethally shred your opponent."

Huffing out her breath, she gave up trying to tell them. *Fine, if they won't listen, that's their own fault.* She grabbed her temper with both hands and reined it in, holding it in reserve. Skimming past Kieran's eyes, she caught a wary concern flash through them as she stalked out onto the field with Chris. She could hear the empath quietly talking to Donald behind her.

"Donald, you two should have listened to her."

"Kieran, she's a fledge. We need to know where to place her for training."

"That wasn't my point."

Tuning out their conversation, Jessica faced Christoff. Eyeing him, she was glad she had walked briskly here; her muscles had gotten a bit of a warm-up. Bouncing on the balls of her feet, she limbered up a little, waiting for him to make the first move.

He gave her a minute before he lunged toward her at about half speed. She easily slid to the side and walloped him in the ribs with her elbow then bounced away. Waiting.

Slowly straightening, Christoff turned to face her, surprise in his eyes. Then tucking his wings in, he circled her, considering. After a moment, he struck with his fist. Blocking, she jumped to the side, hitting him with a punch to the chest. Not a lot of power behind it, but enough to get his attention. Not waiting for him this time, she attacked.

She kicked him with a roundhouse and got the first to connect with his ribs before he got over his shock enough to block. The next several kicks and punches she threw, he blocked, but she kept him on the defensive.

He spun out of her reach, and she slowed, bouncing, waiting for him to attack. Circling her more warily, intensity started to replace complacency in his eyes. Then he fanned his wings, snapped them back, and darted in. Dodging, she started blocking his attacks. He upped his speed. He wasn't testing her at half pace anymore.

They were right; her new reflexes were different. But she wasn't finding it a detriment. Her faster speed and agility helped compensate for how out of shape she was.

It was exhilarating. She felt heat rise and flash in her eyes. Keeping her wings tucked in—she wasn't quite sure what to do with them yet—she did a forward roll, dodging under Chris and bouncing up out of his range.

All her concentration solely on Chris, she was unaware when all activity on the practice field stopped. In shock and awe, everyone watched the two of them spar.

Sweat started dripping down her neck. Annoyed with herself, she knew that before her incarceration she would have been like Chris, only breathing heavily. Engaging again, she scored on him with a solid kick to his ribs, but it brought him in closer so she missed the quick backhand he threw. Her head snapping back, she hissed and her power flared.

Blocking a kick from him, she jumped back, spreading her wings to launch into the sky.

"No! Jessica!"

Tackling her around the waist, Chris drove her to the ground, her wings spread wide. Her breath left her, but she still managed to pull her knees up, pushing Chris off of her. Then rolling over quickly, she snapped her wings closed and glared at him while trying to get her breath back.

"You stay on the ground!" he ordered.

Baring her teeth, she growled at him in response.

"Don't push me, Jessica." He gritted his teeth. Then stalking her, he backed her up, keeping her off balance. She wiped the sweat away and continued to dodge and block. She could feel her stamina starting to give out, making her angry with herself.

Spinning, she threw a backkick, just missing him. Her knee buckled when he planted his foot in the back of her leg as he went by. Rolling, she barely got out of the way of his next attack.

Violence the likes of which she hadn't been aware of ever feeling before roared through her, causing her to fight past her limits. Her limbs started trembling in fatigue, but she kept pushing them. Stumbling, she went down to her knees, regaining her feet slower than before.

"Enough."

She lunged at him, but he spun out of the way.

"I said enough, Jessica!"

Panting, she sank to her knees in the mud as her awareness of her surroundings returned. The silence had her raising her head to look around. All other activity had stopped and all attention was focused on them...or more accurately, on her.

"Come on, Jess, get up or you're going to get stiff." Wariness and respect filled Christoff's eyes. Groaning, it took her a moment, but she regained her feet and started walking around to cool off. Joining her, Christoff stretched then ordered those around them to get back to work. He turned back to her. "Well, that was certainly a surprise."

Tiredly, she smiled at him while she kept moving. "I tried to tell you, but neither one of you would listen. I'm a black belt in tae kwon do."

Comprehension and something more, a look of puzzle pieces falling into place, crossed his face. "Ah, that would help explain how you were able to elude Nick and I during the recovery, and your actions in the Hub."

Shrugging, she stretched her arms over her head. "So now what?"

He caught a bottle of water Kieran threw at him, handed it to her, then caught the second one for himself. "Well, you're certainly up to speed as far as fighting goes. It's just going to be a matter of getting your stamina back...and learning how to use your wings."

Sipping slowly, Jessica made her way over to the side of the field and sat down on a bench, then looked up at Chris. Shivers started now that she was cooling off. "I want to fly, Chris. Why did you stop me? You already know I can."

He sat down beside her and took a drink himself before answering. "Well, for starters, you were reaching the end of your energy. One previous flight doesn't give you the experience to handle difficult flying situations. Second, there are very good reasons why we have rules that we follow when it comes to fledglings starting to take wing. If you don't have a spotter and get into trouble, it's so incredibly easy to be killed falling. It's my job, or Donald or Nick's, to check over your musculature to make sure you're strong enough. We also need to fly with you for a while to teach you how to take off and land, how to handle different weather conditions. But more importantly, we need to watch and make sure that you don't overfly yourself."

She thought about what he said, then nodded. "Ok, I can see that. I can even agree with that. So what do I do?"

Smiling, he watched her. "Well you're going to be really sore tomorrow after the bout we just had, but I'm willing to bet that you have a little left in you now that you've had a rest. What if we fly back over to the courtyard? I know it's not far, but it's a start."

Excitement flooded her, and she immediately capped her water bottle. "Let's go."

A laugh burst from him, and he stood up. "Ok, stand up and spread your wings." He walked around her, pushed at her muscles, and examined the wing membrane minutely. Testing the struts, he pulled and bent them, causing her to wince slightly. Finally he pronounced her good enough. "Now, listen. Before, you didn't have to fight gravity when you took off because you dropped over the river cliff."

"It was so amazing once I was in the air."

Smiling at her, he nodded his head. "Your first flight is always memorable. Well, here's to your first official flight. Bend your knees, then with a strong down sweep, push off with your legs to help get off the ground."

Slowly fanning her wings, she followed Christoff's instructions. Bending her knees, she launched into the air. The sounds of cheering had her quickly glancing back down to see everyone on the field watching her and yelling encouragements.

Thrilled by the sensation of the air rushing over her body, she didn't even feel cold anymore. Christoff took up a position like he had during her first flight, making her smile. She climbed altitude and circled the practice grounds, losing track of time in the joy of flying.

Jessica, remember I said short. Start heading toward the longhouse now.

Sighing, she finished circling, then started in the direction of the public compound when she saw something in the trees by the practice field. *Chris, look over there, in the trees.*

It's Marcus and Robin. They must have been watching our people work out.

Even thinking about her brother didn't dim the joy she felt right now. Landing in the courtyard, she stumbled then she caught herself, laughing. She spun to watch Christoff land, and he touched down with complete grace. "Practice is all it'll take, Jess. Remember, until I give you the go ahead, no flying alone, understand?"

Too exhilarated to argue, she nodded her head.

"I need to get back to everyone else. You need to rest. We'll all see you at lunch."

She watched him take off again then turned to go tell Nickolas all about her morning.

♦ ♦ ♦

Marcus stood with Robin and watched Jessica take her first flight. Both sighed, remembering their own first. The thrill was never completely forgotten as time passed; the wonder of the very first time always remained special. Marcus shook his head and turned to Jessica's brother. "I'm surprised. She held her own with Chris. Watching you and he fight briefly gives me an appreciation of the level of skill that would take. I would guess that when she regains her strength, she'll best both of you."

Robin smiled proudly and shook his head. "It shouldn't have surprised you. Remember, I could fight when I arrived too. I made sure Jessica was trained. I knew we would both change eventually. Why make it more difficult than it needed to be? I remembered watching the Hunters fight when we were kids, so I had some idea of what was in store for us. Jessica received her first black belt in tae kwon do just before I left. From the reports I've gotten from May over the years, she kept up with it, thankfully."

"That was smart, thinking ahead." Shielding his eyes, Marcus watched her circle slowly. "She had good form for her take off. But Chris had better pull her in soon; she doesn't have the stamina." Almost as if they had heard him, Jessica turned toward the longhouse. "Good."

Both of them backed slightly into the shadows of the trees as they watched the two Valkyries pass by.

"Do you need to see any more, Marcus?"

Marcus turned his attention back to the practice grounds and watched the Facility Valkyries resume their interrupted sparring practice. "I don't think so. I wouldn't mind seeing Christoff work against Nickolas sometime, though. From what Dad described, it's pretty intense. I imagine watching Jessica and Nick spar will be exciting."

Flight

They turned and started walking along the path that would lead them back to the creek. "I saw enough to give me a rough idea of what they are capable of as fighters. To give them credit, they work incredibly well together. Doesn't much surprise me though. They haven't needed to worry about everyday affairs like we have. Where their food was coming from or where they were sleeping was all taken care of for them; they had all the time in the world to hone their skills with practice. That would make them very efficient killers. Our people could learn something from their skills, I think."

"The question still remains, though; how do we get them to integrate with us? I didn't expect them to balk so strongly, Marcus."

"If I'd been thinking, I would have. They have a strong culture of their own, with strong leaders. It was easy for us to assume that since we have the larger numbers and it's our home, they would just join us."

"Well, we need to do something. We can't have them running around at odds with what we need to accomplish. It's too dangerous. For us and for them. Gabriel will pluck them like overripe fruit."

They passed out of the trees, and Marcus shook his wings out. "I thought that maybe we could ease them into it. We don't try to split them up among the septs at first, but get them to join work parties and scouting groups, only a few individuals in each so that our people outnumber them. That way they are more inclined to follow our leadership and hopefully become comfortable working with us. As a group, they will have the strength to stay separate. But individuals will be less prone to. We need to reassure them that we aren't a threat. The key is to be quiet and subtle. We need to work as one group as soon as possible."

"What about Nickolas? And for that matter, Jessica? You were right about them having strong leaders. How do you propose we get them to listen? So far, I'm not getting the impression that they are interested in letting anyone else lead them. What do they think they're going to do? It's not like they've ever led themselves before. They've always gotten their orders directly from Ian."

"True. They'll just need to come to terms with losing Ian in that role. Dad sent them to me; they need to figure that out. Regardless of how they feel about it, they don't have the experience or the knowledge, either in day-to-day life or in the situation we have with the Facility and Gabriel, to be able to make sound decisions."

"Good luck convincing Nickolas of that."

Marcus blew out a breath. "Yeah, he isn't too keen on listening to anything I say at the moment. I wish Dad was here.... He'd be able to snarl Nickolas into submission."

"Do you think he's going to be a problem?"

"Oh yeah, I think he'll be a problem." They crossed the creek, walking quietly for a moment. "I don't know about Chris. They all seem to follow him, but Nickolas hasn't been available. He submitted to me once already, which is a good sign that he might be willing to accept my leadership. But that was without Nick to fall back on."

He glanced at Robin as they rounded the corner of the longhouse and headed for the door. "By the way, I thought you handled that punishment well. The two of you really started to work together. Possibly—hopefully—that might influence Christoff into listening to us more. If he will respect you enough, it could help balance out Nickolas's hostility."

The two of them walked through the common room, and Marcus could hear laughter coming from the kitchens as lunch was being prepared. He opened the door to his office and let Robin close it while he went to sit behind his desk. The younger Hunter leaned up against the cabinets, folding his arms.

"I don't know. We kind of reached a truce, but neither of us really gave in. I think we're pretty evenly matched." His surrogate son avoided his gaze. "I am sorry, Marcus, for causing trouble. I didn't mean to screw up your message from Ian."

Marcus stared at Robin until he finally looked up and met his gaze. Marcus could see his concern and the pain in his eyes. "Why did you?" he asked evenly. "I had told both you and

Christoff that I didn't want you fighting, and believe me, I knew how bad the two of you wanted a piece of each other."

Robin pushed away from the wall and started to pace restlessly. "The instinct was so strong, Marcus. I've never been around anyone besides you who has pushed me like that. At least with you, there's no question of my position. But with Christoff...." He shrugged. "He was so on edge, because of fleeing the Facility and Ian's death, meeting you, but mostly he was sick with concern over his brother's condition. Then he discovered the microchip planted in Nickolas and lost it."

Robin raked his hand through his hair and continued. "Both of us escalated the other. I was having trouble because of Jessica's rejection of me and her acceptance of him; I wasn't able to fight the instinct anymore. Before I knew it, we both had gone feral."

A sheepish grin crossed Robin's face, and he glanced over briefly. "It was the most amazing fight, Marcus; I wish we could have finished it."

Marcus shook his head at his Hunter and regarded him seriously. "I need you to follow protocol, Robin. I must be able to trust that."

His Hunter Prime stopped in front of his desk and bowed his head. "Yes, sir. I will, sir."

Silent for a moment, Marcus watched Robin stand, assessing his strength and commitment. Judging that he had left him hanging for long enough, he cleared his throat, waving for him to relax. "Moving on, we need to determine how much extra hunting will need to be done. That was one of the ways I was hoping to encourage the Facility Valkyries to join with us. If I can get Chris to release some of his Hunters to you in the name of learning how to hunt game in the wild, it would be a step toward integration. They are doing really well with Kevin's classes so far. He's gotten those that are free of the inhibitor proficient with their telepathy already. They soak up knowledge like sponges. But they are still hesitant to separate.

"We also need to check on our storage items. We hadn't planned on fifty extra mouths to feed for the winter. I believe this is a time we'll need to tap our financial card. I'll talk to

Beth and have her go over the inventory of what we have and write up a proposition of what she thinks we will need. Then we'll be able to budget our resources, and you'll be able to head to town for a supply run.

"We need to be extra careful now when you head into Lynden. You were right to cut Dustin's communications when you pulled the Flight out of there. If Donald had managed to contact Dustin on that phone Ian gave him, they would have led the Facility straight to Dustin and his family. We'll really be up a creek without their aid. If they can't get to the bank for us, or go to the stores, life will be much harder for us. I would like to aim to get this done right after the holidays."

Robin took his place back against the cabinets. "Dustin fixed his electronics as fast as I figured he would. But boy was he pissed at me. I didn't see that I had much choice though. After Gabriel had almost succeeded in trapping Nick and Chris up in Bellingham I knew the Facility was too close to them."

The Hunter paused, a pensive look crossing his eyes. "Do you ever think we'll be free? Able to walk the streets without fear of being forced into the camps, to do things others take for granted?"

The weight of all the responsibilities he held over the Valkyrie species descended on Marcus's shoulders. The realization that his father, who held the path in his head that they were all taking, was really and truly gone, hit him like a rock. He closed his eyes and leaned forward, head in hands, onto his desk. "I hope so, Robin, I really do. I can't allow anything else."

"Are you ok, Marcus?"

He took a deep breath, grounding and centering, taking strength from his power, then pushed the doubts and pain aside. "It's just hard sometimes, Robin, when I remember Dad is gone. We had always held out some hope that he would join us one day. I've had to grieve for him and both of my sons twice now. Once, when we lost them all so many years ago, and again now, when my father is truly dead and my sons wish I were."

He scrubbed his face then sat up and swiveled to look out the window. "I'm not sure what to do about the situation. I can't change the past no matter how much I wish I could."

"Maybe time will help, Marcus. I know that sounds like a lame excuse, but they only just found out you're alive. Hopefully, after they see what you have done and come to learn what it's like living out here, maybe then they'll understand."

Marcus didn't hold out much hope for that. He turned back to his surrogate son. "Maybe you're right. One thing is certain though. Definitely only time will tell."

Christoff sat with Donald and Kieran at breakfast several mornings later. He reached for another piece of bacon while Kieran drew their attention to their Alphas across the room.

"See, look."

They all watched Nickolas and Jessica while they ate. Oblivious to anyone around them, the two Alphas talked animatedly over their food. Until Dev pitched an orange at Nick. He caught it on reflex with his injured arm.

"He winced, but not too bad. I'm afraid I set Dev up though." Kieran laughed. Jessica was giving the Flight leader the sharp side of her tongue about throwing the orange.

Chris chuckled. "We should make sure Dev isn't paired with her today."

"Wise choice," Donald added.

"Nick's had a week of healing since he woke," Kieran said. "And he's reached the point of restlessness. He isn't ready to work out. But we have to start structuring challenges for him or he's going to go out on his own and likely overdo it."

"What's he capable of at the moment?" Chris asked.

"Not as much as he wants. Beth has him on faster walks and arm stretches. She thinks the splints will come off his wings today, and from the way he caught that orange, she will probably get him started on very light weights."

"How's his memory?" Donald asked tentatively.

"Still gone. But he's questioning more now. So hiding the truth from the outside is becoming more difficult. Beth doesn't want the memories or his power level to be returned yet. It would be so easy for him to reinjure himself if he pushed his body to do what it isn't ready for out of grief."

"And we all know how Nick likes to outrun his demons." Chris sighed. "It's not likely he'd be stupid enough to harm himself on purpose. Especially not with all of us watching him. But why take away a good coping mechanism for him. If he can safely fly and fight, he'll be able to sweat off the demons that way. Otherwise, who knows what sort of coping skill he comes up with?"

All three continued to watch the Alpha pair.

"What about moving them out to the south quad with us? He would have more opportunity to stay busy in a way we can structure. Jess is only staying in sick bay because that's where Nickolas is." Donald looked at Kieran.

Kieran rubbed the knotwork medallion he always wore between his fingers. Chris refilled his coffee.

"I'll talk to Beth. I suspect she'll want him to stay where she can keep a closer eye on him. But I don't know that that is the best thing for him. He tolerates his parents care, but he isn't happy about it. I wish Jays could help. They don't know Nick the same way he does. Or we do, for that matter."

"You're the closest to his care, Kieran. I leave it up to you. But we need to do what's right for us. Not the Aurorans." Chris caught each of their gazes in turn.

"Agreed," Donald said.

Kieran sighed and let his necklace drop to the end of its chain.

Chris held up the coffee carafe, silently asking. The others nodded so he refilled their cups.

"Jess's stamina is improving in leaps and bounds," Donald commented. "She took me down in the ring yesterday."

Chris tipped his head to look at his Second. "Sorry I missed that."

Donald rubbed his shoulder but still smiled.

Chris grabbed another slice of bacon. "She's still not full of grace on her landings, but she's got the strongest take off of any fledge I've shadowed. She's building up in the ranks fast and is already working on storm maneuvers. You should take her flights for a few days," he told Donald.

His Second nodded and took a drink of his coffee.

"Have you looked at Jays recently?" Kieran asked.

"Not closely." He glanced over at Jays plowing through a huge plate of food a few tables away, pausing occasionally to snap at something Dylan said. The Flight leader sat escort with him, looking like he was trying to cajole Jays out of a foul mood. Then Jays shifted his wings, and Chris couldn't stifle a gasp. They were already half grown.

His gaze snapped to Donald's, then they both focused on Kieran, who nodded. "Since he's not in the Hub, he isn't on the usual cocktail of drugs. It's affected how fast he's completing the change."

"But twice as fast?" Chris whispered.

"It looks like it. And more, he's already showing signs that he'll be a Seer."

"What were they doing to us?" Donald asked.

Kieran turned to look at the fledgling. "I don't know. I'm not a doctor, and it was only during Jessica's isolation that I spent any appreciable time in the Hub beyond our tests. Jays might be able to tell us more if he makes it through the coma. I think Bethany knows more than she's letting on, too."

"More and more I wish Ian was here to answer these questions." Chris gripped his coffee cup and stared at the table top. "Is there any point in asking Jays now?"

"Not really. We don't want to be stirring up memories of the Hub and Ian. You could try Beth, but I don't know how much they are willing to trust us any more than we trust them."

Chris sighed and looked back up at his friends. "The more I think about it, the more I like getting the two of them moved out with us as soon as he's physically able. It'll be easier to keep him in the loop. I finally got to go over everything that's happened with us. He was surprised to hear we have fifteen off the drugs already. Obviously his time sense is a bit loopy. It doesn't feel like we've been here that long to me either."

He pulled a piece of paper out of his pocket and handed it to Donald. "Here are the names of the next five Nick and I decided should be weaned off the inhibitor. And, Kieran, as of now you are the acting Prime for all of our combined Casters and Seers. Though at the moment, that's just you."

He and Donald chuckled at the look on Kieran's face at that news. "But it gets better. In the latest group, Dev seems to be a Caster and, lucky you, so does Aiden. I'd like you to make time today to meet with both of them. After talking with Nick, we decided that, for now, we didn't need a Prime for each caste. There's just not enough of us for that."

"If they're right about the percentages for the castes, there will only be a dozen mixed Casters and Seers, approximately, out of the fifty-five of us," Kieran said, then he got an unfocused look and paused.

Donald met his glance before Kieran said, "Beth just called me; David's rousing out of the coma."

Chris pushed back his chair and started to rise, the others following suit. "We'd better head over there then."

They wove through the tables in the common room, making their way out of the longhouse. The chill of the morning air slapped them as they crossed the courtyard. The sky looked like they'd see more snow before evening. Then they were in the medical building and crossing the main room for David's room. The door was slightly ajar; pushing it open farther, they found Beth sitting in a chair while a very groggy David sat with his head in his hands, moaning.

Chris caught her gaze, and she nodded, rising, and left the room. Chris squatted down in front of him. "David."

The new Valkyrie raised his head; he looked at Christoff, squinting in pain. "What happened? I felt fine last night. Now my head's going to explode, and I feel like I could eat the cart that the horse I ate last night pulled." Rubbing his eyes, he sat up straighter, then looked at all of them gathered around him. "What's going on?"

Chris raised his eyebrow at Kieran, who said, "He's a Hunter."

Chris turned a smile on David and lightly clapped him on the shoulder. "I hate to break this to you, David, but you didn't go to sleep last night. That was a week ago. You just woke up from a coma. We all go into one when we enter stage three. It's not mentioned because it's a dangerous time and worry can stack the deck against you. Congratulations, you made it. You are now fully fledged."

The new Hunter stared then sputtered, "Coma? What?" He shook his aching head carefully then looked at the other two for confirmation. "So now what?"

Chris stood and moved over as his mother brought in a tray with food for David. "Now, you eat. It'll take a couple of days for your head to stop hurting and for you to become accustomed to the changes. After that, you'll learn what it is to be a Valkyrie."

David blinked at him then took a sip of the broth. Waving Donald and Kieran ahead of him, they left the room, with his mother following.

In the hall, she stopped them. "Dylan is bringing Jays over now that breakfast is done. He says he's had a hard time with the fledge. Jays woke up argumentative." She looked at Kieran. "It's been a week. And those signs show me that the block you put in is fading. The timing is about right."

"What do you mean?" Chris asked.

"Depending on the talent and the application, the average duration of effectiveness is variable. Without previous examples of Kieran's work, I didn't have a base line to judge the length of his effectiveness. He could have been more like a Caster talent. They can only hold their casting for as long as their power well will allow. Which is usually anything from a few minutes to a few hours. But I had a feeling from the way he was utilizing his talent that he might respond more like an imbuer. They use their talent to set something in motion. In this case, Kieran placed a block and walked away. But the power held within that block is running out. So he needs to go in and recharge it basically. That's what the imbuers need to do every week."

"So Jays is starting to remember?" Donald asked.

"Yes. He hasn't yet, but he will soon if Kieran doesn't reinforce it."

"Nick," Chris stated.

"Already on my list. Especially for Nick, the block needs to come down in a controlled manner, since his full strength talent is tied into it. It was either that or he was going to swat us like flies the first time we were in his mind. As soon as we are done with Jays, we can bring him in for his exam and deal with it then."

"Chris, if you want to stay here with Kieran, I'll head over to the practice grounds and get everyone started on basic drills," Donald suggested.

"That works. We'll be over as soon as we can."

Donald nodded then turned to go. "Hey, Jays," he said as he passed the fledgling stomping down the hall.

Jays ignored them all and tried to skirt around them. He sighed heavily when Beth gestured for him to follow her into his room.

Jays cast them an irritated glare when Chris and Kieran followed him and shut the door. The fledge paced the room and flexed his half-grown wings in agitation. "Where is Ian? The more I think about this…. He should be here. But he couldn't have come. Which means we left him behind, and that's not an option."

"Please sit, Jays," Beth asked.

"This isn't making any sense." He raked his hand through his hair and cast a sharp glance at Kieran.

"Jays, sit," Beth said.

The fledgling made another pass before he stiffly sat on the edge of the bed. He kept a wary eye on them as he stripped his shirt off then flexed his wings, allowing her to measure their span and to check the musculature developing.

Clucking at him, Beth ran her hands over the joint. "Jays, you need to do those wing exercises I showed you; you're growing adequately, but I'd like to see more bulk."

You're right, Kieran. Look at those wings; they're easily half grown already.

I can feel other differences in his development as well. And I think I can actually feel the block thinning.

Chris intercepted an irritated glance from Jays. *Kieran, he senses us talking; did you catch that?*

Yes, I did.

"Why won't any of you answer my questions?" He jerked his head out of Beth's hands.

"Jays," Chris's mother reprimanded quietly. "You know I need to monitor your internal changing as well."

He dodged her hand again and raked them all with a malevolent glare.

"What is going on?" he demanded, flicking a glance at Kieran before he continued. "I'm confused, but it's more than that. I shouldn't be this complacent, Kieran. And don't try to lie to me; I've more experience with the change than any of you, including Beth. I understand why I'm changing so fast, but the rest of this?"

"Kieran, come here," Beth called softly.

Jays scooted back on the bed. "Why?" he asked suspiciously.

Chris folded his arms and watched Kieran sink down onto the mattress beside the recoiling fledgling.

"Because he's an empath, and he has skills I need. I still have your internal exam to finish, Jays, and he is going to help me."

"I don't think..." Jays stammered as he pressed into the wall at the head of the bed.

"Just relax," Beth soothed as Kieran reached his hand out and laid it on the fledgling's bare chest.

"Let me in, Jays," Kieran murmured.

Jays gasped, and as his body snapped tight, Chris saw that his eyes suddenly grew unfocused.

Both men's breathing slowed. Glancing at his mother, Chris decided it was safe to move now and sat down in the other chair to wait.

Chapter Nine

Kieran stood once more on the rocky shore of the river of Jays's dreamscape and watched him patiently throwing rocks into the water. His friend sat on a boulder on the little island he'd cut out of the bank. It wasn't day or night this time. It just *was*.

Interested in how this mental construct differed, Kieran took a moment to visually examine his friend across the water. Unaware of him, Jays stayed on his task. His bodily changes mirrored his real world changes, even though he seemed mentally disconnected from himself.

How long do you think you can keep him there?

Kieran turned his head to look at the voice speaking next to him before he answered. *As long as I need to. Are you trying to reach him?*

The twin Jays shrugged beside him and rustled his half-grown wings. *It's hard to stay apart. The water's receding though; soon I'll be able to cross.*

Kieran murmured, *I can't allow that yet, Jays; you know that.*

Pain-filled eyes searched his before Jays whispered, *He needs to know, Kieran. It's his right to know.*

Kieran buffered himself against the onslaught of pain and held onto Jays's gaze. *Of course it's his right, and he will know. But at what cost? Changing is so hard on the body to begin with, but adding on an emotional burden of this nature? There's a high chance that you won't make it out of the coma.* He put everything he could into his eyes as he pleaded with this half of Jays to trust and understand.

Jays turned away and stared across the water at himself. *The need to get out of this trap, to reconnect, is strong, Kieran. You *won't be able to keep us apart for much longer without causing permanent damage. I'll try to wait, but I don't know how long I'll be able to.* *

   **It'll be easier if you aren't fighting me, trust me.* *

Jays flared his growing wings, then the fledgling turned away without answering and walked off down the river bank. Kieran's heart felt for his friend, but he sighed and returned his attention to the part of Jays who sat oblivious to his presence.

That Jays still skipped rocks, but the stones more and more often hit the muck on the bottom as the water level surrounding the island receded. Studying the situation, Kieran raised his arms and brought his own power to the surface of his mind.

He pulled a strong current from the river and cut the channel around the island deeper and wider, then watched it fill up again. Kieran's shoulders slumped, and he wished there were some other way, but he agreed with Beth that this was Jays's best chance at survival. Examining his work carefully, he made sure that the block on Jays's memory was thoroughly reinforced before he left his friend's mind.

Kieran's accelerated breathing was the first sign that he was coming out of the trance. Chris sat up in his chair. Beth had never taken her attention off of the two in trance.

When Kieran opened his eyes, Jays's body relaxed and slid out from under the empath's hand. Beth caught the fledge before he tipped off the bed to the ground. Rising from the chair, Chris helped his mother adjust the unconscious man flat onto his back, his growing wings tucked securely underneath.

Kieran rose and stretched. "It was exactly how you said it would be, Beth."

"You got the block reinforced?"

"Yes. He fought a little."

"Understandable. But this is what is best for his health at the moment. There's no point in taking chances if we don't have to. His is the easy one, I'm afraid. When he wakes, he shouldn't remember what happened. He'll just be waking from a normal nap like he takes every day. Nick on the other hand...."

She tucked a blanket around the sleeping man then led them out the door.

In the main treatment room, Marcus leaned against the wall, waiting for them. "I asked Robin to go get Nick."

Chris turned a chair around at the table and straddled it, watching the room at large. Beth nodded at his father and squeezed Kieran's elbow as she passed him on her way to the supply room. Raised voices reached them from the foyer as his mother pushed a small cart out of the supply room.

Nick shoved the doors open and stomped through, Jessica on his heels, glaring over her shoulder.

"I had already started on my walk. Why couldn't this have waited until our normal time?"

Jessica swept everyone with a lethal glance. Chris hooked a second chair out from under the table and pointed at it, his gaze locked with hers. He could see she was ready to refuse, so he pulsed a little energy down their link; she narrowed her eyes but stalked over. After she sat, he returned his gaze to his brother.

Nick prowled the room. His wings twitched restlessly, though Chris could see the control he exerted to keep from snapping them open.

"David woke from the coma today and changed our schedule around," his mother said.

"Besides," his father added. "I would think you would want the splints off sooner rather than later."

The hopeful look in Nick's eyes quickly withered under the heat of anger. He rotated his shoulder then raised his arm over his head in a stretch. His gait was smooth but still slow. If Chris looked carefully, he could still see the remnants of pain in his brother's body language.

"Come and sit." Beth patted the center table.

Grumbling, Nick worked his way over to the table. He'd never been a gracious patient, now even more so since he had to deal with their parents. He yanked his shirt off and tossed it at the foot of the table. Beth poked and prodded the healing wound on his shoulder with ungentle hands. Nick hissed and twitched away; she just followed the movement.

"You've followed the stretches well enough that I'll allow you to start with the weights." She looked over her shoulder. "Chris, you supervise. I don't want him overworking it."

He nodded. The masses of bruising that had covered his brother's chest had faded to a sickly yellow.

"All right, stretch out your wing," Beth said as she stared intently into Nick's eyes then wrote something on a clipboard. Marcus had started to pull and prod at the injured wing, and Nickolas winced. "Anything I should be aware of? Have your memories started to come back?"

Chris felt a stirring down the link he shared with Nickolas, and his gaze snapped to his mother. She must have felt the power move because she looked deep into Nick's eyes again.

"I've mostly had feelings instead of memories," Nick said roughly. "The sensation of falling. Spinning green rushing up to meet me."

"Kieran?" Beth called. "Nick, I need you to relax and let us in. I can use Kieran's talent to take a look at your web and see how it's healing. It's going to feel a bit strange. You were unconscious the last time we did this."

Chris felt Jessica tense, and he reached his hand out, gripping her upper arm, holding her in place.

Nickolas winced again as Marcus pulled, then he gasped as Kieran laid a hand on his bare chest, Bethany gripping the back of the empath's neck.

Marcus was the only one of the four who moved. He worked the lacing free from the lacerations in Nick's wing membrane, quickly it looked like, probably hoping to get it done before they came out of the trance.

Nick took a huge gulp of air and opened his eyes as Kieran removed his hand.

"What was that?" Nick shuddered.

Beth leaned forward and opened Nick's eye wider, peering in. "It's a really intimate experience when an empath enters your outer mind. I'm sorry. Your power well looks undamaged, and your web is healing. You still won't have access to your talents for a while, though, it looks like. So don't worry too much about that. Nothing looks permanent. You just have to be patient and let everything heal."

"I don't even have my telepathy."

"I know." She brushed her hand over his head and down his hair. He ducked away.

Marcus tossed the last of the splint lacing onto the tray. "Stretch your wing out please."

Nick complied, and Chris could see the angry red scar that zigzagged through the membrane.

"That's healing extremely well. It's going to fade nicely and be hardly noticeable." Beth ran her fingertips across one of the lines. "And no ridge to speak of. As long as you don't stress it, Nick, you will have full wing integrity."

Marcus held his hands out and liquid light flowed along the seams like quicksilver. Even after he moved his hands to press against the red starburst on Nick's shoulder, the glow continued. Nick groaned as the healing heat penetrated the wound.

Marcus shook his hands out. "You may start stretching the wing. Nothing vigorous. And no strengthening exercises yet. Just stretches for mobility. We will start working on speed in a few days then graduate up to strengthening."

"No sparring still, but you may move up to gentle jogging as soon as you feel up to it," Beth added.

Nick slid off the table and worked his shirt back on, avoiding his parents' gazes.

"You still want to walk, Jess?" he asked.

Chris let her go, and she rose. "Of course."

Without another comment or a look back, Nickolas walked out of sick bay, Jessica on his heels.

Chris looked at Kieran and his parents and said quietly, "I assume you managed to repower the block on his memories?"

Beth nodded. "And made sure his talent remains in lockdown."

"Why? The memories I understand, but why are you keeping his talent confined?"

Beth sighed and fiddled around with the stuff on the cart. "He's so strong, and when we were in his head before, he attempted to use his talent in a way that would have killed me and Kieran. And maybe anyone who was standing close enough. I'm not sure because I don't know what talent he was attempting to use. He hasn't been graded, so we don't know what he can do. But I can't have him lashing out uncontrollably through pain or grief."

Chris rose and slowly paced around the room. "He never tried anything like that in the Hub."

"No one was breaching his barriers and invading his mind either. Plus, he was only coming into his power then. Now he's at full strength and untrained."

"And from what Dad said, a full strength we have never seen before." Marcus scooted Beth to the side and finished gathering up the supplies, wheeling the cart across the room to put it away. "If he would trust us, it would be different. But you've seen him. He won't even look at us if he can help it."

"Is that really such a surprise? I don't have anything to offer. Nick's emotions have always been volatile, even more so since he fledged." Chris ran a hand over his head and watched Marcus run his hands over his face.

"I pick up anguish when he sees the two of you. That's the emotion that circles around him. He's deeply hurt by the fact that you didn't come back for him," Kieran said softly.

"I'm not exactly thrilled either," Chris added. "But I was much younger than he was when you left. He remembers you very clearly." He glanced at his mother, and she fiddled with the covering on the table, avoiding him.

"Chris, we didn't want to leave you," his father replied hoarsely, stopping in the middle of the room. "If there was one thing about the past I could change, it would be that."

Marcus held his hand out tentatively toward him; Chris could tell his father was braced for his rejection. *I'm not Nick. I don't have the same memories to overcome. I can give them this. I can give us all this.* He took a step toward the offered hand. It came to rest lightly on his shoulder, and when he didn't pull away, squeezed, then pulled him into a rough hug. Unexpected tears burned in his eyes, and he turned his head toward where his mother was standing, her hands to her lips. He held his own hand out; she ran forward with a sob. Surrounded, his father wrapped his wings about both of them, holding them securely.

After a moment Chris pulled away, brushing at his eyes surreptitiously, and noticed his father do the same.

"We took comfort knowing the two of you were alive and well. We received regular reports on your progress, so for us, we feel like we know you. It's important for us to try and remember that the two of you don't actually know anything about us," Marcus added.

Chris cleared his throat and looked at both of them before answering. "It's hard. I can see both sides. I understand how Nick feels. A part of me feels the same, but I can get past that and see how it affects you too. Maybe it's just easier for me since I don't have so much to worry about like Nick does."

"I'm glad you're willing to try, son." Clearing his own throat, he looked at his wife. "When you're ready, Chris, I have a last message for you from your grandfather. He recorded messages for us when he knew he wouldn't be leaving the Facility. When you're ready to see it, come to my office."

Chris nodded and ran the back of his hand across his eyes again. "I don't know that I'm up for that right now...." he trailed off.

His father squeezed his shoulder. "I understand. It'll be waiting. Why don't you two go join the rest out on the practice grounds? I saw them getting started."

Chris flexed his wings then joined Kieran near the door. He looked over his shoulder as he walked out. Kieran's shoulder bumped up against his, bringing him back to reality. He looked at the empath but felt too many conflicting emotions to even try to express.

Reassurance and understanding radiated from Kieran. "Forgiveness is a long road, Chris. You've only taken the first step. Give yourself time."

◆ ◆ ◆

Jess's hand slid into his, and Nick slowed down his headlong walk with a sigh. He allowed their pace to change to an amble along the paths, happy to be outside even if it was cold and cloudy.

His wings fidgeted, and he suppressed the desire to snap them open, making do with a slow controlled stretch, flapping them gently to exercise the muscles but not stress the healing sail. "I want to fly."

"Now that I'm getting to take to the air, I can understand the sentiment."

They took the path to the north to see where it led. He already knew the path to the east would lead them to the bridge that crossed the creek, leading to the practice grounds, and right now he wasn't interested in anyone else's company. "It's more than just being able to fly, at least for me. Being confined like this makes my claustrophobia harder to control."

Their feet crunched on the gravel of the path. They passed through the open snow-splotched field beside the fallow vegetable garden. "You're claustrophobic?"

"I have been ever since my isolation. You think you didn't like being confined to the Hub? At least we managed to keep you from getting shot up with Xanthar. There's nothing like being trapped in your own body for hours at a time and not being able to do anything." He shuddered and tried to push the memories away. "Ever since then, flying has been the only way I've felt free of it. I would wake from the nightmares and fly around the dark city for hours sometimes. At first they tried to stop me, so I let them think I'd quit the habit. It wasn't until Chris and Donald caught me, when they had me confined a few weeks ago, that they realized the truth."

Jessica's hand squeezed gently. "So what happened?"

He sorted through the vague memories of those few weeks. "What do you think? Same as you basically, though my choice was twenty-four hour guard in my room or confinement in one of the cells in the Hub."

"But why?"

"Turns out none of us had been allowed to finish our change. In an effort to maintain control of us, we were never allowed to develop our telepathy or, in the case of those of us who were Seers or Casters, our talents.

"When I changed...I was a lot like you. Uncontrollable, irrational. I caused problems, and they didn't want to see a repeat of that, especially not with my talents thrown in. They were also worried about my getting hurt if they couldn't control my environment. Well, being placed into one of the cells was a death sentence as far as I was concerned, and they knew how I felt, though that wouldn't have stopped them from doing it if they decided it was necessary. I didn't like it, but I had to put up with someone watching my movements at all times. Unfortunately they didn't feel in control of me if I was in the air, and I must admit they were probably right. So they grounded me."

"Why are they doing this? Why did they have all of you in the Facility like that? Acting like guinea pigs. Using some of you as trained circus animals, or as the media called Kieran, "the face of the Valkyries." There's something I do seem to remember about my time in the Hub...none of you knew about Aurora. But the Facility does."

"Are you sure? How do you know the Facility knows about what the wild Valkyries have managed out here?" A sudden sharp pain pierced his head, and he pressed his fingers to his temple. He quit trying to trace down the memory that teased him because of it.

"Ian knew. He made it quite clear to me in the Hub. He knew my parents."

"Ian? No. He couldn't have..." He hissed when the pain grew. Jess squeezed his hand and he took a deep breath. "I guess that's something I'll have to ask him."

She cast him a funny look but then continued. "They have to know that everything they were doing to you guys wasn't necessary, because all of Aurora isn't on those drugs. Or what about what they were doing to me? Plenty of people have changed here without all of the interference they forced on me. So why?"

"And who?" Nick asked. "That's something that has been running through my head since I woke up. I don't know much about Gabriel because I was sheltered from him. We can ask the rest of the clan. But my intuition says that while he's a player, he's not the team."

"I'd ask Marcus, but I wouldn't trust anything he said." She shrugged nonchalantly.

He sighed in agreement. "I still can't wrap my head around them being here. If what you are saying is true...then Ian knew they were alive the whole time?"

They reached a branch in the path and followed a side trail that led them alongside the deep pool that the waterfall crashed into. The mist created by the torrent of water coated the rocks of the cliff wall in a sheet of ice. The noise almost drowned out his thoughts of the past. He paused at an overlook to admire the falls.

"I wish I knew why they all feel justified in their choices," Jess said. "They certainly don't seem to care about the collateral damage they cause to the people dependent on them."

This time he squeezed her hand then turned back to follow the trail to the bridge. They walked in silence for a moment before she returned to the previous topic. "That had to be hard when they confined you, losing the one outlet you had to run from the memories."

"It was the hardest thing since my original confinement. In some ways, it makes this injury seem easy. Probably because here I can at least get away on my own, and the reason I can't fly is rather obvious."

They crossed a wooden bridge then walked slowly, still holding hands, and admired the winter landscape that surrounded them. "True. But you're moving better now than you were a couple of days ago."

"I'm still too slow and my shoulder aches, but it's healing." He gave her hand a gentle tug, and they turned down a side path that led to a couple of low buildings. The sound of livestock permeated the air as they entered the dim barn.

Several stalls lined the interior of the building, and they approached the first one on their right. The soft nose of a little goat pressed into his hand when they stopped by the fence, and it braced its tiny front hooves on it. Three other goats gamboled and jumped around behind it, chasing and running into each other. Nick and Jess both laughed as they watched the antics. The playful innocence eased more of Nickolas's tension.

He turned his focus back onto the Alpha next to him. The determination and brittle fear he remembered from the start of her isolation was gone. Now her eyes were alight with amusement as she watched the animals play.

"So what about you? How're you doing now that you've finished the change?" Following after her as she moved down the barn to look in other stalls, he waited for her answer.

"Fine. I don't feel so out of control anymore. I feel like I've passed out of the worst case of PMS I've ever had. Having no control over my life really sucked."

"Yeah, I'll second that," Nick said with a grin.

She chuckled. "I suppose you would. I was always so irritated. My emotions were completely out of control. It's nice to be back to a more even keel." She reached over a wall and scratched the neck of a cow who was patiently chewing her cud. "It's taken a little time to get used to hearing and seeing differently. I like my quickened reflexes and feeling my muscles move when I'm sparring." She grinned to herself. "I enjoy fighting your brother."

That surprised a laugh out of him. "I think you're probably the only one besides me who thinks so."

"So I've seen. The complaining was amusing." Her smile started to fade as she continued to scratch the cow.

He pressed closer to her back and reached over her shoulder to scratch the cow as well. The heat of her body soaked into his chest, and he rested his chin on her shoulder. "So that's the good side. Now, what's bothering you? I can feel it sometimes through the bond."

She sighed and leaned into him. He brushed his cheek against hers. He wasn't sure she was going to answer, but then she took a deep breath.

"A couple of things. The first is the connections to Chris, Donald, and Kieran. I wasn't awake when that happened."

He brushed his lips across the juncture of her shoulder and neck and felt a shiver run through her. "And that bothers you?"

"Yes. No. I don't know." She tipped her head to the side to allow him better access.

His tongue didn't need a second invitation. He tasted her skin. "What bothers you about it? That you don't remember? Or that you didn't have a say? Would you choose to bond with them now?"

Her hand stole up to run through his hair. "Yes to all three. I guess I just wish that I remember it happening."

His teeth scraped across her skin and she gasped, then he followed with a slow swipe of his tongue. "From what they've said, they did it to save both our lives."

She sighed. "I know. It's just taking some time to get used to. They aren't any more experienced in using this connection than I am, but they sure seem like they are with the way they can use it against me."

He chuckled. "Then stop pushing it away. Embrace it and learn how to use it back."

She yanked his hair then let go so she could turn in his arms. He pressed her back against the wood of the stall. His hand lifted and his fingers traced her cheek. "So, what was the second thing?"

The soft brown of her eyes met his gaze, and her tongue flicked across her bottom lip. "I don't want to be in Aurora. I never wanted it. That's why I ran. Part of me is glad to see Robin, but there's another part of me.... He never came back, Nick."

He closed his eyes and dropped his forehead to hers. "I understand how that feels."

She ran her hands along his back, underneath his wings. "I guess you would."

They stood quietly for a few minutes. The neigh of a horse or the baa of a sheep the only sound to break the stillness.

Then he continued. "They aren't real. My parents wouldn't have left me. Not like that. Then I see or hear them and the pain hits me. I can't help but think how our lives could have been different. Not growing up in the Facility."

She tugged his head back and looked into his eyes. Together they bridged the distance, their lips touching. Both offering comfort. His tongue swept out along the seam until she opened and invited him in. He savored the sweet taste of her breath as they twined together. Her hands clutched his shoulders, and he only winced slightly. He let his hands skim down her sides and around back to pull her to him. They both gasped.

She broke the kiss, breathing heavily, and looked down the barn aisle then back into his eyes. She tipped her head. "You know...there's a hay loft here."

He studied what he could see in her eyes. "Are you sure?"

A smile teased the corner of her lips, then she turned in his embrace and grabbed his hand to drag him to the ladder. Laughing as he followed her up, he thought this might be one of the better days in his life.

◆ ◆ ◆

A few days later, Kieran raised a water bottle to his lips while he took a rest and watched Jessica spar with Chris across the grounds. *I don't think Chris is holding back at all now. Ow.* He winced when she landed a particularly good hit on the Flight leader.

He smiled into his bottle. *Moving out of sick bay was good for all of them.* It had taken some convincing to get Beth to agree to the move. She wanted to keep both of the Breeders under observation. And for all the improvement Nick had made, he was still in more pain than he let on, and his healing was far from over. It took the Facility Flight leaders insisting en masse before Beth would give in. The move buoyed Nick's spirits, which translated into stronger healing. Consequently, Beth was calmer now. So Nick, Jessica, and David all moved into housing in the neighborhood with the rest of the Facility Valkyries. Which meant that he was also able to stay full-time in the cabin he shared with Donald finally. With Jays being the only Facility Valkyrie left in sick bay, it was easy enough for Kieran to check on him every morning.

"Kieran, back up. You've had enough rest. Dylan, you too."

He sighed at Donald but capped his water bottle and stood. He stretched as he entered the ring with Dylan and waited for Donald to call the time.

He stepped to the side as soon as the match started and slipped past Dylan, giving him a leisurely kick to the midsection followed up by two more kicks as the other Hunter turned to defend himself. Blocking with his forearm, he bounced back and spun, just missing Dylan's head with his heel.

As they traded blows, Kieran felt a shiver run across his senses that distracted him and allowed Dylan to land a kick to his stomach. Gasping, he dodged and went on the defensive while trying to trace the source of his uneasiness.

Still backing, he blocked and turned, lifting his head to scent the psychic winds. His attention no longer on the match, he missed Donald's annoyance with his inattentiveness.

He dodged a few more blows instead of engaging. "Stop, wait."

They didn't hear him; instead Donald tried to bring him back to task. "Kieran, pay attention. The time isn't over."

He shook his head at Donald and still scanned, trying to trace the source. It was fleeting. Like the slight tremor one would feel before an earthquake. Absentmindedly, he blocked another blow from Dylan, then tuning back into the fight, he realized that Donald had joined the ring, apparently tired of Kieran's lack of attention.

The two attacked at once. Doing a back flip, Kieran leapt out of the way. He grabbed Dylan's foot when he kicked and twisted, sending the Hunter to the ground, then he caught Donald's fist in his hand an inch or so from his face. Staring into his cousin's eyes, he repeated himself. "Stop. Something isn't right. Look." And he pointed over to Jessica.

Her face pale, Jessica slowly spun, searching like a bloodhound who was casting around for a scent. Beside her, Chris had his wings flared and looked like he would attack anyone who came near her.

"Shit. Sorry, I didn't realize. I'm still not used to these power things."

"None of us are." Fear started to work its way through him, and he called over to her. "Jessica? I can't locate him."

"I'm working on it. I can't...wait. He's.... No, Nickolas!"

She spread her wings, but Christoff grabbed her around the waist at the same moment he yelled across the distance to stay.

A psychic wave of darkness rolled toward them like a tsunami. He barely had time to shield himself before the emotional storm reached them. Jessica collapsed to the ground and Christoff went to his knees with her. Fortunately, no one else seemed affected by the storm. Only empaths, or those who had bound themselves to Nick, were having difficulties.

"Go, Donald," Kieran snapped when his cousin tried to help him. He shook his head to clear it, glad he'd gotten his shield up in time, then jogged in Donald and Dylan's wake as they raced over to Chris and Jessica.

"Chris, are you ok? What's happening?"

"Donald, Jessica's unconscious," Dylan said.

"Something's happened to Nick," Chris groaned.

"The wall crashed down, Chris." Still scanning for their Alpha, Kieran called Marcus. *Marcus, this is Kieran. Do you know where Nickolas is?*

No. I've been trying to locate him. What's happened? Beth just collapsed.

She has empathy. The wall around Nick just came down; we need to find him now! Turning to the north, he felt an echo. *The barn, Marcus. He's in the barn. Get Robin and meet us there.* His gaze fell on Chris's pale face. "Are you up for this?"

"Where is he?" The Alpha Hunter slowly rose to his feet.

"He's in the barn. I've told Marcus and Robin to meet us there."

Chris shook out his wings and took a deep breath. "Dylan, get Jessica to the infirmary." Then he turned and launched into the sky, Donald on his heels.

Kieran followed the two into the air. The closer he flew to the barn, the more his shields eroded. They landed beside Marcus and Robin, both of whom looked grim. The roaring showed why. They couldn't enter the barn. The emotional storm that had knocked Jessica unconscious wasn't the only response Nickolas was having. A very physical storm was taking place inside the structure.

"I didn't know he was a telekinetic. I was under the impression that his abilities were in the Seer half of the code," Marcus said.

"He did make that shield against Gabriel," Robin pointed out.

"I told Beth he'd almost gotten a strap off when he first awoke," Kieran said absentmindedly. Debris, tools, anything not nailed down, and some things that had been, were whirling through the building. Boards creaked as nails started loosening and pulling free. The bedding from the stalls made a haze in the air that the five Valkyries couldn't see through. An irreverent thought crossed Kieran's mind. *Now all we need is the wicked witch and we'll be on our way to Oz.*

He pulled his mind back when Chris asked, "Can anyone see him?" Then he called out. "Nickolas? Nickolas where are you?"

No verbal response. But Kieran was sure the debris picked up.

"I can't see more than a couple of feet in. There's no way we'll be able to get through all of that." Donald sounded stunned.

"I can get us through," Marcus said and looked at Kieran questioningly. "But will you be able to do anything for him?"

"I don't know. But I have to try."

At Marcus's direction, they moved closer together so the Auroran Alpha could create a physical shield around them. Then as a unit, they started through the debris storm.

Kieran winced away from the objects that hit the shield, but he kept searching through the shadows for Nick. He could feel a knot of emotion ahead and to their right, so he had Marcus direct their shield that way.

They stumbled to a halt about ten feet away and stared at the shimmering bubble that surrounded Nickolas. Nickolas himself crouched, kneeling on one knee, his head bowed in grief, his wings a dark mantle arched around him, his arms wrapped tight about his middle.

Kieran had a brief thought that they were the only thing holding him together at all, that without their support, he would break into a million pieces right there in the middle of the barn aisleway. He reached out with his empathy and tried to make contact with Nickolas, but he was too locked away. "I can't reach him. I need physical contact to break through his inner barriers."

"I told you to bind to him, Kieran. Then you'd have the conduit you need now," Chris snapped.

He turned a glare on Chris and yelled over the noise. "We've been over that. The risk was too high that he would have sensed what I'd done to block his memories and talent."

"And I told you I thought it was worth the risk."

"Enough. Your bond, Chris? Can you reach through to him now?" Marcus looked intent, waiting for his son's answer.

"Yes, I can feel him, but I can't do anything. He won't or can't hear me."

"Good enough. I think it's enough of a chink in the armor that I can use you to breach through his shield. It won't be pleasant." Marcus stepped up next to his son and held his face in his hands and stared into his eyes. Kieran saw Christoff stiffen.

He could feel the currents floating around them within the bubble, so he was able to see where Marcus sent a thread of energy that connected their shield with Nickolas's. A large object hit the side of the bubble and he jumped. When he looked back, the line had expanded into a tube, then the tube grew and grew until it was just large enough for a person to squeeze through.

As soon as Marcus called out in a strained voice to go, Kieran darted through and paid no attention to the others behind him. Nickolas's shield encompassed enough floor space to allow all of them room.

He crouched down in front of his leader and placed his hands on Nickolas's bowed head.

At first everything was dark. Then lightning forked across the sky, and Kieran was able to make out a silhouette. He left the shelter of the cliff face and walked forward into a heavy wind that buffeted him, threatening to pitch him over the edge of the cliff he was approaching. He stopped a couple of feet away from where Nickolas stood at the edge, his arms wrapped tight about himself. Kieran looked at the raging sea far below him. He also noticed that the ground in front of Nickolas was slowly eroding away. The power unleashed by the collapse of the block ran out of control, amplifying reactions that would have been bad on their own. Soon the bank would give way and Nick would fall with the dirt that rained down into that dark, cold place.

Instinctively Kieran knew that if that happened, Nickolas would die. The power that raged would tear apart his mind. There was no way Kieran would be strong enough to pull him out of that deep, vicious water. More lightning shot across the sky, leaving the dreamscape eerily lit with an amorphous green glow.

"How did I not know this?" He heard Nickolas whispering to himself.

"You needed to heal your body, Nick."

His Alpha stared blindly out, immersed in himself. "I don't understand.... How could I not remember? I saw him die." His wings flexed open then shut. He shifted his foot and the ground crumbled away from his toe. "I could have gotten you out..."

The dirt rained away and Kieran yelled, "Nickolas!"

He grabbed Nick's arm to haul him away from the edge, but as soon as they touched, they both screamed and yanked apart. Thankfully, Nick fell back with the movement.

The Breeder turned his gaze on Kieran, seeing him for the first time. Power raged, twined with grief so magnified it was almost insanity. Uncontrolled, it was like lightning in a box, burning everything in its path.

"What happened? Did you do this? How could I have forgotten everything?" His voice broke and the waves crashed below them as a counterpoint. His gaze jerked away to sweep their surroundings. "Where are we?"

Kieran took a step closer. "In your mind. Your doctors, when they triaged your injuries, felt that delaying the emotional trauma would benefit your healing."

"My mind? Doctors?" His gaze snapped back to Kieran's. "My mother," he said after a pause.

"Yes." Kieran took another step.

"You did this."

"I didn't want to. But you were in so much pain. Beth would have had me take the block out soon, you were healing so well."

Nickolas groaned and pressed his fists to his temples. The flooding tide of power crashed as it cascaded through him from the broken dam.

"Let me help you, Nick."

"No!" He spread his wings and backed up. "I don't want to forget again, Kieran."

"Your power is out of control. You are too strong; no one can contain you. Remember, you and Jessica are the only hope for us. We had to give you the best chance. We had to protect you."

Nick shook his head.

"Nick, please. You have no idea the damage your talents are doing in the physical world right now."

"Jessica?" he whispered.

"I don't know. She passed out. They took her to the infirmary. Let me help."

Nick furled his wings, a strange calmness spreading across his features. Kieran threw a nervous glance over his shoulder and saw the violence of the waves stilled and captured in glittering, razor sharp ice that continued to spread, freezing the ocean and then creeping up the cliff walls.

"Nickolas, what are you doing?" he whispered.

"I don't want to hurt anyone. And I won't forget."

The ice drew closer and Kieran shivered from the frigid air preceding it. This wasn't good. He turned back, speaking fast. "You still need medical care. Your body isn't fully healed. Don't do this. You don't have to face this alone, let us help you."

The ice crawled across the rocky ground. Kieran skipped back farther, trying to stay out of its reach as stones shattered. It reached Nick's feet and the Breeder groaned.

"Please, Nick. Don't shut us out."

His Alpha turned his frozen gaze on him, the ice twining up his body like a poisonous vine.

"A blood bond? Will you consent to a blood bond at least?" He asked Nick and stepped farther back as the ice consumed more ground.

Nick's gaze remained unblinking. "You. No one else."

More stone shattered, forcing Kieran away. He took a last look at his Alpha then pulled his mind out of Nick's.

The fierce howling as the psychic storm roared around them assaulted Kieran's outer ears. He took his hands away from Nickolas and looked up at Chris. "Give me your knife."

The surprise in the Hunter's eyes didn't slow him down any. He handed the blade over, and Kieran nicked the underside of his wrist then grabbed a fistful of Nickolas's dark hair and pulled his head back up enough that he was able to force the bleeding cut to his Alpha's mouth.

Slowly, he felt Nick's body start to cooperate as the rich blood flowed into his mouth. Kieran pulled his arm away after a minute and was surprised when Robin was there and ready to wrap up the wound.

Barely pausing long enough for the Hunter to tie it off, Kieran pried one of Nickolas's arms away from its death grip. This time Chris used the knife to cut his brother so Kieran could maintain his hold on the arm. Bracing himself, he raised the welling cut to his lips. The bolt was pure electricity.

He drank until he was sure the connection to Nickolas was as strong as possible then reluctantly pulled away. He tried to clear his vision while Christoff bound up Nickolas's wrist.

The last of the psychic storm dissipated as objects clattered to the floor. The shield surrounding them shimmered then disappeared. Holding his breath, Kieran waited on his knees, watching Nick.

A remnant of the chill psychic wind from the dreamscape circled him, then Nickolas lifted his head.

Kieran felt everyone around him become immobile as Nick swept those assembled with a look. Their shock at what they saw in Nick's eyes pounded into him.

Nick forced his body to unfold, and without a word, fled the barn.

Voices moaning and animals crying woke them all out of their stupor.

"What the hell happened?" Donald finally whispered.

Marcus shook his head. Chris's wings shivered, and he snapped them closed and asked, "Do we go after him?"

"No," Marcus said roughly. "Not yet. Whatever he's done...we have to help whoever's here first. I hear voices."

Kieran rose unsteadily to his feet. Christoff supported him for a moment as he got his balance. "He wouldn't accept help. As soon as he realized he was hurting people, he did the only thing he could on his own. He froze his talents, froze his emotions."

"Can we help him?" Marcus asked.

"I need to talk to Beth, but I think we're back to waiting. He won't be able to keep it locked up forever. Hopefully as it thaws, it will dribble out in a manageable way."

"Well, we're depending on your and Chris's blood bond with him for the time being," Marcus said as he turned to search the barn. The other's joined in.

A few minutes later, Robin called out from the other end. "Over here."

They converged and found two bleeding but alive Hunters. They had stuffed themselves in behind some grain barrels, trying to save themselves from the worst of the airborne objects. Robin and Chris helped them out of their cranny. They looked a bloody mess, bruised and covered in punctures from the whirling straw.

"Let's get you two over to sick bay. Did either of you see anything before the storm started?" Marcus asked.

They both nodded their heads painfully, and one of them tried to talk. But it came out in a rasp from all the dust damage to his throat. "We didn't know he was in here. We were talking about Ian. I think...we mentioned his death when all hell broke loose. We heard a scream, then this wind started to kick up; we looked up the aisle and saw the glow of the shield start. We tried to throw all the doors open so the animals could escape, but as we were trying to get to these last stalls, it became impossible to move anymore. We took cover."

Kieran glanced over the stall wall and swallowed hard then looked away. The two Hunters were lucky they had found what cover they had.

He followed in the other's wake as they helped the two Hunters out of the barn. Kieran looked out across the snow-covered ground, finding more warmth in it than he had when looking into Nickolas's eyes.

Chapter Ten

The next afternoon, Christoff walked with Kieran into the common room of the longhouse. He cast a quick glance at the gathered Valkyries assembled for lunch. No sign of Nick.

Not that it was a big surprise. Both he and Kieran had a general idea of their Alpha's whereabouts through their blood bond—along with his patent desire to be left alone. With a sigh over Nick's stubbornness, Chris and the empath slipped along the wall to stand uncertain and staring at the different doors in front of them. He was familiar with the last one on the left since it was Marcus's office, but they'd been told to come to the conference room.

About to randomly pick one of the other four doors, they stopped as a Hunter—Chris thought his name was Michael—casually pointed to the third room as he walked by, telling them that one was the conference room they usually used.

They thanked him and opened the door. Inside, a large table laden with a buffet lunch filled the center of the room. Marcus, Robin, Kevin, and Nathan paused in their conversation, their plates already full, to watch them enter.

His father waved his hand, indicating that they should help themselves. Accepting a plate from Kieran, the two of them made selections from the dishes on the table as the conversation resumed around them.

"The loss of the sow and her piglets was the hardest hit. There were also a few sheep that didn't survive, but the majority of our livestock made it out of the barn and were easily rounded up." Robin took a quick bite, then continued, "We're going to need to replace the sow; our supply of pork will be lean for the next year until we raise a replacement or decide to bring one in from the outworld. On the good side, none of it will go to waste. Lynx Sept slaughtered all of the casualties yesterday, so our freezers are extra full at the moment."

Chris sat down and looked up the table at his father, who was nodding his head in understanding at Robin's report. "I'll make sure Matt knows. What about the two Hunters, how are they doing?"

In the middle of taking a drink, Kevin swallowed before he fielded that question. "They're unhappy that their conversation hurt Nick and caused the storm yesterday. They inhaled dust from the air. It was bad enough that Beth had them on oxygen for a while; they were able to get their wings tucked in tight, so the damage to the membrane was minimized, but they still won't be flying for a bit. They received quite a few pinholes through the sail. The rest seemed to be superficial cuts and abrasions from the flying debris."

Chris cut into his lasagna with a fork and listened to the summary of the damage Nickolas's breakdown had caused. Like feeling out a sore tooth, he reached down his link to Nickolas until it turned too cold to continue. His brother was nearby, and alive, but that was all he had been able to read all night.

After talking to Beth, he had been convinced that leaving Nick to his own devices for a time was best. Nick would eventually seek them out. Convincing Jessica had taken them all night though.

"Any word on him?" His father asked suddenly.

Chris set his fork down and ran his hand through his hair, throwing a glance at Kieran. "No. He's avoiding everyone, including Jessica."

Robin reached for the pitcher of water and refilled his glass. "I've seen him. Early this morning, I went into the weight room, and he was there. It looked like he had been there all night working out, maybe sleeping."

The Hunter Prime shrugged his shoulders, but the nonchalance of the movement didn't hide his worry. "Not very many people go in there at the moment with the festival going on. That's probably why he chose it. I worked out for a while and observed him. He's still not recovered enough for what he was doing, I think, but he was being careful. I did let him know about the meeting, Marcus. He didn't respond."

Marcus sighed and dished up a second helping of the lasagna. "If he needs time to process and come to terms with the memories he's regained, we shouldn't interfere with it. It won't help to push him into feeling too soon. Getting him involved in everyday affairs may be good, but we need to keep a careful eye on him."

Conversation paused when they heard a commotion outside in the hallway. Marcus half rose from his chair, looking perplexed. Christoff groaned and waved his father back down, then glared at Kieran who had the audacity to chuckle.

"Told you, Chris," he spoke softly.

Before he could explain to the others at the table, the door opened and an annoyed Jessica walked in. Tossing her hair, she glared at him.

"Thank you for inviting me to the meeting, Chris. I hope I haven't kept everyone waiting."

"Jess, you have enough to deal with right now. You just finished your change, and you're still learning to be a Valkyrie, with flying and fighting practice, and dealing with Nickolas. I didn't think you needed any more stress added right now," he placated.

Pacing around the perimeter of the room, she raked everyone with a glance. "Did anyone tell Nickolas about the meeting?" No one spoke, but Chris could tell that Jessica was able to read her brother quite clearly. "I thought so."

She rounded on Chris again and continued. "It's fine to include him, but not me? I'm healthy and whole, while he is several steps removed from that classification."

Her smile turned sweet, and Chris started to sweat. She walked forward, her steps a threat and a promise. She had settled into her power and was obviously ready to take her position in the hierarchy. She placed her hands on the end of the table, leaning toward him and pinning his gaze. Her softened voice did nothing to hide the threat. "You will not exclude me, Christoff. I won't allow it. None of you would let me go when I demanded it. Now you're stuck with me. If I need to make my position clear to you, meet me in the ring, Beta."

Her gaze never wavered, and he held it for as long as he could, but having worked with her in the ring, he understood the difference she meant. She wouldn't be sparring with him as an equal but fighting him, using everything she was, and the reprimand he received during it would not be pleasant. He was the first to look away.

He stared at the tabletop. "My mistake. I won't make it again, Alpha. I'm sorry."

After a brief pause, she pushed away from the table. He let his breath out in a sigh of relief and glanced up at the startled faces of the other males at the table. The wary calculation in their eyes showed the beginnings of understanding. An understanding he'd had about Jessica since the first time he had to chase her through the woods.

Like Nickolas, she was not someone to cross. He dropped his eyes from the others then snarled softly at Kieran when the empath snickered at his predicament. He silently made it clear that he'd deal with him later, *the annoying Beta*.

Kieran lost his amused look as he recognized the threat from someone higher up in the hierarchy. To break the tension, Marcus offered Jessica a plate and helped her dish up some lunch. She took a chair across from him. Chris looked up briefly then grimaced at the smile Marcus aimed at her.

The other Alpha looked like he was about to throw a right curve at the batter. "So, Jessica, how are you doing? Are you settling in ok?"

She cast a glance at Chris's father then cut a piece of garlic bread to add to her plate. "Physically I feel fine. Much better than I have in months. I'm still uncertain about my talent though."

"You're a light weaver, aren't you?"

A scowl settled on her face, and she glanced at Marcus. "Yes. I don't know what else though."

The lazy smile that Marcus wore seemed to discomfit her, and a flash of childish pleasure shot through Chris. He knew her reprimand was justified. He couldn't help the desire to protect her any more than she could stop the need to know what was going on. But it did help the sting a bit to watch her dance the dominance and hierarchy with a more experienced Alpha. One who was strong enough to not let her get away with more than she should. He stared into his food and tried to suppress his smile.

His father continued, "I'm the ranking light weaver, and it will be my pleasure to take you through the basics."

Chris's grin broke through when she sent a scathing glance his way, letting him know that she saw his joy in her situation.

Robin's snort drew her glare next.

"But I suppose lessons like that will need to wait for a bit, until we have things more settled." Laughter laced his words. He let the subject drop and allowed her to get her feet underneath again before he asked, "And Nick? How's he doing?"

The question jarred her, but she recovered quickly. "I don't know. He's blocked off all of his emotions."

Chris glanced at Kieran. The empath nodded. He'd felt the surge down the link from Jessica too. She was more distressed than she let on. *No wonder she came in ready to pick a fight with me,* he sent in a narrow band to Kieran.

You were right about not telling her; she hasn't been awake long enough yet to know what she wants or how to handle everything she is. Though she's enough like Nick, we probably should have guessed.

True.

Ice water washed through him, and Kieran's eyes widened next to him. They both glanced at Jessica who had set her fork down and stared at the door.

"Well speak of the devil," she said.

The door opened and a shadow-filled Nickolas slid into the room.

His brother didn't utter a word, just pulled a chair in the corner and straddled it, his arms resting on the back as he watched them all with a detached air.

Chris pulled his wings in tight. The unexpected feeling of being prey instead of predator didn't sit well, and he wished

Ian were here to help settle Nick. *But then we wouldn't have this problem in the first place.* He sighed.

He met Marcus's gaze, and the memory of the killing storm in the barn looked back at him.

Marcus cleared his throat. Careful not to startle Nick with any aggressive movements, he held out his hand. "There's food?"

A curt headshake made it clear that Nick didn't want anything.

Marcus scanned the occupants of the room then got started. "Now that everyone is here, let's get down to business. For our newest residents, this is a regular meeting I hold with the caste Primes. I asked all of you to join us," he slid a smile at Jess, "to see how we work and get an idea of how best you can contribute. We'll start with the caste reports. Kevin, you go first."

Kevin pushed his plate aside and folded his arms on the table. "Nathan, your dreamers have made my imbuers extremely nervous with their vague warnings. I've had to carry a couple to the infirmary for Beth to treat for psychic burnout. They've been wearing themselves out working to keep on top of renewing our current charms and to stockpile new ones as fast as they can."

"I can't help that they aren't able to fine-tune their Sight," Nathan drawled. "It's only the dreamers who have received any inkling of Gabriel. The scryers and distance Seers haven't found anything of note. The forest is calm."

"Robin?" Marcus asked.

"Same for the Hunters. We increased the patrols, just in case, but other than bringing in extra game for the new mouths to feed, they haven't found any Facility activity beyond what was documented when Nickolas was found."

"We've had to sit on the imbuers to make sure they are resting enough," Kevin continued. "The talents that are able to mesh with the imbuers aren't as exhausted; they've fared better because there are more of them to go around. But even they are wearing thin."

Chris intercepted a sideways glance from the Auroran Caster and huffed out a breath, figuring he had a good idea where this was now headed.

Marcus turned his gaze on him. "What sort of numbers do you have clean now, Chris, and are any of them Casters or Seers?"

He met Kieran's gaze and did a quick tally in his head before he answered. "We have eighteen out of our original fifty-five clean. Every week, give or take a day or so, we pull another five off. Kieran?"

"Nick, Jess, Dev, Aiden, and I are the only ones in a higher caste so far. But three more are coming off who seem like they might be more than Hunters. They should be done in a day or two, but other than my empathy and Jess's light weaving, we have no idea what any of them can do."

"Once the new three are done," Robin said, "let me know, and we'll bring all of you up to the workroom in the control tower. We have someone whose talent is to judge what someone else's talent is and determine their strength. We call them a Grader. She can test everyone and see what we've got to work with."

Jessica shifted in her seat and drew his attention. She studied her brother, then looked across the room at her mate with faint challenge in her eyes. Nickolas just gazed back at her impassively. Chris could feel the tension between the two Breeders through his bonds with them. Nick's struggle to keep Jessica at arm's length and Jessica's formidable will bent on thwarting it. Something about the possibility of learning about their abilities had caught the two's attention.

The conversation continued on around the silent byplay of the two mates.

"Grading is definitely the first step, Kieran," Marcus said. "After everyone is graded, then it's a lot easier to determine what sort of training they need and who is the best suited for it."

The older Alpha smiled at Jessica and cut a slice of pie, offering it to her, his subtle dominance not lost on her. Chris couldn't help the amused look he shared with Kieran over Marcus's silent reminder about who would be teaching her later. Jess growled but slid her plate down anyway, accepting the sweet.

"Anything else with the Seers, Nathan?"

"No. Nothing more than what I said already. Just disturbing dreams. If anyone gets a more concrete warning about the Facility, I'll let you know. I've continued to have the Seers on duty in the tower cover a larger territory more often, but there's still no sign of Gabriel or the Facility after the close brush with Nickolas."

"I've stationed extra bodies in the tower to help with the increased telepathic traffic," Robin added. "Though, just as Nathan has said, the increase in scout groups haven't reported anything different in the forest either."

"That's good to hear. But I still think we should be wary. With the control group gone from the Facility, I just don't believe they will give up this quickly." Marcus cut a second slice of pie for himself and pushed the tin back into the center of the table. "Who's on duty in the tower right now?"

"It's my watch; I have my Second there now." Robin snagged the pie tin. "Kevin's on watch next. Kev, are you going to be there, or is your Second taking this shift?"

"I'm taking this one. I need to make sure the imbuers actually stop for the day."

"Then I'll see you at the shift change. I want to go over a few of the Casters who've been working with the scouts. I think we may need to make a substitution or two."

"No problem."

"Oh, Marcus, Beth wanted me to remind you that you're scheduled to judge the snow creations this afternoon..."

Talk turned to discussion of the festivities, and Chris watched the interplay between Robin and his father as he stacked his own dishes, then he looked around. The tension between Nickolas and Jessica was thick; he shared a look with Kieran. The empath just shook his head. *There's nothing we can do, Chris.*

Are you sure?

He needs time. The grief is too raw, and his injuries still complicate the situation.

Yeah, normally he'd try to outfly his demons.

Yes. His coping mechanisms aren't available. Let Jessica have the first crack at him. He's not going anywhere, and as long as he isn't destructive, he should have the respect of time to come to terms with everything.

Nickolas watched them all with a frozen stare, and Chris shivered.

"Well, if no one has anything else to add, I think that's all for this meeting." Marcus looked around. "In that case, we'll set the next meeting for the same time next week."

Jessica pushed her chair back and rose without a word, her gaze glued to Nickolas. Nick remained silent and walked away from her without an acknowledgement. Slamming the chair Nick had been sitting in, Jessica swore low and stalked after him, determination in her step.

Marcus finally broke the silence from the rest of the room. "Kieran?"

Kieran studied the Aurorans for a moment. "Like I told Chris, he needs time. Let Jessica handle him for now. Beth doesn't think we need to worry about another spell like the one in the barn unless something incredibly bad happens. Something on the scale of Ian's death."

"Everyday stress won't bring it on?" Marcus's face was carefully neutral as he asked the question.

Kieran shook his head and leaned forward. "No, not now that he's recovered his memories. Now he's just trying to assimilate them and come to terms with the pain and guilt. It doesn't mean that I don't think he's not dangerous. I think the state he's in now is the most dangerous I've ever known him to be in. To cope, he's closed off all feeling. He wouldn't have any difficulty taking someone out in the ring for instance, but I don't think his power will go rogue again like it did yesterday. Not with the iron grip he has on it."

His father closed his eyes then nodded.

Everyone stood, pushing chairs in and picking up the rest of the dishes to take back to the kitchen. Chris watched his father leave as he picked up a stack of plates and followed Kieran out the door.

◆ ◆ ◆

Flight

White clouds from his breath floated away, and Kieran watched them rise up into the clear blue sky. He stood on the edge of the practice field in the cold sunlight and tuned back into the conversation he was having with Christoff and Donald.

"So how long should we let him do this?" His cousin stared out across the grounds to the circle scratched in the frozen mud where Nickolas moved slowly through some complicated warm-up exercises.

Let him? How can you be so delusional, Donald? "I don't think it's so much a matter of letting him. We aren't in the Hub anymore, Donald. We don't have Ian's authority to fall back on to force his compliance."

Next to him, Chris resonated. The steel that ran through Nick's brother caught him off guard.

"While that may be true, Kieran, I think that Nicky will find that if he pits himself against enough of us, even he won't come out on top." Their Alpha Hunter drew his wings in tight and folded his arms across his chest. "We'll let him do a few more moves before I order him off the field. He's pushing himself, but I only see minor muscle fatigue starting to hit."

Nickolas did a slow crouch and spin, coming up with a backhand followed by an elbow to an imaginary opponent. His footwork was only slightly shaky, but Kieran could see the sweat bead down his cheek. Chris was right. He was pushing, but he hadn't gone past his limit yet. Kieran shifted his attention over a couple of circles to Jessica, and he winced, glad that he wasn't the one to have the misfortune of being in the ring with her today. Nodding his head, he drew the others' attention to her.

Chris smiled slightly. "And that's the advantage I have to being the one to assign the drills. There was no way I was going in the ring with her today unless I had to. She can take her frustration out on someone else."

Glad that he hadn't done anything in the last day or so to piss off Christoff, he watched Jessica decimate her latest opponent. From the looks of it, this was her third; the other two unlucky sacrifices were sitting slumped, exhausted, on the nearest bench. This one looked close to joining them, while Jess was barely sweating. The single-minded savagery she had on her face as she attacked made Kieran cringe.

He shook his head and looked back at Christoff. "Maybe today's the day I should take everyone up to the control tower to be tested. The last three finished coming off the drug yesterday, and the new group will be all Hunters, I think. So there's no reason to wait any longer."

Christoff stared out across the field, his gaze shifting over the different circles before answering. "Yes. I think that's a good idea, Kieran. Getting them both out of here is probably good."

He folded his own arms and took a breath then let it out in a quick relaxation. *Robin?*

Yes?

This is Kieran. If now is an acceptable time, we're ready to have our people tested.

There was a brief pause that felt like he had been placed on hold, then Robin replied, *Now's fine. Are you out at the practice grounds?*

Yes.

Good. I'll head over there and meet you. Then I'll take you all up to the control tower.

Kieran switched his focus and cast out over the moving hoard of Valkyries before him. *Dev, Sam, Miguel, Jenny, Aiden, stop your bouts and report to me.* Four heads snapped up, then they started to make their way over to him.

Kieran sighed as he scanned the grounds, looking for the fifth. *This is going to be so annoying. Why did he have to turn out to be a Caster?* He spotted the one he was looking for. Of course he had not stopped his fight.

Kieran aimed his thought in a narrow band directly to the recalcitrant Caster then sent just enough of his power through the sending to let the boy know he was serious. *Aiden, I said stop. Unless you want me to come out there and take over?*

Aiden's frustration and reluctance flowed to him loud and clear. Frustration because he didn't want to obey but knew he couldn't take on Kieran and hope to win, and reluctance because he was enjoying the fight and didn't really want to find out about his talent. Kieran smiled at the sullen look he received.

The others had all gathered around while Kieran watched the young Valkyrie slowly walk over. The teenager maintained eye contact as he pushed his pale hair back out of his face and secured the length behind his neck.

Kieran kept his face impassive. He was still amazed sometimes at how young Aiden was, the youngest of all the Valkyries at only sixteen; but even more to the point was the fact that he underwent the change when he was thirteen. To date, that was the youngest anyone had seen.

Even so, Kieran watched the young man carefully. He had twice the aggressiveness of the average Hunter and the skill to keep him at the top of the pack. The only fighters Aiden seemed to fear were Nick, Chris, and Donald. *And myself. Though I bet Jessica has made that list now too.*

The teen's gaze flashed upward with a hint of—was that fear?—and Robin landed. *So maybe he fears more than we had thought. He'd be wise to be cautious around Robin.* Not that he usually let wisdom get in his way. Kieran sighed. *Maybe it's a teenager thing. If we're really lucky, he'll grow out of it.*

The silent wave of laughter hit Kieran's empathy, and he glared at Chris. The Alpha Hunter found immense amusement knowing that Aiden was now Kieran's problem, since he was in charge of the Casters and Seers.

He pinned Aiden's ice blue eyes with his gaze and warned softly, "Don't push me, Aiden."

The boy's face remained blank, but Kieran felt the brief tremble that coursed through him. Relaxing slightly, he waited for Chris to bring in Jessica and Nickolas.

Jessica grabbed a water bottle and didn't even notice her half-dead opponents as she quickly made her way to join them. Her gaze swept those assembled. A smile broke as she took the towel Kieran handed to her and vigorously started to rub her ponytail to dry it in the frigged temperature before it froze.

Chris growled next to them, his wings snapping open then closed before he prowled to the edge of the ring

Nickolas was using to practice in. "I said enough, Nick. It's your first day back, and you've pushed yourself to the edge of your endurance. That's far enough."

Kieran held his breath as he watched Christoff face down his brother. Nickolas did one more move but then consented to leave the ring. He shied away from Chris's hand as he passed, then stood just outside of their gathering. He accepted the towel and bottle of water Jessica silently handed him, his gaze roving over them all.

Ignoring his brother, Christoff looked at Robin. "How long do you think this will take?"

"It'll probably take the rest of the day. I'll have lunch brought up to the tower for everyone. I think we'll be able to join you for dinner, barring any major surprises."

Nickolas snorted, and Kieran snapped his head to look at his Alpha. Nick had draped the towel around his neck and ran his fingers through the length of his dark hair as he walked away from them.

"Nickolas, where are you going?" Chris snapped.

Nick stopped then slowly turned to gaze at them, his hair falling around his shoulders. "Not where they are." His voice was quiet and made Kieran think of the shards of ice he'd seen in Nickolas's dreamscape.

A wave of heat came from Christoff, and Kieran waited for the inevitable steam to erupt as fire and ice met. "Nickolas, you need to be tested. Just like everyone else."

"No."

A flash of something in Nickolas's eyes, too quick for him to catch, had Kieran alert. Tendrils of his power wisped out to taste the currents surrounding them.

"What's wrong with being tested? You don't know everything you can do."

The barest traces of fear floated down their link at Christoff's words. Kieran suddenly understood.

Nickolas's eyes glowed ever so slightly and the wind ruffled his hair, but that was the only movement around him before he spoke. "And how are they planning to get there, Chris?"

Sudden understanding dawned on Chris's face. "Robin and I made it to the top of the cliff handcuffed together, Nick. It's easy enough to carry someone up to the top. Or a net could be used from here, so you don't have to walk all the way to the base of the cliff."

A much more definite surge of emotion was quickly cut off. Kieran knew the argument would do no good.

"No. No one touches me. No one messes with my head. No." He turned away again and walked off the field, extending his wings open and giving them a vigorous flap before closing them with a snap.

Kieran grabbed Christoff's shoulder, and Jessica gripped his forearm. "Let him go, Chris. He won't tolerate anyone touching him yet, and there's no other way to get him up there."

"The net."

Kieran gave Chris an incredulous look. "You really want to be around when Nick is tied up? With his claustrophobia?"

Chris closed his eyes, his shoulders sagging. "That telekinesis storm has me worried, Kier. What else can he do?"

"Who knows? We'll find out someday. But not today."

Chris turned back to the practice grounds and folded his arms as he brought his thoughts and emotions back under control. "In case you don't make it back for dinner tonight, tomorrow is the holiday dinner they have been planning, so we won't have practice tomorrow. You can give me the test results then."

Kieran watched Nickolas walk away and answered softly, "Yes, sir."

The stares on his back made it itch as he left everyone standing on the practice ground. Nickolas snapped his wings open. With a sigh of pleasure at feeling them stretching to their full extent, without needing to worry about the tears, he flapped them vigorously before closing them. It was good to be able to open and close his wings normally again, even if they couldn't bear him in flight yet.

He still had two days before they would allow him to start the strengthening exercises that would rebuild his flight muscles. Three weeks of inactivity had atrophied his muscles too much.

The shin-high snow crunched underfoot as Nickolas forged a trail across the meadow separating the practice grounds from the cabins they were staying in. He opened his damaged wing again and curled it around so he could look at it. The scars were almost unnoticeable, faint silvery lines in the dusky membrane.

The pain and itching had subsided days ago with the help of the healing oil he'd been given to rub into the skin. He folded his wing back and shaded his eyes as he looked out across the rest of the field, deciding that he was at least half way across.

He stretched his arms above his head, pulling to one side then to the other. The gentle pull on his sore muscles caused by the workout relieved some of his tension, as well as frustrating him in how little he could do. He rotated his shoulders and checked the mobility on his left.

The healing gunshot wound didn't pain him anymore, but the weakness from the torn muscles continued to hamper him. Time and working them would solve that problem. He passed the first cabins as he wove his way through to the center, where his and Jessica's house was.

He knocked the snow off his boots as he stomped up the steps and unlatched the door. The blast of warm air hit him as he left the cold outside, and he glanced at the pile of wood near the woodstove. Satisfied that it would be enough for an hour or two at least, he closed the door.

The living room was sparsely furnished. The refugees had little in the way of belongings; he and his brother had even less, since they hadn't gotten the opportunity to grab anything personal because of needing to run down Jess.

He crouched in front of the cast iron stove to add a couple of small logs then retreated to one of the two chairs facing the flames. He sank back into the cushions, adjusting his wing slightly, then closed his eyes for a moment to let his body relax. The darkness brought his sense of smell to the top of his awareness, the scent of smoke and evergreen from the fire, the clear cold scent of the air from outside, Jessica. She permeated the cabin. Growling, he fought the thawing of the ice around him.

Opening his eyes, he watched the flames dance through the glass door. When he thought about it, he regretted causing her sadness. But better sad than destroying her. He had heard the others talking about how long she had been unconscious from the mental blast he'd released.

He turned his hand up and looked at the scar on it, the jagged reminder of shattering the observation window in the Hub so many years ago. Jillian's forgiveness still echoed in his head. Something he couldn't bring himself to accept yet. Not for the death he'd caused that day, or his attack on her. He didn't care what she said about the drugs being responsible. He should have been able to stop. He didn't want to hurt anyone.

There were other scars of course, but this specific one never left his sight, reminding him of what had happened. The deep slice had nearly fulfilled his dream of escaping that nightmare permanently.

He remembered waking from the tranks they'd hit him with, once more strapped down, to see his hand stitched and an IV dripping blood back into his body. He'd looked up in despair to meet Ian's sad eyes. "Why? Why do you keep doing this to me?"

"Nicky, please understand. It *will* get better, trust me. When the change is over, you'll understand."

"I don't want it to be over, I want it to end." Closing his eyes, he had tried to stop the shivering, a reaction from the tranks. "Just let me go."

The soft touch of his grandfather's hand had smoothed his hair back, giving him the unnerving feeling of both craving the comfort and wanting to reject the person who he had viewed as causing him all the pain. "I can't, Nicky. I'll always be here for you," Ian had soothed.

Nickolas opened his eyes and stared back into the flames. "But you weren't, Ian. You wouldn't let me go when it was too much for me, but you took the out. You took the out."

He clenched his fist and looked at the table between the two chairs to stare at his phone. The same dual feelings of wanting comfort but hating the source poured through him. Ian's voice was there and waiting. All he had to do was call his voicemail.

Finally not able to fight it anymore, he picked up his phone, turning it on and checking the power level. Plenty, since it'd been off for weeks. He hit the button to take him to his voicemail and listened to it ring. But instead of his stored messages playing, an unfamiliar voice answered.

"Nickolas?"

He froze at the unexpected masculine voice and caught his breath.

"Nickolas Sinclair?"

He exhaled softly. "Yes. Who is this?"

"It's good to hear your voice. We had your phone forwarded to us in case you used it. We've been worried about your injuries."

Chapter Eleven

The fire snapped and Nickolas's eyes darted around the empty room, looking for anything out of place. His thoughts racing, Nickolas listened to the voice on the other end of the line.

"Please don't hang up, Nickolas. There's something we would like to discuss with you."

"Why don't you start with who you are and why you would care about my injuries? You caused them in the first place."

A throat clearing on the other side of the phone reached him. "Actually, no, we didn't. It was never our intention for you or any of the other Valkyries with you to be harmed. That was Gabriel's doing."

"Gabriel? You mean the same Gabriel who you created and who answers to you?"

There was a long pause before the voice replied. "That's what we would like to discuss with you."

Concern asserting itself, Nickolas looked at the timer on his phone. He'd been on for one minute. How long did they need to trace a location? He couldn't remember. Did he need to be on the phone or just have the phone on? He needed to hang up and turn the phone off.

"Nickolas, relax. I can hear your breathing accelerating. Please don't hang up until you've heard me out. I'm not trying to keep you on the phone to trace your location. We already know where you are."

"I wouldn't still be here if that were true."

"You are in Aurora, the valley that Marcus, your father, settled with the first group of Valkyries who escaped the Facility. It is located in the higher foothills of the cascades, north of Marysville and south of Bellingham. Am I warm?"

A chill ran through him, and Nickolas closed his eyes. "I'm listening."

"Not everyone is happy with the direction things have been going in regards with how to deal with you and your people."

"What is that supposed to mean?"

The man on the other end sighed quietly. "It means that not all of us approve of what has been done to you or what is planned. We would like to try and change the direction. But to do that, we would need your help. We would like you to consider coming back to the Facility."

"You have to be kidding me!"

"Far from it. I do feel the need to inform you first, though, that your grandfather's remains were recovered during the cleanup from the fire and explosion that destroyed half the Facility. I'm sorry."

"I already know he was gone," Nickolas stated flatly.

"We thought as much. We are still missing a couple of other employees as well...?" Silence followed the question, which Nickolas had no desire to break. Another sigh followed, stating as clear as words that he knew Nickolas had to know something. "If you should find out what happened to Jays Anderson, a doctor in the medical division, and Jules Osmer, a communications technician who I believe is a member of your recovery team, we would appreciate knowing. We're still sifting through the rubble for their remains, however."

"I have no idea. When I left the Facility, it was nearly deserted. I was already in the air and flying away when the explosion happened."

"I see."

The texture of that phrase made Nickolas alert. Beneath it was a wealth of undertones, leading Nick to believe that the mysterious man on the other side of the line knew more than he was letting on and that he didn't believe Nick's protestation of ignorance. His wariness rose.

"Since you can't help us with this matter, let us return to the original one. If you would consent to returning to the Facility, all of you, of your own free will, we would make sure that Gabriel couldn't touch you. We need someone like you in a leadership capacity; you would have autonomy over your people, answering only to me."

"Why? And what about the rebels? My parents? Are you expecting them to return after all these years?"

"We have left Aurora alone all this time, Nickolas. Why would we need to do anything to them now?"

His head aching, Nick just wanted this day to be over now. "I'll think about it."

He took the phone away from his ear, the voice still speaking reassuring nonsense as he hung up on it and powered the phone down. Very carefully, he placed it on the table next to him then leaned back to stare into the flames again, thinking. *I notice he didn't actually answer any of my questions. Convenient of him, don't you think?*

The fire popped.

And a very important distinction to keep in mind, Nicky. A voice whispered through his mind. *Luther has a lot of power, whether he really would wield it in your favor or not, I wouldn't want to guess at.*

Jumping, Nickolas twisted around and scanned the empty room. No one.

But that voice, the same voice he'd hoped to hear in a recording, was resonating in his head. He shook it, trembling slightly as he sank back into his seat. Flashes of memory from when he'd been fleeing Gabriel jumped into his awareness. He hadn't been running just from Gabriel but from his own memories; the fever caused by his injuries had produced the hallucinations. The conversations he'd had with Ian, Ian's directions and encouragements, were just a way for his subconscious to get him to safety...weren't they?

His fever was gone and his injuries were mostly healed. A surge of emotion flowed through him, trying to break the ice that now encased him.

That's right, Nicky, you need to let the ice thaw.

He scrambled after the cold, trying to wrap it back around himself, but fear kept him from fully succeeding. On the hearth, next to the dancing flames of the fireplace, dust motes floated in the air, reflecting strangely in the sunlight.

He blinked and rubbed his eyes. They were swirling around, and Nickolas was sure they were taking on form. His breath suspended, he started shaking his head in denial. *No, this isn't happening. I'm going insane. That's the only answer for this.*

Ian's unmarked face gazed back at him in sympathy. He looked just like he had the last time Nickolas had seen him in the Hub, barring the fact that he was somewhat see-through.

While I'll agree that you may be going insane, Nicky, I assure you it's not because you are seeing me.

Heat burned through him, and Nickolas felt his emotions surge again, briefly, before he smashed them back down into the ice by sheer force of will.

Ian shook his head in reproof, crossing his arms as he studied him. *You can't stay locked up forever, Nickolas, or you're right. You will go insane.*

"What did Kieran do to me?" Nick whispered. "You're not really here. I saw you die. Why wouldn't you come with me?" The last had a plaintive note to it that grated on Nickolas. He looked away to stare out the window into the sunlight and felt the ice crack some more.

This has nothing to do with what Kieran did. He only put a temporary bandage on you. An emotional tourniquet. But like any bandage, it needs to come off eventually to allow for full healing. And I couldn't come with you, Nicky. As it was, you barely made it here. There was no way you would have escaped with me in tow.

Fighting with himself, Nickolas could feel the conflicting aspects he held within. The comforting cadence of Ian's voice lulled him, weakening his resolve and causing him to want things like love and contact with others again.

Even in death, the doctor couldn't leave him alone. Ian had to keep pushing, forcing him to feel again when all he wanted was to stay frozen, where the pain didn't bother him anymore.

Cracks formed throughout the glaciers, and he could feel the volcano simmering underneath, threatening to erupt once more.

The pain struck, and groaning, Nick bent over his knees, covering his eyes, scared at what he might do. "Go away," he told the figment of his imagination while he turned inward, attempting to fortify his barriers.

A hand barely touched his hair, and Nickolas froze. *I'll go for now, Nicky, but please be careful. Listen to your dreams, and don't trust the Facility.*

Counting his heartbeat, it was a while before Nickolas gathered the nerve to raise his head and look at the fireplace. He leaned back and watched the flames dance across the wood almost desperately while he contemplated the concept of insanity.

Excitement slithered through Jessica as she scanned the sparkling valley spread out below her. She couldn't wait to find out what everyone could do with their talents. She flew in the middle of the larger group, Kieran behind her and Dev and Aiden flanking her. She shook her head at their overprotectiveness. Her flying was skilled enough, but this whole Breeder aspect tended to hone their instincts. She tried not to let it smother her.

The sounds of hammering echoed off the rock walls as repairs got underway on the damaged barn. She smiled as she watched the wooly lumps of sheep and the playful jumping of goats interspersed with placid cows wandering around in the fields surrounding the barns. A handful of people were busy coming and going from the structures.

Then they were at the cliff wall, and they skimmed up the vertical stone to break above the surface and rise over the dark waters of the lake. Gaining altitude, Robin led them a little ways out over the lake before he circled in toward the tall building that stood in a wedge of land between the lake shore and the cliff edge.

It had to be at least forty feet square and four stories tall. The entire top floor looked like it was made up of windows. *Getting the glass here must have been a chore. No wonder they call it the control tower. That's exactly what it looks like, an air control tower.*

Snickering to herself, she broadcast, *Tower, this is Valkyrie One coming in for a landing, do you copy, over.* Her laughter rang out into the crisp air when she saw her brother's disgruntled look cast back at her and heard Kieran's soft laugh echo in her head.

They followed Robin, and she managed an almost graceful landing beside him on the flat roof of the building, the other six Valkyries touching down around her. Aiden's voice mingled with Dev's as she stepped to the edge to look over the railing. The entirety of the valley was spread out before her. From the barns and animals at the base of the wall, she could follow the meandering course of the creek as it cut the broad length in half.

The sparkling expanse of snow-covered meadow made up most of the acreage; the major buildings had been built nearest to this end and the large groups of cabins filled the opposite end.

On the other side of the building the large mountain lake, its dark waters sparkling in the sunlight and the light breeze ruffling its top, helped create the wedge of land that the tower sat on.

Robin let them admire the view for a minute but then quickly ushered them inside. Through the stair rail she got a good look at the room as she descended. No walls blocked the space, and glass filled all four exterior walls, giving a spectacular view.

This has to be the best place to watch storms from. The people who were in the room gave them all a curious glance but otherwise refrained from bothering them. Kevin, who had been sitting in a chair by the north window, stood and approached them.

"Finally come for testing then, Robin?"

"Yes. Good timing too. Kel was going to take this next shift, but since I need to be here now anyway, I'll take it."

"I'll come down with you for a bit then before I take off."

"Anything I need to know?"

"Nope, nothing's been reported."

The two Primes led their little group to another stair down as they continued to fill each other in. Jessica filed in after Kieran and was surprised to find that the stair emptied out into a tiny room barely large enough to be a landing.

Hurried out to make room for the others to finish descending, she looked around, confused. This room had no windows, so all light came from the fluorescent fixtures on the ceiling. Comparing the space to the room above it, it seemed maybe half the size.

Then she noticed Kevin open one of many doors that encircled the room. From the number of doors she counted, each room had to be small.

"These are our workrooms," Robin said. "This is where the imbuers work, or any Seers and Casters who need quiet—or a controlled, protected environment."

He opened one of the doors to show them an empty room. Maybe ten feet square with a little table and a couple of chairs, not much to look at.

The main center room they stood in seemed to be about twenty feet square with a large table in the center, but other than size, it resembled the little rooms.

Kevin returned with a middle-aged woman. She pushed her graying blonde hair back behind her ears in an absent-minded gesture that seemed habitual to Jessica. The woman's gaze roamed over them but paused when it landed on her, and Jessica went completely still as a wave of something passed over her. Her shield rose automatically before she realized it, and Kieran sent her an inquiring glance. She shook her head.

Robin pulled a chair out from the table and sat, gesturing that everyone should take a seat. "Kev, could I get you to see about having lunch brought up here for all of us when you head over?"

"Sure, no problem."

He smiled his thanks then looked at everyone sitting around the table. Jessica felt that odd brush again. She caught the woman looking at her once more.

Her gaze flicked back to Robin when he spoke. "This is our grader, Ellie. She'll be able to tell us what talents you have and at what strength."

Ellie had moved to stand beside Robin. She folded her wings closer and smiled slightly at them. "With this many, it will take a while, so you should make yourselves comfortable."

Aiden sighed next to her and slouched down in his seat like a put out teenager, which made Jenny and Sam scowl at him from across the table. Ellie just ignored him. "So, who's first?"

Jessica glanced at her people. They all looked from her to Kieran.

I've been using my talent, Jess. I'll go first.

Kieran stood and absently shook the feathery ends of his hair off his collar then walked casually to the grader. "I will. What do you want me to do?"

Ellie studied him from head to foot before she spoke. "We normally use one of the workrooms, but with this many to test, I think we'll stay out here, Robin. Please set the protections."

"Protections?" Kieran asked as he sat in the chair she pulled out for him. She sat down in front of him, close enough that their knees where touching.

"All of the rooms on this floor of the building have strong shields that can be invoked when a working is started. The imbuers spend one day of every week renewing these shields and the major sight and defensive shield that covers the entirety of the valley."

"There's a shield over the whole valley?" Jessica asked.

Robin nodded when Kieran looked at him. "Yes. The sight shield is in place at all times. It stops air traffic or people walking through the woods from seeing anything we've built in the valley and surrounds, including this tower. The defensive shield is only raised if we're threatened. It would be a pain otherwise. None of us would be able to come or go very easily."

Kieran placed his hands in his lap and looked at Ellie.

"Now this will feel a little weird. I'm going to sort of go through your mind in a way. Try to stay relaxed and it will be easier." She reached out and took both of his hands in hers. "What's your name?"

"Kieran."

The woman flinched ever so slightly and looked at him closer. "You're Kieran? The one with the projective empathy?"

Nodding his head, Kieran waited.

"Well, in that case, from what I've heard you'll be familiar with what's about to happen. Please hold still. Sometimes strange things happen during this process as I work through what talents are present."

Kieran took a deep breath and placed himself into a trance. Ellie paused, looking at him, then smiled slightly, following his lead. The two sat perfectly still, but Jessica could have sworn that she felt movement from them.

She narrowed her eyes and looked closer, not sure what she was seeing but certain that she was seeing something. She wanted to get up and actually touch Kieran, to bring it into closer focus. She clenched her fist. After a few minutes, Ellie gasped slightly, and her eyes came back into focus. Kieran's slowly opened, and he returned her stare without moving.

Swallowing, Ellie shook her head. "This can't be right." She looked at Robin, who sat up straighter, looking at her in concern.

"What's wrong, Ellie?"

"I need to check again. This can't be right. I can't measure his strength."

"What?"

"He's a five, but it's deeper than that. He goes deeper than a five, Robin."

The slight tremble of fear that Jessica picked up from her had her cocking her head again and looking at Kieran, who caught her eyes, a smile in their depths. *The twit. He already knew.*

Wait until she measures you, Jess. His laugh rippled through her. Her lips twitching, she returned her attention to the grader.

Visibly steeling herself, Ellie smiled at Kieran. "Let's try this again, ok?"

Shrugging his shoulders, he closed his eyes. "Sure, but nothing is going to have changed."

Jessica watched them as their breathing synchronized. She leaned back into her chair as she waited with the others. Fifteen minutes passed before Ellie took a deep breath and pulled herself out of the trance.

Kieran opened his eyes, watching her intently. She released his hands and stood up, stretching her neck and arms out. Jessica got the impression it was more to buy herself time before she had to address them than that she was stiff.

Ellie turned back to them and made eye contact with Robin. Then standing straight, she put her hands behind her back, looking for all the world like a professor about to deliver a lecture. After a glance at Kieran, she started.

"As everyone already guessed, Kieran, you are an empath. Receptive empathy is fairly common, though not at the strength that you have it at. The strongest empaths that I know are all around a three. What isn't so common is that you are also a projective empath. I have only known one projective, and she died about ten years ago. Both talents are at equal strength from what I can tell, which is another new development. I have never found someone with two talents that were equal before, though they are closely related since they are the center of the talent scale.

"In effect, I cannot place you in either caste effectively. You are both a Seer and a Caster of equal strength." Shaking her head, she looked stunned. "But that's not all. I cannot gauge your strength; all I can say is that you are a five plus. You are incredibly strong with a talent that can do irreparable harm to others, so please use it wisely."

She took a deep breath then looked at all the rest of them. "There is no one I can think of who *can* train you fully. Beth and the other empaths can give you guidance, but you're going to be largely on your own to work it out. I did a deep scan and found no trace of other talents."

Jessica sent a quick look at her brother and saw a similar stunned expression in his eyes, though he tried to hide it.

Kieran stood, swept them all with a gaze, settling on Sam. Crooking a finger, he pointed to the chair. "Your turn, Sam."

The lanky young man stood, brushing a hand through his short, sandy hair and pushing his bangs out of his eyes. He took the seat Kieran vacated and held his hands out to Ellie.

Jess shook her head at the laughter in Kieran's gold-flecked eyes and moved her chair over a little when he decided to squeeze in next to her instead of taking the big open space on the other side of the table.

Robin made amused, pointed looks at the empty space, and she tossed a glare his way before turning her attention back to the grader. This time she was ready when Ellie went into the trance, and Jessica extended her awareness, trying to follow what she was feeling.

It led her to Sam's hands. Little wisps of light were dancing off of his fingers; they weren't very bright, and Jessica didn't think anyone else was noticing them. She felt a tingle in her own fingers, but when she looked at them, they were the same as they had always been, except for the awareness. It was like she could somehow feel his talent manifesting within herself. She clenched her fists and tried to relax and go back to just watching what was happening.

Several minutes later, Jessica elbowed Aiden who sat on her other side and had started to snore because he had fallen asleep slouched on his hand. Dev's long face peeked over the teen's shoulder at her, grinning as Aiden jumped and his head nearly hit the table when it slipped off of his hand.

"Aw, Jessica, it's the baby's nap time. You don't want to wake him or we'll never get to sleep tonight."

Jessica was always amazed at how fast Aiden could become alert from a sound sleep, lunging at Dev for his comment. He didn't get far; Jessica stopped him by grabbing a fistful of his hair and yanking him back into his seat at the same time that Dev pinned him with a hand to his throat. Aiden's hot gaze raked his Flight leader and promised mayhem later.

Exasperated, Kieran quietly rebuked, "Aiden, knock it off. Dev, let him go and move to the other side of the table."

Grinning, Dev released him, and pushing his chair back, rose and moved to the other side to sit next to Miguel. Jessica released her grip on his hair and let Aiden sit up. Robin chuckled, looking at Kieran.

"I see you have your hands full." Then he addressed Aiden, a mixture of amusement and steel in his voice. "You're lucky you're not in my Flight or I would thrash you for the insolence."

Whatever else might have occurred was forestalled when Ellie pulled them both out of the trance.

"Well the good news is I was easily able to measure the depth of your power well; you grade out at a level two. The bad news is that I haven't a clue what your talent does. It's been a while since I've run across anything new that has stumped me like this. I can tell it is in the Caster half of the scale, but what it is..." Pursing her lips, she sunk into thought.

How odd? How can she not know? She's the experienced one. Jessica waited but finally couldn't keep her tongue any longer. "He casts light."

The middle-aged blonde opened her eyes and pinned Jessica to her seat. The sharp look took Jessica's breath away after the fuzziness of all of her other stares.

"What?"

Squirming in her seat, Jessica repeated what she had said. "He casts light. Couldn't you feel what he was doing? I know you had your eyes closed so you wouldn't have seen the light at his fingertips, but couldn't you feel it?"

Embarrassed by the scrutiny of everyone at the table, Jessica dropped Ellie's gaze to look at the tabletop.

"You could feel what Sam was doing?" Ellie asked carefully.

Nodding her head, Jess elaborated. "I had to concentrate though."

"Sam, I'll finish your assessment in a little bit. Jessica, please come here. I would like to check something out."

Kieran squeezed her arm as she rose and went around him. Then she gingerly took the seat and placed her hands into Ellie's cool ones. Closing her eyes, she tried to relax. There was a light brush against her shields, and she had to restrain herself from flinging the intruder out. Ellie's voice filled her head. It wasn't quite the same as the telepathy that she shared with everyone else. It was closer, more intimate. Something more like what she shared with Nickolas, or the times she had talked to Kieran in the dreamscape. She cringed a little from it.

Relax, Jessica. If you tense up, it will make it much harder, and it will take longer. I'll do a complete scan in a moment, but first I wanted to look for something specific.

The feeling of the stranger rummaging through her mind made her feel like she had fleas crawling around on her skin and that she needed to scratch, so she took deep, even breaths to calm herself. A wave of reassurance engulfed her, and she recognized Kieran's presence. Through their bonded link, he'd been able to tell that she was uncomfortable.

That's what I thought, Jessica; you have a talent in grading. You must have been picking up traces of the energy I raised to show me what someone can do. I enter a person's mind looking for their power well. Located near it will be the threads that represent their talents. I gently pluck the strings, listening and feeling for those that resonate. Sometimes that results in a physical manifestation of their talent without their conscious control. That's why it's important to do this in a protected place. Occasionally that's the only clue I get that allows me to know what it is that they can do. After I have identified what talents they have, I locate the anchor threads that lead into their well. By following the length to the end, I can determine how deep a well they have to draw on. Each talent anchors at a different depth usually. Is this making sense to you?

So far it is.

Good. I can help you with it when we test the rest of your group. For now, let me check to see what other talents you have, then I can show you your well and we'll see how deep it goes.

Following Ellie, Jessica watched her gently start plucking the threads that she had described. Until the grader had mentioned them, she hadn't noticed the web-like construction in her inner mindscape. Intrigued, Jessica examined them.

There seemed to be a great deal of the silvery things draped in the darkness; some were thicker than others, a few as thick as her thigh, a lot almost rope-like, while some were gossamer thin. Most ran up and down, while a few ran crosswise, connecting each other together. Ellie was staring at the cross threads as she plucked a strand here or there.

Jessica stood back from where the grader worked and reached out to gently touch one of the threads near her. She felt it vibrate and yanked her hand back, startled. Ellie turned to look at her.

It would be easier if you didn't touch while I was looking. I get mixed messages if you try to use power while I work.

Sighing, Jessica found a rock that had appeared out of nowhere next to her and sat on it. It seemed that everyone was always telling her to wait or not to touch, or in general not to do anything. Exhaling sharply, she vowed that eventually, sometime soon, that wouldn't be the case anymore. Well at least not the standard. Ellie's hum of uncertainty brought her attention back to the grader.

I think I'm finding at least five talents here. I'll need to do a few tests with you outside of trance work, Jessica. The troubled gaze of the Seer turned to her. *First Kieran, now you. What have we gotten ourselves into?*

They did tell you that Nickolas and I are in a different caste, didn't they?

Yes, I could feel the difference just being near you. But it's still a surprise to look at it like this. I have been grading all new fledglings in the valley for the last twenty years, and to find more than three talents...is odd. Let's go take a look at the depth of your power.

Ellie placed her hand on one of the ropes and led Jessica to a place within herself that had a pool of shimmery water glowing faintly in the darkness. At least it made Jessica think of water. It rippled oddly, until she realized that the movement was in time to her breath.

As an experiment, she drew in a breath and held it. Ellie stopped at the water's edge, her hand still on the rope, and said without turning around, *You'll be more comfortable if you breathe, you know.*

Exhaling in a rush, Jessica watched the ripples start again. She moved so she could look over the grader's shoulder. Ellie had her hand on a tube as thick as her thigh that disappeared into the rippling water.

Jess watched, waiting for something, though for what, she didn't know. She realized that she felt calm and reenergized at the same time as she stared into the pool.

Lost in the contemplation of the water, she jumped when Ellie stepped back. The Seer took a couple of deep breaths before turning to her. The complete blankness in her eyes made Jessica wary.

I really don't know what to think or say.

What's wrong?

Before Kieran, I had never run into anyone where I couldn't gauge their strength. Where I couldn't swim to the bottom of their well and gauge their depth. But compared to you, he was a shallow puddle. You are like a deep ocean. I can't even begin to imagine how much power is at your command.

Really not sure how to respond to that, Jessica backed up, and before she realized it, she was opening her eyes to look out on the real world. Ellie was already speaking softly to Robin, and Kieran was crouched down next to her, his eyes serious.

"You stopped breathing for a moment."

Shaking her head, she tried to reassure him. "I held my breath, that's all. Though I think you were right about them freaking out when she saw my power levels."

His eyes easing, he stood and offered her his hand. "The two of you have been in a trance for over half an hour; Robin was starting to worry. Kevin is coming back with lunch for all of us; we thought a break might be in order."

She rose and stretched, her thoughts centered on what she'd learned.

◆ ◆ ◆

Gabriel stretched his wings to settle the fabric of the vest then checked all of the compartments before he patted the numerous pockets of his pants. The harsh fluorescent lighting glared down on the dozens of Facility personnel running through mission prechecks. The huge garage bay was packed.

He'd finally been called in for the recovery. After more than two weeks. It had taken that long for Kratz to give him the green light. At first Gabriel couldn't believe the delay. The Facility claimed they wanted Nickolas returned no matter what. Which had fit in with his need to hunt both Alphas down. But then two weeks of nothing. *Ah to be a fly on the wall during that infighting.* It was amazing what could change in a couple of weeks though.

His mind drifted to his leave-taking from Pet and Zach. He smiled and slowly licked his bottom lip. At least he'd put the time to good use. Zach was coming along just fine.

"Gabriel, the teams are ready to pull out."

He shivered his wings and snapped back. "Primary teams stay here, Everett. Get all other personnel on the move. We have a lot of miles to cover tonight before we can get set up."

"Yes, sir."

Orders echoed through the cavernous space, competing with the engines roaring to life. Gabriel shook his head to clear his ears but then retreated through the double doors and into a large conference room down the hall.

The primary team leaders started to file in, and he sank into a seat, propping his feet on the table to wait. The noise from the garage bay was muffled through the walls. His mind drifted back to the two he'd left behind in his suite. Amazing how much one could change in such a short time. His need to go after Nickolas that had developed recently no longer pushed him, and he found it almost disconcerting. The suddenness of the shift. But the focus that had been pinned on Nick and Jessica had shifted to Pet and Zach. Now he had other things to occupy his desires. He didn't need the two AWOL Alphas. But, unfortunately, just because he no longer meshed with the current council's dictates, it didn't change his job. Everett gave him a signal, and he sat up.

"I'm sure you all have guessed by now what our assignment is. This isn't an ordinary feral recovery, and we aren't just going after the escaped control group. We are going after Marcus. After tonight, we should have the Valkyrie population back in the hands of the Facility."

He continued the briefing, but a part of his mind wouldn't settle. As he set the plans into motion that he'd been ordered to carry out, he couldn't help but notice the difference a couple of weeks could make. He'd been worried about the delay and what it would mean for Marcus. He hadn't considered he might change.

Oh well, orders are orders. Bringing them in is my job. No matter what.

At least that will be fun.

Chapter Twelve

Marcus replaced the teakettle on the top of the woodstove and carefully hung up the hot mitt, then he turned to look at his surrogate son and held up the sugar bowl. Robin nodded, so Marcus dumped a couple of spoons in and handed the mug over.

The Hunter stirred the sugar into his tea and sat back into the chair, enjoying the warmth from the fire. "So I assume Beth is over at the longhouse overseeing the end of dinner preparations?"

Marcus threw one more log on the fire and closed the stove before he picked up his own cup and settled into his seat. Blowing on his tea to cool it, he answered Robin. "Yes, that's why I asked you to join me here instead of my office. I don't care if Beth hears us, but we can guarantee that we won't be overheard by anyone else in my house. So what happened?"

Robin took a sip of his tea, and his eyes unfocused as he pondered how to answer. "That's a complicated question. We knew it wouldn't be normal, but..." He paused. "I really had no idea, Marcus. You'll have to tell me if Ian warned you or not. I guess the best place to start is at the beginning. Kieran called me yesterday to ask if it was a good day to do the testing. I'd been waiting for them to get ready, so I dropped what I was doing to take them up to the tower. The first difficulty happened before I could even get them off the practice grounds. Nickolas refused testing. He wouldn't allow anyone near him, so getting him up to the tower was impossible. I was going to bring Ellie down to do it instead, but then he said he wouldn't let anyone mess in his head again either, so I recognized a losing battle and let it go."

Closing his eyes, Marcus growled. "Damn it. I really wanted to know what he was capable of. That telekinesis storm has me worried. I don't want any more surprises like that." He looked back at Robin and took a small sip of his tea.

"You're not the only one. Christoff said almost exactly the same when Nickolas walked off."

"That's not reassuring you know, Robin. Chris would be the one most likely to know what the extent of his brother's abilities would be."

"It sounds like Chris is just as much in the dark as the rest of us." Robin stared into the fire and idly stirred his tea. "I took the rest of them to Ellie up in the tower. There were seven of them. Nickolas has appointed Kieran to act as Prime for the combined group of Seers and Casters. We already knew what he could do with the empathy. What we didn't know was how strong he was. We all assumed that he was a five, but when Ellie was in trance with him, she couldn't measure his strength. She's calling him a five plus, and she says that he doesn't have any other talents waiting in the wings."

"Well that's good to hear."

"That's just the beginning, Marcus. She then tested a Caster who has a talent that she hadn't seen before. It turned out that he casts light. But he's only a level two."

"Casts light?" Stretching his legs out, Marcus took a drink of his steaming tea. "How so?"

"It's just like it sounds. He can make light appear. We're calling him a light bringer. He can even cast it in different colors."

Marcus stared at the painting on the wall above the stove as he thought about the new talent. "That could have its uses. Place it into a charm and we can have light without electricity."

"That was our thought as well. Jessica was instrumental in identifying his talent, by the way."

He raised an eyebrow at Robin, who was grinning slightly.

"She surprised the heck out of Ellie. If Ellie was stunned by Kieran, she was speechless with Jess. Untrained, Jessica could tell what Sam was doing. Since she didn't have any preconceived notions about what could happen with different talents, she picked it up faster than Ellie. So she tested Jess next; she definitely has a talent in grading, at a level three and a half. She is also a purifier at a one and a half, has animal telepathy at a three, and is a wind caller at a four."

"Wait a minute, she has four talents? I thought she was a light weaver?"

"She is. This is where I get to the good part. She has three minor talents and two major talents, wind calling and light weaving. The five talents threw Ellie, but not as much as Jessica's power well did. She has no gauge for her strength. She's that deep." Stopping there, Robin waited and drank some of his tea.

Marcus let his mind wrap around the information. "Jennifer did say she would be different." Grunting in agreement, Robin crossed his ankles. Then he thought about his eldest son and froze. "If...no, not if...we know Nickolas is a match for Jessica. This makes me want to know Nickolas's talents and power even more now."

"I don't think he'll be up to letting us near him anytime soon, Marcus."

"I expect you're right. Any other surprises you have in store for me?"

Smiling, Robin brought his mug up to his face. "A few, but nothing quite as spectacular as Jessica. Two more of the seven can't be graded; they're too strong. And they have some spectacular talents. Dev is an electrokinetic with two minor talents, shielding and weather forecasting. Aiden is a storm bringer with low level animal telepathy. He's one to watch out for. He's Alpha material if I've ever seen it, very aggressive and dominant. And he's only sixteen."

Nodding his head, Marcus rose to refill his cup. "Ian mentioned him to me. A couple of years ago, Nick brought in a thirteen-year-old boy who had entered the second stage. I had forgotten. I guess he didn't go to Gabriel."

"I'm wondering if Ian wasn't somehow able to tell what sort of power these people would have. It's too much of a coincidence, the range of talents and the strength."

Thinking the same thing, Marcus decided that maybe he should revisit some of his archived messages from his father and look for clues to what was happening. "You wanted to know if Ian had warned me; the answer to that was no, Robin, he didn't. A lightning slinger and a storm caller, together? You're right, that is just too much of a coincidence. How did Ellie test those two?"

"Dev was fairly simple. As soon as she got him into trance, all the lights started to flicker, and before I could get her out of the trance, the bulbs blew in all the fixtures on that floor. Sam's talent came in handy at that moment." Robin laughed. "Ellie wants to check through our population, looking to see if any of us have a hidden talent in light bringing that she missed. Anyway, Aiden's talent wasn't quite as straight forward. Jessica, again, gave us the clue. Since one of her talents is closely related, she could feel the call of the wind in him. We moved to the roof, and that was all it took. When he has it under control, he'll be able to call hurricanes. With Aiden to call the storms and Dev to direct the lightning from them, I wouldn't want to be pitted against those two."

"What about the last two?" Blowing on his hot tea, Marcus watched Robin's face.

"Not so much to tell. Miguel is an imbuer and Jenny is a Seer with simple clairvoyance; her subsets are remote seeing and locating. Neither of them is out of the ordinary except in the fact that they are part of this group. Something I noticed was the variety, or should I say balance, of talents the Facility Valkyries have to draw on. It doesn't seem natural, which is why I was wondering about Ian."

"I agree with your thought, Robin. I don't know as much about my father's talent as I would like. I also don't know if he had any minor talents. But this isn't beyond what I would call reasonable for a logistical talent like his, just how he did it." He shrugged his shoulders. "Did they agree to help?"

"Yes, that wasn't a problem at all. They were all excited at the prospect of practicing their talents and getting coaching in how to use them properly, so I've set up times for them all to come up to the tower to help. Miguel, he's the imbuer, is already up there with the other imbuers. They're really excited about the strength of Dev's talent. They are already talking about what they can harness in a charm."

"Some of the things they come up with." He finished off his tea and set the cup aside then looked at the clock on the wall. "Dinner should be just about done. Beth will skin us if we make everything late."

Robin set his cup aside and rose before he took a couple of pretty wrapped boxes out of a bag he'd set on the floor by the coat tree. "I brought these over for the two of you."

Smiling at Robin, Marcus pulled his own box out of a pocket in his clothes. "We had the same idea. Beth wanted me to give this to you before we went to dinner, but she told me to tell you not to open it now."

Sighing, Robin accepted the box, placing those he brought on the table against the wall. "She knows how much I hate waiting."

Laughing, Marcus clapped him on the back as they got their coats. "I suspect that's why she wanted me to give it to you; to make you wait. She wanted to see you suffer."

Robin groaned as they left the cabin. It was a beautiful afternoon out. Crisp and clear, the sun sparkled on the snow still trapped in the branches of the large evergreens they walked through. Bird calls filled the air as the little flitters used the last of the warm sunlight trying to find enough food to get them through another winter night.

They walked companionably along the path, and Marcus let all of the information Robin had brought him filter to the back of his mind to simmer and coalesce for later. Stepping out of the protection of the trees, both Valkyries stopped and shaded their eyes until they got used to the glare off of the field. A few passing Hunters waved, but they didn't join any of the groups, instead preferring to make their way toward the longhouse in companionable silence.

When they reached the courtyard, Marcus stopped Robin with a light hand. He glanced at Robin then took a last look out over the fields. "I wanted to tell you, while we had a moment of quiet, how proud of you I am, and that I'm happy to have you as my Second."

Stunned silence fell beside him, and Marcus looked out of the corner of his eye. Hope, fear, longing, love, all chased across Robin's expression, confirming his suspicion that his Second felt vulnerable now that Nick and Chris had arrived in the valley.

He took a deep breath and turned a smile on his Hunter. "So are you ready for this? Tonight's dinner should be interesting."

Robin shuffled his wings then fell into step on Marcus's heels as they entered the longhouse. "That's what you say every year. This year, I think it'll be the truth."

Marcus laughed.

The heat enveloped them as they paused in the foyer and hung their jackets. Both the fireplaces were roaring, and with the number of bodies, it was going to be a hot evening. *It won't be long before all the doors and windows are thrown open.*

Marcus paused with his Second on the threshold of the inner doorway. It took a moment before the milling crowd noticed them. All of the tables had been decorated and laid with place settings for the holiday meal. As the room quieted and everyone found a seat to stand beside, he stepped out with Robin on his left. They crossed the silence of the hall. Only those on sentry were absent tonight.

The Christmas tree rose in splendor in the far corner, colorful lights ablaze, and the pile of presents heaped underneath was enough to make memories from his childhood rise up and choke him. As always, the place left open for them was back by one of the fireplaces. Already sweating, he pulled his chair out. Robin took the seat to his left; the right remained empty and waiting until Beth had finished directing the serving.

The quiet hum of conversation resumed as everyone sat, and Marcus looked around at the tables while the food was brought out. Some of the Facility Valkyries had chosen to mingle with his Aurorans and sat scattered around the room, but the majority still clustered together around Nickolas and Jessica on the far side of the room.

The two Facility Alphas had been placed in front of the opposite fireplace. And they didn't look any more comfortable than he felt. He laughed to himself about it.

But then he caught concerned looks passing between Jessica, Kieran, and Chris. He looked more closely at his eldest son.

Nickolas showed signs of strain; one moment the icy dispassionate mask of the last couple of weeks sat in place, then it cracked, and the emotion he was keeping bottled up would flare.

He held his breath as he watched Nickolas work to keep it contained. The arrival of food platters helped distract him, and Marcus started to breathe again. He did not need another emotion storm like what had happened in the barn. He caught Christoff's eye from across the room.

We're on it. Kieran has already talked to Mom. She feels that he's not a danger. Nicky's just finding it harder to stay aloof from all of us.

Marcus nodded his head and felt relief in the wake of the sending. Robin handed him a platter, and he served himself. As the platters passed from hand to hand, he looked out over the laughter and joy of his people as they embraced the good food and holiday atmosphere. He turned a smile on his wife as she joined him, and he dished up a plate for her, receiving a kiss for his trouble.

She nodded across the room at Nickolas.

"Yes, I saw."

"If it keeps getting released in small bursts like that, it's good. Kieran and I discussed this already. Like a volcano blowing off steam, if the pressure is released, the chances of another explosion are diminished."

Marcus took a bite of turkey, thinking about what Beth said. "But that won't hold true if he gets hit with another calamity, will it?"

Her eyes sad, she shook her head. He watched his son as he fought his silent battle. His boys were finally here, and there was still nothing he could do to protect them.

The evening progressed. He'd been right; it took about fifteen minutes before the first door was propped open.

Unfortunately, the slim breath of cooler air never made it as far as his seat. They ate until they were stuffed, then the good-natured groaning started as the cakes and pies made their appearance. But Marcus noticed there wasn't any difficulty in making the sweets disappear.

As the last few pieces were dished up and most people were leaning back in their chairs looking like they were going to pass out any second, Marcus pushed his chair back and stood. The hall grew quiet.

"First of all, I want to wish everyone a Happy Holiday. This year has been a good one; we have accomplished much. Before the arrival of the Facility Valkyries, we were proud to have fifteen new additions this year." Applause and backslapping accompanied this announcement, and he waited for it to quiet down.

"But the biggest change is definitely the arrival of the control group from the Facility. Though the one loss we received from that escape is devastating, it's better than the sixty we lost the first time. I know that if Ian could be here now, he would have been glad that everyone made it."

He had to clear his throat as he raised his glass into the air. "To Ian. He led us well and gave the final sacrifice so that many could be free, even though he never was." Tears blurring his eyes, he took a drink.

The sound of many voices in unison resounded through the hall. "To Ian."

After a moment of silence, Marcus continued. "So, now I would like to officially welcome all of you who have sought refuge among us. I hope that one day you join us in truth. But for now, we would like to welcome you with a few gifts that we all gathered for you. Normally, we assign people to get gifts for and have all year to gather them. But since all of you arrived only a few weeks ago, this was hardly something that we could include you in.

"Eagle Sept, please rise." Twenty Valkyries rose throughout the room. "Another tradition we have is the awarding of who gets the pleasure of passing out the presents. This year Eagle Sept won. Congratulations."

Excited faces turned to one another then they made their way to stand in a line up by the tree waiting for his signal. He waved his hand and the group started to pull out huge bags and carried them to each of the Facility Valkyries. The stunned looks on all of their faces made Marcus smile. Beth reached up and held his hand. He sank into his chair and kissed her fingers as he watched tears fill more than one of the new Valkyries' eyes.

Each bag held mostly necessities, clothes and personal care items, but there were also some frivolities like books or trinkets.

After all of the Facility Valkyries had their care packages, Eagle Sept started to hand out the rest of the presents. Marcus accepted a package but set it aside and nudged Beth, pointing across the room. Nickolas held a large, flat package in his hands. Unable to look away, they watched as he carefully pulled the paper from it then froze. Even from across the room, Marcus could see Nick's arm tremble.

Jessica turned to him suddenly, dropping the conversation she'd been in and placing her hand on his arm, offering support. Slowly, Nick raised his eyes from the picture collage that Marcus and Beth had made to meet their eyes across the distance. The pain in them made Marcus's heart ache.

They were all held captive until Nickolas flinched like he'd been stabbed with a pin, and he turned to look into the empty space over his shoulder. Marcus could see he was talking. He cocked his head as he watched the curious behavior. After a moment Nickolas looked back at the picture, and Marcus could see that he had his emotions mastered again. He set the picture aside carefully, where it couldn't be hurt.

The care with which his son handled the gift warmed Marcus's heart. Feeling a gaze trained on him, Marcus looked away from Nickolas and caught Christoff watching him.

A smile slowly worked its way across Chris's face, and his son raised his glass in a salute. He'd finally made a break in Nickolas's emotional shield. Clutching Beth's hand, he felt a sliver of hope and thought that if that was all he received for Christmas, he would be happy.

Flight

♦ ♦ ♦

The flickering orange and yellow glow of the fire reflected off of the collage of pictures Nick had propped up beside the hearth, each picture randomly brought out in relief as the shadows danced with the flames. First one scene, then another, and another. His gut clenched in pain as he recognized the moments in his past that they represented. He found himself longing for a drink as he sat shrouded in darkness, unable to keep his gaze from straying to the photos any more than he could block the insistent voice in his head.

"Go away, Ian. You're not real; you're just a figment of my imagination." The low growl of laughter reverberated through his head, and the fire popped, filling his ears. Nickolas rubbed the bridge of his nose.

No, I'm not. And I'll just keep repeating myself until you believe me, Nicky. That one.

Nickolas saw a ghostly hand out of the corner of his eye point at one of the pictures.

I took that one of the four of you. Do you remember? Chris was only three at the time, I think, and all of us had gone up to the mountains to look at the fall leaves. You kept hoping there would be snow.

"It was right before everything changed."

Yes. Your grandmother was still alive, and none of us had changed yet. I'm glad to see that they put that picture in.

"Go away! Why are you doing this to me?" More of the ice encasing him broke up; Nickolas fought futilely to remain unemotional. "I guess I should say, why am I doing this to myself, since you aren't real."

I'm as real as you are, Nicky. I promised you I would always be here for you. I don't know how long I'll be allowed to fulfill that promise. I can't do much, but I'm here to help you. You've been too successful at suppressing who you are, and if left to your own devices, you'll cause yourself harm at this rate. You can't stay frozen; you need to feel your emotions. You need to come to terms with your memories. I wish I could change them for you, but that wouldn't be right or fair. The upper left picture, do you remember that one?

Against his will, his eyes sought out the picture in question. Remembering the day, Nickolas closed his eyes. He could still smell the scent of baking bread and the way his mother's hair had felt on his cheek as she hugged him when he'd fallen running through the kitchen. The picture showed him, about five, and his mother covered in flour as she helped him knead bread. His infant brother sat in a bouncy seat on the table next to them.

"Stop already. I don't want to remember any of this, Ian. Can't you get that?"

I get it, Nicky; you're the one who doesn't.

The rage grew, and Nickolas ruthlessly tamped it down. He turned in his chair to look at Ian's intent face. "What do you mean, I don't?" His voice began to rise, but he didn't notice. "If I don't get it, then I don't think I want to. Why would I want to remember this? They left without a backward glance. They left us to..."

He trailed off as memories of before they left vied with memories of his life in the Facility. The horrors he had been left to face without their support. "They made a choice just as you made a choice, Ian. Regardless of how I, or they, feel about it, I get to live with what you chose."

Ian shook his head sadly. *You need to let it go, Nicky. Things have worked out the way they were supposed to. Trust me. If you hadn't been at the Facility, Jessica would likely be dead by now. No one besides you would have managed to bring her in, and she would have died during the change because she wouldn't accept help from anyone. That would have been a great loss. And maybe it's selfish, but I would have been alone all those years; you and your brother being there made it bearable.* Turning away, Ian watched the fire.

"I can't believe I'm arguing with myself like this," Nick muttered.

I repeat, I'm as real as you.

"Yeah, right."

Soft footsteps entered the room, and Nickolas looked over the high back of the chair. Jessica pushed her hair out of her sleepy eyes and looked around the room until she saw him in the chair.

"Who are you talking to?"

He ducked his head to pull his gaze away from her and saw Ian smiling gently in the other chair. He exhaled, his shoulders falling.

Jessica added some wood to the fire then looked out the window on the moonlit snow, waiting for him to get around to replying.

Tell her I think she's doing great. Her talents are coming in nicely, and she's looking in good health. Both of her parents are proud of her. As am I.

Nick refused to answer Ian and instead whispered, "I think I'm going insane."

She turned away from the window to lean against the sill. "Excuse me?"

All of his uncertainty and fear rose up; he knew she could see it in his eyes because she approached him and knelt beside his chair. He stared into her face and repeated, "I think I am going insane, Jess. I'm talking to Ian."

"You know the saying; it's only insane if you get answers." The corners of her lips turned up slightly at her attempt at humor.

Ian laughed from the other chair, and Nickolas turned to glare at him. "Shut up, Ian."

Her eyes were wide with shock when he met them again. "That's the problem," he replied sincerely. "I am."

Jessica searched his face in a silence that stretched almost unbearably. He waited while thoughts he couldn't name passed through her eyes, until finally she blinked and asked tentatively, "Can I use my talent on you? I know you don't like people in your head anymore..."

She left the sentence hanging, and he thought about what she meant. It wasn't so much that he didn't like people in his head as he just couldn't take the chance of more pain right now, but he trusted her in a way he didn't trust anyone else. Not even Chris.

He nodded his head and relaxed back into his seat. She cupped his cheek and turned his head so she could look into his eyes. Hers grew unfocused.

All he felt was a strange itching that grew into relief when he realized he wouldn't be subjected to another waking dream like when he had Kieran in his head.

After only a few moments, Jessica's eyes refocused. Her voice quavered ever so slightly, and she looked around the room. "You're not insane, Nickolas."

She licked her lips and looked back at him. "When we were graded, I learned I was a grader too, and she had me help test our people. I don't know what you're doing, but you are using some form of talent."

Ellie probably wouldn't recognize this talent either, Nick. They haven't documented any Seer's with mediumship yet.

Nick blinked in shock, and all he could think to say was, "I see dead people?"

Ian laughed, and even Jessica's lips twitched up, though a heaviness still rested in her eyes.

I'm afraid so, Ian's voice continued seriously. *But this is also something you can't spread around. First of all, everyone would find this hard to believe, even though they all use psychic talents of their own. And it's not something we should encourage anyway. The concept of being able to talk to your loved ones after they have passed would hinder the living from moving on. Sometimes, like now though, the powers that be decide it's a good idea.*

"Nick?" Jessica whispered.

"He says I'm a medium." Nick looked into Jessica's eyes.

"So when we've seen you talking to yourself, you're talking to Ian?"

He nodded his head.

"Can you see him?" she asked tentatively.

Nick let his head fall back wearily. "He's sitting in the other chair."

She stood and looked into the other chair before moving back to the window to watch him. "So what does he want?"

"He claims he's here to help me. Though it seems more like it's to annoy me."

Anything you haven't liked, Nicky, you think is annoying. I will help you all I can, but I have rules and limitations just as in corporeal life. I'm not all seeing and knowing.

"Help how?" she asked.

"He led me to the valley, though at the time, I attributed him to fever dreams. It seems I was wrong."

"That's a good start. What is he trying to help you with now?"

Nick turned away from her uncomfortably to stare back into the fire.

"Nick," she said in exasperation.

You really should tell her, Nicky. It's not fair to leave her in the dark.

He tossed a glare at Ian then turned back to the fire and saw Jessica waiting for his answer. "He wants to force my emotions back to the surface."

"Good."

Irritated with her, Nick shifted in his seat and stretched his legs out.

"I know being made to feel again isn't comfortable, but the rest of us have been worried about you." She sank down to the floor and sat cross-legged next to the hearth then turned to the empty chair. "I, for one, am glad that you are succeeding. Thank you."

Tell her she's welcome, and I'm very pleased that she's doing well.

Snorting, Nickolas relayed the comment.

She's right you know. The storm you produced when you lost control was dangerous; they have every reason to be concerned about you.

Grinding his teeth, Nick attempted to ignore Ian, but he forgot how perceptive Jessica could be.

"What did he say, Nick?"

"Nothing of any consequence. Why am I blessed with so many people wanting to control me?"

Because you're a Breeder.

"Because you're a Breeder," Jessica stated at the same time. "Now you know how I felt in the Hub." She addressed the empty chair with a scowl. "I still hold you responsible for all of that, by the way."

Rich laughter poured out of the adjacent chair, and Nickolas flinched. "I don't think she would appreciate that, Ian. You're immune to her wrath, I'm not."

Now glaring at both chairs, she wrapped her sweatshirt-covered arms around her fleece-covered knees. "Well at least I'm glad I got dressed before I came out here."

Who does she think tended to her in the Hub, Nick? Besides, I'm dead; it's not like seeing her naked will make much of an impact for either of us.

Sputtering, Nickolas started to cough. "I can't believe you said that."

"What do you mean? You want me to parade around naked in front of your grandfather?"

"No, not you, him. And of course I don't want you naked around Ian. Both of you are going to drive me nuts."

Seriously, Nicky, have the two of you thought about what your caste means?

Shifting in his seat, Nickolas gazed at Jessica for a long moment before turning to Ian. "I thought I had, but what are you getting at?"

"What's he saying?"

He held his hand up for her to wait.

Have the two of you talked about the repercussions of being together? You two are the first, so we don't have a base line to go on yet, but I would expect her fertility to be high, Nickolas.

The possibility floored him. He hadn't thought about having children before. And even though Ian and Jays had used the term Breeder, it hadn't sunk in. He turned to look at Jessica. He focused on her, looking for anything different.

She's not yet, Nick, but the two of you should figure out what you want to do soon.

Meeting Jessica's eyes, Nick gasped a breath. He hadn't realized that he'd stopped breathing. Her expression was growing mulish, a sure sign that she was getting tired of waiting. He cleared his throat. "I, um. Well, Ian was just wondering if we had discussed how our different caste would affect us. You know...like how our power is different...that sort of thing."

Nickolas Ian Sinclair! Do NOT misrepresent my words.

Glaring at Ian, Nickolas snorted. "I'm not a child."

Then stop acting like one and repeat what I said.

"You're not repeating what he said, are you?"

Glaring at both of them, Nick threw his head back into the chair. "Fine, but don't blame me, Jess. He said that you aren't pregnant yet, but you will be soon. That was the difference that he was referring to."

Her mouth dropped open, then swallowing convulsively, she stood up and started to pace. "I see. That's...I see."

"Exactly. He's right though, it is something we should be aware of."

She sank back down on the hearth and looked at the chair Ian was sitting in. The expression on her face was clearly stunned. "I've been so busy my whole life with plans about avoiding anyone associated with Valkyries that I never once considered having a family."

"Growing up in the Facility doesn't lend itself to planning for the future, either."

Well now that I've planted that little seed, it's time I—

Ian's pleased voice cut off abruptly and sent a sense of alarm coursing through Nickolas. He sat up and looked at his grandfather's pale face. The vacant look in Ian's eyes reinforced Nick's concern, and he turned to search out the window into the dark night. Even with the snow cover, the lack of moonlight still left the surrounding terrain black.

Jessica rose and moved away from the window. "Nick, what's happening?" she whispered.

The valley is under attack, Nickolas. Gabriel has found you. That's the extent of what I can find out immediately.

"Thanks, Ian." Rising swiftly, he grabbed Jessica's coat and threw it at her before grabbing his own. "We're under attack. We need to get out of the building." *Chris, Gabriel's here. Do you see anything out there?*

A thrum of shock and then alarm coursed along his connection to his brother.

Nothing unusual. Are you sure?

Yes.

I'll let the scout group know.

Donald, wake up. I need you to get everyone up. The Facility has found us.

Securing his coat, Nickolas stepped out onto the little covered porch and looked around carefully. *Dad, do you hear me?*

Nickolas?

Yes. I believe the valley is under attack. I'll know more in a minute.

After a brief moment of silence, his father replied, *Be careful.*

With Jessica protected behind him, Nickolas listened to the sounds of the night. The lack of moonlight was going to be a problem. They may have better eyesight than a grounded, but they still needed some light. The starlight wasn't enough. Wisps and tendrils of fog were just starting to drift among the buildings and across the grounds.

It was about four thirty in the morning, still two hours until dawn. *Damn, Gabriel knows what he's doing.* The fog was starting to grow and Nickolas grabbed Jess's hand, pulling her down the stairs, hoping to get to Donald's cabin.

Dark, silent shapes drifted by overhead, and the two of them crouched down in the snow next to their building, looking up. Black blobs released from the silhouettes plummeted, leaving a trail of white to drift through the air. And the fog grew.

"Gas!" Jessica whispered next to him. "Hold on a minute."

He turned to look at her as she went into a trance. Her eyes started to glow lightly, and he froze. She came back in a rush, quickly shaking the trance off like a wolf sheds water.

"It's a concentrated form of inhibitor, Nickolas. It'll incapacitate all of the Seers and Casters. I don't know what it will do to the Hunters, but I expect it'll have some effect."

Dumfounded, he stared at her for a split second. "How do you know this?"

The corner of her mouth quirked up slightly. "It's one of my talents. I'm a purifier. I can detect and nullify poisons, or by extension, drugs. I guess I'm kind of like the fabled unicorn, you could say."

He felt a grin break across his face, and he looked at her intently. "No self-respecting unicorn would have anything to do with you anymore."

Snorting, she punched him in the arm. "I can call the wind and direct the gas into the south end, away from the inhabited areas."

"Fine, do it." He pulled her to her feet and checked between the houses. The blanket of gas was thickening, creeping around the buildings and seeping into the structures. It crawled its way knee-high across the ground toward them.

Swearing, Nickolas cast a shield around Jessica and himself. "Ok, Jess, the clock's ticking. We only have as much air as I have contained in the shield. So hurry up."

She closed her eyes, and he watched her concentrate. The trees started to sway lightly. Then the gas swirled and started to flow slowly toward the south instead of drifting aimlessly.

Leaving her to her task, Nickolas broad sent a wakeup call to the entire valley. *Aurora is under attack. We're being gassed. The gas is concentrated inhibitor. If you can make an airtight shield, do it. And take as many under it as you can.*

This is Hunter Prime Robin. There are forces in the woods; the shield is going up.

Everyone do what Nickolas says. And if you can, get above the gas. Anyone who is able, meet at the tower. Marcus's strong mind voice echoed through Nick's head, breaking in after Robin's.

"Nickolas, Chris is outside the shield."

"Keep working, Jess. We can't worry about him until we can get to him." Turning his attention away from Marcus and the Auroran Valkyries, Nickolas called Donald again.

♦ ♦ ♦

Wiping his eyes, Donald clutched the doorframe to Kieran's room, coughing. Covering his nose and mouth with his shirt sleeve, he stumbled over to slam the window shut. His cousin coughed violently on the floor next to his bed.

Donald grabbed Kieran's arm and dragged him out of the bedroom, yanking the door shut behind them. After lowering Kieran to the floor, Donald heard Nickolas calling him. Closing his eyes to concentrate better, he listened to his Alpha.

Donald, where are you? I need you and Kieran to come and protect Jessica.

We can't make it, Nick. The gas is too thick here. It's already in the cabin. I can barely hear you.

Can you get out? Can you get to any of the others?

Coughing again, Donald sank down next to his cousin. Kieran's coughing hadn't let up, and the empath was starting to shiver violently. He placed his hand on Kieran's shoulder and focused hard to push his reply to Nickolas. He could barely get the thoughts past the gravity of his own mind. *I don't think so, Nick. Kieran's in bad shape.*

Stay pu...

The sending dwindled away to nothing. The barrier that filled his mind was all too familiar. *Funny how this thickness never bothered me before, and now I feel like I'm deaf.*

He shook his head at the stuffed-up feeling and pushed the unexpected wave of nausea away. First he tried to make Kieran comfortable on the floor, then he rose and started ripping strips from a towel. He soaked them in the wash basin near the door, then tied one around his face and crouched down next to Kieran.

His cousin's eyes were wide and dilated; his coughing was more sporadic, the breath wheezing in his lungs. Donald reached out and tried to tie the wet cloth over Kieran's face, but his cousin suddenly came to life and started to fight him.

"Kieran, stop! It's me, Donald. I'm trying to help."

"Donald, help! Where are you?"

The hoarse, panicked voice ripped through him. "I'm right here."

Donald forced his smaller cousin down and held the cloth over his face while searching his eyes. *He can't see. I don't think he can hear, either.*

He grabbed Kieran's hand and gripped it, hoping he could convey that it was his touch and provide some comfort. But he soon realized that Kieran couldn't feel either. The gas had stripped away all sensory perception. Kieran was lost.

Donald tied the cloth in place and let go of him. The empath immediately curled up into a fetal position, rocking. Anger at Gabriel, and all of the others who had a hand in creating them, pulsed through Donald as he stood. In some ways, he was one of the lucky ones. He still had family, while most of the others had to abandon everyone they knew. He had at first too, at least until Kieran started to change and was brought in. After that, he never took family for granted again.

Breathing deeply through the wet cloth, Donald tried to settle his rebelling stomach. *They must have put something in the inhibitor to try and incapacitate all of us.*

He looked around the room and saw gas starting to leak in under the front door. He grabbed a second towel, rolled it up, and stuffed it against the crack then checked the rest of the windows and doors. Peering out into the darkness, he could see how thick the gas had accumulated around their cabin—and its source.

A gas canister had dropped against their house, right under Kieran's open bedroom window. *Now that would be our luck, wouldn't it? Damn.*

After a glance at his cousin curled up on the floor, Donald's resolve firmed. Nothing would take Kieran if he could help it. He grabbed his *boken*, the wooden practice sword he kept by the door, and settled down into the chair nearest Kieran.

To watch and to wait.

Gabriel stood in the snow and shook his wings, flicking the dripping water off of them. The battery torches, stuck into the ground around the perimeter of the small clearing, illuminated the slushy morass their booted feet had made. He cocked his head and eyed the melting snow on the branches above him. Drips of icy snow from the tree or squelching mud from the field? Sighing, he chose drips and stayed where he was.

Crossing his arms, he listened to his people relay their progress. Several of his men were on radios, staying in contact with the different arms of this operation. The scurrying of the others through the clearing churned the mud deeper as they continued to set up their retrieval equipment. When he chose this clearing for their base of operations, he founded it mainly on the distance from the rebels' valley; it wasn't so close that they would notice it easily, but it was barely close enough for them to work from.

Gabriel stepped back closer to the trunk of the tree, trying to stay clear of most of the drips, when one of the radio men caught his attention.

"Excuse me, please repeat. Hold on." The young radio man looked up with trepidation in his eyes.

"Yes. Is there a problem?" Gabriel asked.

"Sir, my teams report that they cannot enter the valley. There is some sort of barrier blocking the way. And the last barrage of gas canisters hit something as well and slid to the ground outside of the perimeter."

"Hmm. A physical shield? It's one thing to have a sight shield of that size. How did they manage a physical one?" He rubbed his chin for a moment. "Let's concentrate on subduing their forces outside of the shield."

He looked back at the communications man. "Tell all teams I want as many alive as possible. Nickolas and Jessica are the highest priority. Capture Christoff, and you have Nickolas. Marcus and any other high-ranking leaders are next. If we can't breach the valley's defenses, we need to thin their numbers. Take as many of their sentries as you can. After we have control of the region and have them under siege, then we'll worry about how to enter the valley."

"Yes, sir."

The young communications man relayed his orders, and Gabriel looked past the lights into the darkness.

"Besides," he spoke more to himself than to any of his underlings, "by that point, the gas that did make it into the valley may have done its job, and the shield might be down."

Flight

Gabriel leaned back against the trunk of the tree and pondered. "How did they create that shield? And what else can they do?"

Christoff jumped a low log and landed in the snow on the other side at a dead run. He dodged through the trunks of trees in the darkness trusting that the other three members of his scout group still paced him. All hell had broken loose in the forest on the heels of Nick's call. He caught sight of Adam briefly when fire blossomed several hundred feet to their right, followed by the distinctive sound of Facility-issue trank rifles.

The Hunters fled the invading force, trying to avoid the herding action. An unnatural fog wisped along the ground, kicked up by their passage, and Chris tried not to cough as he got a lungful. He saw scouts from different teams go down in the chaos. The thickness of the wilderness trapped them to the ground and allowed the recovery teams to pick them off.

Battling nausea, he ducked a branch unnecessarily, his shield taking the hit, and noticed that the still night was gone. The trees were beginning to dance around them. A soft call reached his ears and he tracked through the slush after his teammate. He jumped into a hole left by the death of one of the giant trees when it was toppled some time ago. Breathing hard, he counted all three of his team mates huddled in the muck.

"Have you heard anything?" Chris asked Ben, the Seer for their group. "I'm having trouble pushing my telepathy out."

"They've dropped gas on us, and Robin has raised the shield. We're on our own until Marcus can send us reinforcements. But he'll have to drop the shield briefly to do that. Not knowing what the situation in the valley is, there's no way for me to know if they can send help. I haven't been able to reach anyone since that initial flurry of broad sendings. Too much gas in my system too."

A gust of warm wind hit them then skittered away. "They're sending help all right. That has to be Aiden bringing the wind down on us."

"Good, that should help dissipate the gas, and if he brings in enough wind, it could help with any aircraft."

"What is your procedure for this sort of circumstance?"

"Try to defend and stay free. That's about it."

"Nice and simple. I like it. They're using trank weapons, so they want us alive. We don't need to be hampered like that. We need to meet up with some of the other groups to try and set up an ambush of..."

"Quiet, I hear something."

The sound of boots squishing through the melting snow reached Chris's ears too. "Let's spread out a little."

Pulling out a pyrocone, Chris got ready to take the shield off of it while Ben got his staff ready, then the first of the Facility people came into view.

"Meet up again at the big maple in the center of our range," Chris whispered, then he triggered the timer spell and threw the pinecone into the midst of the invading group.

The sudden explosion of fire took them by surprise, felling the two whose feet it had rolled under and igniting a third. Several others were singed when they didn't fall back fast enough. As the invaders were trying to beat out the flames, Christoff leapt out of the hole, the rest of his scout team following.

Shouts from behind let them know they'd been seen. Something impacted on his shield. He chanced a look over his shoulder and saw a Facility rifle aiming a second shot. Dodging around a tree, he lost track of the rest of his scouts as two more recovery people stepped out from behind some bushes.

He spun and struck one in the head with his heel while pulling the knife out of his boot; as he finished the spinning kick, he slashed the second man's throat.

Red dots prismed around him as several new arrivals targeted him. The gas masks they wore made them look like aliens.

"Crap." Reforming his shield, Chris pulled it in tighter, forming a layer just above his skin. Then Chris spread his wings and launched over their heads, doing a somersault, and landed running. There wasn't enough space to get much use out of his wings.

The sounds of shouting followed him into the darkness. Slipping, Chris slid to one knee in the slushy snow, regained his balance, then heard voices. He froze and pressed up against the trunk of the nearest tree, hoping to be overlooked.

"There's a group of three we have surrounded about a hundred feet over, sir."

"Where's the fourth?"

"Unknown. He slipped by us."

"Then he can't have gotten far yet. The trees are too thick for them to get airborne. Keep searching. Gas the others."

No! I need to warn them. He looked over his shoulder and around the edge of the tree. Four moving through the brush. Slipping his knife back into his boot, he leaned his head back against the trunk and slowed his breathing, centering himself. He tried to reach out to Ben, but Chris couldn't find him. *Damn it, where is he? Why can't I be better at this already?*

A small red eye winked on some distance in front of him, and Chris dropped to the ground. The small dart meant for him quivered in the tree. He rolled to the side then dove through some bushes, right into the path of several more invaders.

Tackling one around the knees, Chris pushed off of him like a springing cougar and slammed his fists into the midsection of another. They reacted to his presence quickly and spaced out, surrounding him.

Chris lunged at the nearest, shoving him over and backhanding him as he hit the ground. He felt the impact of several darts hit his shield, and he rolled off of the man, gaining his feet. He dove across the circle they now had him caged in. Pulling his knife, he stood looking at the Facility people.

"Stop!" The command echoed through the woods from his right.

Chris turned slowly and stared narrow-eyed at the Facility man who took a step into the circle and slowly removed his mask. His eyes widening slightly, Chris stared at Flynn.

"Hello, Chris." His former teammate smiled then turned to one of his men with a radio. "Call Gabriel. Tell him Christoff is outside of the shield."

Chapter Thirteen

Concentrating on bringing the wind to her hand, Jessica blocked out Nickolas's mental sendings. The wind was a fickle playmate; it wanted to go where it pleased, not obey another's will. She coaxed the little tendrils of breeze to blow gently but steadily as she gathered up as much of the dispersing gas as she could, urging it along a path against the cliff face to flow southward toward her.

She regulated her breathing while checking the flow of her power, slowing it and making sure she was maintaining a steady, even draw. The rustle of Nick moving next to her pulled part of her mind away from her task. "What's happened?"

"Donald and Kieran got gassed; they can't make it here," he said quietly as he shifted behind her. "From what Donald managed to send, it sounds like Kieran is in bad shape. Dev and Aiden made it above the gas though and are on their way."

"No, Nick, they are two of our best weapons. We need them out where they can do the most good."

"The most good is making sure you are protected."

Growling, she pulled back on her power. Her irritation had caused her power to pulse and the wind started to eddy and kick up stronger. "I can protect myself, Nickolas."

"They *will* defend you."

She didn't have the time or power to spare to fight the strength behind that order. Snarling at him, she turned back to the gas.

"Jess, is all of the gas gone from our immediate vicinity? Dev says they're circling above us."

"Tell them to drop down as close to the shield as possible. You need to be ready to open the barrier quickly in case their wings stir up some of the gas."

The rush of colder air circled around Jessica as Nickolas let the other two in. She took a deep breath and realized how much easier this would be if she could feel the wind on her skin as well as in her mind. She threw a quick glance at Dev and Aiden then nearly dropped her hold on the wind when she saw Nickolas beyond them, looking at her from outside of his shield. "Nickolas what are you doing?"

"Ok, Dev." She heard his voice distorted through the shield just as she felt the Caster impose another shield just inside of Nickolas's, then her mate dropped his.

"Nickolas Sinclair!"

"I need to get to the control tower, Jess. It's more important for you to clear the gas from the valley; Dev can hold the shield while you work. They will protect you," he shouted through the shield.

"Who's going to protect you? You idiot! You're the one who's still hurt. You can't even fly yet." She shrugged Dev's hand from her shoulder as she grabbed her power with both mental hands to maintain control.

Raising his hand, Nick pressed it up to the shield. "I'll be fine, Jess. You need to protect everyone in the valley."

She took a deep breath as she touched his hand through the shield. Then he turned and started to run across the valley. "You stupid, imbecilic male," she muttered after him. Then she took her fear and anger and channeled it into moving the gas out of harm's way. "So what did the two of you see while you were in the air?"

"We circled above the whole valley briefly. There were lights on in most of our people's cabins; a few had tried to make it to other cabins but were downed by the gas. There were a few of the Auroran Valkyries who were able to create airtight shields. I asked one of them to go and warn all of our people who aren't off of the drugs yet to stay inside. The others were carefully moving the canisters of gas or ferrying others above the gas, like I did with Aiden."

"Good. If the gas canisters are moved to a centralized location, it'll make my job easier. One of you call Beth and make sure they are taking them south, where I'm sending most of the gas. With the valley shield in place, the flow is just going to run up against the wall, so I need to neutralize it and soon, or everyone will be incapacitated eventually." The wind picked up force, and the fog of gas started flowing quicker.

"The last drop of canisters hit the shield, Jess, and slid to the ground, so there is loose gas outside with our scouts. Even if we opened the shield, it couldn't guarantee that we would get clean air in exchange. Besides, we would just be sending our scouts more poison to contend with." Aiden's voice sounded far off to her as she concentrated. "I could do what you are doing and call up a major wind to blow the gas outside away. Besides, if it's big enough, it'll keep any aircraft away."

"Go for it, Aiden; anything that will help is a good idea."

Dev's voice broke in. "Beth says to tell you that she has them moving the canisters to the bank of the stream where it exits the valley in the south. She's left Jays in charge of sick bay and is out starting to collect those who've been affected."

"Tell her as soon as I've neutralized the gas, we'll join her." Ignoring them now, Jessica closed her eyes and visualized the place Beth was talking about. She imagined all of the gas that she had been herding forming a thick bank trapped up against the wall. Then reaching her mental hand out, she tried to touch it. A growl tore from her throat when she realized that this wasn't going to work.

"Dev, we need to move. I have to be closer to the gas to neutralize it."

"How much closer?"

"Closer. Now move." She stared at the Caster then spread her wings, letting him know they were going.

With a sigh, he expanded the shield enough to allow all three of them to fly. "We need to be careful, Jess. Flying in the shield is a bit more difficult than normal."

She nodded her head, then they all launched together. It wasn't too far to the stream's exit point, and after a moment she could see the bank of gas swirling where she had it trapped up against the cliff wall and the shield.

They dropped down to land close to the surging edge of the gathered gas. She studied it for a moment then took a deep breath and looked at Aiden and Dev. She knew they weren't going to like what she was about to do. She didn't like what she needed to do.

"Dev, can you make a hole in the shield like Nick did for you guys? Or do you need to drop the whole thing?"

"I think I can make a hole. But it's not like I've had a lot of practice."

"None of us have. Fine, I need you to make a second shield around the two of you then either drop this one or make a door for me."

"Wait a minute. You're not going out there."

Turning, she trapped their gazes. Aiden hadn't said anything, but she could see his objection in his eyes. She stared them down. "There's no choice. If I'm to neutralize the gas, I must touch it."

Waiting, they both finally looked away, but not without promises of retribution later for making them do this. She moved up to the edge of Dev's shield and watched the second barrier form between them. That would protect them from any of the gas leaking in.

After taking a deep breath of the warm but still clean air, she nodded. When she turned back to the shield, a hole just big enough for her opened. She stepped through it, and the cold of the night air slapped her. Not giving herself any time to reconsider, she walked straight into the cloud of gas.

Diving into her well of power, she arched through it, turning with her momentum and rising back to the surface, dragging as much of her power with her as her wake would pull. She burst through to the surface, and her power fountained up around her.

She glowed with the strength of her energy. Jessica reached out into the blankness around her, and pouring everything she had into it, she started ripping the nebulous stuff apart. She worked as fast as she could, but there was still too much for her to reduce back to its component parts before she needed to take a breath.

Her vision grayed from lack of oxygen; she had to face the inevitable. She started to take shallow breaths hoping to keep most of the crap out of the deep part of her lungs. But too soon she was suppressing her coughs, and her effectiveness dropped as more of her energy had to be spent neutralizing the gas she was inhaling.

Finally, a tendril of fresh air wound its way around her, and she realized she'd closed her eyes. Opening them, she found herself on her knees, but most of the fog was gone. She pushed through and finished neutralizing the rest of the gas then fell to her hands, coughing.

Nickolas ran through the darkness and formed another shield to protect him from the tendrils of twisting gas flowing across the fields. He nearly fell over objects he couldn't see but found the going easier once he cleared the buildings and struck out across the snow-covered meadow. He was not happy about leaving Jessica, but he knew she had to stay to clear the gas, and he had a strong feeling that he really needed to get to Chris. Something was wrong, but he couldn't tell what through their link.

Thankfully, Jessica had been too preoccupied neutralizing the gas to notice Chris through her bond with him. His breath rasping through this throat, Nick pushed his body on. The sight of the gas flowing like a river across the valley was encouraging.

The desire to spread his wings was overpowering, and he growled, pushing harder, taking his anger out on his body. The irrational feeling that it had let him down flooded him. He couldn't reach the top of the cliff himself. And he hated that.

Lashing out with his thoughts, he broad sent, *Someone come pick me up!*

Nickolas? I'm on my way. Where are you? A familiar voice sounded in Nick's head.

I'm almost to the base of the cliff.

As he neared the cliff wall, the mist of gas was gone, pulled by Jessica to the south end of the valley. The dark shape of Robin dropped to the ground in front of him as he came to a halt and dropped the shield, breathing the fresh air. He placed his hands on his head and walked for a moment, gaining control of his breath, feeling his weakened muscles burn from the strain.

"Nickolas, are you ok? Will you be up for this?"

Nick glared at Jessica's brother as he took a deep breath then stopped before him. "Get me up there."

A grin flirted with the corners of his mouth as Robin nodded. "Hold on tight."

Nick hooked his strong, uninjured arm around Robin's neck then snugged his left hand into the Hunter's belt while Robin carefully wrapped his arms around him, pinning his wings to his back.

"Ok, here we go." And spreading his wings, the Hunter Prime launched into the sky. "Marcus just arrived and is getting a head count."

Nick tried his best to relax and not make this more difficult for Robin. They ponderously rose up above the cliff, and he saw the dark glassiness of the lake for the first time. A four-story structure rose up beside it. Torches lit the dirt courtyard in front of the door where close to a hundred Valkyries milled. A few carried boxes out of the building.

They touched down at the edge of the lit area, and Robin let go of him after making sure he had his feet under him. Nick carefully stretched his wings then followed Robin up to where Marcus listened to an older Valkyrie.

"Some of the scout groups are not reporting in any longer, and we haven't been able to reach their Seers. Those that are still responding have reported fighting throughout the woods."

"That would account for the fires we've glimpsed in the distance, Nathan."

"And the explosions," Robin added.

"Hello, Nickolas," Marcus murmured.

Nick nodded an acknowledgement.

Nathan eyed him briefly, then continued. "There have been reports of pockets of gas throughout the woods as well, and the winds are steadily picking up."

"Thank you, Nathan. Kelley, what have you got to report?"

"The gliders managed to drop at least two runs of gas canisters before the shield went up. Those that managed to escape the gas have Nickolas's warning to thank. Gas was blanketing the valley, but someone's moving the wind, forcing the gas into one area for some reason. At least two thirds of the valley is clear now."

"That's Jessica's doing. She's trying to neutralize the gas. I suspect the wind you're noticing outside the shield is probably coming from Aiden."

Marcus nodded and gestured for Kelley to continue. "There've been quite a few who've been affected by the gas. Now that most of it's been cleared, Beth is out with some of the shield casters locating the injured; she's left Jays in charge of the infirmary."

"All right. That gets us up to date, folks. There's close to a hundred of us outside the shield, and the count so far of those who have managed to make it up here is eighty-eight. That leaves about two hundred and fifty injured or incapacitated Valkyries in the valley. There are an unknown number of invaders outside at this time. Their goal appears to be to capture us, but there's no telling if that will change. I don't know about you, but I've found that capture is not really to my liking.

"The best choice we have at the moment is to arm up and go out to try and bring our scouts back under cover. The more able bodies we bring home, the better we will be able to defend the valley until everyone who was gassed has recovered. Besides, I don't want to leave even one of our people to Gabriel if we can help it.

"The imbuers are handing out the stockpile of weapons; once they're done, everyone needs to be ready to move when I drop the shield. I don't want it down for long."

Clearing his throat, Nickolas caught everyone's attention. "Why are you going to drop the whole shield? Won't that give Gabriel the chance to slip people in anywhere along the border? Why don't you just make a hole in the wall, like a doorway?"

The blank expressions facing him made Nick narrow his eyes. "What?"

"You can do that?" Marcus asked carefully.

"Yes."

Marcus's eyes turned to the milling Valkyries. Most were standing watching them, waiting. "All right, it looks like we're ready. Divide up into eight or nine groups. They're succeeding in taking out groups of four, so don't make your groups too small. We're reinforcements and rescuers. Get as many of our scouts as you can and get them back here. Even if you can't get through the shield, you'll have better defense with the lake and the shield on two sides." Turning back to Nickolas, Marcus raised his eyebrows.

Without a word, Nick walked toward the shield. Marcus and Robin fell in behind him, and the rest formed their groups to join them. When he reached the shield, Nick raised his hand and touched the barrier.

His mind quested out until he met the braided energy that formed the defensive shield over the valley. After taking a moment to learn the feel of the energy, he wove his own tendril of power into the cloth of the shield, then parted the curtain of power without breaking the integrity of the casting. It was like slipping a needle in between the threads of a cloth. He held the portal open and stepped back. Everyone stared in wonder at the hole.

"Well, boys and girls," Marcus raised his voice. "Let's get out there." And he was the first to step through.

Once everyone was outside, Nickolas stepped over and let the hole close up behind him. Most of the groups had taken off already; the only people left were his father, Robin, and about ten other Hunters.

"I didn't think you'd have the sense to stay put," his father said.

"Chris is out here."

Nodding his head, Marcus turned, and they all walked into the woods.

Flight

♦ ♦ ♦

Gabriel rolled his shoulders then stretched his wings, closing them with a snap. A cold drip splashed on his neck. With a low growl, he shook the melted snow out of his hair and started seriously considering the merits of mud. This strange, warm wind was quickly melting the snow accumulation.

He sighed as he listened to the radio reports coming in. His teams were managing to capture some of the rebel Valkyries, but at a cost. He had fifteen confirmed injured or dead so far, but he suspected the real number was higher. He had three hundred men here. His people, at best guess, assumed that there could only be about two hundred Valkyries in the valley. But from the looks of this mess, he thought his people were wrong. His officers were estimating the forces outside of the valley at about one hundred. Gabriel seriously doubted that they would put a full half of their population on guard duty.

One of his communications officers jumped up from the table he was sitting at and started over to Gabriel, excitement shining in his eyes. "Sir, Flynn just radioed in. His team has a group of four captured. Christoff is among them."

A slow smile creased Gabriel's face. "Christoff? Fate does favor me. What luck. I think I'll go and say hello to Ian's grandson. What is their location?"

"They're in the northeast quadrant center, sir."

Leaving the dubious protection of the trees, Gabriel strode down into the muddy clearing. Once he was clear of the trees, he spread his wings and flew up above the buffeting treetops. He had chosen a clearing a few miles south of the reported sentry perimeter that the rebels used.

He skirted the actual location of the valley to fly over the contested land. He adjusted his wings as the wind slammed into him. Small fires lit the landscape below, marking spots where his people had clashed with the feral Valkyries. Entering the northeast quadrant, he felt the effort to fly through the turbulent winds in his chest muscles. He reached the center of the quadrant and started to scan the terrain more closely. A large fire drew his attention, and skimming along the treetops, he saw through the waving trees some of the portable lights his people had brought with them set up in a ring.

Within the circle he was able to see Christoff fighting two full recovery units. As he circled, he watched the Hunter break the neck of one of the men as another tried to take him to the ground by leaping on his back, only to get thrown across the clearing.

They finally brought him down with ropes. Like an unbroken stallion, four of the recovery team members ran at him with lines, tangling him up long enough for the rest to tackle him.

Gabriel slowed his speed as much as possible in the difficult flying conditions, located the biggest gap between the tossing trees, and folding his wings, he dropped down through the canopy. At the last instant, when he was clear, he opened his wings, breaking his momentum, then back-winged to a landing in front of his newest captive.

Christoff still struggled as the recovery teams roped his arms and legs, trying to immobilize him. They got the rope over him then held his wings down, pinning him to the ground.

Gabriel looked over at the dead man then to Flynn. "Why didn't you trank him?" he asked, nodding at the still struggling Hunter.

"He has some sort of shield. It's the only explanation we can come up with. Every shot we took at him bounced off."

He looked back down at the still futilely struggling Hunter. The six recovery men had just finished lashing his hands behind his back, pinning his wings along with tying his knees and ankles together. They left his heaving body lying on its side.

"Flynn, let's get him trussed up for pickup. I want him out of here and in the helicopter."

Christoff looked up at him, and Gabriel could see the fear in the depths of his eyes. But that didn't stop the daggers when he looked at Flynn. Gabriel smiled.

"There's a problem, Gabriel. I just got word that the helicopters have been grounded. The sudden storm winds are too strong," Flynn replied quietly. "They don't think they'll be able to pick up anyone."

Gabriel's eyes narrowed in annoyance, and he looked at the people around him. More recovery personnel were carrying the other three unconscious members of Christoff's team into the small clearing. "Then we'll have to hike him out—"

A sudden shift in the power currents surrounding them caught his attention, and he paused. His mind flashed out, and he tasted the source. A change in the shield around the valley; a lot of new Valkyries just passed out into his arena.

Including one power signature that he would always recognize—Nickolas.

Too many. There are just too many for me to get at him. Huffing in irritation, Gabriel looked at Nickolas's brother. *And there's no way we'll be able to get Christoff out of here now.*

His brain racing, Gabriel hauled Christoff to his knees; the skintight shield may have protected him from the darts, but the way it was made, it wouldn't protect his mind. He snagged the Hunter's gaze with his own and forced his power to wrap around Christoff.

He smiled as he felt the Hunter fight against him and pushed, breaching the surface of Christoff's personal barriers. Just enough to force a small coercion.

"Drop the shield, Chris."

The Hunter fought him, breaking out in a sweat, but Gabriel was patient, even if he didn't have a lot of time. He knew it wouldn't take Nickolas long to find his brother, and Gabriel wasn't willing to lose everything. He grabbed his captive's chin and repeated, "Drop the shield."

Christoff snarled in defiance, but the shield surrounding him dispersed as the Hunter glared, starting to struggle.

Gabriel probed Chris's mind but quickly came to the realization that he would be too hard to break in the time he had. Gabriel let him go and the bound man fell back to his side in the slush. Gabriel reached into his thigh pocket and pulled out a small vial, followed by a needle and syringe. He peeled the paper on the sterile packaging, inserted the needle, then quickly inverted the bottle and drew up the injection. Chris's eyes got wide, and he blasted out a weak mental call. *Nickolas!*

Clamping a mental hand over the Hunter, Gabriel damped any more attempts at communication. "Now, now, none of that." He tapped the syringe for air bubbles. "This is a little present that I brought along, in the off chance I got my hands on your brother, but since it looks like that won't happen this time, I don't mind using it on you."

A couple of the recovery people stepped forward. One grabbed Christoff by his hair, wrenching his head back and holding his throat while the other hooked his arms, freeing one for a third man to stretch out.

The impotent fury that radiated from the Hunter made Gabriel smile. He was looking forward to this. The trials with Zach and the subsequent guinea pigs had been so promising.

And this would be the first field trial.

Deftly inserting the needle into Christoff's vein, Gabriel gave him the injection then stepped back to watch it go to work. The men lashed his arm back then released him, the breath heaving in Chris's lungs.

"What did you do to me?" He groaned, then his back arched in pain. His legs dug into the slush as he writhed on the ground.

Slowly circling the Hunter, Gabriel watched the first stages of the drug take effect. When Christoff was only panting in pain, after the initial convulsions, Gabriel crouched down to stare into his eyes. "Do you feel every protective barrier on your mind as it is peeled back, Chris? Defenses you never even knew you had?" Fear and a glimmer of understanding stared at Gabriel. "You're mine now, Christoff, and through you, I will have your brother and Jessica Reuther."

Christoff shook his head and moaned. "No. You can't do this. Leave them alone." He struggled and tried to push away, but Gabriel grabbed him by the hair, holding his head up.

"This was the primer dose. The effects are worse the first time, but they're still not pleasant on later boosters. It leaves your mind open, defenseless to me. Now, I want the answers to a few questions. How many Valkyries reside in the valley?"

Shaking, the Hunter tried to refuse to answer, but Gabriel gave a soft mental push.

"Three hundred and fifty," Chris gasped.

"Does that count the Facility Valkyries?"

Frustration filled Christoff's eyes. "No."

A smile settled on Gabriel's face as he got the Hunter's measure. "How many Facility Valkyries are there here?"

"One."

Laughing, Gabriel pushed again. "Good try. How many escaped from the Facility?"

Growling, Christoff ground out, "Fifty-five."

"Fifty-five? That's too many; I'll have to look into that. Do you know how many Casters and Seers there are?"

"No."

"Do you know what they can do?"

"No."

He looked into Chris's eyes and was able to detect the barest hint of triumph. "I think you're managing to lie, but I don't have the time right now to pursue more detailed questions to narrow it down. How bad were Nickolas's injuries?"

"Bad."

"What were they?" Interesting, there was something about Nick's injuries that Christoff didn't want to mention.

"Shoulder bullet wound, ripped wing sail, exhaustion, and exposure." The Hunter shuddered with his attempt to refrain from finishing.

"What else?"

"Mental trauma."

"Fascinating. Now I wish I had more time to pursue this. I would like to hear the details. Jessica Reuther, what is her condition?"

Closing his eyes, Christoff's mouth twisted as he tried to refuse the compulsion to answer. He finally stuttered out, "She has completed the change."

"What caste is she?"

"Breeder."

His eyes narrowed and he stared at Nickolas's brother. "Breeder? There is no such caste that I am aware of."

Christoff opened his eyes and stared his hatred at Gabriel.

"What caste is Nickolas?"

"Breeder," Christoff spat.

Whistling, Gabriel released Christoff's hair. "No wonder Ian went to such lengths to protect Nickolas." He stared off, thinking for a moment, but Christoff's groan brought him back to the here and now. The feeling that his time was running out filtered through him, so he pulled Chris into a kneeling position, then holding his prisoner's head securely, Gabriel released his power.

His mind easily overpowered the Hunter's, thanks to the influence of the mind drug. "Christoff, the next time I call you, you are to come to me without delay but without letting anyone else know that you are leaving. Do you understand?" Unsurprisingly, there was frantic fear bordering on panic in the Hunter's eyes. "You will forget everything you have experienced here today until I call you."

Shivering violently, Christoff moaned. "No. You can't do this, Gabriel."

Smiling, he released Christoff once more. "You're mine, Chris, and soon, thanks to you, I'll have Nickolas and Jessica." Striking Christoff hard in the temple, Gabriel watched the Hunter crumple into unconsciousness.

He rose and looked around at the silent crowd. "Ok, people, let's get out of here. We don't have a lot of time before Nickolas and a large group of rescuers arrive."

He turned to look at Flynn. "Call a full retreat. Anyone they have subdued and they can carry out, do so. Otherwise, I want everyone hiking within fifteen minutes."

"Injured and dead?"

"If they were stupid enough to get killed, leave them. If they can hike, fine. If someone is willing to carry them, fine; otherwise, leave them." His attention drawn back to Christoff, Gabriel smiled. "I have what I need now. I have a foot in the door."

◆ ◆ ◆

An explosion of fire to the right had Nickolas ducking behind a tree. The four Hunters Robin ordered to guard him crouched around close by. *Now I know how Jessica felt. At least she only has to contend with two.*

He hoped that the others were in position; he looked around the edge of the tree. There were six Aurorans bound, sitting at the base of some trees. Twenty of Gabriel's men watched the forest intently; waiting for the next batch of detainees to be brought to them.

They had already managed to free four other Hunters who had been held singly. They'd each joined Marcus's group. It was better than trying to make it back to the shield without support and getting captured again.

Another two scouts were carried in and dropped to land in an unconscious thud next to the others. These two looked like they'd gotten gassed. *Marcus? Robin? Are you in place?*

Yes, Nick.

I'm almost there. Robin's mind voice held grim determination. He had the hardest point to achieve. *I'm there. Give it a count of five, then I'm going.*

The guards were nervous, looking in every direction.

Nickolas took a deep breath, then on five he reached out into the clearing with his power and gripped the ankles of as many of the enemy as he could. Robin dropped through the tree canopy, landing in the midst of the guards, his feet a blur as he took out as many as possible.

The stunned men tried to react to the sudden attack, only to find they couldn't move or they tripped over their own people, who Nick had stuck to the ground.

Marcus and the rest of their group charged in while Robin held their attention. Using his light whips, Marcus snapped the necks of the men who got close enough to try and slash at Robin's wings. Other than stick a few more to the ground, there was very little for Nickolas to do. The protection foisted on him prevented him from participating.

The confrontation was over quickly. He crouched down next to the two unconscious Valkyries and touched one, hoping the little bit of healing talent he had might help.

Unfortunately they stayed out cold. He looked at the rest, but their injuries were minor.

The Facility people were collected, a few were dead but more were injured or unconscious. Nickolas bent down to check the pulse of one and got a surprise when the man lunged up at him, grabbing the front of his shirt and swinging a knife. Nickolas grabbed the wrist and dove in a roll to pull the man over and then underneath him. He slammed the hand with the weapon into the slush to no avail, so he grabbed the attacker's throat and squeezed.

He growled and planted his knee in the man's crotch, pressing down. "If you want to live, drop the knife."

Booted feet surrounded them, but they were smart enough to leave him alone for the moment. The Facility man's eyes rolled, looking at everyone before he released the knife. "They aren't who you need to worry about," Nick whispered an inch from the man's face.

"Nickolas?"

Hands grabbed the back of his jacket between his wings, pulling him off of his prey. Snarling, he shook them off and faced his father. Marcus's worried frown was replaced with censure as he turned to the four guards. "You are supposed to prevent that sort of thing," he spoke quietly.

"It won't happen again, Marcus," the lead stated, pulling himself to attention.

Flowing up behind them, Robin leaned over the Hunter's shoulder. "It had better not, or you'll face me in the ring."

Nodding curtly, the Hunter turned back to the other three and, much to Nick's disgust, they immediately surrounded him.

The twinkle in his father's eyes made Nickolas bare his teeth in a snarl, which did nothing to change his position. He rubbed his shoulder; the wound ached from the exertion.

"Are you ok, Nickolas?"

"I'm fine."

"You should go back with this group, Nick. We'll find Chris."

He leveled a stare at his father, and the older Valkyrie sighed. "Fine, have it your way. Robin, once everyone is ready and the Facility people are tied, let's get moving."

He paced the edge of the area and held his arm stiffly at his side, trying not to jar it. The protectiveness that radiated from his guards told him they saw his weakness.

The wash of fear that slammed into him through one of his bond links took him by surprise.

Nickolas!

The strength of the mind call and its abrupt end choked him. *Chris! Where are you? Christoff!*

"Oh no, Chris." Nickolas didn't realize he'd spoken out loud until he had both Marcus and Robin in front of him. "They must have him. I need to get to him, now." Nick started to move toward the biggest open space among the trees and loosened his wings, only to be forcibly turned by his father.

"Don't you dare, Nickolas. You are not cleared to fly yet. Robin will take to the air and start searching; you will focus on trying to use your link to narrow down the search."

Nick snapped his wings closed. He knew his father was right, but that didn't mean he had to like it. The sound of Robin's wings as he took off barely registered as Nick plucked the thread that led to his brother. Christoff's mind was shielded from him, but Gabriel couldn't block the deep bond they shared. Scenting the psychic winds like a blood hound, Nickolas turned slowly until he felt the direction. "He's this way."

"Let's go," Marcus commanded.

Striking off at a lope, they were back to their original number of people. All of the scouts they'd rescued banded together to get the wounded back to the shield. With the onset of dawn, the going became quicker and easier. But it still took too long as far as Nick was concerned. The pain, anger, and terror that flowed down his link pushed him on.

As they traveled through the forest, they were finding fewer of their people, either fighting or captured. It looked like the Facility was abandoning their plan and running. He ignored the amazed grumbles from his guards, who were surprised at his capability given his injuries.

Finally, a shout to his left drew his attention. Shoving through some bushes, he came out into a clearing and found Robin kneeling at Chris's side. The other three members of Christoff's scout group lay nearby, unconscious in the slush.

Nick dropped to his knees next to Robin and stared in disgust at the ropes binding his brother.

"Too much wind. Gabriel couldn't get them out," Robin said. "Looks like they left in a hurry."

Together, they got Chris untied and straightened his limbs. Carefully, Nick turned Chris's head to the side and examined the purple bruise forming.

Marcus crouched down and reached out a hand, gently brushing the slush-soaked, stringy blond hair away from the swelling. Without looking up, he issued orders. "Robin, get the nets ready. Jeff, how are the others?"

"It looks like they were gassed, Marcus."

"All right, two of us per net should get everyone out of here." Marcus rose and handed Robin the net he'd been carrying.

Nick shuddered at the thought of the net; he picked up his brother, settling him against his sore shoulder, and turned away.

"Nickolas, you are going in the net." The quiet order from his father stopped him.

Shaking his head, he just stood there.

Robin approached him slowly then stopped in front of him, catching his gaze. "You know it's the fastest way to get Chris to help, Nick."

"I can't." Reluctantly, he handed his brother over to the other Hunter. "I'll meet you back at the valley."

Marcus's voice behind him was set in stone. "No, Nickolas. We will *not* leave you unprotected. If you want Christoff to get to help, then get in the net."

Whirling back, he stalked to his father. "I. Can't. You don't get it. I can't be confined like that." The two of them stared each other down, neither one willing to give in.

Robin's voice broke into their contest of wills. "What if you sit in the net like a swing? We can still carry it that way, and you won't be confined. Will you be willing to compromise that way? It'll get all of us back to the valley quicker."

Nick broke eye contact with Marcus to look at the sincerity in Robin's eyes. Then he looked at the rest; the others were all ready to go. Chris's teammates were lashed securely in the nets, and Robin had lowered Chris into one and was tying it shut. Nick ran his hand through his hair and winced at the stiffness from his unused muscles. A glance at his father showed that it had been noticed.

He took a deep breath and pushed his insanity deep into himself then looked at his father. "Fine, let's go."

Relief flashed through Marcus's eyes, but he quickly covered it. Two of Nickolas's guards clipped the net between them and spread it out on the ground like a hammock. Nick settled into it like Robin had suggested, his fists clutched in the mesh. He looked to Marcus and Robin, who were transporting Chris, in sick dread.

"You stay in that net, Nick. Your wings won't be ready for your weight for at least another week. Don't break them." Spreading their wings, Marcus and Robin led the group into the sky.

Jerked into the air, Nickolas hissed in pain, his fingers turning white. Frustrated with himself, he watched the trees flash by underneath them while he wrestled with his private demons.

Jessica pressed her forehead to the wet ground, coughing until she felt like she would rip her insides apart. Her muffled senses and the nausea she felt made her disoriented. A gentle touch startled her, and she started coughing again. Aiden pulled her against him to support her while the spasm shook her. She tried to take slow, shallow breaths as she rested her head on his shoulder and looked into Dev's worried eyes.

"You did it. The gas is gone," the Caster said quietly.

Her voice hoarse, she replied, "So is my talent." She closed her eyes and suppressed a wave of nausea. "Dev, can you please call Beth and tell her the gas is gone and that we're going to check on our people." She relaxed into Aiden and started trying to force her body's compliance.

After a moment, Dev asked, "Are you ok? Beth thinks you should go to the infirmary."

"We need to get to Kieran. Nick said he got gassed. He'll need help more than I do. My body will clear the gas quicker than anyone else's. But it'll still take some time." She pushed herself upright and stretched her aching muscles then flapped her wings. "Come on, there are people who need our help."

With the two of them flanking her, they launched into the brightening sky. After a short flight, they landed in front of Donald's and Kieran's cabin, and she bounded up the steps only to get jerked back by Dev.

Aiden pounded on the door and yelled. Pale and shaking, Donald pulled the door open then leaned on his weapon, breathing deeply of the fresh air coming in the door.

"Aiden, throw all the windows open, will you? Air the last of the gas out," Donald instructed hoarsely. "Status, Dev?"

"Jess cleared the gas from the valley. Nick left for the tower saying something about Chris being in trouble. The valley shield is in place, and none of the enemy made it in that we can tell."

Aiden came back to the door, his face a blank mask. Even more worried about Kieran's condition from Aiden's response, Jessica pushed past Dev and scowled at Donald until he let her by.

"The gas might not be clear, Jess," Donald rasped through a raw throat.

"Give me a break," she muttered. Then more loudly, "I've already had full exposure, so there's nothing in here that's going to make it worse."

Once inside, she sank to her knees next to the trembling empath.

Donald used the staff for support as he walked up to her side. "Kieran likes to sleep with the window open, and a gas canister hit the ground right underneath it. He took in a lot before I got the window closed and got him out of the room. It's obviously some sort of inhibitor, because my head feels all stuffed with cotton, and I lost my telepathy, but there's something else in there. The nausea has been intense."

She gently removed the makeshift mask from Kieran's face then looked into his glassy eyes. "I'm pretty sure they put that in to incapacitate the Hunters, so you couldn't fight back."

"But it's worse for Kier. He's spent the whole time curled up on the floor with convulsions hitting him. I don't think he can see or hear at all."

The clamminess of his skin concerned her. "We need to get him to the infirmary. Is there anything else, Donald?"

"He's calmed down somewhat; at first he couldn't stop coughing, and there was blood in it."

She waved Dev over to pick up the empath then stood and looked at Donald. "With both Nick and Chris out of the valley, you're the Alpha Hunter. I want you and Aiden to go gather up our people. With so many still on the drugs, they wouldn't have heard the warnings, and I don't know how the gas will have affected them. Make sure everyone's all right and bring them over to the longhouse."

Aiden shook his head. "I was ordered to guard you."

"I'm fine. You're needed by the others."

"Sorry, Jess, I agree," Donald said. "Especially since your talent is knocked out, and we don't know for sure that no one made it into the valley, do we? Dev's got his hands full with Kieran. I'll be fine, and I'm sure that I'll have help after the first cabin or two. Aiden stays to protect you."

A growl rumbled in her throat at their stubbornness. "Fine, Donald, do it yourself. I hope they give you a ton of trouble." She followed Dev out the door and wanted to kick him when she saw his grin.

"I doubt anyone except Nick could give me more trouble than you," Donald said with a sigh.

She turned her glare on him, but then she detected the uneasy sickness he tried to hide in his eyes. Swallowing back her retort, she stepped off the porch and looked up at the waving trees in the dawn light. She met Aiden's eyes, and he nodded.

"I've managed a good storm. Without proper guidance, I don't know how effective it's been. I've just tried to make sure there was a lot of wind, hoping to keep any of their aircraft out of the area."

"I bet it's helped."

They took their leave of Donald, and the three of them flew across the valley to land in the courtyard in a flurry of wings. Two Hunters stood guard at the infirmary doors, which they opened for them. The usually quiet room was full of hustle and bustle. Orchestrating the chaos, Jays waved them over as soon as he saw them.

Dev held Kieran's small body as Jays checked the Empath's pulse then stared into his vacant eyes. Jess didn't like the worried look he got.

"Bring him over here." The fledgling led them into one of the small rooms then asked an Auroran for some equipment as Dev laid Kieran out on the bed. "No one else who was exposed has looked this bad."

"The stronger you are, the harder it hits you," she said.

He looked thoughtful. As soon as his gadgets arrived, he got to work. She stepped over to the other side of the bed.

"How are you doing, Jess? I hear we have you to thank for getting rid of the gas. Though looking at you, I can tell you were exposed."

"The only way for me to nullify it was to step into it. It's working its way out of my system. I don't feel great, but I can now sense the poison in myself and Kieran. I couldn't do that a bit ago. Hopefully I'll be able to clear it out of my system enough to be able to help Kieran soon."

"Well, that answers one mystery. We wondered why you needed such high doses of inhibitor. Your body burned it up much faster than it should." Jays pulled a blanket up around the unresponsive empath then looked at her. "They've changed the drug's composition somehow. He shouldn't be reacting this way."

A commotion out in the main room drew their attention. They hurried out and found Robin carrying Christoff, with Marcus and Nickolas on his heels. Jays cleared the nearest bed and had Robin lay him down.

Marcus glanced at the full room. "Jays, we need to get back out there. Let Beth know that Gabriel seems to be pulling out. Nick, I know you want to stay with your brother, but we really need you to open the shield."

Jessica studied Nick and could tell his ice was shattering all around him. He still tried to suppress his emotions but with much less luck. He met her eyes, and she saw the concern not just for his brother, but for her. She realized then that he could feel the gas affecting her through their bond.

"I'm fine. Be careful."

He nodded then left with Marcus and Robin.

She looked down at Chris, staring into his face. *I wish I could feel you through our bond.* She placed her hand on his forehead and tried to push past the drug blocking her system. "Jays, I can't be sure, but I don't think he's been affected by the gas. There's something else in his system." She pivoted his head to look at the bruise on his temple.

The doctor pulled back Chris's eyelid. "He was knocked out. I don't know what else was done to him though. Hopefully he won't have a concussion."

Damn it. Push this drug through already. She berated herself as she dragged a chair over, and while Jays performed the exam, she sat down to wait.

Chapter Fourteen

Late that night, Jessica brushed the hair back on Kieran's forehead then laid her hand lightly in the hollow of his throat. The slow rhythmic pulsing of his heart reassured her. He hadn't stirred all day. The inhibitor had done a number on him.

When he hadn't shown any sign of waking after several hours, Beth had called Jillian in to do an internal scan, worried that the gas had done physical damage, but he checked out ok.

The blood he'd coughed up at the start had come from the violence of the spasms, not anything worse. But he still wasn't waking.

Jess had taken enough gas damage that her talents still hadn't recovered fully, so her sensing of their bond was weak. Still, she called out to him through it since it was her only option. She sighed at the silence.

No encouragement to report, she rose, turned the light down low, and left the room.

Back in the crowded main treatment room, she shook her head at Dev and Aiden when they glanced up at her inquiringly. She dug the heel of her hand into her tired eyes as she skirted around knots of subdued Valkyries to intercept Jays and see what needed to be done next.

She couldn't really blame anyone for not wanting to be alone at the moment though. Both the hospital building and the longhouse were full to capacity.

Jays had just finished wrapping the wrist of one of the scouts when she walked up. He ran his hands through his hair, leaving it in spikes.

"So, anything yet?" he asked.

"No. No movement, and no response mentally."

"Damn. I'd hoped that by now he would start coming around. He's the only one left who was gassed that hasn't come to yet. Even Chris is showing signs of waking, but I think I agree with you on him. I don't think Chris was gassed; it's something else, but what, I don't know."

"And my senses are still too muddled to work properly. I can't tell what it is either."

"We'll just have to wait until Chris wakes, I guess, to find out what happened to him."

She scrubbed her face with her hands.

"You need to sit and get something to eat, Jess."

Snorting, she opened her eyes and looked at him ironically. "I need to eat? Jays, you're the one who's still fledging, give me a break."

A tired smile crossed his face, and he stretched his wings—wings that looked pretty full grown to her—before he said, "Ok, maybe you're right. We both need to eat."

She caught Aiden's eye; the youth stood and walked over to her. "Aiden, could you go over to the kitchens and get something for both Jays and I to eat?"

"Sure, Jess. And Dev just found out that they're calling a halt to the search. Nick and the others should be on their way over here soon."

"Thanks." Once the young Caster had walked away, she said, "So, who's next?"

"Nobody. All of the injured have been treated. Beth went to do a check on everyone in the longhouse, but that shouldn't take too much time. All of the worst cases are here in the infirmary."

"Good. Come on." She grabbed Jays's arm and pulled him toward a couple of empty chairs she spotted against the wall. They sank down and she closed her eyes for a moment. "I don't think I've ever felt so tired."

"Sure you have. When you were running from us at the start, remember?"

She opened her eyes and glared at him for the reminder. "Actually, I don't remember much of that day very well. It's all become kind of a hazy blur."

"Interesting. I wonder if the flight here will be like that for me when I'm done with the change."

She shrugged and looked out over the crowded room. Movement near the doors caught her attention, and she saw Nickolas enter, followed by Marcus, Beth, and Kevin.

Kevin held the door for Robin. Her brother had his arm around his Second, and it was obvious that Kelley had been crying. Elbowing Jays, Jessica gestured toward the newcomers.

"Good. I didn't want to have to walk anywhere to meet with them." The doctor yawned.

Silently agreeing with him, she caught Nick's eye as he scanned the room for her. She could see suppressed pain in his eyes, and the flares of emotion that reached her through the inhibitor in their link told her how difficult this day had been for him.

Chairs scraped as people moved to give the Alphas and Primes a place to sit.

"Hey," Jess said softly.

"Hey," Nick returned. Then, "How are Chris and Kieran?"

Jays scrubbed his hands over his face. "Chris is starting to move around, finally; I'm hoping he'll wake soon. Kieran has me more worried. He hasn't moved or responded to anything since Dev carried him in at dawn."

"We know he had a high exposure to the gas," Beth said. "But there were others that did as well. He's the only one left who hasn't come to."

"Jays and I have been talking about that," Jess added. "We think that it has something to do with how strong he is in his talent. The stronger you are, the more it affects you. That's our theory anyway."

"I wish I knew what they did to it," Jays groused. "This drug is not responding like any of the forms of inhibitor that I'm familiar with. It's a new compound."

The smell of cooked food reached her nose, and Jessica's stomach growled. Looking up, she saw Aiden and a couple of other Hunters carrying trays across the room to them.

"I saw everyone coming in here, so I thought all of you would be hungry," Aiden said as he handed both her and Jays plates piled with food while the other Hunters passed out food to the rest of the leaders.

"Thank you, Aiden. Have you and Dev gotten dinner yet?" Nickolas asked.

"No."

"Find Donald, make sure he's eaten, and the two of you grab something as well."

"Yes, sir," the young Caster said, and Jessica watched as he went and collected Dev and left.

Digging in to her stuffed pork chop, Jessica wondered how anyone had found the time to cook anything more elaborate than soup. But she was thankful. The moist meat blended nicely with the herbed stuffing. She closed her eyes as she savored another bite. Nickolas chuckled softly next to her, and she looked at him out of the corner of her eye.

"What?" she said with her mouth full. He just shook his head and took his own bite. Turning her attention back to her food, she continued to eat.

Aiden arriving with food must have been a signal, because it wasn't long before more people arrived, carrying food for those Valkyries in the hospital building that couldn't go next door to the longhouse to eat.

She finished her dinner and set her plate aside, then looked at the rest of the group. They were all just finishing as well.

Handing his plate to the Hunter who had come over to pick them up, Marcus leaned back into his chair. "So, time to debrief. Beth, what's our totals?"

She cleared her throat and looked up tiredly. "Only a few injuries in the valley itself. A couple of sprains, a concussion when someone fell; the worst was a gas canister that fell through someone's roof. That Hunter got a bad dose and a shard of wood through the leg from his broken roof. He's doing ok. As for gas exposure, we have one hundred and sixty-two cases in the valley alone. The interesting thing was the Facility Valkyries that haven't yet been weaned off of the inhibitor were the least affected by the gas. Most of them were still able to function, though they did have to deal with nausea. Of the hundred scouts outside of the valley, forty-eight were injured. Some have symptoms of gas exposure but most were brought in with injuries. The worst of those cases are still here in the infirmary. Of all the injured, Chris and Kieran are definitely the worst."

Robin set his plate aside and picked up where she stopped. "We have four dead. It looks like one was a Caster that got trapped and took his entire team with him when he overloaded his power."

"Who was it?" Marcus asked roughly.

"Brent. He was a level four light weaver. He took eight Facility people with him." Everyone was silent for a moment before Robin continued. "There are still six people unaccounted for. I don't know if they were gassed and can't mind call, or if they are injured somewhere out in the woods, or the option I like least, Gabriel has them."

Nickolas cleared his throat. "They were taken."

Marcus looked surprised. "You seem very sure of that, Nick."

"I am. I'm a Seer, remember? I know they were all taken."

A glance at his eyes and Jessica realized that Ian must have told him. The Hunter sitting with Robin sucked in her breath at his statement, and her brother put his arm around her. "Don't worry, Kel. We'll get Leslie back. You'll see."

"You better believe it, Kelley," Marcus stated. "We aren't leaving anyone with Gabriel again. Not now that we finally have a location for that containment facility. Now, we have a problem. We have a lot of Facility personnel sitting in the indoor arena, along with a lot of dead Facility people. The question is, what are we to do with them?"

"I think I have a contact who will come and get them," Nickolas said.

Silence greeted that statement. After the others exchanged looks, Marcus stared at his son for a moment then said, "I think you had better explain. What sort of contact?"

A tremor shot down their link, and Jessica watched Nick's eyes flare briefly before he shut down his emotions again. She wondered what he was thinking.

"Someone named Luther rerouted my phone. When I tried to use it a day ago, he answered it."

"Wait a sec," Marcus cut in. "You have a cell phone, and you've used it? Didn't you learn anything in the Facility? There's a reason we don't have phones or computer access here, and it's not because we can't. Who the hell were you calling?"

Nick looked down at his hands. "I just wanted to listen to a saved message. I wasn't on long. Besides, he already knows where Aurora is."

Marcus sighed and rubbed the bridge of his nose and said softly, "Ian left a recording for you. When you're ready for it. What did Luther say?"

"He wants us to return. 'Us' being the Facility Valkyries. He said that he has known your location for years and hasn't bothered you, so why would he now. I would be willing to bet that if I called him and told him to come and get his people, he would."

"At least it's Luther," Jessica heard Marcus say under his breath.

"You can't seriously be thinking of letting someone from the Facility come here?" Robin asked worriedly.

"Not here, Robin. But the idea has merit." Marcus raised his head and pinned Nickolas with a look. "We can march them out of our vicinity then let Luther pick them up. That way we won't have more Facility people on our doorstep. Of all of the factions of the Facility, Luther is the only one I would agree to do this with."

"You trust him?" Kevin asked.

"About as far as I can throw him. But that's still more than I would trust anyone else in that place. Before we escaped he was the only one who seemed to actually listen to us and he's never cared for how they run Gabriel."

Her eyes still red, Kelley spoke for the first time. "Sir, do you think the Facility is going to come back?"

"Yes. But their attack will probably be different. I'm also wondering how Gabriel's keepers are going to like the fact that he left so many people behind." Marcus shrugged his shoulders. "We'll see. We need to keep our vigilance up."

"Nickolas!" Dylan shouted and waved wildly by Chris's bed.

Everyone rose, but Jays and Beth pushed past to reach him first.

"He just started mumbling and tossing his head," Dylan said.

Jessica could see that Christoff's face was flushed, and sweat ran down from his temple. He jerked his head, yanking it away from Jays. Then he yelled hoarsely, "Gabriel, no!"

And his eyes snapped open.

Everyone froze. Christoff stared about him blankly, then he started to shiver. Sound resumed within the infirmary as the injured Valkyries started to talk quietly again.

"Where am I?" Chris asked, his voice raspy. Bethany and Jays continued with their examination, and he looked at them all, his gaze unfocused. "What happened?"

Nickolas reached out and picked up his brother's hand. "We have you back in Aurora. We don't know what happened; we were hoping you could tell us."

Chris raised his free hand to his forehead and rubbed the space between his eyes. "I don't know. I can't remember. My head is killing me."

Shining a light into Chris's eyes, Jays said, "Don't worry about it now. You need to rest. Hopefully it will come to you later."

"Jays is right, Christoff, rest is the best thing at the moment," Beth said while she examined the huge bruise on his temple. When she was done, she looked up at all of them. "Ok, everyone, I'm sure there are things that still need to be done. Let's give him some peace."

Jessica felt Nickolas tense next to her, then Marcus chimed in as well. "Beth's right. Now's probably the best time, Nick, to go and call Luther, then we can go inspect our guests."

Jess placed her hand on her mate's arm. "I'll stay with him."

Nick pressed his lips together but nodded and then turned to Marcus. Robin gave Kelley a quick kiss and told her to stay in the infirmary, then the three of them left sick bay. Jessica looked back down into Chris's glazed eyes and squeezed his hand, brushing the hair off of his forehead. The fuzziness in her mind was still stopping her from being able to tell what was in his system. She sighed and had to accept Beth's reassurance that what she was sensing was probably a drug that the Facility had given him to knock him out since they had found him trussed up for transport.

Nickolas shoved through the door and inhaled the outside air deeply. The thought of who probably waited in the arena among the prisoners weighed heavily on his thoughts. Friends, acquaintances...most definitely people he'd worked with. The crisp cold air flowed through his nose. The chill had returned as soon as Aiden had stopped pushing the warm southerly wind to keep the invaders off balance. They now had a lot of ice to contend with from the melted snow. And it looked like more snow was soon going to fall. Another result of Aiden's wind. The clash between the warm and cold air masses made for a perfect recipe to make snow. Walking with his father and Jessica's brother, they crossed the courtyard to the longhouse, running into Donald on the way.

"Donald, would you please fly over to my cabin and pick up my cell? It's sitting on the table in between the chairs in the living room."

"Yeah, sure, Nick."

"We'll be in Marcus's office."

The Hunter took off, and Nickolas followed the other two into the longhouse. He hadn't seen the building so crowded except for the night of the holiday dinner. *Likely no one wants to be alone*, he thought.

He stifled a yawn and pushed the door to the office closed behind him then dropped into one of the chairs in front of the desk. His father took his own seat, and Robin perched on the corner of the desk.

"Well, Nicky, I hadn't expected you to know about Luther," his father said.

"I don't really." Nick shrugged.

"From my understanding from Dad, Luther had pulled back from most of the day-to-day decisions in the Facility. Kratz had taken over the running of the Facility about the time you fledged. I wonder what's brought him back into activity."

"No idea. We avoided Kratz as much as possible. I know nothing about any other leaders, but this general Luther wants control of us."

"That's been the main aim of the Facility from the get go, Nick. But Luther Faulk does seem to be the best choice for ridding ourselves of our uninvited guests."

Swinging his leg, Robin asked, "How should we go about it?"

"I was thinking about that. There's a forest service road that ends about twenty miles to the southwest of us. It might even be the road Gabriel used to get his people in. If we wait a day or two, so enough of our people recover from the gas, then we could walk them out. At that point, we could spare enough Hunters to make sure nothing happens to either our group or the Facility people and still have plenty to defend Aurora. If we start them out early, they should be able to cover the distance in one day."

"Will Gabriel hear about it through the grapevine when Nick tells Luther? We might be setting ourselves up for him to try us when we're divided."

Nickolas, tell them that won't be a worry. As soon as the attack started, I traveled to Gabriel's superiors. They don't have enough support to move again that fast.

Nick shot a glance over at Ian where he leaned up against the wall on his right. "You're sure?"

Watch yourself. He nodded at Marcus, who was looking at Nick questioningly. *And yes. Kratz has overstepped.*

Nick shifted his attention back to his father, ignoring the quizzical frown to relay Ian's words. "They won't be able to attack us when we move them. They don't have enough people."

"Huh?" Robin said in confusion. "And just how would you know that?"

Sighing, Nickolas looked at him. "I'm a Seer, remember."

Well technically that is true, Nicky. It is a Seer talent that allows you to see me, but somehow I don't think that this is the talent they're thinking of.

Snorting, Nick looked at Ian again and shook his head.

Do you want them to question your sanity?

"Didn't we already have this discussion? You know my opinion."

"Nick, what are you talking about?" Robin asked.

"Or more importantly, who?" Marcus asked quietly.

He looked away from Ian and caught a concerned look pass between the other two. *I told you, Nicky.*

"Oh shut up, Ian," he said under his breath, but he caught his father's eyes widen and knew he'd heard.

At that moment Donald walked in. He tossed Nick's phone at him then took the other chair in front of the desk. Marcus glanced at the Hunter, and Nickolas knew that as soon as he was gone, his father was going to tell Donald to sic his Hunters on him. Annoying. He stabbed the talk button and raised the phone to his ear. After only two rings, it was answered.

"Nickolas?" the cultured voice queried.

"Luther?" he responded.

There was a shocked pause before the gentleman on the other end of the line cleared his throat. "I'm impressed. You've certainly surprised me. You have also proven that I was right in pursuing you to return to us. How did you learn of me, perchance?"

"It doesn't matter."

"Of course it does, Nickolas. To survive, I need to be sure of my people; a slip like this could cost lives."

"Then don't worry; I didn't find out through normal channels. It's not something another would likely be able to do."

"If you say so." The voice sounded skeptical. "So to what do I owe the honor of this call? Have you decided to return to us?"

"No. I'm not coming back. I'm calling because we were attacked last night."

"What?"

"You heard me. Gabriel attacked Aurora before dawn. Four Aurorans died, six are missing, and a lot are injured. You claim you don't have anything to do with Gabriel, but how do I know that is true?"

"I assure you, we knew nothing about this attack. Why are you calling me?"

"He gassed us, and we want to know what it was and how to counter it. We want our people back, and we don't want yours."

"People?"

"We have thirty-five dead, along with fifty-two injured and captured Facility personnel. We don't want them."

"We want those people alive, Nickolas," the general said in a deceptively soft voice.

"That's why I'm calling you, Luther."

"I'll have someone look into the gas. There's nothing I can do for your captured people, though."

"I figured that would be the case. I'll get back to you on when and where you can pick up your people."

"I can send helicopters out tomorrow morning."

"Don't. They won't come back," he promised.

Luther's voice was starting to sound slightly strained. "We didn't have anything to do with the attack—"

Nickolas hung up the phone. It rang back in ten seconds, and he powered it down.

♦ ♦ ♦

General Rembrandt Harrison Luther Faulk gently hung up the receiver when what he really wanted to do was slam it down. "Stupid puppy," he said softly.

"What happened?" Jared asked. His secretary pushed the door shut and walked up to his desk.

"Find out what occurred last night, Jared. Carl's giving Gabriel too much rein, and now we're going to have to clean up the mess. He attacked Aurora. Nickolas is not amused. He's going to call back to tell us when and where we can pick up the survivors and the dead."

"Pick up? We could just fly into Aurora," Jared said as he cocked a hip on the corner of the desk.

"I've been assured that that would be a bad idea. I'm thinking that it might be a good idea not to push Marcus. We'll do it his way. For now."

"I assume that this has influenced Nickolas's decision?"

"It certainly hasn't endeared us to him," Luther replied caustically. "Damn Carl Kratz anyway. Pulling Nickolas back is going to be more difficult now. Gabriel used a gas on the Valkyries. They want to know what it is; please get someone on it. I would like to be able to offer them something when Nickolas calls back. Then get transportation set up. I want you to go with them, get a feel for the situation. You might find something we can use against him."

"Sir, I shouldn't leave you."

"Nonsense. I'm hardly incapable, and the man you've trained is almost as good as you. I need you to extend your expertise, Jared. I think you're the only one I have who stands a chance of getting close to any of the Valkyries. You're much like them."

Chewing his lip, his secretary looked like he wasn't sure he liked that comparison, but Luther knew that if Jared got to know the Valkyries, he would change his mind. *I expect I'll lose him to them eventually.* Luther sighed.

"And Nickolas, sir? What should I do about our schedule?"

Leaning back in his seat, Luther thought for a moment. "Finish securing the contract for Sandpoint so we can get the new base started. An opportunity to bring him in will present itself eventually. Gabriel is not through with them."

"Yes, sir," Jared said and quietly left the office.

"Well, Nickolas, that seemed to go well," Marcus said.

Nick slipped the phone into his pocket and shrugged at his father's facetious tone. "Hopefully he'll be able to tell us what the gas is the next time I talk to him. Unless you want to call him?"

"Hardly. I was content to go the rest of my life without talking to any of them again. Well, let's go inspect our guests. Maybe we can find out something to help us get Leslie and the rest back. Someone has to know what Gabriel is planning."

His father gave him a searching look as he rose. "Are you feeling up to this?"

Nick met his gaze and held it.

Nick, Ian snapped. *Let it go.*

"I'm fine." He addressed both of them and turned away from the desk to follow Robin out the door. Ian's presence dissipated, and he breathed a sigh of relief. Donald caught up and cast a sideways glance at him but wisely kept quiet.

As they passed the longhouse, it looked just as full, and people were bringing blankets in. No one was going anywhere.

They continued across the courtyard again, but this time they entered the third building. The interior of the gym was open, like a gigantic barn, at least a hundred feet across and a couple of stories tall, with high windows to allow natural light. It was large enough to accommodate the whole population of Aurora, but not if they were all trying to work out at once. He could see why Chris favored the outdoor practice grounds. Even in the cold. There were a couple of doors that led off of the main room. They housed the weights and a full bath. As far as an indoor arena went, it was nice.

The Hunters who were guarding the door nodded at Marcus as they entered. Just inside, the first thing they encountered were the dead Facility personnel. They were arranged respectfully in neat rows. Aurora didn't have sheets or blankets to spare, so they were uncovered, and Nickolas looked at several of the faces. Sadness hit him when he saw Danny, the Delta team leader, and Matt from Gamma.

He felt irrationally like he'd betrayed them somehow and heard Donald murmur something and suspected it was a similar sentiment. He turned his face to the rest of the room. The prisoners were tending to their wounded with his mother's help. *There* was something he should demand from Luther. Aurora shouldn't be losing precious medical supplies.

Hunters lined the interior wall, standing silent guard over the intruders. With Marcus leading, they crossed the room; heads turned in their direction, and he saw a few more familiar faces. Some pleased, some not so pleased. They stopped next to Jeff, and Nick saw that the Gamma leader was tying off a bandage on another prisoner's leg. Nickolas recognized Rick, who moaned in pain even as his eyes remained shut.

Jeff took a deep breath before he turned his head to look up at him. "Hi, Nick."

"Is Rick ok?"

"He should be. I don't think he'll lose the leg."

"I just saw Matt. I'm sorry."

"Yeah, me too," the Gamma leader said. After an awkward pause, Jeff continued softly, "We didn't have a choice, Nick. They didn't tell us what we were walking into. It was just supposed to be a feral recovery, though when we saw the size of the operation, several of us suspected we were coming after you. That many teams were called out during Jessica's manhunt, so while it wasn't usual there was precedent. Some of us tried to pull back when the fighting started, but our own turned on us. Then it became a matter of life and death."

"Who?"

"Most of us didn't want this, Nick. We just got our orders like normal from the section leaders who presumably got them from Kratz, since Ian is gone."

"Who was it, Jeff?"

The Gamma leader sighed. "Everett. He heads the new Alpha team. They were pulled to the side and were briefed by Gabriel. I got the impression that they knew what we were going in to do."

Nick closed his eyes.

"Damn," Donald said softly beside him.

"Where's Chris?" Jeff asked. "I thought he'd be with you."

"He's in the infirmary. Gabriel got a hold of him."

"God, Nick, I'm sorry."

Shrugging, Nick looked over at Robin's and Marcus's impassive faces. "Can you tell us anything else, Jeff? What was the gas? What did the Facility really want? Why did Gabriel leave so suddenly? Anything could help."

Jeff rested his head in his hands, and Nickolas knelt down next to someone who he had always thought of as a friend. He hoped that he had been right.

"I don't know, Nick. This wasn't like any recovery I've been a part of. Since you all fled and Ian destroyed the Valkyrie portion of the Facility everything has been in turmoil. We didn't know who was running things. Many new faces have been coming and going at the Facility. But it looks like it's shaken down to Kratz running the whole complex."

Jeff looked back to Nick, his expression drawn. "Sorry, Nick. That word sure is getting a lot of use, for all the good it does."

"Thanks, Jeff. I hope Rick recovers."

"Stay safe, Nick."

Standing, Nickolas looked at Donald. His Hunter was keeping his face carefully blank, but Nickolas could see the pain in his eyes. As one, the two of them turned to look across the room at Everett. Marcus and Robin stood quietly, leaving them to handle the Facility people. Everett sat within a small group, staring straight at Nick. Anger and hatred blazed from him. Nickolas pushed his feelings back down under the ice. This man had once been his friend as well.

Donald and Nick crossed the distance side by side then stopped in front of Everett. The other man looked Nick up and down, then his gaze took in Marcus and Robin, who had followed behind, and lingered a moment on Donald before returning to Nick. "So they didn't get you, I see. That's a shame. I was hoping they'd get all the traitors."

Ice crackled over the anger Nick felt rising up. "First Flynn, now you. What makes me a traitor? Not rolling over and letting myself be a lab rat? Not giving up my freedom and very probably my life? Would you do that, Everett?"

"Don't be so melodramatic, Nick. You would have been well cared for, with nothing to worry about, and every need supplied."

"Nothing to worry about? I don't think you'd submit to that kind of captivity quietly." Nick shook his head and changed the subject. "But let's talk about traitors, shall we? Who was it that left you behind?"

Everett's mouth thinned to a fine line, and he stared at Nickolas with hard eyes. "I'm sure every possible action was taken to make sure we all got out."

Snorting, Nickolas stared at him in disbelief. "You have got to be kidding me. You can't actually believe that. Wait, what am I saying? If you believe that I would have been safe in Gabriel's hands, of course you could believe that." He looked at his companions for a moment. "Everett, I need to know what Gabriel is up to. What was the gas, and why did he pull out so suddenly?"

"I don't need to tell you anything."

"Actually, yes you do. Or had you missed the fact that you are sitting in the middle of the feral Valkyries' home. Do you really think the police patrol here? It's not like anyone is coming to save you."

"None of you will kill us, or you would have already."

"I can't believe how stupid you are. I really hope you never fledge. I wouldn't want you around." Having had enough of Everett's idiotic self-righteousness, Nickolas drew upon his power, and like quicksilver, it ran beneath his skin. He turned his eyes on the Facility man.

Power lashing out, Nick pinned him and held him still with a thought. Gasps echoed around him but barely penetrated Nick's concentration. He reached out mentally and wrapped his thoughts around Everett's, forcing the man's compliance. "Now, Everett, please answer my questions. What was the gas?"

"Damn it, Nick, if I had known you had this ability.... This should have been done in private," his father hissed.

Ignoring him, Nick continued. Breaking out into a sweat, the Facility man stuttered, trying not to obey, but it was a useless effort. In the end, he stumbled over himself. "We were told it was inhibitor. It had something added to it to incapacitate quickly, so none of you would be able to use your strange abilities. It also had something else added to knock out the Hunters. It was supposed to be fast, then we would be able to come in and pick you up like fallen fruit."

Donald growled beside him, but Nick ignored it. "What was Gabriel after, and why did he leave so suddenly?"

"He was ordered to bring back you and Jessica. Anyone else he got was icing on the cake, he said. I don't know why he left the way he did."

Withdrawing his mind, Nickolas released Everett. Fear shone out of the man's eyes as he looked back at them, and when Nickolas looked around, he saw that fear reflected on all of the Facility people's faces.

Then he looked at the Valkyries. Donald just displayed his normal, open trust, but all of the Aurorans held wary respect.

"They're right," Everett stammered. "They need to leash all of you."

"You made us," Nick pointed out. Weary of the fear, he continued, "We're still human. We started out just like you. And remember, you could become one of us at any time. All we want is to be left alone."

He turned away from the former Beta team leader and caught Jeff's gaze from across the room. A shimmer of fear, quickly suppressed but there nonetheless, stabbed at Nickolas, and he started to look away from his old friend, but Jeff quickly held up his hand in a salute before sitting back down with Rick.

Bowing his head, Nickolas closed his eyes, another crack in his ice, and this time it wasn't from Ian.

◆ ◆ ◆

"Damn it." Gabriel slammed the door to his suite shut. "Almost a complete failure."

The joyful reprimand that Kratz had given him still echoed in his head. One of these days he would skin that man. *Alive. In the arena. In front of the audience he loves so much. I'm sure they would appreciate that sort of blood sport.*

He threw the filthy vest he'd taken off into a corner with a loud thud as he walked through the suite. The lights brightened, and he glanced at the cage. Zach watched him with glittering eyes, curled around a sleeping Pet.

"Get up."

Zach carefully pulled away, trying not to wake her, then with deliberate slowness rose and crossed to the edge of the cage near the small commode. "Problem?"

Gabriel grabbed him by the throat faster than the Seer could dodge and yanked his face against the bars. "Don't fuck with me tonight, Zach."

The insolent Seer just cocked an eyebrow at him and said, "Are you sure? That's what you normally want."

"I can send you back to the labs."

"But you won't. It's not like you to use empty threats. What happened?"

With a growl, Gabriel ripped his hand away and spun on his heel. He snapped his wings open then closed before he returned and jabbed in the combination for the lock. Zach pushed through the cage door.

Gabriel fell back to pacing. Zachary stretched his wings and gave them a vigorous flap before sauntering over to sit on the foot of the large bed to watch him.

"Next time you're going to be gone so long, the least you could do is make sure we can get out to stretch our wings."

Gabriel cast a slashing look at the Seer. "You're really pushing tonight..."

Zach shrugged.

After a few moments of silence, Gabriel asked, "Carmine brought your food on time?"

"Yeah. With a side of Freddie, who sat and watched us the entire time. Talk about indigestion."

Gabriel growled and turned back to his Seer, raking him with a gaze from head to toe. He looked normal. Gabriel's mind arrowed into Zach's, and he swayed on the bed with a groan.

"Y-you...j-just...had to ask," Zach bit off in pain.

"Well? I'm waiting."

Zach pressed the heel of his hand into his eye. "He tried to get the lock open, yes. When that didn't work, he got help and pinned me to the side of the cage with poles. The guards were willing to do that for him. They weren't willing to court your wrath by getting through the cage."

Gabriel caught the blue of Zach's eyes, even though he tried to dodge, and stared hard. The Seer's breath quickened. "What did he give you? Was it the same thing?"

Fear and remembered pain flashed through Zach's eyes. "I don't know."

"I'll find out tomorrow. Did it have any different effects?"

Now Zach actively sought to break eye contact. Gabriel swept into his mind and ordered his reply. Zachary's body grew stiff as he no longer controlled it, and he gave a detailed account of what had happened. Once satisfied, Gabriel released the Seer, who slumped over on the bed, shivering.

"Climb into bed," Gabriel ordered. He removed his boots then stripped the rest of his clothes off before going into the cage and gently picking up the still sleeping Pet. "Move it, Zach."

The subdued Valkyrie crawled with his head down into the bed. Gabriel tucked Pet in between them and pulled the covers up. The lights dimmed as soon as the movement in the rest of the room ceased. Zach's trembling breath sounded harsh in the darkness.

"I needed to know, Zach. You may not have liked it, but I had to know what I'm dealing with."

◆ ◆ ◆

Snow fell thick as Donald carried the tray across the courtyard. The dawn light barely penetrated the swirling velvet. The two Hunters stationed at the infirmary doors stepped out from the overhang and opened them so he could enter without juggling the breakfast tray.

He nodded his thanks as he stepped inside then shivered his wings to rid them of the snow and shook his head. Quietly, he walked across the floor and listened to the sounds of people sleeping. The room here was just as full as the longhouse. He stepped carefully as he made his way to one of the back rooms and pushed the door open. He found Jays and Christoff inside, along with Kieran. Chris sat up in one bed, but Donald's cousin still hadn't moved, from the looks of things.

He set the tray down then handed food out. "Anything, Jays?"

"Sorry, Donald, nothing. Not a change in breathing, not a twitch of a muscle. His eyes aren't even moving, and they should be. I don't know what to do to bring him out of this."

"What about Nick? Do you think that since they have a blood bond he could reach Kieran?"

Jays stopped with his fork halfway to his mouth, thunderstruck. "Boy, I feel stupid."

Christoff chuckled slightly. "These talents are new to all of us, Jays. Besides, you're still fledging; you shouldn't be doing all of this anyway." He took a bite and winced from the bruise that had spread across the side of his face.

Donald glanced over at Kieran then returned to his food. "Jays, Nick said he'd like it if you'd stay in the infirmary and out of sight of the Facility people."

"Anyone we know, Donald?" Chris asked.

"Yeah, quite a few."

"All right. It's not like I want to go back there or anything," Jays said.

"Nick was able to get a few questions answered but nothing earth shattering. He had to use his coercion, which resulted in scaring the shit out of the Facility people. It also apparently alarmed the Aurorans. I overheard Marcus and Robin talking about it afterward. Marcus really wants to know all of Nick's talents and how strong he is. He doesn't like getting surprised like this."

"He's not the only one who wants to know what Nick can do," Chris muttered.

"Yes, well I get the impression that the number of talents Nick keeps cropping up with is a shock. They're wondering what else he has waiting in the wings. The reason I managed to catch this conversation, by the way, is because Marcus asked to see me. Without Nick around. Marcus and Robin are worried. They caught Nickolas talking to nothing yesterday. They wanted to know if we had seen any abnormal behavior, and if not, to watch for it. Marcus is concerned; with Nick's strength...if he were to go insane...well, Gabriel's name was on everyone's mind."

"Something is going on; I just haven't been able to figure out what. Ask Jess, she might know," Chris replied.

"I'll do that." Realizing that Jays had been pretty quiet, Donald looked over at the fledgling. Jays was eating slowly, almost absentmindedly, and his forehead was creased. "Jays?" he asked.

Jays looked up at him, and Donald could see his eyes come back into focus. "Huh? Sorry, I feel like I've forgotten something, and I was just trying to remember."

Donald exchanged a quick look with Chris then smiled at the fledge. "Hey, don't worry about it. It's been a busy twenty-four hours. You should get some rest; it'll come to you when the time is right."

"Yeah," Jays said uncertainly and looked over at Kieran before he finished his food.

Sound still traveled funny in his ears. And the big blankness within himself scared Kieran. Jessica assured him it would fade, that he would regain his empathy, but at the moment, he felt locked away from himself.

It had been twenty-four hours since Nick had called him out of the darkness. Twenty-four hours since that first sound echoed in his head; the silence had felt like eternity. The first touch, the first sensation that had penetrated the shell that had been forced around him had been excruciating.

And he had fought.

But Nick was stronger, and he had grabbed Kieran by the scruff of the neck and hauled him back to the surface, spluttering like a soggy kitten. The disorientation was overwhelming. Sight, sound, touch, and smell; everything returned in a rush. Kieran had fallen into Nickolas's arms, sobbing in pain and relief.

That had been yesterday. He was still piecing together what had happened two days ago, when the valley had been attacked. It gave him something to do at least. They weren't letting him out of sick bay yet.

Flight

They let Chris go, even though he still had no memory of the entire day of the attack, and he hadn't been out cold for it. He was now off with the rest at the practice grounds.

There's nothing physically wrong with me, so why won't they let me go too? Shuddering at the quiet of the room, he got up and started to pace. He hadn't slept last night. He'd probably driven Chris nuts with his incessant chatter.

But he couldn't face the dark and the silence.

Thankfully the Hunter had understood. Restless, Kieran's wings half opened then closed. *I need to go find Jessica.* That was the only thing he could think of that would help. *But she's at the practice grounds, I'm sure. If I show up there, Donald will kill me.* Rubbing his upper arms just to feel something, Kieran looked dispiritedly out the window at the snow. *It's really quiet, maybe I can get out without anyone seeing me. Once I was in the air, no one could stop me.*

Now with a direction, Kieran spun on his heel and left the room. He walked down the hall and stopped in the doorway to the main treatment room. It was now empty of patients, but Jays was still there picking things up and organizing equipment. His friend's movements were agitated, and Kieran frowned for a moment as he watched the fledgling. Jays seemed preoccupied and irritable, so Kieran didn't say anything to him. Instead, he quietly skirted the edge of the room, leaving Jays to his tasks.

"Where do you think you're going, Kieran?" Jays asked sharply over his shoulder as Kieran stopped halfway to the door. He slammed a drawer then yanked another one open, tossing something in before treating it to the same. "You were told to stay here today."

"I was just going to fly for a bit," Kieran replied reluctantly. Violence visibly circled the fledgling, and Kieran took a step back. He felt deaf and blind without the added input his empathy normally gave him; Kieran tried to interpret what was going on with Jays.

"What part of stay here did you not understand?" The fledge kicked a chair out of his way then shoved a couple more up against the wall. "Has your empathy returned? Can you mind call?" he snapped.

Kieran shook his head and wrapped his arms about himself.

"That's what I thought," Jays said as he looked at Kieran closely then ran his hand through his short blond hair, and his expression suddenly turned confused before his focus returned. In that moment, Kieran saw his friend's eyes clear for a second before the clouds scudded across them again.

Kieran felt the blood leave his face. *Oh God, it's been a week. Jays's block is breaking down.* The sudden realization flooded Kieran with fear. Desperately, he tried to reach his strength, to find his talents, but he was locked away more securely than he had ever been in his whole life. Even in the Facility, when he was on the drugs, his talent had been so strong that he had unconsciously used it. Now he had to stand and watch as Jays remembered leaving Ian behind, and there was absolutely nothing he could do for his friend.

Jays was getting close to the coma. This could make an already risky time much more dangerous.

Jays paced slowly through the room, stopping and starting erratically. Kieran stood apprehensively near the wall, halfway to the door, and waited while Jays worked his way through the mental barrier. Clamping his wings down, Kieran watched in sympathy when Jays fell against one of the empty beds, his arms bracing him as he leaned over it, his head bowed. A low moan escaped from Jays, and Kieran saw the fledgling's wings shiver before his entire body tensed and froze. Then slowly his head rose, and he pinned Kieran with blazing eyes.

"You made me leave him, Kieran. You and Donald made me leave him. Then you made me *forget* him." His voice was low and dangerous.

Tensing, Kieran replied, "We had no choice. You know that. We couldn't leave you behind; you know too much, as much as Ian. And you would have had no protection from Gabriel since you'd gone into the second stage."

Jays pushed away from the bed and stalked him. "But you left *him* for Gabriel!"

Kieran shook his head and said quietly, "He's dead, Jays. Nick saw it happen. He's gone."

The fledgling stopped like a rope had pulled him up short, his face blank, but anguish shattered his eyes. "Damn you, Kieran," he whispered, and twisting away, he slammed the door open and ran out.

Groping blindly for a chair, Kieran sank down into it. Silence filled the room, and he wrapped his arms around himself, unable to feel any warmth.

The crisp cold air puffed through Nickolas's nose, streamers of mist rising away from his fluidly moving form. Rhythmically moving—block, kick, spin, kick, block—he twisted to the side to avoid an invisible opponent, then repeated a mirror image of the movements. Speeding up his moves, he switched forms and started a more complicated pattern, pushing his mostly recovered body.

He wanted to spar, but no one was willing to be his opponent until he was pronounced completely healed. And that wouldn't be until he had flown again. The strengthening exercises were building his flight muscles back; the latest estimate from his mother put him in the air in a week. *Which is good, because I don't think I will be able to wait much longer than that.*

Sweat started to bead at his hairline as he spun and struck. The sounds of the other practicing Valkyries faded into the background. He reveled in the movement of his body once again and thought that it would be a while before he took such basic joy for granted.

Nickolas! Ian's frantic thoughts broke into his workout.

"Not now, Ian." Nick sighed.

Nick, stop!

Ian's sudden appearance and concerned attitude forced Nick to pause. Counting his breaths to slow them, he grabbed his bottle of water from the edge of his practice area.

"What?" he asked as he downed half the bottle.

He watched Jess spar very lightly with his brother a couple of rings away. Chris was on half duty for a couple more days. Normally, his brother would be fighting such a constraint placed on him, but the amnesia still occupied his mind. Beth felt that it was just a result of the blow Chris took to the temple, but Nick wasn't so sure. Something didn't feel right.

Jays is breaking through Kieran's memory blocks. He needs your help. There's nothing Kieran can do.

"Where is he?"

He was last in the infirmary. Kieran needs help too, Nick. You need to hurry.

He capped the bottle then dropped it and spun on his heel. Sprinting off of the arena grounds, he heard shouts behind him then felt both Christoff and Donald brush his mind.

Nickolas, where are you going?

Jays is breaking the block. Chris, stay on the grounds. Donald, take Jess, Kieran needs help. Feelings of assent flowed down the link from both them, and Nickolas concentrated on running across the valley. The sound of wings passed by overhead as Donald and Jessica went to Kieran. Cursing his grounded state, Nickolas pushed harder, his feet thudding across the bridge, and he paused briefly on the other side to catch his breath.

It's happened, Nick. Jays has left, Ian whispered into his mind.

Nick looked across the fields to the north and saw Jays disappear into the woods surrounding the base of the waterfall. Altering his course, Nickolas sped along the trail beside the creek. He jumped off the path, slipping in the slush to get around some people, ignoring their startled looks as he ran by. His breath rasping, he ducked under the drooping evergreen boughs at the edge of the field that hid the twisting pathway to the pool at the base of the falls. When he turned the last corner, he stopped.

Jays was ransacking the small clearing that overlooked the water. He heaved up basketball sized rocks and violently hurled them into the pool below. He kicked apart rotted logs, sending moss and chunks of spongy wood everywhere, his voice savage as he cried out incoherently.

Nick watched his friend rend the woodland and knew the activity was useless. It was only putting off the inevitable. Much like he had put off the inevitable himself by trying to ignore the reality and bury it in ice.

"Jays."

He'd spoken softly, though he might have yelled from the way the fledgling spun at the sound of his voice. Their eyes met across the distance, and Nickolas could see the devastating grief contained within their clear blue depths. The ragged wound that Jays's soul bled from triggered the release of Nickolas's own grief, and he felt the overwhelming sense of pain and loss that he'd been bottling up flood through him once again. They stared at one another, their eyes mirroring.

"Is it true?" Jays asked raggedly.

Nodding his head, Nickolas watched the dam break in Jays, and the fledgling sank to his knees in the soft loam of the forest floor, tears running down his face as he stared sightlessly. Nickolas winced as flashes from his memory shot through him. He watched Ian die again. Felt the helplessness. And his own grief started to choke him.

Tears of his own slipped down his cheeks, and he took the last few steps separating them to sit down on the ground next to Jays.

"Why?" Jays asked hoarsely.

Nick closed his eyes and shook his head slowly. "I don't know. I've been asking myself that incessantly since I broke though Kieran's block."

"What happened? Kieran said you were there?"

Swallowing, he shuddered. His voice sounded hollow to his own ears. "I'd gone back to the Hub to make sure everyone had gotten out. I found Ian still there. He'd rigged the place to explode and was destroying the computers in his office. He'd blocked himself in. I tried to move the stuff, but I couldn't."

Nick spread his hands on his knees and stared at them. "He wouldn't come with me. He said I wouldn't be able to get away with him weighing me down, and he wouldn't let Gabriel take him. He asked me to leave. He ordered me to leave, but I wouldn't. I kept trying to break the door. Then he...h-he shot himself."

Nickolas swallowed before he looked back at Jays. "I watched him *kill* himself, Jays. I couldn't do anything to stop him. Why did he do it? I could have gotten him out. I could have." He turned away from Jays's watery blue eyes and bowed his head, tears falling steadily onto his hands.

Jays sniffed and cleared his throat. "He probably wouldn't have lived past a week away from the Facility. But he could have tried."

"What? What do you mean?" Nick asked, looking up.

Mud streaked the fledgling's cheek where Jays had wiped at the tears with his dirty hand. "Ian was on a special inhibitor. He had been since his messed-up change twenty-five years ago. The council kept control of him by only allowing him a one week supply. He was constantly trying to figure out how to make the damn stuff, but he was never able to break the recipe. He needed it to keep the change suspended in his system. Without it, he would die. Just like the rest of his change group."

Shocked, Nickolas stared at Jays blankly for a moment. "I never knew. Why did he keep that from us? Why all the lies, Jays?"

Jays closed his eyes and sighed. "The situation is so complicated. I don't know how many factions there really are or what their individual goals might be. Ian was performing a constant balancing act. Trying to keep the Facility believing that he was dutifully doing what they wanted while protecting you and your brother, plus helping Aurora. You have to understand it's not that he didn't trust you, but the more people who know something, the higher the chance of a slip. He just couldn't take the risk, Nick. And when you changed, it got even more complicated. He knew that you held the key for our survival. But if the others had found out about your differences, they would have destroyed you trying to learn everything they could."

"Damn it. I don't know what to think."

"Me either." Jays said softly.

Flight

They both stared silently out into the forest, the mist from the waterfall blending with their tears.

Chapter Fifteen

Marcus sat back in the chair and pushed his breakfast plate away before picking up his coffee cup. The breakfast rush was thinning and the common room was emptying. Beth sighed next to him, so he glanced at his wife. "Did you want to join us for the meeting, love?" he asked.

Worry passed across her face before she answered. "No. I don't have the time to at the moment. I need to get the infirmary ready for Amanda and Jays. They should be going into the coma any day now. Cameron, Amanda's mentor, said that she was starting to show the signs, and I've spotted them in Jays."

Blinking, Marcus took a drink. "It *is* getting close to that time, isn't it? It doesn't feel that long since Robin and Kev brought her in from Bellingham after Gabriel's attempt on Nick and Chris. So much has happened that I hadn't realized how close they were."

Beth smiled without much humor then shook her head. "I think they'll both be ok. Amanda is a Hunter, but Jays is a Seer, and now that he knows about Ian...I'll admit to a touch of concern for him."

Marcus reached out and brushed a strand of hair away from her eyes before saying, "He's strong, dear. He'll be fine."

"I know, I know." She sighed again. "Chris is doing well. Physically he's fine, but he's still upset about his memory loss. I keep trying to reassure him that it's just from the blow to the head he took and not to worry about it, but he won't listen."

"And this comes to you as a surprise?" He laughed softly. "How's Kieran doing?"

"He still doesn't have full use of his talent yet. It comes and goes erratically. I think he's covering up other damage he sustained as well. He won't let me get close enough to tell." She sat back and folded her arms across her chest with a scowl.

Sipping his coffee, Marcus thought about it for a moment. "Maybe you should talk to Jess or Nick. They're both stronger than he is and could force the issue if need be."

She chewed on her lip and nodded. "I've thought about it. If he doesn't improve significantly in a few days, I'll do that."

They sat quietly together for a moment, then Marcus grimaced when he saw Robin approaching.

"Everyone's here," the Hunter said.

Marcus drained the last of his coffee then asked, "All Primes and Seconds?"

"Yes, ours and the Facility's. I also asked Jays to come."

"Good. I haven't wanted to press him on what he knows from working with my father, but now that the block is down, this might be our last chance since he's almost to stage three." He pushed away from the table and rose then bent down to give Beth a quick kiss. "I'll see you later, love."

Side by side, he and Robin crossed the half-full hall to join the gathering in the larger conference room. He glanced at the occupants as he walked over to take his seat. Nickolas was still making a habit of sitting off by himself, he noted.

Vexed at his eldest son's behavior, Marcus looked closer and smiled to himself in relief. He could see that Nicky wasn't as successful at maintaining the cold as he had been right after his psychic storm. He didn't look terribly happy about it either. He pushed the worry he held for his son aside and turned his attention to the rest of the gathering, alarmed by the division he could see among those in the room.

Jessica, Chris, Donald, Kieran, and another Valkyrie that he wasn't familiar with all sat on one side of the long table. While his people sat on the other. Interestingly, Jays seemed to straddle the line, choosing a seat between the two factions. *We need to work together if we're going to make this work*, he thought as he sat down between Robin and Kevin.

All eyes were turned to him. He cleared his throat. "Well it's been three days since the attack. Everyone who was exposed to the gas, with the exception of Kieran," he made an apologetic gesture to the Seer, "has recovered. With our strength returned, we were able to send our uninvited guests home. Robin, you took care of that task. I'll leave the floor to you."

The Hunter Prime leaned forward and rested his forearms on the table. "I divided us up into two groups. My Second oversaw hauling the dead and severely injured out in the nets while I walked the rest out. It took all day for us to cover the distance through the wilderness; we reached the forest service road, where Kelley and her Flight stood guard over the dead and injured by supper time." Robin shook his head. "I don't know how the Facility managed to time it, but we were only there for maybe half an hour before a fleet of SUVs arrived. They also had four helicopters in the air, circling.

"They brought a lot of personnel. I'm not sure how many people they had, but I wouldn't have wanted to tangle with the numbers. I kept three Flights back with me and sent the rest of the Wings into the woods, in case there were orders to try and bring us in as well.

"I did find it interesting that the survivors did not have the air of being rescued. They seemed to remain prisoners. When I noticed that, I drew a little closer to see what was going on.

"We appeared to make the grounded uncomfortable...all except for their leader. He moved with complete confidence. His lack of fear of us stunned me." Robin took a quick sip of water. "His body flowed like a Hunter, a predator among the sheep, and he pushed my buttons on purpose. Dominant, challenging. The way he met my gaze...I could tell he knew what he was doing. And the thing that got me was...I'm not sure I could have taken him in a fight."

That dropped into silence.

Marcus cleared his throat. "Other than that, was there any interaction between you and Luther's people?"

"None."

"I was hoping Luther would have sent them with some sort of information to help us get our people back. We know the location of Gabriel's camp now, but that's not enough. I want our people back. Not just the six that were taken during the attack, but everyone we've lost over the years. I know not all of them will have made it. The research my father passed on to us from the camp's scientists has shown that. I don't know how many Valkyries they are actually holding there. But we can't leave a single one for them to continue their research on."

Jays cleared his throat and Marcus looked at him. "Ian and I speculated that Gabriel is holding somewhere upward of five hundred."

Marcus's eyes widened. "Five hundred...that's a bit more than I had expected. He never mentioned that."

Uneasy murmuring flowed around the table. "What are we going to do with that many, Marcus? We don't have food to take that many through the winter," Nathan, the Seer Prime, asked in concern.

Marcus leaned back in his chair. "This is going to take careful planning. We're only going to get one chance. We shouldn't rush into it." He paused, thinking, and then looked back at Jays. "Is there anything more you can tell us? How did my dad finally get the location?"

Pain flashed across the fledgling's face, but Marcus couldn't hear a trace of it in his voice. "We were finally able to get someone planted into his compound. Unfortunately, Jack compromised himself to warn us of Gabriel's attack on the Facility. That's how we were able to get all of the Valkyries out in time. Jack's situation was worse than he realized. Ian said that he was about to enter stage two, so I don't expect that he's been treated too kindly by Gabriel's staff after giving us the warning."

Grunting, Marcus agreed. "No. I don't suppose he has been."

Kevin broke into the conversation. "Marcus, we need to know the layout of the place. Was Ian able to get anything at all?"

"Nothing more than the GPS coordinates, as far as I know," he replied to the Caster Prime and then looked to Jays, who only shook his head.

"What about Nickolas's contact? Can he do anything?" Kelley asked.

Alex, Nathan's Second, said, "Would you want to trust anyone from the Facility, Kel?"

A low growl issued from the side of the table that the Facility Valkyries occupied.

"Dev," Nickolas commanded sharply.

Marcus saw Alex stiffen when he belatedly realized what he'd said. All of the Facility Valkyries were now on edge and one step away from violence. Needing to smooth ruffled feathers, Marcus looked pointedly at Alex, who slicked his wings down tight.

"A little tact please, Alex."

"Sorry, sir. That wasn't what I meant."

Shaking his head, Marcus pulled the conversation back to the original topic. "To answer your question, Kelley, I don't know if Luther could or would do anything. And I don't know whether or not we could trust him in a situation like this. He is part of the Facility machine."

"Marcus," Jays said, "Nick told me yesterday that they're still looking for me. Apparently they don't know that I'm here in Aurora or that I've fledged. My access codes into the Facility network will likely still be good. If you get me to a computer, I can look into what's happening in the Facility. How much damage there was, what they're repairing, what, possibly, their plans are. I could also look closer into Luther, maybe find out more of his agenda based on what he lets slip in the ether. It could give us a direction."

A slow smile stretched Marcus's lips. "That's a very good idea. But you're not the one to do it. Give your codes to Robin. He'll take them to Dustin to do it."

The fledge shook his head. "That won't work. Dustin won't know what to look for or even what he's looking at. He wouldn't be able to get through the different areas."

Slowly drumming his fingers on the table, Marcus watched the fledgling. "You can give him a list, Jays. We don't have internet access here in the valley. It would have allowed Gabriel to trace us too easily. The only place we access the internet is at Dustin's house, which is a good six-hour flight from here. You, my friend, are much too close to stage three to be allowed to leave the valley. Give the codes to Robin."

A low growl rumbled out of Jays before he said, "If you want this to work Marcus, I need to be there."

Stilling, Marcus stared him down. "Give the codes to Robin." There was silence for a moment as everyone waited, then looking mulish, Jays sat back in his chair, and Marcus continued. "I recognize that you are much better equipped to get us information that could prove useful but *you can't leave*. Robin will give the codes to Dustin. Dustin is a computer genius; the only person better than him was his twin brother, Zach. If anyone besides you can get anything out of the Facility net, it'll be Dustin."

Nickolas spoke up for the first time. "Jays, he's right. If you're that close to stage three, I'm not comfortable with you being away from us. Besides, what good would you be to the job if you were out cold? It's not like you can type in a coma." Nickolas paused and looked at Jessica for a moment. Marcus wondered what they were saying to each other, then his son looked at him and continued. "I'm not overly enamored with the idea of trying to enlist Luther's aid. He's already pushing to have Jessica and I return to the Facility. I'm not interested in paying that price."

"Don't worry, Nick, we aren't willing to give you up," Christoff cut in.

Nickolas smiled at him and snorted softly. "Anyway, he isn't likely to give us up, either. Every time I've spoken to him, he's made it clear that he wants us to return. At the moment, he's still asking, but when that doesn't work, what will he try next? I don't trust him to leave us be."

Reflecting on what Nickolas said, Marcus nodded his head. "You're completely correct. He'll switch to a different tactic. But that doesn't mean that we should ignore the path. Any information, whether we use it to try and enlist his aid or just use it defensively, should be sought. Knowledge is power." Glancing around the table, Marcus looked at each person individually. "We have a direction to take our first step. Please, everyone, think about the questions we've raised today. We'll meet again after Robin returns from Dustin's to discuss what he's learned and hopefully any solutions that have been thought of." Rising, Marcus nodded at everyone. "Till then."

♦ ♦ ♦

Zachary took a foot to the stomach. He allowed it to double him over and fell into a roll to get out of the way. The Hunter charged again, hatred on his face. Zach tried to not let it bother him. He knew what the others thought. Even if he could somehow have missed it from their reactions, he could hardly miss it now that his new talent of empathy had cropped up. He didn't blame them...

Exactly.

He lashed out with his wing and spun, clotheslining the Hunter. The Hunter didn't stay down, and Zach was soon on the defensive again. He didn't want to hurt anyone, but Gabriel wasn't giving him any choice. The bastard Alpha had made a point of not giving him any orders. Careful not to take any responsibility over this choice, he'd made sure Zach would have to consciously choose to hurt or be killed—because it was abundantly clear that his fellow Valkyries viewed him as a traitor and were more than willing to use the exercise in the ring to punish him for it.

He did wish they could look past the obvious.

His arms vibrated from the force of the blows he blocked. Gabriel's still thunderous face watched him without blinking.

Punishment from all sides.

His sight clouded again, and he took a roundhouse to the ribs. *Damn those visions. Why can't I just block the fucking memories? I don't need to know this.*

He shook his head clear and blocked the next attack. Breathing hard, he started to fight back; he couldn't stay on the defensive, he was wearing out.

The phantom pain of the memory shredded him inside, and he turned it outward, using it against the Hunter.

Gabriel's control of him was secure enough that the Alpha had left him alone in his suite while he took Pet for some exercise earlier in the day.

Zach's fist connected with the Hunter's firm stomach as the memories continued to mix with his reality. He'd just wanted a nap. He was tired.

He grabbed the Hunter's wing and yanked him down as he tried to get airborne.

The drugs fucked with him. Gabriel fucked with him. He didn't need his own goddamned conscience fucking with him now too.

The Hunter swept his legs out from underneath him. He fell, taking the Hunter with him.

His primary talent, and until now his only talent, was psychometry. The ability to psychically read objects that he touched. Something had pulled at him. Something under the bed that wouldn't let him sleep.

He grappled with the Hunter on the ground. He no longer felt the punishing blows.

He only saw the visions released when he'd touched the object he'd found under the bed.

The struggling grew limp and stopped. That brought him back enough. He convulsively jerked his legs away from the stranglehold he had around the Hunter's neck. He scrambled back and only started breathing again when he saw the man's chest rise.

He dropped his chin to his chest then slowly lifted his head to meet Gabriel's eyes across the ring. The memory of Gabriel's screams trapped within the threadbare stuffed animal under the bed reverberated in his mind.

Guards dragged the semiconscious Hunter off the grounds, and Gabriel curtly waved another to take his place. With a sigh, Zach rose to meet the fresh opponent.

His punishment for trespassing wasn't over. He wished they could beat the memories of what he'd seen out of his mind as easily as they damaged his body. But the truly horrific thing about this? Sympathy caused by the knowledge of what had broken Gabriel now mixed with his hatred of the Alpha and all he had done.

He would never be able to look at a teddy bear again.

◆ ◆ ◆

Three days later, Nickolas cupped the air underneath his wings for the first time since he was injured. High above the valley, he soared on a thermal, watching the sun glint off of the heaps of snow blanketing the fields, feeling the strain in his unused flight muscles.

How long? Weeks? I'd only just managed to get back in the air before the evacuation. Ian had me grounded for about three weeks. No wonder my muscles are in such bad shape.

The air currents washed over his body. *A week or two back in the air after my first grounding isn't much to recover muscle.*

Beth and Marcus had finished going over his wings during his morning exam and pronounced him flight worthy, though he could see in their eyes that they wanted to wait a little longer. They smothered him, following him out to the courtyard to watch him take off.

He ignored their fussing. Too little, too late.

A shadow shot by underneath him, and he glared over his shoulder. Not the person he wanted in the air with him. Kieran flew in the standard escort position below and behind; Nickolas ground his teeth at the sudden pounding in his veins. He wanted to wrap wings with Jessica, not with his shadow. That need brought too many other thoughts and feelings to the surface. The intimacy they had managed so far had only fed the fire that grew daily. He turned back and pumped his wings; as he rose in altitude, his muscles started to burn.

Nickolas, it's time to land.

Ignoring Kieran, he found a new thermal and started a lazy spiral.

The sound of wings drifted to him, and Kieran's shadow blocked the sun as the empath moved to a position above him. **Nickolas, you heard me. It's time to land.**

Side slipping, Nick kited to the side, and Kieran shot a burst of annoyance down their link. **Damn it, Nick, land your ass now! Or I'll broad send a call across the entire valley. You can bet your wings that Chris, Donald, and way too many of the other lieutenants will be on you before you can count to five.**

Flight

Exhaling in irritation, Nickolas dropped altitude. Back-winging, he touched down in the field near the barns—far enough away that he wouldn't need to interact with anyone. Except his shadow. Wind kicked up as Kieran landed next to him, a scowl on the empath's face.

A growl rumbled in Nick's throat as he stretched his tightening wing muscles then folded them across his back. "I'm not a new fledge, I do know how to be careful and gauge my own abilities. I know how to strengthen my flight muscles properly. I don't need a nursemaid."

Kieran flipped his hair out of his eyes. "You know the rules, Nick."

Nick lifted his arms and pulled the muscles in his back, giving them a different stretch. "Rules? Whose rules do we have to follow now? Ian's? Marcus's?"

"Don't get snippy. It's common sense, and you know it. What's really eating at you?"

Nick turned away and continued to stretch.

"Nickolas, don't forget, I'm an empath."

Spinning, Nick struck out low with his leg. Kieran leapt with a wing beat then landed with his own growl.

"You're not doing a very good job keeping your feelings locked up anymore, are you? The thunder surging down our link is almost deafening. I can receive your feelings, Nick. I can feel the uncertainty, the worry, the pain. But I have no idea why, or what causes them."

Nick stretched his wings out and gave them a vigorous flap, then crouched to take off again.

"Stay on the ground," Kieran snapped. "You haven't rested sufficiently yet."

Nick snarled and slammed his wings closed.

"Nick, you've always tried to outrun your demons. Has it worked yet? Talk to me."

Nick sliced a glance at the empath but finally, grudgingly, broached the subject that had started to obsess his mind now that he was healed enough for his body to make other demands. "How many partners do you have, Kieran?"

Kieran cocked his head, surprised by the sudden sex question. "Three. Jen and I still like to dance, and we have learned a few of the complex aerial dances the Aurorans developed. I've enjoyed having Kevin as a new partner."

The want, the need to learn the aerial mating dances, to be in the air with Jessica now that he could fly again, sank talons into him, and he walked away as he fought with his new need, not sure how to deal with it. It didn't seem to matter that they'd become intimate, it wasn't enough. The realization that this was because of his caste didn't help him figure out how to cope with it. For the first time there wasn't anything to stop either of them from coming together fully. She was through the change, and he was finally flight worthy and physically healed enough, and his body knew it. But...he remembered the questions he'd had about himself since his fledging. His inability to conjure up any desire for either sex. His certainty that something was wrong with him. Look at what he'd done to the nurse tech during his isolation. And now he struggled with this overwhelming need. A need he really didn't want displayed for the joy of the rest of the clan. *They all may like to play peacock...* He spread his wings.

Kieran's hand yanked him to a stop, but he wouldn't look at the empath. "There is nothing wrong with you. Get that out of your head."

Ashamed that Kieran had picked up on that, he tried to shake off his keeper's hold, but he was stronger than he looked. "Damn it, Kieran."

"Everyone knew you weren't like us sexually. No one thought badly about you for it. We respected your needs or lack thereof, and yes those needs are changing. That's not really a surprise, is it?"

Nick's wings flapped, and he shifted from foot to foot.

"Becoming curious about such things is normal, Nick. You just have to ask..."

Mental static interrupted whatever Kieran was saying, and Nick turned back to him. Kieran's eyes flared, and Nick saw anger spark in them, but underneath it, driving it, was concern and fear. Swearing a blue streak, Kieran dropped his hand from Nickolas's arm.

"What's happened, Kieran?"

The empath clenched his fist. "No one can find Jays. He somehow managed to slip out after his breakfast was delivered."

His emotions settling down with something else to focus on, Nick shrugged his shoulders. "So? He probably wants to be alone."

Anger flashed in Kieran's eyes again, and he snapped, "You don't understand, Nick. *No one* can find him. They can't sense him."

Surprised at Kieran's insistence, Nick shook his head at the empath. "He'll come back when he's ready. Just leave him alone."

"He's going into the coma, Nick."

Finally understanding, he closed his eyes briefly. "Crap. We need to go find him."

"Yes. Beth hoped I might be able to locate him since I've had such a close mental link with him for the last few weeks."

"Good idea."

Kieran took a deep breath as he went into a trance. Nickolas could feel the surge of energy around them as he worked.

After a few moments, the empath resurfaced, frustrated. "Nothing. It's like the line I have to him disappears when I get too close. I can see it from a distance, but when I try to get closer, it goes invisible."

"Let me try." Nick dropped down into the trance, then using his blood bond with Kieran, he caught Jays's line and traced it. With the same results. He looked at it from all angles then got an idea. *Kieran, join me, will you? Maybe together we can get through.*

Kieran's presence winked into existence next to him in the trance. Together they both followed the link, pouring more energy into it when the line started to fade from view. It fought them, wanting to hide itself, but after a brief struggle, it flared back into view, and Nick and Kieran quickly traced it to the end. *He's on the bluff. What is he doing up there?*

"Better yet, how did he get up there?" Kieran said in surprise, dropping out of the trance.

Nick shrugged his shoulders and extended his wings, taking the few moments necessary to do the preliminary stretches that were required until he was fully back to normal. Together they took off, heading for the cliff face above the practice grounds.

Do you see him yet, Nick?

His eyes skimmed over the Valkyries working out on the practice grounds before he returned his attention to the top of the cliff. *Nothing. Let's land and look on foot.* Landing side by side about thirty feet from the edge, Nickolas and Kieran looked around but still didn't see the fledgling.

"What is going on? Why can't we see him?" Kieran's calm voice belied the concern Nickolas received through their link.

He closed his eyes and let his senses waft around him. The subtle buzz of power in use penetrated his awareness, and he looked at Kieran. "He's blocking us somehow. Remember, he hasn't been on the inhibitor for the duration of his change."

The empath's gaze grew thoughtful, and Nickolas felt Kieran join with him once more. Together they sent their power out, and suddenly there was Jays. He sat on the very edge of the rocky cliff, his legs hanging over the side of the flat boulder. Nickolas didn't like the set of his wings; depression was written plain in the fledgling's body language. Kieran met Nick's eyes briefly before the two of them carefully approached him.

"Hey, Jays," Kieran said softly. "Everyone's looking for you."

"Yeah, I know," he said without looking at them. The fledge stared out over the working Valkyries three hundred feet below them.

Concern in his eyes, Kieran looked at Nickolas before he continued. "So, what're you doing up here? Beth told me that you didn't eat your breakfast."

Jays finally turned his head slightly and looked at them with one eye. "Did you see the size of the breakfast they brought me, Kieran? I'm not stupid. I know I'm going into the coma."

Wondering why that surprised him, Kieran said, "You do?"

Jays snorted and looked at them like they were stupid. "Give me a break. I've helped enough of you through. I think I know the signs."

Kieran tucked his wings in and asked Jays a second time. "So, what are you doing up here then?"

Jays turned away and looked back out over the Valley. Several aerial dances had started up over the practice grounds, and Nickolas thought that the fledgling wasn't going to answer, but then he drew in a deep breath.

"Thinking. Remembering. Wishing. Personally, I think it's a blessing for all of you to have no idea the coma is coming. I wish I didn't."

He looked even more listless, if that were possible, and Kieran's worried expression grew worse. Suddenly afraid for Jays, Nickolas moved closer to his friend and could see the bleakness in his blue eyes.

"Will I wake up? Or is today the last day of my life? This is the most dangerous time in a wild Valkyrie's change. Did you know that? If I remember the records correctly, almost a quarter of the fledglings who have changed outside of the Facility didn't make it out of the coma. The ratio was different in the Hub. We hadn't figured out why yet." Jays paused, swallowing. "I watch everyone down there, sparring, fighting, flying. Ian never got to know what it was like; that's why he avoided the obstacle course as much as he could. He longed for fully developed wings."

Nick sank down next to him. "I never knew," he whispered.

"He didn't want you to know, Nick. But today, I watch everyone down there, and I realize I don't want to die not knowing what my wings feel like."

Sucking in a breath, Nickolas stared out over the cliff in apprehension. "Jays, you can't," he said with understanding. "You know the protocol."

Anger swirled up around the fledgling, and Nickolas looked at Kieran, who had placed himself on Jays's other side.

"So?" Jays snapped. "It's not like you let rules stop *you*. Besides, Jessica flew."

He sympathized with Jays's irritation about the constraints, since he'd just been complaining about the same. "Kieran wouldn't be here if that were true. As much as I dislike it, he's spotting me until everyone else is sure my wings are strong enough. And Jess doesn't count. First off, she didn't know the protocol; second, she took off from a river bank. If her musculature hadn't been able to support her, she wouldn't have gotten far and the drop would have been negligible. Unlike leaping off a cliff face," he said grimly.

"Which *I* see as thinly veiled suicide," Kieran added softly.

Jays's wings fell again, and he tried to block them out once more. Nickolas studied him closely, watching the emotions drift across his face.

"Do you want to die?" Nick asked him quietly.

Jays's eyes tightened, but he didn't take his attention away from the valley below. "I don't know, Nick," he replied almost under his breath. "Part of me has wanted desperately to give up, but then the other half of me fights back."

Nick brushed his shoulder against him. "I don't know if it's normal for most at this stage of the change to feel that way, but I sure did, Jays. I can tell you, though, that if I had been given the opportunity to sit on a cliff like you are...I wouldn't have hesitated." Jays met his eyes and Nick could see that he understood what he was telling him. "Ian wanted you to live. You know that. That's why he sent you. Don't throw his gift away."

Tears glistened in Jays's eyes but didn't fall. "I'm scared, Nick."

"I know. We've all come through the coma. We'll be waiting for you on the other side."

Jays studied him for a moment longer then turned to look back out over the valley, but Nick could see a slight lessening in the tension around the fledgling. He looked back up at Kieran; the empath still looked worried but managed a small smile.

They sat there in silence for a few minutes, then Kieran broke it. "So, Jays, you still haven't answered *how* you got up here."

Jays looked over at Kieran. "I walked."

Nick looked over the cliff and was able to see the zigzagging deer trail that wound down the steep face. He met Kieran's gaze, smiling as he shook his head.

"That's not what I meant," the empath said. "No one knew where you were. There's no way you should have been able to scale that cliff without someone noticing; it's completely visible to the entire valley. You shouldn't have been able to get past Beth in sick bay either."

He shrugged his shoulders. "I can't answer that, Kieran. I don't know. It just seemed like no one saw me, and I walked right by them."

Kieran hummed under his breath, and the two of them exchanged looks while Jays continued to stare. *He's definitely using his talent,* Kieran sent to Nick.

He nodded in reply. "Jays, what did you feel when you were able to walk by people? What were you thinking?"

The fledgling furrowed his brows in thought for a moment. "I wanted to be alone. I remember that. I kept thinking I just wanted outside, to go somewhere quiet and alone. Then when they brought in my breakfast tray, I took one look at it and it confirmed my suspicions. I wasn't sure, at first, that I was correct when I started seeing the preliminary signs for the coma. It was too early from all of my experiences. I'd forgotten that the rate of change outside of the Hub was so drastically different. When I saw the food, it hit me, and I just needed to get out. When I walked into the main room, everyone ignored me, so I kept going and didn't look back. Now that I think about it, though, I did feel a warm tingle ripple through my body. It wasn't so strong that I noticed it at the time though."

We need Jessica to take a look at him, Nick sent to Kieran.

I agree. What he's describing sounds like he was using power to me.

We'll need to keep a closer eye on him. If he can drop off the radar like that... Nick held Kieran's eyes, and he knew the empath understood what he meant.

Let's get him down from here.

"Come on, Jays, let's get you back to sick bay," Kieran said, and he reached out and took the fledgling's elbow, gently urging him to stand. "We'll walk back with you."

"Don't trust me, Kieran?" Jays said with a last wistful look out over the valley.

"Should we?"

He shrugged, and Nick saw a slight smile tug at the corner of his lips. *No, I don't think we can trust him at all,* Nickolas thought with a chuckle. With Jays in between them, they started down the steep, rocky path. Concentrating on his footing, Nickolas heard Kieran's voice drift up.

"Well, Robin finally left today, Jays. Hopefully he'll get something useful with your access codes."

In front of him, Jays snorted. "Don't count on it. It won't work. I tried to tell Marcus that."

"How can you be so sure? It's worth a try," Kieran replied. Nickolas felt the brief stirrings of power flowing around him, and he looked up. Jays had paused, and his eyes were unfocused. Kieran looked away from the fledgling to catch Nick's eye. *Talent number two, I would say,* the empath sent.

You felt the stirring?

Yes.

Gently nudging Jays, Nickolas got him moving back down the mountain. "Come on, Jays. You've got a busy week ahead of you."

The fledgling tossed a glare over his shoulder, but Nickolas saw the fear he held in his eyes. "You'll be fine, Jays," he whispered. "We'll all make sure of it."

◆ ◆ ◆

Robin skimmed the dark treetops and passed the last sentinels surrounding Aurora. He dropped lower to descend past the cliff wall and fly over the darkened valley. The only movement he saw was the occasional ripple of desiccated grass poking through the patchy snow. A warm, southerly wind had blown in when he'd left four days ago, and there wasn't much left of the snow.

Every year he hoped that it would herald the start of spring, but it was almost always just Mother Nature playing a trick. After two weeks of wonderful weather, they would have a last four to six weeks of rain and snow before true spring struck.

Back-winging, he dropped into a tired landing in the courtyard. The shadowy form of Kelley waited for him. Light spilled out onto the cobbles as she opened the door. Her hand brushed his shoulder when he passed, and he reached up to give it a quick squeeze. Warmth enveloped him, and he sighed as he wove across the room, entering the kitchens.

He opened the fridge but just stared at the contents until Kelley pushed him out of the way then shoved him into a chair, taking over getting him food herself.

"I called Marcus. He said he'd get Nickolas and come over here to meet you," she said.

He rested his head on the table for a moment and mumbled, "Oh good. I wasn't really looking forward to going anywhere else tonight except our bed."

Kelley tsked. "What'd you do, fly straight from Dustin's?"

Raising his head, he narrowed his eyes at his Second. "And what if I did?"

She just shook her head and sliced the sandwich in half before she placed it on a plate with a couple of pickles and an apple. After setting the plate down in front of him, she got a glass of water and pulled out a second chair. "Was there an emergency? Any reason to push yourself?"

He bit into the sandwich and shook his head. "No," he mumbled. "I just needed to be home, Kel."

Her expression lightened, and she passed over the cookies that she'd been palming. Smiling tiredly at her, he picked one up. Footsteps echoed through the open door, and Marcus and Nickolas entered the kitchen. Nickolas still looked distant but not as cold as he had been for the last couple of weeks. The two Alphas pulled out chairs, joining him and his Second.

"What brought you in so late, Robin? Why didn't you wait until tomorrow?"

He looked sheepish as he wolfed down the last of his sandwich. "We got locked out of the system this afternoon. Jays was right, we didn't get anything too terribly useful, and I don't see us getting a second chance. They had to have detected us, because we were completely locked out."

Marcus sighed then thanked Kelley for the cup of tea she handed him. "We knew that was a high possibility. But I don't have to like it."

"What *did* you find out?" Nickolas asked quietly.

Robin drained the last of his water then sat back. "Nothing of use for going after Gabriel. Dustin and I stayed up all hours trying to get what we could. They even had their personnel and food requisitions locked down. So we couldn't even make a guess how many people we face in Eastern Washington.

"All we could find out was how much of the Facility had been destroyed and damaged. Ian did a good job on it. All of the Valkyrie portion was completely demolished, and any area attached was heavily damaged. They have repairs underway. They're razing the most damaged sections. But the most discouraging part is how quickly they've reestablished isolation facilities for emerging Valkyries. No one has been brought in yet, but according to the documents that Dustin found, they have a small three-cell lab ready to go into operation as soon as they have need."

Nickolas growled but fell silent at a look from Marcus.

Huh. Didn't think Nick would take direction from anyone. Robin supposed it just depended on the circumstance. He took a deep breath before he plunged into the next topic. "Ian's remains were located. After they were examined, a General Faulk signed the orders for him to be buried in a place of honor next to his wife."

Robin paused then. Marcus's face was set in stone. Nickolas's eyes were far from cold anymore, and he glanced quickly away from the Breeder's gaze.

Marcus cleared his throat. "You said General Faulk, Robin?"

"Yes, that's what the paperwork said. Why, do you know him?"

"That's Luther's last name."

Nickolas's head snapped around at the mention of Luther. At Marcus's nod, Robin continued his debriefing. "With Ian gone, there's no one to oversee the Valkyrie portion of the Facility, so a General Kratz, who apparently had been in charge of the military segment there, has taken command of the whole complex."

"Kratz," Marcus snarled. "He's one of the worst of the faction leaders on the council. He's the one, last I knew, who was personally holding Gabriel's leash."

Too tired to really ponder that, Robin ate the last cookie and looked at his Alpha. "So now what? We didn't find anything that would help. Jays was right."

Marcus sat back and sipped his tea. "I can't believe Luther took care of Dad."

"Who exactly is he?" Robin asked. He pushed back his chair and rose to make himself a cup of tea, but Kelley waved him back to his seat and took over. "What is his position in this mess we call a life?"

"General Rembrandt Harrison Luther Faulk. Thank you, Kelley," Marcus said when she refreshed his tea as well. He leaned forward, placing his elbows on the table, and wrapped his hands around his warm cup then looked at Nickolas. "Do you know any of the generals, Nicky?"

"I know Kratz, of course. We usually avoided him though. He kept to his section of the Facility. Ian had pretty solid control over his area. But I also recently found out that everyone had been protecting me from a lot of things, so what I do or don't know isn't necessarily a good gauge. I'd suggest that you ask Chris. Anyway, he's the only general I know."

Marcus nodded his head, and Robin drank his tea, watching the two. "Carl Kratz and Luther Faulk are two generals on the council. I don't personally know all of the members or how many there are; I think Dad did though, we should ask Jays. When the experiment that created us escaped and the military got involved, the council formed. Together, mostly, they decide how the Facility is going to proceed, but they all have different agendas. And they pursue them regardless of the others on the council. So there's always jockeying amongst the factions to gain support for their own personal aims. Kratz is dangerous. But in some respects, I fear Luther more than any of the others I know. He gets what he wants with careful planning and manipulation."

"If Kratz was in charge of the Facility, what is Luther in charge of?" Robin asked.

Raising his mug, Marcus saluted him. "Now that's a very good question. I have no idea." Marcus held his eyes, and Robin could see the resignation forming in them before he turned to look at his son. "But we must have more information if we want to take down Gabriel's compound."

Nickolas shifted uneasily. Robin didn't blame him; if he had been the one hunted by Luther, he wouldn't like the idea he was sure was coming. He glanced away from Nick and caught Kelley's eyes. He could see her fear for Leslie that she tried to keep hidden. Reaching out, he took her hand and pulled her onto his lap.

"I don't see much of a choice, Nicky," Marcus said reluctantly. "We need to ask Luther if he can or will help us."

Nickolas shook his head in denial, opening his mouth to protest, but Marcus sighed, cutting him off. "Do you have any other ideas? I'm open to them. But so far, nobody has offered any other alternatives."

Nickolas closed his eyes. When he opened them again, all emotion had been removed, and Robin felt Kelley shiver in his arms.

"Fine. Let's see what he has to offer. I'll put it on speaker, so everyone be quiet." He reached into an inside pocket and pulled out his cell phone, powering it up. After the chime sounded, he punched the talk button, then after pressing another button, he laid the phone down on the table in front of him.

After two rings, Luther answered in a clipped tone of voice. "This better be good, Nickolas. You have a bit of explaining to do. I don't appreciate being lied to."

Taken aback, Nickolas straightened in his seat. "Excuse me?" he said, and Robin could see him going on the defensive.

"I asked you if you knew where Jays Anderson was, remember? And you said you didn't know."

Clearing his throat, Nickolas responded, "Well, I didn't actually know right where he was at that moment in time."

There was a tension-filled pause before Luther replied in a curt tone, "I see that I'm going to have to be very specific in what I ask you from now on. I don't like being lied to. Someone with Jays Anderson's access codes hacked into our computer system in the last few days. Where is Jays, and is he all right?"

"Jays entered stage two the day we left the Facility. Ian didn't want him remaining behind, so he sent him with us. He was just fine as of this morning, but he entered the coma four days ago, so his health is still uncertain. It's a day-to-day thing."

Even though Robin knew Jays had been close to the coma, it still came as a surprise to hear that his childhood friend was walking that line. Kelley ran her hand over his hair, and he relaxed, bringing his attention back to the conversation.

"But otherwise he's unharmed?" Luther asked sharply.

"Of course!" Nickolas exclaimed. "We don't hurt our own."

A satisfied sound came across the line, and Robin frowned, wondering what exactly had just occurred.

"So, what is it you want? You're obviously looking for something. What is it you need, and why did you call me?" The general asked, and Robin didn't like the hint of silkiness he detected in that voice.

"We're going after our people, and we need more info on Gabriel. Can you get us access to the documents we need?"

"Your people? I wasn't aware that Gabriel took any of the Facility Valkyries in his raid. I thought he only got Aurorans."

"Just because I'm not personally familiar with an individual doesn't mean that I would want Gabriel to have them. They are still Valkyries. And they were taken against their will," Nickolas replied coldly.

"Good," Luther said softly, and this time Robin was sure there was more behind his goading than what was on the surface. "I can do better than give you access to documents,

Nickolas," the general continued cautiously. "There are things I can do to help. But there is a price."

Silence descended before Nickolas asked in a flat voice, "What?"

"You know what I want, Nick. We need you to return. You, Jessica, Jays; we'd like Kieran as well, since he's so well known, and at least a small contingent of other Valkyries."

Robin watched Nickolas fall completely still. "No. Not happening."

Luther continued on as if Nickolas hadn't said a thing, and Robin watched Nickolas's jaw clench. "I have people inside Gabriel's compound, Nick. I can get you the layout, the locations of all Valkyries, how many people Gabriel has on hand, any pertinent information you might need. They can also disable the radar when you are set to arrive, along with the alarms on the perimeter fencing."

Robin's eyes snapped to Marcus, who looked back at him with a mixture of trepidation and hope on his face. This was more than they could have wished for. But could they live with Nick paying the price? He looked back at the Breeder; leaning with his elbows on the table, Nick had pulled the band out of his hair, and his hands clenched at his temples so his dark hair fanned out over his arms.

"No. I won't sell any of my people back into that cage, no matter how gilded."

"There's at least five hundred Valkyries being held at the compound, Nick. A lot of them are injured, maimed, or in some way incapable of flight. How do you propose to get them out of Eastern Washington? And how does Marcus plan to feed and clothe that many? We've been watching his investments, and while they are ingenious and much more lucrative than we would have expected, they are not enough to solve this problem, even if they liquidate everything."

"You can't really expect us to return to the Facility. Not after all we've learned and done."

"That's not quite what I'm proposing," the general said persuasively. "I was thinking of installing you in a new location. We have recently acquired the buildings that are located at the old naval base at Sandpoint in Seattle. You would have the advantages of a city location, but still be separated. You would have aerial access from Lake Washington, so you wouldn't bother too many people. I would allow you almost complete autonomy over the complex; but in exchange, Ian's research would need to be continued, and my people and I would have unlimited access to it and to the complex. You would be free to come and go as you want. Within reason. We can't have you creating enemies with the people in the neighborhood, for instance.

"Movement between Aurora would be highly encouraged. It would allow Marcus and his people access to the city, which they haven't had for two decades. I would also insist that all injured Valkyries, and not just those from the compound, be checked out by my psychiatric team. For all that you are different, you're still human.

"Besides the inside information, I can supply buses to carry everyone away from the complex, blankets, clothing, and food to support the extra mouths for the time it would take my people to get the naval station remodeled enough for you to occupy it. I also want you to continue your recovery and fledgling work. The only other requirement I have is that you and Jessica must reside there. You would be free to visit Aurora as much as you like, but I want you in Seattle." He paused, letting it all sink in. "So do we have a deal?"

Nickolas looked trapped. "I can't make a decision like this on my own. It affects too many other people. I'll call you back."

"I'll be waiting, Nickolas."

Nickolas reached forward with exaggerated care and picked up the phone, pushing end and powering the unit down before setting it back on the table. His hand rested on the phone, and he bowed his head for a moment, his dark hair falling to obscure his face. Silence hung heavy in the room before Nick looked back up at all of them. Robin could see a mixture of fear and anger in his eyes from the trap Luther was setting for him. His eyes fixed on Marcus, Nickolas asked, "Well, what do you think?"

"The help he can give is invaluable," Marcus said evenly.

"You don't have to pay the price."

"Don't be so sure of that, Nicky. He wants *you*, but I suspect he would settle for anyone else if worst came to worst. I also wouldn't put it past him to use any of us against you if he felt it would work."

Nickolas slammed his fist down on the table then took a deep breath as he exerted a tremendous effort to stomp his feelings down. "I don't like it," he finally managed to say. "But I think you're right. He won't give up until he gets what he wants."

"Think about it. Talk to the others. If you accept his offer, maybe this way you'll retain some control on your lives."

Nickolas shook his head. "I'm starting to think freedom is just an illusion." Rising, he walked out of the kitchen. Marcus swore, and Robin glanced at him.

"Just when I start to hope I might get my son back..."

"It's not over yet, Marcus." Robin caught his Alpha's gaze. "He might find a way out of it."

Shaking his head, Marcus rose and rinsed out his tea cup before following his eldest son out.

Luther quietly reached forward and punched the button that disconnected the speaker phone. He made sure it was truly off before he leaned back in his chair and looked over at the man whose overt job was as his secretary. Jared Roberts sat on his customary perch on the corner of Luther's desk, his face thoughtful. A slight smile tipped the corner of Luther's mouth, and he asked, "Did you hear what I heard, Jared?"

His secretary cocked his head and met his gaze with clear eyes. "He had us on speaker. Who else do you think was there?"

Pleased with his pupil's astuteness, Luther thought for a moment before answering, "Marcus most definitely, and I expect Robin. Marcus would have sent his Second to their contact in Lynden. Dustin is the most logical choice to help them with computer issues. May assures me that Martha's grandsons are the best there is. And with Zachary out of the picture, Dustin has to be the one who attempted to breach our security. And the timing is right for Robin to have just gotten back to Aurora after they were shut out."

"What do you think they're going to do?"

"They'll try and figure a way around my proposal. We'll give Nick a little more time. It won't take him long to realize that he really doesn't have much of a choice. Soon he'll be back with us. So, on a slightly different topic—my business trip went well, though I wasn't pleased with the timing. I've been keen to hear your observations from when you picked up our errant personnel."

Jared stood and started to slowly pace in front of the desk. "I got into position just after dawn. The first wave of Aurorans arrived carrying the dead and injured. I listened with the parabolic and watched, so when the bulk of the rebels arrived with the prisoners, it didn't take me long to figure out who was who from their behavior. Then I slipped out of my blind and made my way to the rendezvous down the road to meet up with the fleet so I could arrive with them.

"Wild Valkyrie behavior differs drastically from the tapes I've studied of the Facility Valkyries. Their behavior patterns are not like what we have recorded."

"Really? Isn't that interesting? That should make bringing the control group home a learning experience. I wonder how the Facility Valkyries have changed since being with the feral group."

"How many do you think will return? Do you think any of the valley people will come with?"

"No idea. I suspect Nick would try and keep the numbers as small as possible, but I don't think he'll have control over that. Not from what I've seen. His people won't want him alone and unprotected as far as they are concerned. So, please continue."

"As soon as we arrived, Robin pulled the majority of his people and only kept a couple of Flights of Hunters in sight to watch us. Gone was the civilized, normal behavior I'd observed secretly. As soon as they felt threatened from our arrival, they turned to instinct, and the animalistic traits shined through. I had to keep a tight rein on our people; the Valkyries' behavior unnerved them.

"It was a little freaky, I'll admit. The way Robin's groups watched us—I felt like I was watching a half-starved wolf pack that had recently been beaten with a stick."

"They have precious little reason to trust us, Jared."

His secretary nodded and stopped in front of the desk. "Robin was interesting. The strength that seemed to pour off of him, the kind of invisible, intangible strength that you see when you watch a horse running across a field, completely unconscious grace. He was the uncontested leader of over a hundred; I watched him smack down a few of the Hunters the way a wolf would reprimand a subordinate, swift but almost absent-minded, yet even with the prisoners that obviously worked for Gabriel, he remained incredibly gentle. He was a fascinating mix of behaviors."

"I'm hoping he will join his sister, at least in part, at the Seattle base. We've never had the opportunity to observe a Valkyrie that has undergone the change completely out of our control before. We'll have Jays, but with his experience from his work in the Hub, it won't be quite the same."

Luther watched the thoughts swirl in Jared's eyes. "You seem very sure that Nickolas will take your bait."

Luther raised his eyebrow and stared at his student. "You heard his responses when I pushed him. There is no way Nickolas will leave even complete strangers at risk when he has the ability to help them. All I have to do is wait. We've set the snare; he will willingly walk into it. Watch."

"From my debriefing with Jeff and some of the other Facility personnel that have now joined us, they agree with your assessment of Nickolas's temperament."

"Speaking of that, how is it going?"

"Well, it was easy enough from watching Robin and his Valkyries interact with the prisoners to judge who was working for Gabriel knowingly and who wasn't. Past that, I was also able to tell who was particularly sympathetic to the Valkyries. Jeff, his remaining two team mates, and about a half dozen more have joined our group. The bulk of the personnel were returned to their previous posts, but we have a few 'guests' left. I've deflected inquiries on their whereabouts already. Carl is looking for them."

Luther pursed his lips and frowned. "I'll look into that. I can keep Kratz at bay. The dead were taken care of?"

"Yes. After examinations, the next of kin were given appropriate stories, then they were buried in a mass grave in the Facility graveyard."

Luther pulled out a note pad and jotted down some reminders. "I'll need to put together my report for the council meeting next week. They are going to want to know what has happened. They will hardly have missed an addition of that size in the graveyard."

Returning to his seat on the corner of the desk, Jared studied him before he asked, "So how long do you think it will take Nickolas to bow to the inevitable?"

"Truthfully? I'm not sure. It depends on the circumstances he's in. If Gabriel makes another grab at him..." He shrugged his shoulders. "How has the remodeling been going?"

"We gained access to the buildings last week. Our engineers and architects spent three days going over the place. The architects have finished the first of their plans and turned them over to me for approval, and I sent them on to the builders to get the ball rolling. They've already started on the kitchens and the first of the living quarters. The estimates I've received have them completing the basic living accommodations in about two months. After that, they will focus on the labs and training facilities."

"Good. To twist Nick's words, let's make it a gilded cage."

Chapter Sixteen

Robin walked across the field, the early morning breeze warm as it blew through his hair. He'd had very little sleep for the three days he'd worked with Dustin, and he was still exhausted from his flight home, but that hadn't let him relax enough to sleep.

After tossing and turning all night, Kelley had kicked him out of the house and told him to go and see Jays.

He pushed open the doors into the infirmary and walked into the dimly lit room. The place was deserted. His boots rang on the wood, then he paused outside Jays's room. The soft sound of a voice on the other side of the door stayed his hand before he carefully opened it. His sister sat in a chair, her back to the door, holding Jays's hand. His friend had the waxy complexion and slack features of someone who was in the coma.

Robin held still, with his hand on the knob. Jessica hadn't heard him enter. He could tell from the set to her wings and the tone in her voice that she was upset.

He shifted his weight and looked over his shoulder back into the hall. She still wouldn't have much to do with him, preferring to stay close to the rest of the Facility Valkyries. He'd missed her so much, but she would hardly talk to him. This was the closest he'd been to her alone, when she was unguarded and acting like herself, and he couldn't seem to make himself leave. Even though it was obvious that she wanted a private moment with Jays. Her voice floated out through the room, full of uncertainty. Frozen, he listened to her talk.

"Don't worry; you're going to be just fine. I know I don't have any experience in this sort of thing, not having seen anyone else in the coma before, but I'm very stubborn. I won't let anything happen. I know everyone else feels the same. In all respects but wings, they already considered you theirs. You were an acknowledged member of Nickolas's clan. And Nickolas may even be more stubborn than me, Jays, so don't worry. If they have anything to say about it, you're going to wake up right on time."

Robin watched her smooth out the blanket then pick up his hand again before going on. "I'm really sorry about how mad I was at you in the Hub. It was just such a shock seeing you again, and under those circumstances. I envy you the change you had here in Aurora. I don't know why I felt or feel the way I do. I have no one but myself to blame. I could have come here to go through the change, well, if I could have gotten away from Nick, that is. Then I wouldn't have been subjected to what you and Ian did to me in the Hub. But now I'm just circling around and second guessing things, aren't I? If I hadn't been in the Hub, I wouldn't now be with Nick, so maybe it worked out for the best. Who knows?"

Jessica paused as she ran the back of her hand across her face, and Robin gripped the knob tighter, realizing that she was crying. "I hated it there, Jays. I really hated it there. And at times I hated both you and Ian, but you knew that, didn't you?" Her voice trailed off. "I don't want to go back. Nick told me what that general wants, and he promised me that he doesn't want to return either. But...for him it would almost be like returning home. Wouldn't it? He didn't know any other way of life until the last couple of weeks. If this general succeeds in convincing Nickolas, I won't have any choice. I'm scared, Jays, really scared. I don't want to return to the Facility."

Clearing her throat, she wiped at her face again then gently brushed Jays's bangs out of his eyes. "Your hair has gotten longer since I was brought into the Hub. It's darker than I remember from when we were kids." She brushed her fingers through it again. "I wish you hadn't gone away. Everyone seems to leave me. First you, then Mom and Dad, then Robin. We missed you a lot, you know. I felt like I had lost a brother, but it hit Robin the hardest. You two were inseparable. Do you remember? He didn't know what to do with himself after you were gone. It took months for him to start to get back to normal."

Robin felt his heart clench when she rested her forehead on the mattress next to Jays. "Jays, what am I supposed to do? He left. He left and never even looked back. I miss May. She's always been there. She would be able to help. She could tell me why he wouldn't come back. Couldn't she? I needed him, and he didn't care. He went off and started his new life with Marcus and forgot all about me. Why was I not important enough? I don't know how to talk to him now."

His heart breaking, Robin shut his eyes as memories flooded him. He could see her at fifteen, the last time he'd seen her. He had just gotten his wings and had flown back home, disobeying direct orders from Marcus. He had needed to see Jessica, to let her know he was ok. But when he got there, she was so angry at him she wouldn't listen to anything he had to say. He could tell that she felt betrayed because he'd gone to Marcus, but where else was he supposed to go? It wasn't like he could control his body and make it not go through the change. He'd tried to talk to her, and May helped him, but he couldn't spend enough time to calm her.

Marcus had had a very good reason for not wanting him to go back. The Facility had been watching for him to return and had almost finished setting up a trap when he realized what was going on. He'd barely managed to get out of the region. When he'd gotten back to Aurora, Marcus had taken a piece out of him for disobeying and endangering not only himself, but Jessica and the rest of them. Then he had forbidden him from going anywhere near Jessica again until she had changed.

He'd begged Marcus to bring her in. If she was relocated to the valley, she'd be safe from the Facility. Marcus had looked so sad then and had sat the young Robin down to explain the last request that he had received from Jennifer, his mother. He couldn't, in good conscious, interfere with such a strong vision from a Seer, he had told Robin. They needed to trust her Sight; there had to be a reason that she wanted Jessica to remain where she was. Bowing to the inevitable, Robin had agreed and thrown himself into his new life. But he had never once forgotten his sister the way she seemed to think he had.

Clearing his throat, Robin closed the door, and Jessica whirled around in her seat. "You were important enough, Jess," he said roughly. "The Facility nearly took me the time I came to see you. After that, Marcus refused to allow me to try again. May kept an eye on things and made sure to let us know that the Facility never gave up their hope that they could get one of us by watching you."

His feelings ricocheted around, and he couldn't bottle them back up. He crossed the small distance between them and grabbed her by the shoulders when she rose and tried to move away from him. He stared into her eyes, the same eyes that he saw in the mirror every day. He could see the sheen of tears that filmed them. "I didn't want to leave you. Can you get that through your thick skull? You're my baby sister. I love you. Why can't you forgive me?"

The tears spilled over in her eyes, and he pulled her into his arms. He laid his cheek on the top of her head and slowly rocked to the side, his own tears getting her hair wet. After a while, she started to draw away, and he tipped her head up, wiping at the tear tracks on her cheeks with his thumbs. "I really am sorry, Jess. I have thought about you every day. I worried constantly that you would start to change and the Facility would get you. You don't know how hard it was for me when that's exactly what happened."

"I-I'm sorry, Robin." She hiccupped. "But couldn't you have at least written or sent some sort of message through May? You didn't, though. Nothing for ten years, Robin."

He closed his eyes briefly then looked back at her before he answered. "I didn't think you wanted to hear from me. After the last time I saw you..." He swallowed. "I couldn't take it if I had tried and you kept rebuffing my attempts."

"I was a hurt teenager. I didn't know what to do."

"Shhh. Just stop trying to shut me out now, ok? Please?"

She nodded her head, and this time when she tried to draw away, he let her. He pulled up another chair then sat down next to her and looked at his unconscious friend.

"How has he been doing?" he asked, changing the subject.

Sniffing, she replied, "So far, so good. Beth said that he hasn't shown any of the warning signs that they look for."

He relaxed at that news. "Good, that's good to hear. Has she said how much longer she thinks he'll be out?"

"Another three days, probably."

Jays's chest rose and fell slowly; Robin reached out and touched his cold cheek. If it wasn't for the slight movement, he would think his friend dead. He always hated this part of the change. Waiting was so hard. To distract himself, he looked at Jess. "Do you remember Dustin and his twin?"

Jessica's eyes unfocused, and she chewed on her lip. Robin smiled at the old gesture that he remembered. "I think so," she said. "What was his name?"

"Zach. Zachary and Dustin Donovan. We used to go over to their house for barbeques in the summer before Mom and Dad died."

"Oh yeah, I remember now." She glared at him. "The three of you used to love tricking me into following you into the woods and then leaving me."

Robin laughed. "We never actually left you. But it did make it so you weren't always following us everywhere."

"I remember one time when I came back, Mom took one look at me, and you were grounded for a week."

He ducked his head and felt his face grow hot. "Yeah, well that was her showing her talent again. Zach and I had come up with a new plan to keep you out of our hair. I guess she didn't think it was a good idea."

"I probably wouldn't have either."

"No, I suppose not."

"So why are you bringing them up?"

"That's where I spent the last four days. Dustin's family is our outside liaison. He's a computer whiz, so I took Jays's access codes to him, and the two of us attempted to get what info we could. Unfortunately, Jays was right, and we didn't get much."

"What does Zach do?"

Robin cast a quick look at her before he looked back at Jays. "He changed sixteen years ago. He was here in the valley until he was captured by Gabriel almost ten years ago. None of us have seen him since. Dustin was devastated. He hasn't ever given up hope that Zach will come back."

"Zach changed, but Dustin didn't?"

"Yeah."

"Weird."

He laughed at her. "Really? And how long have you been fledged?"

"Ok, point."

"Zach was flying to see Dustin when Gabriel caught him. He wasn't supposed to go by himself, but for some reason he headed out on no notice. He was a Seer, but he hadn't reported any visions. It came as a surprise to all of us here. And Dustin blames himself."

"How do you know Gabriel captured him?"

"I suppose we don't, really. He could have gotten hurt in the forest and died without help, but like a lot of identical twins, Dustin and Zach had a special bond. Dustin is sure that Zach is still alive, and pretty much every time a Valkyrie has disappeared, it's because a feral recovery team got them."

"That's what almost happened to you?"

"Yes. I only managed to escape them by the skin of my teeth. You were heavily watched after that for several years. It's only been the last few years that they lightened up on the surveillance. May has always kept a close eye on the situation."

"I just can't imagine her doing that."

"You would be surprised at what she can do. She's a retired spy. She was the best when she was in the field. Only the best live to old age like she has. I don't know how Mom knew her, and I doubt she'll ever tell us, but I trust her more than anyone, except Marcus."

"I feel like I'm in a dream, Robin. My perfectly normal life turns out to be something that could be shown on primetime television. My nanny is a spy, my brother disappears and comes back with super powers. I get superpowers and get kidnapped by a hot superbabe. Things blow up, and then reality strikes and people I know die. For real die. I was happy with my boring, normal life, Robin. I don't want to be wanted by secret government agencies; I want to just live my life."

"That's all any of us want, Jess. Trust me, that's what we all want."

◆ ◆ ◆

Christoff sat at a table in the longhouse and picked at his lunch as he listened to the conversations of his friends with half an ear. The room held few people. Lunch was the least busy meal of the day. Most people preferred to grab a sandwich or something to eat at home. Taking a bite, he chewed it automatically. He just hadn't felt right since the night of the attack. And it bothered him. *Beth is sure it's just from the knock on the head I took, that or the sleep drug they gave me to haul me away. But...* He shook his head. Ghost images blurred through his mind. A burst of laughter brought his attention back to the table.

"...told you that." Kieran laughed.

"So," Jays mumbled.

"What was that, Jays? I didn't quite catch that," Kieran prodded.

"I'm just glad my head doesn't hurt anymore," Jays said more clearly.

"Only two days?" Nick added in. "You're lucky. I was incapacitated for three, then it lingered."

Snorting, Chris remembered Nick waking from the coma. Incapacitated? He'd been like a bear just out of hibernation. Shaking his head, Chris took another bite of his lunch.

"Yeah, I think he needs to spend today in the infirmary too, just in case. It might come back. Don't you agree, Nick? He doesn't really want to take his first flight today. Better safe than sorry, I say."

"I'm still a fully qualified doctor you know, Kieran. I can harm as well as heal," Jays snarled.

More laughter erupted from the table. "Come on, guys, leave him be." Jessica laughed. "Or he'll go without you, Kier."

Chris saw the twinkle in Jays's eyes and knew that Jessica was right. Looking back at his plate, the conversations around him drifted off once more as he returned to his current obsession, poking at his faulty memory. Phantom fingers trickled up his spine and he caught his breath. With a conscious thought, he unclenched his hand from around his utensil and forced his lungs to work.

The last thing he remembered of that night was leaving dinner to head out with Adam and the rest of his scout team. He couldn't even remember gaining their quadrant position. From all of the other accounts, the attack didn't start for several hours after he had been on duty. What had happened? Adam and Ben both told him what he had done, both before and during the fight, at least until they were knocked out. But the recitation wasn't any different than hearing a news report. It didn't trigger his own memory of the night.

Pushing his food around on his plate, Chris could almost catch the tail of a memory, something he needed to know but really didn't want to know. A whisper scratched across his mind. Absorbed in his thoughts, he missed the concerned looks that everyone at the table kept throwing at him.

Agitated, he stabbed at his food but then a shiver rippled down his spine, and he paused with his fork halfway to his mouth. The mental storm winds that had been buffeting his mind for the last hour intensified. Panic flushed through him, and he looked up at his brother in desperation. Nick had stopped his conversation to look at him. His panic reaching through their link. Then a soft melodic voice drifted through his thoughts.

Christoff Illya Sinclair.

The singsong quality of the voice as it whispered through his consciousness brought pain in its wake. Like cobwebs, the barrier that had obscured his memory was shredded, and Chris shivered, dropping his fork to grab his head with his hands as the pain took his sight for a moment.

Chrissstoffff, the voice purred softly.

The memories swamped him, and his head filled with a silent scream that he wasn't allowed to release as Gabriel's laugh echoed through his mind.

It's time, Christoff.

Leave me be, he shouted silently.

That's not likely to happen. Are you alone?

No.

Then remember your orders, and make sure you cover your behavior. I don't want anyone to guess what's happening. Tonight after moonset, you are to leave the valley without anyone knowing. I'll be waiting for you four miles to the south.

No, I won't leave the valley, Gabriel, and you can't come in to get me.

Laughter followed that declaration. *Oh, you'll come, just like I ordered. You won't be able to stop yourself. I implanted the order deep, Chris. I can't alter it without another dose of the drug, which is too bad. I would love to cut this exercise short and have you bring your brother and Jessica out with you, but except for the command to be silent and come when I call you, your will is still your own. For now. I'll call for you at moonset.*

Silence filled his mind, and Christoff became aware of Nickolas's hand resting on his shoulder. Opening his eyes, he saw concern in his brother's gaze. Everyone around the table was staring at him. Gabriel's implanted orders kicked into effect, and try as he might, he couldn't make his mouth form the words to get help. He shouted them inside his mind, but nothing would come out. No words, no actions.

"Are you ok?" Nickolas asked him.

Almost choking trying to tell Nick no, he even tried to shake his head, but finally he said, "Sure, I just got hit with a massive headache. Maybe I should head over to the infirmary."

Nickolas stared into his eyes, and Chris could feel him trying to probe down their link. He pulled away and smiled, trying to block him. "I'll be fine. I'll just go and get some aspirin or something."

He rose and backed away from everyone at the table, then turning, he walked out the door. But instead of crossing the courtyard to sick bay, Chris took the path that led to the waterfall. Once he was under the thick overhanging evergreen boughs, he stumbled to a halt and sank to his knees against a thick tree trunk. The pain was stunning. His head felt like it was on fire. Not even realizing that he was crying, Chris curled up into a ball in the soft pile of fallen pine needles, the memories of his missing day running through his mind. Moonset was an awfully long way away...but still too near.

◆ ◆ ◆

"He did very well. Better than any other fledgling I've seen, except Jessica. His takeoff was flawless," Kieran said.

"How was his stamina? Was his musculature well developed?" Donald asked and leaned his head back in his chair to watch the fire glow in the fireplace while Kieran gave him the report on Jays's first flight.

Kieran crossed his booted feet and settled deeper into his chair. "Good on the stamina. It won't take him long to be up to full flight. He's lean though. Maybe it's just a trait for his entire body, but I would like to see his flight muscles more defined. But the way his stamina was...we'll just have to watch him develop."

Donald nodded his head, and they drifted into silence. The fire popped, and Donald jumped slightly. That was when he noticed his cousin staring at him, waiting. Sometimes Kieran's gift was unnerving. Coughing, he looked back at the fire. "I'm really worried about Chris."

"He has been acting odd."

Relieved that he wasn't the only one to notice, Donald continued. "He stayed away from everyone today after he got that headache or whatever it was. I checked in with Beth to see how he was doing, and I found out that he didn't actually go in to see her."

Frowning, Kieran got up and added another log to the fire. "Then where was he all day?"

"I don't know. And neither did Nick when I asked him."

Crouched down next to the wood pile, Kieran looked into the distance. "I was too far away from him at the table to get much of a reading from him. Since we don't have a blood bond and I haven't ever needed to go into his dreamscape, I don't have a direct line to him. The best I got was pain, a lot of it, with just a touch of fear. Really nothing more than you could get from plain old observation."

Donald sighed, and his shoulders sank. He hadn't realized he'd been hoping Kieran could tell him something more. "I think I'll head over to his house and make sure he's fine. I'm not going to be able to sleep otherwise."

Rising from his chair, he grabbed his coat from the peg by the door. Kieran had returned to his seat and watched him. "I'm not tired. I'll wait up for you."

He glanced back over his shoulder at his younger cousin and gave him a smile. "I shouldn't be too long, I expect."

Pulling the door shut, he waited a moment for his eyes to adjust to the darkness. The moon had just set, so even with his enhanced sight, it was dark. He remembered that when he'd still been unchanged this would have been pitch black to him. But the faint stars overhead cast just enough light for him to not run into things.

He walked the short distance to Chris's cabin but paused a house away when he saw furtive movement on Christoff's porch. A figure slipped to the side of the building then quickly made its way along the creek, heading downstream.

Gaining Chris's porch, Donald could feel that no one was inside. Certain now that it *was* Chris who had left, Donald set out to follow. *Where does he think he's going at this time of night?*

He kept the figure within sight, past the rest of the houses in the south quad, then crossed the bridge and followed the creek where it curved to flow along the base of the cliff wall. Once in the woods, they took the trail past all of the new cabins until they left the valley proper.

He must be joining one of the scout groups. I didn't think he'd been cleared for work yet. Donald had just decided to call out to his Flight leader when he saw Chris drop down into a crouch. Following suit, he waited to see what had alerted Chris and saw a Hunter from one of the scouts.

Surprised, Donald watched Chris use all of his Hunter abilities to slip past the sentry line, unnoticed. Concerned now, he approached the sentry quickly. He was afraid that he would lose sight of Chris by delaying to talk to the scout, but he needed to alert someone.

As he approached, the startled scout dropped into a fighting crouch.

"I'm Donald, Chris's Second."

The sentry flicked his eyes over Donald's shoulder then lowered his hand. The glow from whatever charm he held started to dissipate. A glance over his own shoulder showed him one of the other scouts disappearing back into the brush.

"What are you doing out here tonight?" the scout asked quietly.

Damn it, he's out of sight already. "Chris just left the valley and slipped past your line."

The sentry looked affronted. "No one has gone through here," he stated.

Not in the mood for it, Donald growled, "I just watched Chris pass you. I have no idea what's going on, but you should be on the alert."

"Why would he leave?"

"That's what I'm going to find out. Keep the perimeter."

"Yes, sir. I'll make sure we include this when we make our next report."

"Good." Donald left the scout and moved through the heavy forest as quickly and as silently as he could, trying to catch up with Christoff.

Kieran, he called.

Surprise flowed down the link, and Donald realized that Kieran had picked up the distance between them. *What's happened?*

He sent everything in a complicated thought burst. Donald waited for Kieran to digest the contents before he added in words, *I'm going to keep following him. If I need help, I'll call Nick.*

Be careful, Donny.

Smiling at the childhood nickname, Donald leapt over a fallen log, landing in a crouch in the leaf mold on the other side. Tracking in the direction Chris had gone as best as he could in the darkness, Donald followed his Flight leader another two miles. He finally caught sight of him through the trees, dropping down over a hill. Donald slowed.

When he reached the crest of the hill, he dropped to the ground behind a fallen nurse log, shock coursing through him. Scattered amid the ferns that covered the floor between the wooded slopes were a dozen people and a ring of lights. Chris stiffly made his way to the center, where he fell to his knees at Gabriel's feet like a puppet. Gabriel's angelic face smiled down at the trembling Valkyrie.

"Oh shit," breathed Donald as he took in the scene. Backing away, he mentally gathered himself and blasted out a mind call. He knew the distance was at the edge of his range, but the need was too great to wait until he got closer to the valley. *NICKOLAS!*

Gabriel's head snapped up, and for one second, Donald looked into insanity before he felt a mental vise clamp down around his thoughts, stopping him from completing the warning to Nick. Turning, he took off as fast as he could through the darkened forest. His sight hadn't recovered yet from the lights, and he stumbled over a log, the sound of pursuit loud in his ears.

He ducked a low branch then sprinted through a more open space, looking up, hoping for a break in the tree canopy clear enough to get into the air, but the interlaced branches of the trees were too thick. Swearing, he dodged around a large tree trunk just as he felt something whiz by behind him. Forcing his breath to slow, he took cover and continued to move more slowly through the underbrush.

Radios crackled all around him as the recovery members made a tremendous amount of noise tromping through the woods trying to find him. He tracked as many as he could by sound while he crawled through a large thicket, then groaned to himself when he heard Gabriel's voice directing them back toward where he had managed to slip past them.

The sense-blind grounded he could avoid, but getting away from another Valkyrie was always harder. Rising, Donald ran again. Beams of light shot around him, and he dodged. A clearing lay ahead, and judging the size, it would have a large enough opening to get into the air; he put on a burst of speed.

Flight

Spreading his wings, he gave a hard push off and a strong down sweep, but after two wing beats, a sound ricocheted through the woods, and he grunted with the impact as something twined around his wings, fouling them. He hit the ground hard.

Rolling, he shook his head and pulled a knife from his boot as he regained his feet. He pushed his body as he raced to the edge of the clearing. More of his pursuers entered the open space. Reaching over his head, he tried to slice the cord wound around his wings. He kept moving, but his speed was seriously reduced.

A figure stepped out from behind a tree in front of him, and he spun to the side, dodging. Too many had caught up with him. He didn't have another direction to go for, and too soon for his liking, he found himself surrounded.

He dropped into a crouch, looking for any way out. The faces surrounding him were grim and determined. Instinctively trying to spread his wings, they pulled against the cord, and he growled in frustrated anger.

Without his wings, he didn't have much of a chance against so many, but they still wouldn't find him an easy target. He pushed at the mental barrier clamped around him and tried unsuccessfully to get another call out for help. Growling, he lunged at the first person who got too close, slicing his knife through the multiple layers of cloth covering the man's chest. Blood slicked his hand and he leapt over the falling body to grab another man by the throat, spinning so that the hapless person took a bola instead of him.

It was more difficult than he had thought to maneuver with his wings pinioned. Diving into a roll, he came up and sliced another man in the throat, then he felt the snake of a bola tangle his feet, and he fell into a tree. Rolling onto his back, he kicked out with his bound legs, impacting someone in the gut from the sound of the grunt.

There were too many; he managed to slice a couple more before they succeeded in disarming him. They flipped him roughly and wrenched his arms back over his wings, securely tying them. He pressed his face into the soft loam and groaned, not so much because of the physical pain but because he knew that he hadn't been able to get enough information to Nickolas.

They freed his legs then tugged him upright and forced him back through the forest to the lighted circle where Chris waited, bound the same way, kneeling at Gabriel's feet. Dropped unceremoniously next to his Flight leader, Donald saw the anguish in Chris's eyes when he struggled up to his knees.

"So, who do we have here?" Gabriel asked.

His gaze still locked with Chris's, neither one of them answered. Donald felt a hand cup his chin and turn his face away from Chris. Looking up at Gabriel, Donald shivered and cast his eyes down.

"What is your name, Hunter?"

Gabriel brushed his thumb along Donald's chin when he didn't answer, then before he could realize the intent, Gabriel slapped him hard across the face. Knocked off balance, he fell onto his side, and Gabriel grabbed him by the hair to haul him back upright.

Snaking his tongue out, Donald caught the blood from his lip and probed at the split that Gabriel had caused. He raised his gaze to look into Gabriel's blue eyes and remained silent, refusing to tell him his name.

The Alpha Valkyrie's hand clenched tighter in his hair and pulled his head back, exposing his neck. Donald felt the pinprick of a sharpened nail cut into his throat. "Who is he, Christoff?"

When the other Hunter stayed silent, Donald felt the warm trickle of blood as Gabriel incised a thin line in his skin. After the fourth such cut, Christoff started to fight his bonds, and one of the grounded came forward to hold him down on his knees.

"Leave him alone, Gabriel!" Christoff shouted.

"Tell me his name," Gabriel said without looking at Chris and continued his work.

"No! Let him go. It was me you wanted."

"Not quite, Chris, but you already know that." He dug deeper on his next cut, and Donald couldn't hold back a hiss of pain. Donald closed his eyes, blocking the sight of Christoff next to him. "If you take too long, Chris, I might accidentally get too close to the jugular. That would be a shame, wouldn't it?"

Growling, Christoff bit out, "Donald. His name is Donald."

Donald opened his eyes and saw Gabriel smile down at him. "Isn't that the name of your Second, Chris? Interesting." Gabriel turned to one of his men. "He comes with. He could prove useful." Then Gabriel released Donald's hair and he slumped forward, the warm stickiness of his blood saturating the front of his shirt.

He raised his head then glanced at Chris. He saw concern and fear in the depths of his eyes. A low thump registered in his mind, and Chris quickly looked up. Doing the same, he saw the trees start to sway then move more violently as a helicopter came to hover over their position, dropping a rope down. Frantic, he pushed with his mind and tried one more time to reach Nick, then Kieran.

Gabriel smiled at him. "Don't worry, Donald, they'll know what has happened to you soon enough." Stepping away from them, Gabriel ordered, "Let's get them loaded."

Kieran sat in his cabin, watching Dev and Aiden verbally spar with each other while they waited for Donald to return. They had stopped by just after Donald left for Chris's. Kieran shifted slightly in his seat and glanced out the window. He thought Donald should have been back by now. Hopefully Chris was doing ok.

A niggle of guilt wormed through him as he wondered how long he should wait before telling Nick. If it wasn't for the fact that he could tell through his bonds that both of his Alphas were busy...his lips curved in a slight smile. *Most definitely not something I'm going to let slip to either one that I can sense. I'm not suicidal.*

"Try it, Aiden, and I'll slap you down." Dev laughed, pulling Kieran back to his current companions. He hadn't caught what they were arguing about this time. "Or better yet, I'll get Chris involved."

"Fine," the young Caster growled, then opened his mouth for another retort.

A sudden shock of emotion shot down Kieran's link with his cousin.

"Donald?" *Donald!*

No answer.

He lurched out of his chair, the concerned faces of the two Casters a blur.

"Kieran?" Dev asked.

He grabbed his coat and yanked the door open, Dev and Aiden on his heels. "Something's happened."

The next slam came from his bond with Nickolas, and he went to his knees. Fear and panic that his Alpha couldn't suppress fast enough reached him. Dev helped him up, and they launched into the air, covering the short distance to Nick and Jessica's in a matter of moments. They met the two Alphas as they came down the porch.

"I just got a cut off call from Donald. I can't raise either him or Chris," Nick said.

Kieran stumbled, fear and guilt blinding him for a second. He grabbed Nick and blasted the same thought burst Donald had sent him earlier down their link. His Alpha grasped him by the throat. He went limp submissively.

"You didn't think I needed this right away?" he said softly. "He sent this to you over an hour ago."

"Donald said he'd call you if there was a problem," he whispered.

"Well it looks like there is one."

Dropping his eyes, Kieran stared at the dark ground, his mind going numb. A broad-sent mental shout broke the silence.

Nickolas. This is Robin. The scouts just checked in and reported that Donald and Chris left the valley.

I already know. Something else has happened to them. I just got a cut off call from Donald. We're heading out to find them.

Not without me, you're not. You don't know the area like we do. And the moon's already set. I'll get Kel to take over for me here in the tower and get Kevin. We'll come meet you at your cabin. WAIT for me.

Nickolas loosened his hand and released Kieran, stalking away a few feet.

"Nickolas?" Kieran whispered.

His Alpha looked over his shoulder at him. "I'm sorry I snapped at you, Kier."

"But what if you're right? If something has happened..." He swallowed. "And I didn't tell you soon enough..."

"There's no telling if my knowing could have made a difference. You listened to your Flight leader, right?"

He nodded.

"We just need to deal with the situation as it presents itself," Jessica interjected.

Kieran felt the shiver of energy as Nick tried his brother and Donald again. The Alpha clenched his fist. "Come on. I'm not waiting."

Wing beats overhead heralded the arrival of Robin and Kevin. The two Primes landed next to them.

"Anything, Nick?"

"Neither one is answering."

"Let's go. We'll start with the scouts Donald talked to, then we'll know our next step. They're in the southwest quadrant," Robin said.

The silence felt ominous to Kieran as they all took off. Wings heaving, they pushed their flight chasing after Robin; the short time it took to locate the scouts felt like an eternity. His concern for his Flight and Wing leaders was escalated by the link he shared with Nickolas.

They touched down in a dark clearing next to Kevin. Robin had already gotten most of the scout's report by the time Kieran approached, and all he caught was, "...took off. About five minutes, tops."

"Which way did they go?" Nickolas asked.

The scout looked to Robin instead of answering. Kieran moved to stand behind Nickolas, and he felt his Alpha's barely concealed annoyance. Robin must have sensed it too, because the Hunter Prime threw Nick a quick glance before addressing the scout. "Just the one helicopter? Any other sign of intruders?"

The scout shook his head, and Kieran flexed his wings. He needed to move, he needed to be looking for Donald and Chris. He didn't want to—could not—acknowledge what had likely happened, not yet. He needed to try to find them.

"What direction, Robin?" Nickolas growled low.

Compassion shone brightly in Robin's eyes, but the Hunter still shook his head. "It's too dark, Nickolas. You aren't familiar enough with the environment. You'll destroy any evidence if you try to go through the dark forest. We need to wait until first light."

Hissing, Kieran spun away to start looking anyway, Nickolas hard on his heels. But the scouts blocked their way.

"Nickolas, if they're still here and ok, they'll be fine for the rest of the night. If they were in that helicopter...well, it hardly matters if we wait; they were gone before we left the valley shield. We can't hope to catch them, it would be like trying to run after a car. The most we can do is gather as many details of what happened as we can," Robin said softly from behind them.

Frustrated, angry, and scared, Kieran stood next to Nickolas, whose mix of emotions mirrored his, blending together. Jessica joined them.

Kieran could feel her reaching down their bond, sharing her fear and concern. He pulled away and spun, snapping his wings out and launching through the opening in the trees. Pumping his wings hard, he pushed his body, flying fast and reckless back toward Aurora.

Chapter Seventeen

Lifting his face up off of the metal deck, Christoff blinked in the sudden light that had sprung up to fill the interior of the helicopter. Next to him, Donald groaned as he turned his head to rest his other cheek on the floor. The bruises were starting to rise on his Second's face, and Chris looked away, not wanting to see the evidence of his injuries, knowing that it was his fault that Donald had gotten them.

The shift of a boot brought Chris's eyes to the feet in front of him. Following the legs up, he met Gabriel's gaze. The other Valkyrie stared impassively down at him, and Christoff shivered at the feeling of being a bug under glass.

The helicopter dipped then slowed; Chris braced himself for what was coming when they landed. Twisting his bound wrists, he tried to relieve the pressure on his trapped wings. With a light thump, they touched down and the rotors started to slow.

He stiffened at the sound of several bodies rising behind him, and he wanted to lash out with his legs, but Gabriel clucked at him and smiled. Baring his teeth in a silent snarl, Chris didn't resist when he was hauled to his feet and out of the helicopter into the darkness. Donald swearing behind him made Chris smile grimly as they were shoved across the empty ground and into the nearest building.

It was a small building, and Chris looked around in confusion at the shelves, which stored various food stuffs. Certainly not big enough for prisoners. But then Gabriel opened a door in the back wall. As the lights came on, Christoff saw a wide sweeping staircase. A rough shove to his shoulder pushed him through the door and down the stairs.

His eyes widened at the opulence of the room he descended into.

It was as grand as any theater or opera house lobby that he had ever seen portrayed in movies. Red velvet draped the walls and couches and matched the hue of the carpeting, all of it offset by gilt. And the size was much larger than the room above it could ever hope to contain.

He didn't have long to wonder what that room was all about. Gabriel quickly moved across and swiped a key card in a reader next to a door. An elevator opened and they were ushered into it. When it opened again, Christoff heard Donald gasp behind him, and the guards chuckled. In front of him was a nightmare. A modern recreation of a Gladiator coliseum. An oval of dirt was surrounded by a concrete wall about ten feet high. At the top of the wall, bleacher type seating started, rising for several tiers before the concrete ceiling stopped them.

Another shove broke him out of his shock, and he snarled at the guard behind him.

"Save it for the arena," the man chuckled.

Still growling, he followed Gabriel across the dirt, envying the way the older Valkyrie was able to spread his wings. They were taken through another door on the far side. This room was dark when they entered, but only for a moment. Fluorescent lights switched on, and they saw the true horror. They were in an immense room. Easily the largest room that Chris had ever stood in.

And it was filled with cages.

Like some horrific dog pound, row after row of barred cages stood in a maze of blocks and alleys. In the nearest, bleary-eyed souls raised their heads to see what was happening.

"You told me that you would only be bringing one back, Gabriel. I only made one room ready."

A dark-skinned man folded his arms across his chest to their right and leaned against the wall. The open door beside him showed a glimpse of a luxurious suite.

Gabriel sighed before he shrugged. "So, they can both stay in one for the night. That will be the least of their worries. You need to learn to cope with the unexpected, Edward."

Snorting, the man walked forward to examine them. "Huh, they've got good musculature. They could go far in the arena."

"We'll see." As Gabriel waved his hand, the guards pushed them forward again. Following in Edward's wake, Gabriel led them to an empty cell. The door clanged shut with finality. "Get them started on basics in the morning, Edward. I'll want to put them through their paces in the arena tomorrow."

"No problem. I'll have them ready by morning practice."

Feeling chill, Christoff looked up to see Gabriel studying him, his ice blue eyes full of amusement. "I can't tell you how many times I've visualized you or your brother here. I'm looking forward to your stay. Try and get some rest. Tomorrow's going to be a busy day."

Smiling, the Valkyrie turned and walked out of the room, the men who had escorted them following.

Twisting his uncomfortable hands, his shoulder brushed against Donald's, and the two of them stood looking at their new keeper.

Edward studied them for a few minutes before grunting then gave them a malicious grin. "Well, boys, you should probably do what Gabriel said and get some rest." And with that he turned and started to walk away.

"Hey, wait a minute. My hands are numb. Untie us," Donald said.

The man stopped and turned his head. "Now why would I want to do that?" Grinning again, he started whistling. When he reached the doorway to his suite, he flipped the light switch and the room was once more enveloped in darkness.

After his eyes adjusted, Chris realized that the room wasn't completely dark. There were soft lights spaced throughout the ceiling. Sighing, Chris turned to his Second. "Come here. Let me look at your neck."

Donald lifted his chin. The slices were mostly shallow but a couple looked deep enough that Chris worried about infection setting in. They were still bleeding sluggishly. "I'm sorry, Chris," Donald said softly.

"What the hell were you doing out there anyway?" Christoff said gruffly.

"What were you?" Donald countered. "You walked right up to him and gave up. I saw you."

"I didn't have a lot of choice. We need to get untied. Can you move your fingers?"

"No. I wasn't kidding about my hands being numb."

Chris turned to look at their cell. The tiny space was barely big enough for them to stretch out and lie down in. Not even enough room to extend their wings, and nothing with which to free themselves from the ropes binding their arms.

He looked through the round iron bars and saw several Valkyries awake and watching them.

"Would you untie us?" he asked one of their neighbors. Three sides of their cell shared walls with other cages. The man looked unsure but stood up.

"Don't do it, Dan. Edward will make you pay, you know it," someone from down the line called out.

"We can't leave them like that. They'll never be able to fight in the morning," someone else added.

"Yeah, well you wouldn't be the one getting the lashing, now would you," their neighbor on their other side called back. The debate continued, so Chris turned to Donald.

"Let me try to get you untied." Back to back, Chris fumbled at the knots holding Donald's hands. They were slippery, so Chris assumed that he wasn't just numb but cut as well.

"Hey, who did Gabriel bring in?" a feminine voice called from a couple of aisles over.

"Come over here."

Looking up, Christoff saw the Hunter someone had called Dan standing at the bars, reaching through.

"Are you sure? I don't want to get you in trouble."

"We're always in trouble around here. At least this will do something good." Backing up to the bars, he felt nimble fingers tease at the knots until they loosened. "What's your name?"

His arms fell to his sides. Shaking his wings, he wished there was enough room to stretch them out. "Thank you. My name is Chris."

Dan called out across the room. "He says his name is Chris."

"Chris? Christoff is that you?"

He returned to Donald's back, knelt, and started to untie his Second. "Who is that?" he called back as he dropped the rope and looked at the abrasions on Donald's wrists.

"It's Leslie."

"Are the others here too?"

"Most of us. Two were taken away as soon as we arrived. It would really be nice to get out of here soon."

"I'm sure that's being worked on, Les." He got the cord still wound around Donald's wings off, then rubbing his own wrists, Chris stood up. "Your wrists aren't as bad as your neck, but keep an eye on them anyway."

"So now what?" Donald looked tired and shook his wings out before sinking down to lean against the bars of the cage.

"What other injuries do you have, Donald?"

"I think they cracked a couple of ribs, but otherwise just bruises, I think."

"Hey, you two."

Glancing over, Chris saw one of their neighbors look up at the ceiling meaningfully. Getting the point, Chris nodded his thanks.

The Valkyrie nodded back. "You should get some sleep. They wake us pretty early."

Sighing, Chris sank to the floor as well. "Somehow I'm not surprised by that." He grabbed the one thin blanket that had been left on the floor of the barren cell and tossed it to Donald. "Here, you need it more than me."

Wrapping himself up, Donald stretched out on the hard floor before he cleared his throat. "I'm sorry, Chris."

"I know, Donny, so am I." Then he too lay down on the floor and closed his eyes.

◆ ◆ ◆

"I can feel him coming, Beth." Marcus turned to his wife, who was waiting in the door of the longhouse. "Robin had trouble getting them to swallow coming back here to wait. But I don't need them running rampant through the dark forest, destroying evidence. They have no experience in this sort of thing."

"They're more capable than you think."

"Maybe. But they won't follow orders, and they aren't familiar with this fight. Not like we are."

"That's going to change now."

He sighed and closed his eyes. Her arms came around him, and he bowed his head to her shoulder. He didn't want to think about his youngest son in the hands of that branch of the Facility. But he had no choice. "Nickolas is going to be hard to keep leashed. If you could talk to Kieran, I'm sure his talent—"

"Kieran won't be able to help."

He lifted his head and looked into her eyes.

"Robin said both Chris and Donald were missing. Donald is Kieran's cousin and his emotional anchor. I remember Zach talking about both of them, especially how he and Donald protected Kieran. I've spent some time going back through the old records that Ian sent us, researching what I could on Kieran. So I could try and understand him and his talent. He was strong enough that he was using his empathy before he started to change. Now that I've met him, the documents and test results Ian sent over the years make more sense."

"So what are you telling me?"

"That we have two potential explosions waiting to happen."

"Great. Let's hope that Jessica will choose to be a voice of reason."

They both turned and entered the empty longhouse then walked in silence to the kitchen, where they helped each other put together some plates of food.

Marcus watched Beth as she precisely placed sandwiches on the platter. He reached over and pulled her into his arms. A tremor ran through her body. He rested his cheek on her hair and breathed in her scent. "Don't worry, we'll get him back."

He felt her head bob, acknowledging that she heard him. They stood that way until Marcus heard the outside doors open and several people come in. He kissed her head before he left to join the others in the great room.

"Dev, Aiden, could you please fetch in more wood and stoke up the fires," he asked as he crossed the floor.

"Sure, Marcus," Dev said. "Come on, Aiden."

Marcus stopped close to his Hunter and Caster Primes and watched his son take a seat in front of one of the fireplaces, Kieran pacing before him. Jessica slipped off through the door into the kitchen.

"Kev," Marcus said softly, "go roust Nathan and have him take over the tower. Robin, I want you to get Kelley. Have her get a group together and start tracking what happened. Be quick. They'll notice if you're absent too long. Nick's telepathy is too sensitive to chance arranging anything here. I'm not going to be able to hold him past first light, if that. We need all the information we can get. We have to assume that Gabriel has them."

"Yes, sir," they both said.

Marcus watched them pass Dev and Aiden at the door as the two came back in with the wood. Once the two fireplaces were blazing, Beth and Jessica started bringing out the trays of food and coffee, arranging them on one of the tables near the fireplace. Then the wait truly began. Marcus felt like he was standing vigil, waiting for the doctor to bring unpleasant news. Before long, Robin rejoined them, bringing Marcus a plate and leaning in close.

"It's done."

Taking the plate, Marcus nodded. "It will be dawn in another couple of hours. Do you want to catch a nap?"

"No. I'm too keyed up. Is there anyone else you want ready to head out with us?"

He took a bite of his sandwich and thought for a moment. "No, I don't think so. We'll have Kelley and her scout group as well as the four of us. That's plenty. Nick has just been sitting there, waiting, so I don't think we need to worry about any more Facility Valkyries joining us. We still have the advantage of numbers."

"Do you really think that will make a difference to Nickolas?"

"Not really. He'll do whatever he damn well pleases. There's very little we can do to stop it."

The bright lights flared on, and Christoff groaned as it drilled into his aching head. He rolled to his side and saw Donald had flung his arm across his eyes. He pushed himself up to a sitting position and nudged Donald with his foot. "Come on, rise and shine."

Down the aisleway, Chris could hear the keeper, Edward, harassing caged Valkyries as he passed them.

"That man is distinctly annoying, Chris," Donald said quietly as he rose to his feet and folded the blanket.

Joining his Second, he nodded his agreement. They didn't have long to wait. The keeper stopped in front of their cell, smiling at them maliciously.

"Sleep well?" he inquired.

Not bothering to answer, Christoff stared at him. After a moment, soft clicks echoed throughout the room, and Edward's smile stretched as he waved one of his two guards forward to push open the door. Chris shared a glance with Donald then stepped through, his Second at his back.

The aisles were full of Valkyries slowly plodding nose to tail to some unknown destination. Joining their ranks, Christoff looked around. There were more guards standing at the walls watching, but he and Donald were the only ones with a personal escort. They were about halfway down their particular cage block; he could see several aisles to his left but only one more on his right.

This place must house at least a hundred, Chris.

Easily. I don't think we're getting out of here without effort.

They reached an open space at the end of the large room, where their line merged with the rest of the Valkyries, and the large group was funneled through a door. Leslie caught his gaze, and she smiled reassuringly.

When their turn came, Chris was surprised to find a giant bath facility. To the left was a long row of toilet stalls, on the right were sinks. All of them were occupied, and as one emptied, the next in line was sent to fill the vacancy. They were first directed to relieve themselves, after which they were given a disposable toothbrush.

Watching the other Valkyries go through the routine, Chris dumped his foam brush in the can at the end of the sink aisle and followed Leslie through another door. Steam billowed around his face.

A hand grabbed his, startling him. Hissing, he half spread his wings before he realized that it was Leslie. She pulled him to the side.

"Watch it. The guards don't like it if you spread your wings. They're going to want your clothes." She pointed to a pile of discarded garments. "We leave yesterday's clothes here, then after we're clean, we pick up new ones on the other side."

He looked at Donald, who had joined them, and scowled.

I can't see any help for it, can you? his Second asked.

No. I hope Nick gets here soon. Christoff sighed in frustration. Stripping, he tossed his clothes onto the pile and joined the group under the communal shower heads. They got clean, then after a last rinse, Chris made his way to the other side of the room, where there were shelves of thin cotton pants and T-back tank tops in various sizes. He found a pair that he thought would fit, slipped them on, then looked for Donald. His Second was shaking the water out of his hair, so Chris grabbed some clothes for him.

Handing Donald the clothes, Chris quickly inspected the damage to Donald's body. "Did you wash out those cuts well?"

"Yes, Mom."

"Let me see." Donald lifted his neck, and Chris could see that most of the superficial cuts were already sealed shut. A couple of the deeper ones were a little red though. Bruises were still developing all over Donald's body. "How are the ribs?"

"Definitely cracked from the way I feel this morning."

"Damn. I was hoping you were wrong about that."

Shrugging his shoulders, Donald put the clothes on.

They followed more departing Valkyries and found themselves in a small hallway. There was a line of people slowly filtering past a desk at the other end. It wasn't until they were closer that Chris could see what the holdup was. Each Valkyrie had to stop at the desk so that a white-coated grounded could place an injection gun to their upper arm.

"What do you want to bet that's an inhibitor?" Donald leaned over his shoulder to say in Chris's ear.

"I don't take losing bets."

Snorting in grim amusement, Donald pulled back. When their turn came, Chris held out his arm, and the doctor placed the gun against his skin. But the guard behind the doctor stopped him.

"Not those two. Gabriel's orders."

Surprise on his face, the doctor turned to look at the guard. "Are you sure? That's highly irregular."

"Yes, he insisted that the two he brought in last night not get dosed."

After a short, concerned pause, the doctor waved both of them through the door. A sigh of relief escaped him, and Chris continued on. The other side of the door revealed a large cafeteria. More Valkyries than he could count filled the room. More than could have come from where he and Donald had spent the night.

Surprised at the number, he took a moment to get the lay of the room. Not only were there Valkyries, but there were also grounded sitting down to eat as well. The room was large enough to seat at least five hundred. And it looked half full already. Donald nudged him to keep moving, so they both joined another line of Valkyries who were picking up trays. It was eerie how quiet the room was. In contrast to the noisy boisterous crowds at meal times in Aurora, there was only a very quiet hum of conversation.

Flight

A dour looking human dumped a bowl of thick, pasty-looking oatmeal on his tray then slapped a scoop of watery scrambled eggs and two strips of flabby, greasy bacon on top. Wrinkling his nose at it, Chris looked around for something to thin and sweeten the cereal but found nothing. Sighing in resignation, he and Donald found a table to sit down and eat. Trying not to taste the food, Chris took a bite.

Leslie and the other Aurorans who had only recently been captured joined them. "So what do you think of the food?" Leslie asked as she started shoveling it in.

"Do I need to answer that?" Donald asked as he let a glop fall from his spoon.

Snorting, Leslie downed a piece of the bacon. "Not really. But FYI, they don't give you long to eat, and you are going to really need the energy. Trust me; it's a lot harder if you're hungry. So bite the bullet and get it down."

Taking her word for it, Chris started to eat more quickly. He noticed Donald cringe, but his food started to disappear also.

"What's next?" Christoff asked Leslie in between bites.

He noticed her glance around without making it obvious before answering. "Next is the arena."

I don't like the way that sounds, Chris.

Me either. Choosing to let that subject go, he scraped his bowl then asked Leslie, "How have you guys been doing?"

"As well as can be expected, I guess. We haven't seen Todd or Aaron since we were captured. We're just holding on day by day, hoping that Marcus can get here soon."

"I expect we won't have much longer to wait now that you're here," one of the others added in.

Chris exchanged a look with Donald.

The sound of a bell reverberated through the room, and Leslie and the others shoved the last of their food into their mouths. Following their lead, Chris scraped the last of his eggs up and grabbed his bacon when everyone rose. He followed the large group through yet another door and found himself in a barren waiting area. Everyone immediately started to stretch and do warm-up exercises.

A few minutes later, a door opened, and Gabriel walked in with Edward and another unknown Valkyrie on their heels. Donald stifled a gasp, and Chris shot a look at him. His Second slowly shook his head. Gabriel scanned the crowd until his gaze located Donald and Chris. Pointing at them, he gestured for them to approach. As they made their way through the crowd, Edward started reading a list of names.

"So how are you enjoying our hospitality, Christoff?" the Valkyrie asked.

Not bothering to answer, Chris folded his arms across his chest.

"I see you still haven't learned any manners. We'll rectify that in time. Come." And Gabriel turned, leading them out the door he had just entered. Gabriel's Hunter fell in behind them, and a couple dozen of the other Valkyries followed.

The door led to the huge arena that they had walked through the night before. Chris once again shivered at the significance of the space. All the Valkyries that had followed them out, except for their Hunter escort, spread themselves out in pairs and started to spar. Gabriel led them to a scuffed ring in the center of the coliseum then turned to look at the two of them.

His scrutiny was unnerving, and Chris resisted the urge to flex his wings under that stare. Though he felt Donald fidget. Then Gabriel smiled slightly. "This is going to be a challenge. But I expected nothing less, Christoff. You would have disappointed me otherwise."

He waved his hand to encompass the room and continued. "I'm sure you recognize the purpose this room is put to. Look around you. This is the daily exercise regimen. We punish slacking, and no one wishes to disappoint me."

Stunned, Christoff watched the groups fight. Because fight was what it was, all right. This was no sparring practice. The couples were just a hairsbreadth from killing blows. Forcing all emotion from his face, Chris turned back to Gabriel.

The older Valkyrie nodded his head in a satisfied way before calling his games master. "Edward, who's up today?"

The keeper looked up from where he was watching a match. "Edana!"

A tall, willowy redhead back-winged out of reach of her opponent, disengaging from her match, then walked over to the center of the oval room. Christoff met Donald's eyes before returning his attention to the ring. The female Hunter's eyes held a cold hatred that Chris could see from where he stood.

She waited in the center of the ring while Gabriel paced a slow circuit around the outside of the perimeter. "So, Edana, still refusing Edward are we? You shouldn't be such a rebel. Your life would be so much easier if you would just do what you are told instead of arguing about it." Flaring his wings, Gabriel gave them a brisk flap before crossing the line. "But at least your recalcitrance gives me the opportunity for some action."

"Like you ever need an excuse." Disdain dripped from her words. Flexing her knees, she moved, keeping the older Valkyrie in front of her at all times. When the two came together, it was fast. The speed surprised Chris. The female Hunter had no hope of besting Gabriel, but she gave it her best shot, succeeding in landing several good hits. Still, it was obvious that he was playing with her; a cat with a mouse.

Chris pulled his attention away and turned to Donald, but his Second was talking intensely to the Valkyrie that had accompanied Gabriel. Startled by the obvious familiarity of the two Hunter's, he started to join them, but then Edana screamed, whipping his attention back to the fight. Clawing her way out of the hold Gabriel had her in, she beat her wings to help her back up. Gabriel swiped at the blood that ran down his face, smearing a large streak across it. Chris watched her breathing hard as she tried to put weight on her right leg, but he could see from where he was standing that it was broken. Spreading his wings, about to go out and help her, he was stopped by a hand on his shoulder. Their Hunter escort shook his head. Gritting his teeth, Chris stood and watched.

Gabriel's movements were fluid and menacing as he circled her again. Strength poured off of him. But then something strange happened. Christoff felt something shiver across his senses, and Gabriel paused, cocking his head.

Edana went down onto her knees, her wings settling around her, but through the pain on her face, Christoff saw something else. Her eyes flashed, and her hair stirred lightly, like a breeze had drifted past her. Curiosity replaced the cold indifference on Gabriel's face, and he took a couple of steps toward her. Her image distorted, as if a heat wave on a highway road had swept between her and the rest of the room.

The hand on his shoulder squeezed harder, and Christoff heard the Hunter whisper, "No, Dee. Don't."

Then flames leapt to life around her.

Gabriel stumbled back with a shout.

Watching her face through the flickering light, Christoff saw her hatred blaze, and a fireball the size of a cantaloupe was flung from her hand straight at the Alpha Valkyrie. Gabriel dove to the side, rolling away neatly as it exploded, taking out a section of the wall and bleachers behind him. Before she could get another shot off, he sang out in a clarion voice. "STOP!"

All movement in the arena crashed to a halt. Chris found his body frozen. The flames flickered out, leaving black scorch marks on the sand. Gabriel rose to his feet and walked to stand over her, singing softly. Chris couldn't make out what he was saying, but he could feel the power as it flowed around her. Slumping, she bowed over her knees in defeat.

"Zachary, please take her to the labs," the Alpha called over his shoulder.

The hand clutching Chris's shoulder tensed then released, and the Valkyrie standing behind him moved forward, carefully picking Edana up and making sure her wings were tucked securely. Gabriel reached out and touched her face, but she jerked away. "Very rare. Pyrokineses. And through the inhibitor, no less," he said with some awe. "Have Fredrick set her leg. I'll see to the rest tonight."

Bowing his head, the Hunter left the arena carrying the increasingly voluble Caster.

"Well, wasn't that exciting. She shouldn't have been able to do that through the inhibitor," Gabriel said to thin air. Then the Alpha turned and pinned Chris with a glance, a smile lighting his face and making Christoff shiver. "Your turn, boys," he said.

♦ ♦ ♦

"You traitor," Edana hissed in his ear.

Zach pulled her tighter to his chest and booted the door to the arena closed.

"Shut up. You don't know what you're talking about, Dana." Struggling to free her arms, she tried to bite his neck, but he tipped his head and blocked her. "Knock it off. What are you hoping to accomplish? It's not like you can even walk to get away."

"What do you mean I don't know what I'm talking about? Everyone can see that you're working with *him*. You sold out. You make me sick. And to think I called you a friend."

He heard the sob catch in her throat. *I make myself sick too, Dee.* Marching down the hallway, Zach kicked a door open, more to take his temper out on something than because he couldn't open it. Stepping inside, he gently set her down on a desk. "How is your leg?"

"What do you care?" she snapped, immediately trying to push him away.

He grabbed her wrists, pinning both of her hands to the table, and leaned in so he was face to face with her. "I care way more than you give me credit for, Dee."

After a pause where she searched his eyes, she asked, "How could you?"

The pain in her pale green eyes twisted the knife in him even more. "It's not like I've had much choice." He backed away to look at her leg. She still tried to pull away, but he held on firmly, knowing that it hurt her. She yelped then glared at him, but she quit her pulling.

"No one, except for you of course, has been seen again if they were taken to the labs. And here you are, doing his bidding. What do you expect us to think?"

Relaxing his grip, he felt the break in her lower leg. "I suppose I expected you to actually think." Prodding the swelling flesh, he ignored her hiss and found what he was looking for. "It's a clean break. You're lucky, it should heal relatively easy."

"What do you mean by that?"

Starting to feel the mental pull, Zach took a deep breath to try and resist for a few more minutes. "I thought it was pretty clear. It's a clean break, so it will heal quickly."

"Don't be stupid, Zach. Think about what?"

He glanced up at her then stood. "Why do you think the others have disappeared, Dana? What do you think they're doing to us?"

She shrugged her shoulders, and he could feel her trying to push the aching pain away from her mind as best she could. Zach knew that she handled fear and pain by lashing out. So he wasn't surprised by her attack. But he needed to get her to think before he got her to the labs.

"Why are you doing this, Zach?"

"I don't have a choice, Dee. None of you understand what's really going on beyond the pens and coliseum. I've seen beyond our narrow world. I won't excuse anything he's done, but Gabriel isn't the one to fear."

"Then stop helping him," she snapped.

"It's not that simple," he said, exasperated. "He controls almost every move I make. And if you're lucky, he'll control yours too."

"What do you mean?"

"The alternative is death. So far, I'm the only one who has survived. Though trust me, I tried to make sure I didn't." He ran his hand through his hair and turned away to pace but quickly realized that Gabriel's order wouldn't allow him to leave Edana's side. Snarling in frustration, he turned back. "Fredrick has been developing a drug designed to control us. Something to make them able to utilize our powers without the inconvenience of giving us any say in how we use them. I can think for myself, but I can't do something like set your leg. I was ordered to take you to Fredrick to do it, so I can't make myself do it. My mind is free but not my body."

"Why are you telling me this now?"

Snorting at himself derisively, Zach told her, "When have I had another opportunity alone with anyone? I won't be able to delay here with you much longer. I can already feel the pull to get you to the labs."

"That's where I'm going?" Edana asked in a horrified whisper.

He felt her shock and pain, and he leaned in, resting his forehead against hers, trying to offer them both some comfort. "I'm afraid so. They would love to have control of your power. And to be able to cast through the inhibitor, you have to be at a level five, at least."

He framed her face with his hands and looked into her eyes. "There is nothing in this world I want more than to be able to spare taking you there. I know what is waiting for you." Kissing her forehead, he picked her back up. He pulled the broken door shut behind them with his mind and felt Edana stiffen.

"Zach? Did you just do that? You aren't a Caster."

"Yes, I know. I've changed. The drug changed me."

"I'm scared, Zach."

"I know. Me too, Dee, me too."

Marcus glanced at his watch again then shifted his feet on the stool. He knew it wouldn't be long now. Aiden was sleeping with his head on the table, snoring. Robin, Kevin, and Dev were playing cards while Jessica and Beth talked quietly in the corner. Kieran had stopped pacing a while ago and was just standing at the mantle, staring into the flames. Nickolas hadn't moved all night, but now he shifted in his chair. Kieran turned to look at his Alpha. They must have had a private conversation, because Nickolas rose and they both turned to face the others in the room. Kicking the stool away, Marcus got up.

"It's light enough; we're going," Nickolas stated.

"All right." Everyone else got up, but Marcus held his hand out. "But...this is our territory, Nickolas."

His son's eyes flashed, but he didn't respond. Holding the door for everyone, Marcus let them all file past him into the courtyard. "Ok, Robin, take us to where you met the scouts." In a flurry of wings, they were all airborne.

Flying next to Beth, he met her eyes. The sorrow of their missing son had to be pushed down if they wanted to have any chance to formulate a rescue. It would take all of his skills to herd and protect his eldest. His thoughts turned to Nick.

Beth's voice whispered in his head. *His wing has healed well,* she sent.

He turned his attention forward and studied his eldest son's wing stroke. *Strong. I don't detect any weakness in the membrane.*

This is going to be hard on him.

I know.

The flight didn't last long, and they were soon landing at one of the scouting check points on the perimeter. One of the quadrant scouts waited for them, along with Kelley and her search party. Folding his wings, he joined Robin and his Second.

"What did you find out, Kelley?"

"We hadn't reached the end of the trail yet when Robin called to let me know you were on the way. But we did find evidence of a fight and that at least one man fled from a group of people."

Marcus closed his eyes. It wasn't anything he didn't expect, but he still wished it wasn't so. Nickolas and the rest came up, and Marcus could feel Nick simmering.

"You've had people out searching?" The question was spoken softly, but Marcus could tell that it was covering a volcano waiting to erupt.

"We are experienced in night tracking through these woods. This is our home. As you were already told, we didn't need all of you destroying the evidence."

"No, you just wanted control of the situation, Father, that's all. You don't know what we are capable of. These aren't your people, they're mine. My responsibility, not yours. And the fact that you made a decision to block us out just proves my point."

"Chris is my son, Nick," he growled.

"You lost all rights to claim that responsibility when you chose to leave us behind enemy lines."

They both stared at one another. Stalemate.

Beth and Jessica jumped between them. "Stop it! Both of you," Beth ordered, her voice hard with restrained emotion.

"Now's not the time. We need to finish the search," Jessica added. But she threw a glare at Marcus.

Taking a step back, Marcus took a breath and tried to rein in his temper. "They're right. Let's move on."

His son stared at him, and Marcus knew there would be no working together. "Kelley, how far away did the trail lead?"

"Half hours brisk walk. It's about two miles southeast."

"Lead the way."

Nickolas stalked off to join Kieran where the trail started. Jessica turned to look at Marcus, anger etched into her face. "You haven't changed a bit. You still feel justified doing whatever you want to get your own way."

Jessica turned on her heel and joined the rest of the Facility Valkyries. Marcus watched them close ranks as they all headed off into the forest.

It took a bit longer than half an hour. There were two trails. One very faint and another of utter wreckage that crossed the first. Following the traces of the second trail, they found the clearing where a big struggle had taken place.

There were footprints and broken foliage caused by a number of people. A grim look on his face, Nickolas studied the tracks. Marcus didn't blame him; this didn't look good. Nickolas started back to where the trails intersected, and Marcus rushed after him, the rest of the party right behind. They all arrived at the rim of a small dished valley and looked down. The ferns and small bushes were trampled; signs of a large number of people were unmistakable.

They picked their way down and started trying to piece together what had happened. The largest disturbance was at the base of a huge fir tree. When Nick reached it, Marcus saw something pinned to the trunk at the same moment Nickolas reached for it.

The wave of power took him utterly by surprise. Marcus dropped to his knees as his vision grayed out. Both Beth and Kieran screamed. When he could see again, Beth was gripping her head, and Kieran was unconscious where he fell. Nickolas knelt and stared into space, whatever he had pulled off the tree clutched in his fist.

Both Robin and Dev rushed to Nickolas's side. Marcus lurched to his feet and saw Jessica picking herself up, dazed.

Moving as fast as his aching head would allow, Marcus approached the tree. Robin finally managed to pry whatever it was out of Nickolas's grasp. The Hunter Prime hissed when he looked at it.

"What is it?" Marcus asked when he got near enough.

"This was pinned to the trunk with a knife, Marcus."

Holding his hand out, Robin gave him the square of paper. It was a picture. Posed to look like the cover of a big game magazine, the kind where the hunter held up their captured trophy. But in this instance, the picture consisted of Gabriel holding both Christoff and Donald by the hair as they knelt, bound hand and foot, on the ground. His son looked unharmed, but blood ran down Donald's throat.

A snarl ripped from him, Marcus handed the paper to Dev. "We need to get everyone back to the valley." This changed the time line. There would be no holding Nick back. Not that he wanted to, with Chris taken.

He glanced around and saw that Kieran was still knocked out by whatever psychic storm Nickolas had released; Beth and Aiden were with him. Nickolas looked unaware, but then Marcus saw that he was whispering something. Jessica pushed past him to reach Nick.

"Nick? What did he say?" she asked.

Perplexed, Marcus opened his mouth.

"Luther," his son said quietly to Jess then rose to his feet. Her face had gone white, but she clenched her fist. There was fire and steel in his eyes. Nick looked in his direction. "I won't leave them there."

"No. We won't leave them there. It's time to get them *all* out."

Nickolas reached into his pocket and pulled out his phone.

Jessica whispered, "Are you sure?"

"I don't want to be. We all talked about this cage and how unlikely it would be to get out of it. Everyone agreed we'd likely have to take the deal eventually. And now the noose has tightened. There's nowhere left to run. Luther has all the resources and help we need." He powered up the phone and placed the call.

Marcus looked into his son's grim eyes.

"Luther? We'll take the deal." Nickolas pulled the handset away and punched a button to turn on the speaker.

"...s sudden. What has happened?"

"Gabriel has Chris. I want in today."

"I need at least five days, Nick."

"No. I can't leave Chris and Donald there."

"I need five days to get everything set up, Nick. I can't do it any quicker."

"Do whatever it takes. I'll be in touch."

Chapter Eighteen

Gabriel ran his hand down the soft silkiness of Pet's hair and looked at Edward. She leaned her head against his thigh where she sat cross-legged on the floor next to his chair. Edward looked over his shoulder at Zach, who stood with his arms crossed next to the exit of the suite, then returned his attention to Gabriel.

"They haven't been cooperating."

Noting Edward's suppressed nervousness, Gabriel snorted. "Of course not. Did you expect them to? They are still waiting for rescue." Leaning back in his chair, he continued to caress Pet. "They've only been here three days. That's not much time to break their resolve."

"True, but I've been hearing things. It's more than the usual certainty that someone will come and rescue them. There is a certainty throughout the entire hold that they will be rescued soon. They have to have a reason for that."

Frowning, Gabriel stilled his hand. "You've been exercising them daily?"

"Yes. They're very good fighters. But even though I have them matched against groups, they will allow themselves to be beaten to a pulp and still not fight, other than to defend themselves from the worst of possible injuries. They just will not fight to the best of their abilities. They insist on not hurting anyone. And it's infecting all of the fighters. It's getting harder to get any of them to fight. And now, no one will go up against Christoff or Donald at all." Edward looked irritated.

"We need to separate them. Move them to a detention cell. I'll deal with this. I had wanted some time with them in the hold to soften them up, but I think I just need to move on with the plan."

Edward straightened his back and continued to stare at Gabriel.

"Was there something else?"

Edward nodded to Pet. "She needs to go back to the hold. It's time for you to have a new toy."

Gabriel's hand fisted in Pet's hair, and she flinched. "No. It's none of your concern."

"You've become too attached. Go pick someone else out, but she needs to go."

"I run things here, Edward, in case you have forgotten. I will decide when I tire of her. Not you."

"You still answer to someone, Gabriel. And they want you to stay focused. They're starting to think that you aren't going in the direction that they want."

"Then they can bring it up with me." Leaning forward, Gabriel half rose, putting his hands on the desk, sheltering Pet under one of his wings. "She stays. And if I find out that you touched her, I'll rip you apart. Do you understand me?"

Edward turned pale but held his ground.

"Now get out and get Christoff and Donald moved to a detention cell."

Edward's mouth firmed to a hard line, but he nodded and left, brushing past the silent form of Zach.

Zachary raised an eyebrow. Growling, Gabriel got up to pace. Pet watched them both. "I don't trust him, Zach."

"You shouldn't."

"I don't like being threatened." He shook his wings out. "You are to protect her at all costs. That is your number one priority." He stopped pacing and ran a hand through his hair then turned to look at Pet. "I have a feeling this came up because of the news I just received."

"News?" Zach asked.

Gabriel walked over, then crouched down and ran a finger over the silent Valkyrie's high cheek bone. She looked into his eyes patiently. "Do you remember the tests I ran on you the other day?" He waited for her nod. "I was a bit shocked, but it turns out that you are pregnant."

Her eyes widened, and she placed a hand over her belly.

"Pregnant? Are you sure?" Zach asked, walking over quickly to stand next to them.

"There's no doubt." He looked up into Zach's shocked eyes. "That's why she's been so sick lately. But it looks like I have spies. It's just too coincidental to have someone trying to relocate her now. Somebody shared test results they shouldn't have had."

"Fredrick?"

"Maybe. I just don't know. But now I know why I get my dander up around Nickolas, and why I'm so different. I just pulled my own records and did a few tests. It turns out that I'm a Breeder, too."

Zach cocked his head, "Huh?"

"It's a new caste that has only recently been discovered. Now the number one question I have is how did Pet become pregnant? She's not in the Breeder caste. So what is going on?" Rising, he held his hand out to the female Valkyrie. Pet looked worried and scared, but she placed her hand in his. "Hush, there's no need to look so worried. This is an exciting time."

In her quiet voice, Pet said, "You're not upset?"

"Upset? No. I couldn't be happier. I'm going to be a father. That is something I thought they had robbed me of years ago. Now come, it's time for you to go to your room. No one but Zach and I have the combination, so don't worry. They would need to take time to break into it to take you from me."

Zach opened the door to the large steel barred cage set up in the corner of Gabriel's bed chamber. It was full of the colorful pillows that Gabriel seemed to like. She settled down onto the floor amid the pillows. "We'll be back soon. Then we need to get you checked out and run a few more tests. Let's go Zach. Edward should have them moved by now."

Zach shut the door, but Gabriel heard him whisper, "Don't worry. We'll keep you safe, Pet," before joining him in the other room. Zach didn't look at him but went and opened the door. Entering the hallway, Gabriel walked with Zach for a few minutes in silence.

"You will take care of her, Zach? I know it is an order, but she needs to be protected. I need to know that you will, no matter what. Drugged or not."

The other Valkyrie was silent for a minute. "Yes. I'll keep her as safe as I can."

Nodding, he continued on. He placed his keycard into a reader, swiped it, then opened the door, stopping to talk to the guard behind the desk. "Has Edward brought them in yet?"

"Yes. They're in cell twenty-two."

He walked away from the station and took the right-hand hallway. He opened the door to cell twenty-two. Edward was watching the transfer guards finish chaining Christoff to the wall. Donald was sagging almost unconscious in his restraints, and blood ran down Christoff's face. They were both black and blue with half healed cuts and lacerations over their torsos. Christoff raised his head and glared at Gabriel out of one eye.

"That will be all, Edward. I'll take it from here."

The keeper of the hold looked at him, and Gabriel could see the assessment running through his mind.

"I meant what I said," Edward reiterated.

Gabriel grinned. "So did I."

The keeper shook his head and left with the guards. Zach closed the door. Gabriel turned back to the chained Valkyries and clucked his tongue. "Looks like you boys have had a rough few days."

Donald coughed and spat out blood.

"We need to have a little chat. Now, we can do this the easy way or the hard way, Christoff, and you've already tried the hard way. Which will it be?"

"Go to hell, Gabriel." Chris swore and yanked at the chains holding his wrists above his head.

Laughing lightly, Gabriel smiled. "No need, I'm already there, Chris. I've been living in hell for the last twenty-five years."

Christoff glanced over at his Second then stared mulishly back at Gabriel.

"The first thing I want to know is why everyone is so certain that you will be rescued soon."

Donald raised his head, and Gabriel could see that his nose was broken. But his eyes held the same assurance that Christoff's held. And both of them kept their mouths shut. Gabriel sighed. "So it's to be the hard way, huh?"

This detention cell was outfitted with the wall restraints that the two Valkyries were currently occupying, but it also had a mobile table that had been wheeled in and placed to the opposite wall. It was large enough to secure one of the Hunters to the surface, but it also contained all of the necessary equipment he was going to need for this interrogation and to complete his assignment of bringing the rest of the Valkyries to heel. Moving over to it, he opened up a couple of the drawers and pulled out his supplies.

"Well, I'll get the answer to that question in time. I might as well get started with the reason you are here. You see, I've been charged with the task of recovering both Nickolas and Jessica, and, preferably to my superiors, the rest of the feral Valkyrie population. They are starting to cause them too much trouble, you see." Gabriel stripped open the sterile packaging on a disposable needle and syringe. Then he drew up a dose of liquid from a bottle he pulled out of the little refrigerator under the table. "To accomplish that task, I'm going to use the two of you to infiltrate Marcus's stronghold."

Gabriel flicked his finger against the syringe. "Now, the drug I used on you, Christoff, is the second generation. Zachary here started out with the first generation but has moved on to the second. The problem with it is that it needs renewal. Without it, new commands can be ignored, though already implanted ones still hold. Fredrick hopes that this gen, combined with a new offshoot, will produce the effects that are desired. Namely, complete compliance with multiple orders over a long period of time, without the necessity of renewing the dose or the commands. Zach, secure Donald's arm."

"Stop it, Gabriel!" Christoff yanked aggressively at the restraints. "Leave him alone."

Zachary moved forward and held Donald's arm still. Donald pulled but to no avail. Gabriel slipped the needle into the vein in his elbow and depressed the plunger.

"I'm sorry, Donny," Gabriel overheard Zach whisper as he disposed of the needle in the sharps box.

"Zachary, haven't you learned by now? No one cares what happens to any of us. Look at how we came into being. The sooner you accept that, the sooner you'll be rid of your weaknesses."

"They are not weaknesses, Gabriel. And it's not true. There are a lot of people who care," Zach countered as he backed up from Donald.

"Not in my experience." The drug was quick. Donald groaned and sagged in the restraints. Gabriel turned to look at Christoff. The Hunter's eyes smoldered with hatred. "This is going to take a while, Christoff. First I need to break you, then train you to the drug. Then you'll be able to bring me Nickolas and Jessica."

Christoff bashed his head into the wall in frustration as Donald started to convulse.

Robin? Nick? Are you in position? A resonant mind voice drifted into Dev's thoughts. He felt Nickolas inch closer to the chain link fence, coming up next to him. The five days it had taken Luther to prepare had almost destroyed his Alpha. The rest of his and Nickolas's teams ranged out behind them, using the darkness for cover.

We're set, Marcus, Robin answered.

Ready, Nickolas replied. *There's guard activity here. We'll make it as quiet as we can.*

Everyone knows their assignments. Make it quick. Neutralize any resistance. We'll meet up back on the surface. If Luther hasn't lied to us, he'll have transport waiting. Good luck, Marcus sent.

Breathing slowly, Dev relaxed into the dirt. He felt Nickolas do the same. The guards were patrolling along their section of fence now. They still had a couple of hours till dawn, and the moon had set, so it was pitch dark out. It was difficult for the Valkyries to see, and impossible for the grounded. *Ok, Dev, you and Aiden take the rest of your team and disable any surface issues we might face. You need to hold the door for us.*

Sure thing, Nick. What about Gabriel? Will he hear us 'talking'?

He might, but he's only one. There are a lot more grounded who would hear us any other way. It's a risk we have to take. The guards had moved on and were now going around the buildings in the center of the above-ground complex. *Now, Dev. Cut the fence.*

Dev quickly crawled forward and snipped the chain link with bolt cutters and held it back so Aiden could rush through. The rest of their team followed and spread out among the shadows of the buildings to take out the sentries. Nickolas came through next with his team, and Dev lowered the fence back into place.

Good luck, Nick. Bring them back to us, Dev sent. A worried wave of reassurance was his answer.

Slipping through the shadows, Dev caught up to Aiden. The young Valkyrie had just finished disabling a guard.

"This was the last one," Aiden said softly. "The others are starting to set the cones."

"Good. Let's get ours done." The two made their way to the front gate. They paused in the shadows of the large posts that held the huge gate in place, and Dev looked around for anything that wasn't on the list they had received from Luther's spies. "Aiden, start rounding up some clouds for me. We don't know what the others might bring to the surface."

The young man nodded, eyes flashing in the darkness as he called up his talent. The wind picked up, and Dev could feel the lure of electricity sparking in the clouds that were beginning to build. Grinning, he pulled an exploding cone out of his bag. Invoking a whisper of his own power, he triggered the timing spell on it, then carefully scraped a depression at the base of the first of the posts. He placed the pinecone into it so that it couldn't roll away.

He placed three more, then slipped over to where Aiden was just finishing up his cones. The teenager was singing softly to himself. Dev shook his head to clear his ears.

"Ring around the pinecones, let's build us a war zone. Ashes, ashes, they all go boom."

"Aiden, you are insane. That has to be the sickest nursery rhyme I've ever heard."

"Then you've never really listened to the true nursery rhymes, have you?" The two of them stealthily made their way over to the helicopter landing pads and started to place the rest of their explosives in and around them. "I have more. This one I made up a long time ago. Baa baa, black sheep, how are you so cruel? Well, sir, well, sir, I'm no fool. One for the master, one for my name, and one for the little boy who'll never be the same. Baa baa, black sheep, have you any soul? No, sir, no, sir, it left me alone. You fleeced this little sheep, and underneath's a wolf, you'd better watch out, or your goose is cooked. Baa baa, black sheep, how'd you lose your soul..."

Dev listened to the teenager sing in his quiet voice and silently cried for the little boy who had made up those songs. No one knew for sure what had happened to Aiden. He was the youngest to have ever made the transition to a Valkyrie. But the more Dev got to know him, the more he knew that Aiden's background was not pretty. He would bet anything that Gabriel had something to do with it too. Especially with the way the Caster was acting tonight. He was always mercurial and prone to aggression. But now, Dev wasn't sure he had been joking when he'd told Aiden that he was acting insane. There was just something in the way he was projecting tonight that made Dev realize he was only holding on by a thread.

He slipped out of the last helicopter, his pinecones dispersed, and crouched on the ground.

Dev! We need that distraction, now! Nickolas's mind voice ripped through him.

Aiden! To the safe zone. We need to blow these! They ran for cover as Dev mentally reached for the clouds. Gathering up some of the lightning, he pulled a bolt down, aiming it for one of the timed cones at the base of the landing pad. Dev knew that if he breached one of the timer shields and released the explosion that it would cause all of the others to blow too. *Green team! Take cover. They're blowing now!*

He dove behind a small fence next to a building just as the crack of the lightning was heard. The thunder that followed the bolt was drowned out by the sound of the helicopters exploding. Alarms blasted all over the compound. *Heads up, everyone. We're going to have company.*

Doors to the buildings opened all over, and a crowd gathered to stare at the burning rubble. Most of the spectators were shocked and talked about a freak lightning storm, but then the soldiers that must have been stationed below started arriving, and they knew differently.

Getting ready, both he and Aiden loosened their wings and started to draw up their power. The wind got stronger, and Dev caught a handful of electricity, shaping it into a ball. Bouncing it in his hand, he threw it at the first guard to rush them. Another lightning bolt hit the gate, and it exploded, throwing the metal into the air. The crowd screamed in panic and fled back into the buildings, leaving the soldiers as clear targets. The rest of the Valkyries joined in and fireballs blossomed.

Voices whispered in his mind, rousing him out of sleep. The soft weight of Pet snuggled deeper against his side. Tilting his head, Gabriel concentrated but couldn't catch anything. He kicked his foot and nudged Zach awake.

"Huh?" the groggy voice answered.

"Wake up. Something's not right. I want you to go over to security and check it out."

"What? Is there a disturbance in the Force, Darth?"

"Go. Now."

Chuckling evilly, Zach climbed out of the bed and grabbed his clothes.

After the door shut, Gabriel closed his eyes, searching his power web, but he couldn't find any trace of a disturbance.

He sighed and rolled over, intending to go back to sleep, but the alarm light flashed on in the suite. Throwing back the covers, Gabriel reached for the telephone just as it rang.

"Yes."

"Intruders have breached the security. They're in the underground complex already."

"What happened to the perimeter alarm?"

"Don't know yet. But it wasn't triggered."

"How many?"

"We haven't gotten an accurate count. At least a hundred, maybe more; there are several groups. They are all Valkyries."

"Lock down what you can."

"Yes, sir."

Zach, change of plans. Go to storage and bring the contents of locker number sixteen back here. Then you are to take Pet out the tunnel to the hidey hole. Do you got that? Instead of a reply, he got a shot of mental static. *I mean it, Zach, don't fight me now. This is an order! You get her out!*

Fine.

Gabriel pulled on his clothes and picked up a sleepy Pet, plunking her into the cage and slamming the door shut on her now wide eyes. Without a word, he swept out of the suite, making his way to the detention block.

The guard at the front desk pulled a gun on him when he thrust the door open but quickly holstered it when he saw who it was.

"Good, stay alert. Nickolas is here for his brother." He swept past the guard and proceeded to the cell holding Christoff and Donald. He shoved the door shut and immediately went to the table and withdrew the latest drug. He hadn't had a chance yet to test it. "Damn it, I was almost there too," he muttered under his breath.

Christoff choked on a laugh and said through bloody, cracked lips, "I take it Nick has finally come?"

"I wouldn't look on that as a good thing, Christoff." Gabriel set the prepped syringe down on the table then went over to where Donald was hanging. Donald looked at him and slowly shook his head.

"Chris..." the injured Valkyrie called.

As soon as he released Donald's wrists, the Valkyrie collapsed into Gabriel's arms. His battered body wouldn't support his weight. He tried to fight, but his arms were like limp noodles, and Gabriel easily pinned them behind his back. He faced Christoff, forcing Donald to kneel before his Wing leader. "I only need one functioning sleeper, and you are much more valuable, Christoff."

Horror dawned on Chris's face. "No," he whispered.

"The drug hasn't broken through your defenses enough yet. Given sufficient time, it would have, but now I need an emotional prod to finish what it started. I need you vulnerable." Lashing Donald's hands behind his back, Gabriel pulled the large knife he carried in his boot.

"No. Don't do this! Please."

"Chris," Donald whispered raggedly.

Struggling against his restraints, Chris begged. "Gabriel, please! I'll do anything you want, just don't do this! Stop!"

"I know you mean what you say, Christoff, but you can't just choose to let your defenses down to the point that I need them. They are an involuntary reflex." He grabbed Donald by the hair and pulled his head back, exposing his throat. "I'm sorry, Donald. You've been a strong and worthy opponent."

Donald tried to struggle, but it was no use. "Chris...take care of Kieran!"

Gabriel sliced the blade across Donald's throat.

"NO! Donald!" Chris screamed. He struggled against the chains that held him securely to the wall, yelling until he was hoarse.

Donald gasped and convulsed. Blood slicked across the blade and Gabriel's hand. The Valkyrie's mouth opened and closed as he sagged sideways, and Gabriel laid him down gently. Donald's eyes held Christoff's for a moment more, then they drifted shut and his heaving chest stilled. The blood continued to pool on the ground.

"Donald..." Chris sobbed.

Swiftly, Gabriel laid the knife on the table and grabbed the prepped syringe. Working quickly, he injected Christoff with the dose of the new compound. Tears streaked down

Christoff's face, and he tried to kick out but was held too securely.

Grabbing Chris's face, Gabriel turned it to look into his eyes. He pushed with his mind and invaded Christoff's thoughts. The Hunter tried to resist, but between the shock and the new drug quickly working its way through his system, he couldn't hold out. Gabriel tore through the last cobwebby barriers and dove straight into the core of Christoff.

Shuddering, the Hunter screamed.

Using his song talent, Gabriel implanted his orders. "Christoff, you are not to let anyone know about your directive in any way. You will go back with the other Valkyries and wait for things to settle down before you contact me. After you have contacted me, you will then arrange for the retrieval of Nickolas and Jessica. You are to operate in a way that does not cast suspicion on yourself. After the Breeders have been retrieved, you will attempt to open the defenses of Aurora so the population of the valley may be recovered. When you contact me, I will update and fine-tune your orders. Do you understand?"

The Hunter's eyes were glazed, but Gabriel could see self-awareness still in them. Christoff fought, and Gabriel pushed harder. A groaning "yes" finally emerged.

"Good. You cannot kill yourself or put yourself purposely in a position to cause harm or your death."

Christoff closed his eyes in defeat, and Gabriel released his face. The Hunter sagged in his chains, his eyes hollow as he stared at his Second lying on the floor.

Picking up his knife, Gabriel slipped out of the room.

Chapter Nineteen

They had barely entered the subterranean hallway when the alarm lights started flashing, creating a bright red, strobe effect. Nickolas led his team quickly down the different corridors, remembering the layout from the information Luther had provided. Kieran was right on his heels. Their last intelligence report stated that Donald and his brother had been moved to the detention block. Nickolas didn't like the sound of that.

They reached an intersection, and his group met up with resistance.

Nick willed a shield into being as the hall erupted with noise and movement. A couple of Valkyries around him fell as the grounded soldiers' guns found targets. Nick's mind flashed out, and he grabbed as many of the guns as he could with his telepathy, yanking them to point down. Shielded Hunters swarmed the stunned grounded as they pulled against their weapons ineffectually.

A storm of emotion flooded through Nick's bond with Chris, undecipherable, and then nothing. Kieran screamed Donald's name. Leaving his Flight to deal with the fighting, Nick leapt after Kieran and they dodged through the melee, ignoring the worried yells of their Wingmates. They were close to their goal; the team could catch up.

Kieran kicked open the locked door when they reached the entrance to the detention cells, and Nickolas surged through, a shield shimmering into being as he launched himself at the guard who was hurriedly drawing his weapon. Nick took the man to the ground and bashed his head into the concrete floor. By the time Nick stood up, Kieran was already typing on the keyboard.

"They're in cell twenty-two. First right-hand corridor," he said.

Kieran vaulted the desk, and the two of them raced down the hall. Nickolas bashed his shoulder into the cell door and forced the lock. They both froze in the open doorway. A strangled sound came from Kieran.

Nickolas had to shake off the feeling of déjà vu as he stepped into the room and took in the scene. Just like the vision he'd had in the Hub weeks ago, Donald was obviously dead with the amount of blood around him on the floor. Terrified for Christoff, Nickolas looked up at his brother hanging from the wall, and a sense of relief washed through him when he saw Chris's chest rise in a shallow breath. He hadn't been sure Chris was alive, the way his blue eyes stared unblinking at Donald. Kieran pushed by, falling to his knees, heedless of the blood. Sobbing, he pulled his cousin into his lap.

Wishing he still had a lockdown on his emotions, Nickolas pushed his grief over Donald to the back of his mind and moved to Chris. His brother's unresponsive form made getting him free difficult. "Kieran, I need help." He looked over to the empath and sucked in a breath. "Kieran?"

Kieran looked up, and Nickolas could see the searing pain in him. He felt it through their bond, and it found a matching place inside him.

"Why? Why, Nick?" the empath asked in a small voice.

"I don't know yet, Kieran. But we'll find out. I need your help getting Chris down."

"Why?" Kieran said again. Looking back down, he started rocking.

Nick worked on the shackles, using his telekinesis, and finally got them open. Christoff's slack form fell into his arms. Carefully folding his damaged wings, Nickolas was just lifting Chris into his arms when the rest of their team arrived. Nickolas handed Chris to Dylan so he could go to Kieran.

Kneeling down next to the empath, Nickolas squeezed his shoulder. "Come on, Kier, let them take him. We won't leave him here. We need to get them out. Let's go."

One of the Hunters stepped forward and gently took Donald's body from Kieran. The empath sobbed but didn't stop them. Rising, Nickolas helped Kieran to his feet so they could all leave the little room.

Nickolas opened his link with Kieran as wide as it could go. The first spark of rage had started to burn within the cloud of grief. The empath stumbled blindly with them in a state of childlike docility. The rest of their Flights saw what had happened and kept them surrounded as they worked their way toward the surface.

In the first attack, he barely noticed the movement of power, but on the next, Nick felt Kieran use his talent against one of the guards. It was just a little thing, projecting fear so the human dodged at the wrong time and the Hunter going after him took him down easily.

That gave the ember tinder. The next group of grounded froze in fear, and the Hunters cut them down.

The sparks inside Kieran burst into flame.

The first kill was sudden.

Kieran pulled away, and Nick felt the empath dive deep into his well. The fighting grew worse as they tried to reach the surface. Kieran channeled his pain and anger, turning it into a weapon. Eyes glazed, he struck out at anything that moved against them. The Hunters pulled back, allowing Kieran to forge ahead, his power an emotional lightning bolt that seared all of the enemy before them. Almost like they had turned mad, the soldiers screamed, either collapsing to the ground or turning on their own in a haze of panic.

Through his link, Nickolas could feel Kieran's anguish. His foundation crumbling beneath him as he tried to push reality away. The empath released his power, using his talent to destroy. Nick hoped his friend retained enough of his sanity to only hit the enemy.

♦ ♦ ♦

"Jessica! Behind you!"

Whirling around, she lashed out with her foot and dropped the guard who had come at her from the doorway.

The sudden empty spot inside her was an aching distraction and she'd missed the obvious attacker. She jumped over a couple of bodies and made her way to Marcus.

"You need to focus. Stop thinking about the others."

"Something happened. I could feel it through my bonds."

"I know, I could tell from your reactions," he said. "But something bad will happen to us if you don't concentrate. We're almost to the labs."

Locking away her thoughts, she ran with Marcus down the hall, followed by what remained of their entry force.

"Here, this should be the door," he said, and they skidded to a stop.

Jessica watched him study the sealed door. "Ok, Jess, go into mind sight and watch."

Changing her vision, she dropped quickly into a lucid trance and watched as Marcus drew on his power pool, noting the finesse and dexterity he utilized in the weaving. Splitting her sight, she watched as he formed a matrix across the door itself, then slowly wrenched down to pull the door out of alignment just enough that he could use his power to set it to the side. A couple of Hunters stood ready, and as soon as the door was out of the way, they flowed in to deal with any guards.

That left the rest to stand watch in the hall. Jessica followed Marcus and the two Hunters in. She found herself in an anteroom with glass observation windows. She stepped past the downed guards and went to look out the windows. The two Hunters joined her.

One of them gave a low whistle.

Below them were a series of gurneys and unoccupied wall chains. When she looked to the right, she could see a short hallway with doors, closely spaced. It reminded her of the Hub. That was where she needed to go.

She turned back to the room, and a quick glance showed Marcus had just finished rifling the desk in the corner. He joined her near the windows. "Ok, Jess, it's your turn. See if you can get this door open like I did."

She stepped back and took a breath then tried to imitate what she'd seen the other weaver do. The door went flying across the room and crashed loudly.

"Just like a toddler. We need to work on dexterity, Jess." He started down the stairs first.

With a growl she followed.

They gained the base of the stairs. The rest of the Hunters swarmed into the room. Jessica was surprised at the lack of people. Marcus turned a slow circle, keeping an eye open until everyone was down, then he turned to the doors on the left.

A surge of grief and anger swamped her from her blood bonds. She gasped and swayed as she cut them off. Her gaze sought Marcus's and she realized he read her reactions because she saw the acknowledgment of what had likely happened reflected in his eyes. She clenched her teeth and stiffened her back.

He gave her a nod. "Ok, we need to hurry, so we're splitting up. Jess, you go check out the cells while I get any records I can out of the offices. Any research we find could help in the recovery of some of these people."

Jessica turned to her right and skirted past the line of gurneys, half the Valkyries following her. At the head of the hall, she paused. Eight doors, four to either side. Steeling herself to what she might find, she approached the first door, but one of the Hunters grabbed her hand before she could open it.

"Let us go first."

Wrinkling her nose at him, slightly annoyed, she backed up. The Hunter opened the door and shook his head. "It's empty."

"One down. Let's get these done. We don't know how long we have here," another Hunter said.

Agreeing wholeheartedly, Jessica moved onto the next door down the wall, waiting for someone to check it.

The Hunter opened the door and hissed. "We have one here, Jess."

She hurried forward and entered the room. The emaciated Valkyrie huddled naked in the corner of the cell.

His large wings were wrapped around him as best he could to form a blanket. He barely stirred when she entered with the Hunter. She could see every vertebra snaking down his back. Approaching him slowly, she reached out. He flinched the moment she laid her hand on him. His head snapped up, and she gasped.

"Jack?" she asked.

His eyes focused on her, and he shook his stringy hair out of them. "Jessica?" His voice sounded hoarse and raspy.

"That is your name, isn't it? Jack?" she asked again.

Nodding slowly, he pulled his legs in and tried to sit up, but his muscle mass was so nonexistent that he was having trouble moving. "I'd hoped that Ian would get here a little sooner. I'd given up."

She exchanged a look with the Hunter. "Well, we're here now, and we're getting you out. Hold still and let me scan you."

"Scan me?" Jack flinched when she touched him again, but other than trembling, he tried to hold still.

She rested her hands as gently as possible over his heart then dove into her well. Racing up, she flooded through him, ignoring his gasp. She started citing her findings so he could be reassured and the Hunter would know what was needed if she wasn't able to take care of it. "Your internal changes are all in order. I can clear out the inhibitor and other drugs they have in your system, but it's going to take a long time to get you back on your feet. You're getting close to the coma, aren't you?"

He nodded. "I figure I probably won't be making it through that."

"I won't lie to you. Your body's reserves are nonexistent, but to have made it this far in your change, you have to be strong. So don't give up yet. We'll get you to Beth and see what she and Jays can do."

He closed his eyes, and she saw a single tear escape.

She looked up to the Hunter and saw his concerned expression. "Get him out of here, but be careful. His body is fragile, and he just doesn't have the reserves to heal anything more."

"Got it, I'll take good care of him."

She rose to her feet and cast a disgusted glance around the cell before she followed them out the door. The rest of the Hunters were checking the other cells.

"Over here, Jess." One of them was waving from the end of the hall. "The rest are all empty, there's just this one."

She peered in the open door and saw a second Hunter hunched over the form of a still Valkyrie. She didn't like the look of this. The occupant was much too still. Kneeling across the body, Jessica reached out for a pulse. *There, one strong beat. And another.* Finally the woman took a slow breath. "Her pulse is incredibly slow."

"Yes, we thought she was dead at first."

Scanning the female, Jessica exhaled in frustration. "She's not in the coma. She's been fledged for a while, from the looks of it. She has traces of some compound in her system. I've cleared it out, but considering her condition, I don't think getting rid of that little bit will make much of a difference. We're going to need Kieran for this one. He'll need to go into her dreamscape."

The Hunter across from her picked the woman up, and Jessica followed them into the empty hallway. Trailing behind the others, she was the last one out of the hall. Everyone was already gathered at the base of the stairs when she heard the rush of steps from behind her. She whirled around and was able to get her arm up to block something swinging on her at the last second. She screamed in pain but still managed to spin and kick out at the white-coated man. He got up and continued to come after her with a metal rod. Cradling her arm, she widened her stance.

Wings brushed the top of her head as Marcus leapt over her. He spun, kicking the man into the wall, then grabbed him by the throat before he could slide down it. The man's hands came up to frantically scrabble at Marcus's grip.

"You bastard." Marcus spat in the man's face. His feet flailed as the Alpha lifted him higher. His mouth worked but nothing more than a gurgle could emerge, and his eyes started to bug out, his face turning red. Surprised that Marcus didn't just break the guy's neck, Jessica watched him slowly suffocate until finally the man gurgled once more and stilled. Marcus shook him like a dog shakes a rabbit before he dropped the body on the ground.

Flexing her hand, Jessica cradled her arm, and when Marcus turned back she snapped at him. "I was more than capable of finishing that fight on my own, you know."

He snapped his wings into place and glared over his shoulder at the dead man. "I'm sure you were." Then he turned his eyes back on her. "But you've never killed. And the first time you do, it changes you. Besides, I had a few things left to settle with Freddie here."

Still a little annoyed, she backed up when he reached for her arm.

He sighed in exasperation and just looked at her. "Is it broken or not?"

Not quite over her irritation, she looked at her arm, extending it carefully. "I don't know. I have no feeling yet." Holding it out, she let Marcus examine her right forearm.

"You're lucky. It doesn't appear to be broken." She hissed at his probing but kept her arm still. "But I can't rule out if it's cracked or not, so be careful with it until we can have Jillian take a look."

She nodded, and the two of them rejoined the group waiting for them at the base of the stairs.

"Ok. We've gotten everything from here that we can. Let's start heading for the surface."

"Why haven't we run into any resistance, Robin?"

"I don't know, Kel, but everyone keep your eyes open." He spoke softly. They'd gotten as far as the lobby of the underground arena, and after a thorough search of that level, had moved on to the arena itself. "With as many Valkyries as I'm expecting behind those doors, I would have thought we'd run into some fighting by now. It's almost like they've deserted their posts."

"More likely they're in a different section of this Facility. They wouldn't need much man power here if they have them all contained, especially since it's night," one of the Facility Valkyries pointed out.

"Huh, that could be it." He reached the ground floor and held up his hand. Fifty Valkyries gathered around him. "There are three different barracks; you know which group you belong in. Good luck, and we'll meet back up in here once we've freed everyone."

They split up, and Robin took his group to the first door. "Craig, set the cones; everyone else, step back." After a loud explosion, the door creaked then fell to the dirt. Alarms blasted on, and Robin rushed in, the others following. Someone found a light switch, throwing the room into sudden relief. The nearest Valkyries were gaining their feet quickly, hope in their eyes. Robin looked at the row after row of caged people in the warehouse-like room and was nearly sick. He clenched his jaw and snapped out. "Someone figure out how to get those damn things open!"

"Robin!" A voice shouted from the center of the room. Kelley shot past him. He watched Leslie reach her arm through the bars of one of the cages and grab Kelley's hand. Closing his eyes in thanks, he turned back to the task at hand. Someone had found a control panel and was working on the code.

"I think I almost have it. There." And all of the cell doors released. The Valkyries didn't waste any time pushing out of their cages.

Kelley and Leslie shoved their way through the gathering mass of bodies to reach him. "Robin! Thank God you've finally gotten here. They took Chris and Donald away a couple of days ago."

"Nick went after them. We just need to get everyone organized enough to get the lot to the surface."

A pounding started, interrupting what he was saying. More people rushed past him to help.

"Yessss," Leslie hissed.

"What's going on?" Robin asked as he watched those freed work at forcing a door in the farther wall open.

"That is where Edward lives. I guess he didn't leave like the rest of the guards."

The angry Valkyries managed to get the door open, and several of them disappeared into the room. After a moment, they dragged a struggling man out into the open of the barracks.

Unfortunately, there wasn't enough of him to go around. Unfettered by guards and with the prospect of freedom, the imprisoned Valkyries made short work of ripping the man to shreds. Robin had been in his share of fights and was an accomplished hunter of game, so he wasn't unfamiliar with death. But their vengeance still chilled him to the bone.

Once they were done, he could attempt to get them focused and organized for a retreat to the surface. But before that, there was just no point in trying.

Another guard came around a corner. Quick as a striking snake, Kieran dove into the man's unprotected mind, found his greatest fear, then amplified it a hundred fold. Screaming, the guard dropped to the ground, his weapons scattering. Kieran didn't even pause as he passed him. The screaming stopped abruptly, changing to a gurgle as the man's heart burst under the strain.

Kieran felt it happen, but he didn't care.

His power shot out ahead of him again, and he sensed three more guards waiting around a corner, getting ready to ambush them. He slipped into one of their minds; he twisted the guard's dreamscape and brought it to the front of his thoughts. The nightmares he produced had an immediate reaction. As he led the large group past the intersection, Kieran saw one guard knifing his teammate, the other already lay dead on the floor. Kieran knew that the third wouldn't survive either, when he turned the knife on himself.

The flash of the knife in the red light made the crack in Kieran's shell widen, driving his grief deeper. The picture of Donald's body on the floor filled his vision again, and he stopped abruptly in the hall, shaking his head. The weight of Nickolas's hand pressed his shoulder as the rest of the Valkyries flowed around him to continue the trek out. Kieran could feel his Alpha bottling up his own grief. *He has more practice at it*, Kieran thought uncharitably.

"You need to pull back, Kieran. He wouldn't want this. You know that."

Kieran clenched his fists, seeing spots of rage flash in his vision.

The hand on his shoulder continued to hold him back as the rest of the party slipped around him in the hall. Understanding and knowing that Nick was right didn't make it easy to do, though.

"I just talked to Jess; we'll meet up with them in a minute," Nick said, urging Kieran to fall in the wake of the rest.

"It hurts, Nick," he said softly after a moment.

"I know, Kier. I know how you feel right now."

They reached an intersection where the hall widened, and their group stopped to wait for Marcus's. It wasn't long before the other team rounded a bend, and Kieran could see Jessica was injured. Shocked, he realized he should have known from their bond when she got hurt, but his mind felt like it moved through molasses. Kieran's gaze shot to Nickolas. His Alpha's eyes looked grim but not surprised. *I should have felt that happen.*

As the two groups mixed, Kieran tried to push his grief aside but failed miserably. Focused on himself, he missed when the whole group went silent. It wasn't until Marcus said "Zachary?" in surprise that he looked up.

A lone Valkyrie stood frozen at the end of one of the long halls. Recognition raced through Kieran and succeeded in accomplishing what he could not, suppressing his grief. Hope blossomed, and he whispered, "Zach?"

With a shake of his head, Zachary slowly backed away.

Kieran pushed his way to the front. "Zach, wait."

"What is he doing free?" Kieran heard one of the Hunters ask behind him.

His stomach sinking, Kieran's gaze jumped to Zach's. His childhood friend looked back at him mutely, but even with the distance, Kieran could see the guilt in his eyes as he continued to slowly back away. Unbelieving, Kieran started walking toward him. "Zach?" As the truth sank in, he moved into a run. "You son of a bitch. You're working with him?" His voice broke.

Zach dropped his pack and fell into a crouch as Kieran slammed into him. The two struggled briefly before the larger Seer pinned Kieran to the wall.

"Kieran, stop!" Zach snapped. His hand wrapped about Kieran's throat. "You know you're no match for me. You never have been," he finished softly.

Not able to struggle physically, Kieran opened his mind, looking for the pathway into Zach's, trying to come at him from a mental direction instead, hoping to get to Zach's core and cause damage that way.

But his control on his talent was slippery from his grief and shock. Kieran gasped when Zachary turned his empathy back at him. Shocked, he stared at Zach.

The sound of rushing feet broke Kieran's surprise at finding that Zach had a strong empathy talent of his own. He struggled against the larger Valkyrie's hold. Zach's hand squeezed, cutting off his air briefly in warning. The older Seer looked over his shoulder at the rushing Valkyries.

"Stop."

Kieran heard them skid to a halt.

"Zach? What are you doing?" Marcus said. "Let him go. We're getting everyone out. You need to come with us. Dustin hasn't been the same since you disappeared."

"I can't, Marcus." Zach turned away. Kieran was watching his eyes, so he saw the anguish the Valkyrie quickly suppressed. "Believe me, I wish I could."

Not sure what that meant, Kieran licked his lips, then Zach's face suddenly turned ashen, and he closed his eyes in pain before slamming his free hand into the wall next to Kieran's head. "I'm coming already! Leave me alone," he muttered, then Zach's eyes opened, boring into Kieran.

"I can't believe this. You really are working with him," Kieran said in disgust. "What happened to all your talk of honor and fair play when we were kids?"

Zach's hand flexed around his throat, and the harsh stare he received nearly made him flinch. He tried to move to defend himself, but he found his limbs pinned to the concrete of the wall. Apparently, Zach also had telekinesis.

"You don't know what you're talking about, Kieran." Zach looked away to the other Valkyries, who were all vibrating with the need to do something, but none of them were willing to risk Kieran's life. Addressing Marcus, Zach asked, "You got Edana out?"

"Who?"

"She was in the labs."

A Hunter Kieran didn't know stepped forward, holding an unconscious Valkyrie. Surprised at the wave of relief that washed from Zach, Kieran tried to tune back into his empathy. The mixed messages he was receiving from Zach started to penetrate his grief-fogged brain. Zachary was terrified for this female. He looked out of the corner of his eye again, but all he could see was fiery red hair cascading over the Hunter's arm.

"Take care of her, Marcus," Zach said before he turned back to Kieran. "Now, for you."

Adrenalin shot through Kieran and he dove for his source to try and shield, but he wasn't quick enough. Zachary slammed through his natural barriers and took them both diving into Kieran's dreamscape.

Kieran found himself standing shin deep in meadow grass, the searing sun deflected by the old elm tree that held a familiar tire swing. Confused, he turned around and looked about him at the old farmstead where he grew up. He hadn't been back here since his change. He didn't really want to be back here now.

What the hell?

A twig snapped, and he spun to peer under the tree. Zachary stood with his forearm resting against the trunk, grinning at him.

"You're strong, Kieran, but you don't have the experience yet to use your talents well. Though, you do seem off to a good start."

Memory returned with a rush. "What do you want, Zach?" he snapped, stung by his friend's, his *former friend's*, criticism.

Zach flared his wings then snapped them closed. "I need you to help Dana. They won't be able to. What Fredrick and Gabriel have done to her has trapped her in her own mind. You're going to need to go into her dreamscape to free her."

Pain swamped him. "No..."

The realization of what he had done with his talent, how he let it control him, how he'd used it to kill...pain and anguish filled him, twisting with his emotions from Donald's death. The entire tangle coiled up in his mind.

"Kieran?" Concern radiated from Zach, and Kieran took a step back. He shook his head, but the other Valkyrie wouldn't let up. "I can feel your pain. What happened?"

Kieran couldn't say it out loud. It was already too real. He used to know Zach. When they were kids, the older boy had always looked out for him. Zach and Donald. They'd protected him on more than one occasion, and Kieran had always looked up to Zach, had always trusted him. But now...how could he work with Gabriel?

"Kieran," Zach pressed.

Swallowing, Kieran finally got the words past his dry lips. "Donald's dead."

Zach stared, his eyes wide. "What? He didn't...no..." This last was muttered, and then Zach started to pace furiously. "Damn him! God damn him!"

Kieran turned his back on Zach and walked out into the hot summer sunshine. The sounds of grasshoppers chirruping in the tall grass filled his ears. He felt his power stir. Felt the heat, the pressure. He wanted the obliteration of the eruption he felt building.

Dozens of childhood memories suddenly flooded his mind, blocking out the view of the landscape in front of him, and he staggered. Donald popping up out of the tall grass, a boyish grin on his face. Zach and Dustin shoving him off the bank to swing terrified out over the river on the rope swing for the first time. Donald and Zach dragging him home by the scruff of the neck after they had beat the crap out of the neighbor boys for ganging up on him. Zach or Donald, one of them always there. Each memory was a knife that pierced a hole in the building pressure and allowed the eruption to dissipate.

"Stop it, Zach." Kieran gritted his teeth as the memories continued to flow from his childhood companion.

"You need to remember who you are, Kieran. You're in danger from your talent."

"None of this is real anymore. The farm is gone. Everyone is gone, Zach."

"No. Everyone is not gone. Gaining our wings separated us, but things always change. Whether you're a Valkyrie or not." The onslaught of memories stopped, and Kieran refocused. The grass waved in the breeze while swallows swooped through the air. He wished he could just stay here. Turn back time. This was before the memories. *No wonder Nick was so hard to move out of his dreamscape. I can see the appeal in not returning to reality.*

The heavy weight of Zachary's hand came to rest on his shoulder. The jolt of power that shot through the contact surprised him. He would have turned, but Zach prevented him from moving.

"I don't have much longer. Tell me you'll help her, Kieran?"

"Why do you care? You're working with him." Kieran could feel Zach's power rising. The other Valkyrie was using Kieran's dreamscape to build something inside of him, a link between them. Not knowing what to do, Kieran tried to block it, but the older empath slipped around him with ease.

"Kieran, knock it off," Zach said, exasperated. Then he leaned in, and Kieran shivered when Zach breathed in his ear, "She's one of the two people I love most in the world, Kieran. Please don't leave her trapped."

Kieran closed his eyes and bowed his head. He wouldn't give Zach the assurance of his help. He didn't know if he even could help. What he had done in response to Donald's death, what he was responsible for, was starting to sink in like a stone into a pond. Where the ripples expanded to, he could only wait to find out. He couldn't trust his talent or himself. The thought of using it made him sick to his stomach.

"I'm out of time, Kier. Marcus has left us alone out of worry of you getting hurt. They won't wait much longer. I've left you a book. When you're ready to help Dee, come find it. It has all of the information that I know about what was done to her."

Zach's hand left his shoulder and ran gently through his hair. Shocked at his response to the touch, Kieran froze.

"Stay safe, Kieran," Zach said, longing in his voice.

His vision wavered, and Kieran found himself back in the corridor. Only seconds had passed in the physical world. His mind was disoriented from the sudden shift.

"Remember," Zach whispered in his ear before the Seer released him both mentally and physically. Kieran slid down the wall and shook his head, trying to clear the mental fog. The other Valkyries started to react as he watched Zach slip around the corner and disappear.

Feet rushed in around him, and he blinked up owlishly at Nickolas and Marcus.

"Are you ok?" Nickolas asked quietly.

He shook his head. Hands reached down and helped him back to his feet.

"Come on. Let's get you out of here. You go with the rest. I'm going to take our Flight and go help Robin. We'll meet you all back on the surface," Nick ordered.

Kieran pressed his temples and fell in beside Jessica as they split up.

Chapter Twenty

Boots reverberated through the stark hallways. The memory of jogging through similar halls in the Facility confused Nickolas's sense of location, but not for long. They rounded a corner, and his Flight ran into yet another group of guards. He threw a shield up and dove into their midst, causing them to scatter. The fighting spread out through the halls.

Nickolas! Where are you?

He spun low and swiped out with his leg, making the man in front of him jump. Then he dove through the hole he made and somersaulted, coming up into a crouch, his knife in his hand. When he looked around, he realized he'd been outmaneuvered. They'd cut him off from the others. They were all a good twenty feet back down the hall. With too many between him and his group. *Crap.* *I've been separated. There's at least ten of them in my way. I'm draining my power too quickly. I can't shield indefinitely.*

Grinning faces closed in. Holding his knife, he backed slowly down the hall. *Hang on, Nick, we're working our way toward you.*

He flexed his wings then refolded them, looking for a way through the barrier of bodies. His people were just on the other side, but that might as well have been miles away for all the help it would give. *I'm not going to be able to last for them to get through. Time for plan B.* Changing tactics, Nick turned and sprinted down the hall.

Just in time. A second group burst out of a door he passed on the right. If he'd stayed to fight, he'd have been trapped between the two groups. The odds now really not in his favor, Nickolas started looking for a way to ditch his pursuers.

They started to slow, and just as he began to wonder why they were letting him get so far ahead, he turned a corner and found himself in a corridor that ended in a closed steel door. He tried the knob. *Locked, of course.*

Behind him, he heard the guards filling up the hall. He reached into his power and pulled a tiny tendril, threading it into the lock, then he felt around until he got the lock to disengage. Quickly opening the door, he slipped through to the sounds of the guards yelling behind him.

He slammed it then braced his back against it as he relocked it. Pounding started instantly, and he used his power to break the lock. Finally taking a breath, he looked at where he was. The room was immense.

This must be the arena.

His gaze scanned the large, oval dirt floor, then he froze. Across the expanse, Gabriel stood with two other Valkyries next to a large metal door. The three stared back at him, and Gabriel slowly smiled before he turned to a keypad on the wall. Gabriel punched in a code and the big steel door popped open. Reaching out, he swung it wide and waved the two Valkyries in.

"Zach, get Pet to safety. I'll join you as soon as I can. Don't lock the door behind you," Nickolas heard Gabriel instruct.

Nick looked around the room for another exit and swore as he realized there would be no avoiding a third confrontation with Gabriel. Checking his shield, Nickolas moved out into the arena.

The other Valkyrie shook his wings loose as he started a slow, prowling circle around Nick. His movements showed how comfortable he was, the advantage of being on his home turf.

"Well, Nickolas. I didn't expect to see you. You've succeeded in tearing the walls of my house down."

Following Gabriel's lead, Nickolas circled his opponent, drawing closer, a spiral that would end with their meeting.

"You killed Donald," Nickolas voiced.

The other Valkyrie shrugged. "It was, unfortunately, unavoidable."

"Unavoidable? You murdered him!" Nickolas took a deep breath. Losing his temper was a sure way to lose the fight. "You need to be put down, Gabriel. You're a rabid dog."

"You don't know the half of it, Nickolas." Gabriel shook his head, staring at Nick with a strangely serious expression. "You are pathetically naïve. You're a baby who's just coming out to play with the big boys. And, like any child, you think you know everything; you think you are invincible."

Not wanting to consider the validity of Gabriel's comments, Nickolas stretched his wings out. They were almost within striking range; he needed to be ready.

"So let's see how invincible you really are, shall we, Nickolas? My orders are to recover you. By any means necessary. It would sure make my work a lot easier to take you now."

The memory of Donald lying on the stone floor uppermost in his mind, Nickolas lunged at the other Valkyrie.

"Robin, there are two other barrack rooms. If we go through the doors over there, it will take us to them." Leslie pointed them out.

Robin shook his head. "Teams have already gone to get them; we're to meet up in the arena." He cast a brief glance at the mutilated mess on the floor. "If everyone is done, we can get ourselves out of here."

Leslie looked over the group. "I think we're ready now, Robin."

"Good. Try to keep them together...and under control. Ok, Les?"

She gave him a half smile and a shrug. Praying for patience, Robin led one hundred and fifty Valkyries back out into the arena.

He had only taken a couple of steps through the door when he froze, Kelley slamming into his back. A grumble started behind him, but he ignored the sound.

The sight before him froze the breath in his lungs. Nickolas was fighting Gabriel. Alone. The attention of the two Alphas was entirely centered on one another.

"Oh my God, Robin, it's Nick," Kelley said. "We need to help him."

"Kelley, that's Gabriel," Leslie said in a whisper.

Robin saw the reactions of the rest of the freed Valkyries as they peered around him, too afraid to enter the arena with Gabriel right in front of them. Totally cowed. None of them would be of any help. *Huh. Funny how they can rip one man to pieces but when confronted with another, they freeze.* Movement on the other side of the arena drew his attention. The rest of Nickolas's team arrived on the run. They froze to take in the situation as well. Robin made eye contact with Kevin.

"Les, you and Kel get all of them across. Kevin will lead them to the surface. We'll get Nickolas."

Nickolas pumped more power into his shield then jumped into the air, and after two wing beats, clamped his wings to his body and spun to the side, narrowly avoiding the lunge Gabriel made. He landed in a crouch and didn't hesitate before launching his own attack. This time the two exchanged several blows; with each one, Nick had Gabriel backing up.

"This is probably the best workout I've had in forever. Thank you, Nickolas."

"If I were to have my way, Gabriel, it would be your last workout."

"Not likely, boy. You're good, but not that good. Yet."

Suddenly, Gabriel threw up his own shield, and Nickolas's next blow felt like it hit a brick wall. Grunting in pain, he started retreating as Gabriel pressed his advantage. The older Valkyrie was relentless, and Nickolas felt his power bleeding out of him in his effort to maintain his shield.

"You're leaking power like a breached nuclear reactor, Nickolas. You really need to work on that. You should be able to divide your talents, using more than one at a time. Look at me. I'm not wasting anything. You, on the other hand, are glowing like a goddamned Christmas tree. I can even see the leakage with my normal sight." Stopping, Gabriel shook his head and studied him.

Nick took the brief respite and tried to control his labored breath, shaking his wings out, rubbing his hand to make sure it wasn't broken. "Well I haven't had the freedom to practice using my talent, now have I?"

Gabriel flashed him a grin before striking out once more. "True."

Nick dodged then swept out with his foot, connecting with Gabriel's shin, which surprised him. Gabriel did a backward somersault. Staying on top of his advantage, Nickolas moved forward. The sound of voices penetrated his thoughts, and he spared a glance behind him. Robin had just freed the bulk of the Valkyries. A fist to his shield brought his attention back right quick, and he dodged the next volley.

He ignored the new arrivals and focused on Gabriel. They continued to exchange blows, but the other Alpha was no longer talkative. It took every ounce of Nickolas's skill in the ring to match Gabriel. A second shield blossomed in front of Gabriel's first, but this time Nick felt the draw and pulled his strike in time. The two stopped to stare at each other for a second. Gabriel grinned, and Nickolas suddenly realized that he'd been toyed with.

Reaching out behind him, Gabriel pulled open the door he'd sent the other two Valkyries through only moments before. "This has been a pleasure, Nickolas. While it would have been nice to best you, I'm not willing to let Robin get involved to keep you. So I'll say adieu for now." Still smiling, Gabriel slipped through the door and disappeared.

Knowing it was useless, Nickolas raced to the door as it snapped shut. He placed his hand on the cool steel surface and reached within. But there was nothing left for him to work with. Gabriel had sealed it tight. *Not getting this door open again without explosives.* Boots on the sand thudded behind him, and Nickolas turned to face Robin.

"I don't suppose you have any exploding cones handy?"

"Sorry, Nick, we used them all up."

Nick sighed. "I guess we couldn't drag the rat out of the sewer pipe anyway."

"Come on, Nick. Let's get up to the surface." Robin shivered his wings, and Nickolas took a closer look at him. Robin noticed and added, "I need to see the sky."

"No one better than I could understand that feeling, Robin." Combing his fingers through his sweat-dampened hair, Nickolas walked with Robin across the sands.

They reached the surface, and Nickolas shaded his eyes from the early morning sunshine. A nudge from Robin drew his attention to his father. Marcus was directing the layout of the sheet-shrouded bodies of the fallen. Nick steeled himself before he walked with Robin to join the older Valkyrie.

"I'm glad to see the two of you." Marcus looked them both up and down. "We were lucky. We only lost a few of our own. But even one was still too many."

"Where's Chris?" Nickolas looked across the dusty ground at the milling Valkyries. Most were blinking and shading their eyes.

"I have the injured gathered by the fence over there." Marcus pointed to the other side of the square. "We still need to organize a group to go in and finish sweeping the tunnels."

The low rumble of shifting gears reached their ears, and the three of them turned to the remnants of the front gate. A moment later, a fleet of buses came into view down the road. At least fifteen of them proceeded up through the open valley until they pulled into the grounds. The milling Valkyries made way for them. With a hiss of breaks, they rocked to a stop, then the door to the lead bus opened and Jules jumped down the steps.

Surprised, Nick broke away from his father and Robin. Laughing, he clasped arms with his friend and ex-recovery team member. "I'm so glad to see that you made it out of the Facility, Jules."

"Same here. Where's Chris?"

Nick's face fell, and he looked across the compound. "He's with the injured. I don't know how bad it is yet."

Jules squeezed his shoulder before saying, "Let's go find out."

"Wait." A second man descended from the bus. His short brown hair shifted in the early morning air. "Not yet, Nickolas. We have some things to discuss first."

Something about this one made Nick's hackles rise.

"Jared, give the man a break. Let him see to his brother first."

Eyeing the new arrival, Nick addressed Jules. "You go; keep an eye on him for me, please. Let me know what you find out?"

"All right, Nick."

Nickolas could see the reluctance in Jules's eyes, but he walked over to the makeshift triage area.

Nick turned back to the man from the bus and sized him up. A compact body that hid the strength of his muscles. "So, you're Jared?"

"Yes."

"And that means?"

"That you answer to me."

A growl rumbled in Nick's throat. "I don't think so."

"I'm Luther's Second, Nickolas. You answer to me."

Nick stared into Jared's blue eyes, but the man didn't flinch. Very few could maintain eye contact with Nick when he pressed like this. A ripple of premonition slid fingers of ice down his spine. The growl in his chest grew and the corners of Jared's lips twitched. It was the arrival of Jessica that broke the dominance.

Jessica's anger pushed ahead of her arrival and Nick ducked her first punch easily then caught her fist in one hand, quickly spinning her until he had her back pulled up against his chest, his arms wrapped about her. She struggled for a moment, but Nick bit down on her neck and her body went pliant, though she growled softly.

After a moment, he relaxed his hold on her neck and kissed the spot, raising his eyes to meet Jared's through wisps of Jessica's hair. The newcomer watched the proceedings with veiled curiosity.

"It's nice to see you too, Jess, though you should be more careful of your injured arm. It isn't up to attacking people."

"If you ever do anything like that again, Nickolas, I'll kill you. Robin was just fine without your help."

"You were injured. You couldn't come with me."

"I don't care. It wasn't necessary for you to take the chance. Don't think that I couldn't tell you were fighting Gabriel."

He rubbed his face in her hair then felt her shift her wings against his chest so he let her go slowly—watching to make sure she was finished attacking him. Robin and Marcus walked up, both trying to hide their grins with little success.

The exchange allowed him to regain some of his equilibrium, so Nickolas turned his attention back to Jared. On closer inspection, Nickolas could see how the grounded held his body in readiness for whatever they might throw at him. He was tense but not afraid. *He's confident in his abilities. We need to watch him.*

Twining his fingers with Jessica's, Nick shook his hair out of his eyes. "I answer to no one," he reiterated.

Jared folded his arms across his chest and leaned back against the bus. "You answered to Ian."

"Ian's dead."

"That's not the point. You are capable of taking orders. You have an agreement, Nickolas."

The persuasive tone that entered Jared's voice told Nick that he had changed tactics. "What does he want?"

"You already know the answer to that, or at least think you do."

"Then spell it out."

"He wants you and Jessica," he nodded his head in her direction, "and Jays, Kieran, and any of the other Valkyries to come back to a new Facility that is being built. You will need to work out the rest with the general yourself." He pushed away from the bus, and Nickolas watched him stare out over the crowd before he turned to Marcus. "Marcus, Luther has been content to leave all of you in peace, but we expect Nickolas to uphold his agreement."

"I don't like being threatened," his father said.

"I wasn't threatening." The unspoken promise hung in the air until Jared clucked his tongue and shook his head. "Look, this doesn't need to be so difficult. Until the new buildings are complete, we have provided emergency food and supplies to see all of you through the next several weeks in Aurora. But there is one more condition."

Warily Marcus asked, "What?"

"Most of the drivers are professional psychologists. They are to come with and do evaluations on everyone."

"Unacceptable," Marcus snapped.

"Shrinks," Nickolas groaned at the same time.

"I don't want strangers with unknown agenda's poking into Aurora."

"Sorry, Marcus, but this is a nonnegotiable item. Many of these people are going to be traumatized. They will need help."

"I can understand that, Jared. But you implied that my people are to be subjected to this too."

"Some of your people have been *here* Marcus," Jared pointed out. "Besides, we need a baseline of healthy personalities to compare to."

"I don't like it."

"We didn't imagine you would. Nickolas, they want to speak with you as well."

"Won't that be fun?" he replied sarcastically. "What else?"

"Nothing for now. I have enough people to secure this facility and deal with the injured and dead. I'll get started on that, Marcus, while you get everyone sorted out and loaded onto the buses. Then we can take you home."

"Home," Nickolas repeated; as he looked out at all of the people, he realized that he didn't have one. And probably never would.

Gabriel sat with Zach and watched the buses pull away from his decimated home on the remote monitor. Pet was curled up asleep on the mats they'd set on the floor next to the fireplace. He'd found this old line shack several years ago a few miles outside of the compound. It was small, with only one room. Designed as a seasonal shelter for the ranchers that used to roam the vast expanses after their cattle. He had slowly set it up with everything he would need in the unlikely event that he had to flee.

"It looks like they left an occupying force behind. I don't think we can go back."

Grunting an agreement, Gabriel glared at the images. "Damn, I'm going to miss my bathtub." He stood and went to look out the window. The midmorning light streamed in. "We will give them a few hours. After Pet has had a rest, we'll start the flight for the Facility. I think we should be able to get there before tomorrow morning."

"Will she be strong enough for an extended flight?"

"We'll help her. Go and get some rest too. I'll wake you when it's time to go."

♦ ♦ ♦

"Gabe, I need to rest."

"She's faltering, Gabriel! Her wings are giving out," Zach shouted.

Gabriel dropped back to come up behind and under Pet. He scooped her up just as her wings collapsed. "Come on, we're almost there," he said softly into her ear.

The moon was setting as they landed in the remains of the courtyard next to the burned out hulk of the Hub. Most of the debris had been cleared away, but there were still scorch marks where the destroyed section had been connected to the rest of the Facility. He set Pet on her feet and turned her over to Zach with orders to follow but stay quiet and out of the way.

He brushed past some of the night guards and marched straight to General Kratz's quarters. Arriving at the general's suite, Gabriel cocked his head at the two guards stationed at the door. *I guess he's starting to be afraid. Must not be as stupid as I always believed.*

"I need to see Kratz."

"Gabriel, it's three in the morning," one of them said.

"How does the time change my need to see him?"

"He's asleep."

"Do you want to wake him or shall I?"

The other guard pinched the bridge of his nose and shook his head. "Fine. I'll go wake him."

A minute or two later, the guard opened the door and waved them in. The general, his florid complexion looking sallow in the single light that shone on the desk, yawned as he sat down in his desk chair. "This had better be good, Gabriel."

The sound of a squealing pig replaced the general's words in his mind, and Gabriel felt his spirits lift with the thought. "I need to cancel tomorrow night's games. Someone needs to go out and fix all of the doors in the compound, and I have a lot of data on the amount of force a light weaver can expend on doors."

"Cancel the games? You woke me up for that?" the general shouted. "We can't cancel. There are some very important people arriving for them tomorrow."

Knocking interrupted the beginning of his tirade and an aide rushed inside. "Sir!"

"What?"

"I have the information you just requested. The holding compound was attacked and closed down this morning."

"Attacked? Luther has to be behind this." The general turned to look at Gabriel.

Shrugging, Gabriel ignored the question in the general's eyes. "Well, I did just tell you that I had a lot of data on what a light weaver could do, didn't I?"

Spluttering, the general turned to the aide. "I want people out there assessing the damage. I want answers. What happened, and who's responsible."

The aide went scurrying out, and the general turned to look at him. "And you. You are to remain within the Facility until further notice. Now get out of my sight."

Gabriel gave him a mocking bow then turned and ushered Zach and Pet out of the room.

"Well that was fun, Gabriel. Now what?"

"I don't remember giving you leave to talk, Zach." His mind racing, Gabriel led them through the halls to his quarters here in the Facility and started contemplating that exact question. Now what?

Chapter Twenty One

The warm spring sun shining down on his head felt good after the cold winter. Marcus turned his face up into it, letting it wash over him and soothe the stresses of the last several months. He stood on the cliff that overlooked the valley and the hive-like busyness taking place below him. The scents of the early spring flowers floated on the breeze, and the soft green of the new leaves from the Indian plums and salmonberries painted the view. A few minutes ago, he'd watched a helicopter land; the sight reminded him of just how much had changed for them all.

The future, ever uncertain, was even more unsure now, and that took a toll on every individual. With the overcrowding within the valley, Marcus found himself searching out places of solitude like this more and more often. Full integration would never happen, though. Too many were damaged or belonged to Nickolas and Jessica.

Finally spying Jared on the path up the cliff, Marcus waited. It had been six weeks since Luther's proxy had left. *Too bad he hadn't taken all the rest of those annoying people with him too.* The man was making good time in the ascent, and Marcus was reluctantly impressed with the grounded. *He's in good shape. He could maybe keep up with us. He might make a good Valkyrie someday...if we could get him to follow orders.*

During the time Jared had spent in the valley, he had slowly won a portion of Marcus's trust. The man was strong willed and cocky, enough like an Alpha Hunter for Marcus to know how to deal with him. Strong enough that Nick was wary around him. But what really decided it for Marcus was watching Jared's ethics and honor that he lived by unconsciously. It showed in the way he treated the injured and maimed. In how he treated Jessica and the other Facility Valkyries…and even Nick, for all they butted heads.

Jared crested the cliff face and grinned before looking out over the valley. "Nice view you have."

"Yes, we like it. Didn't take you long to find me."

"Saw you up here when I came in to land." Jared turned back to him, and Marcus saw his eyes twinkle before he said, "I brought in a truckload of flowers for the wedding. I hope Jessica likes them."

"That was thoughtful of you. Afraid you wouldn't be welcome without a bribe?"

"The thought had crossed my mind. It's not like they want to come home."

Snorting, Marcus said, "I suspect she will love them."

They fell silent for a few minutes before Jared continued. "The workmen have almost finished the first stage of renovations on the new accommodations in Seattle. The living quarters will be complete in a week. General Faulk wishes the residents to be ready to move in then."

Marcus closed his eyes and tried to hide his mixed feelings. He didn't wish to lose his sons so soon, but their presence was also causing contention among the permanent residents of his valley. The sooner everyone was settled, the better. "Nickolas is going to love hearing that," he said cynically.

Snorting, Jared agreed. "I imagine Jessica is just as enthusiastic about her relocation. So how has everyone been adjusting? Not just the freed Valkyries, but all of you?"

Marcus shrugged his shoulders as he looked out over his valley, not seeing anything. "We lost a few. Suicides."

"Not really surprising, is it?"

"No, I suppose not." He looked up at the sky and blinked his eyes to clear them. "A couple of them were friends that had been recaptured early on."

"I'm sorry to hear that."

Marcus shrugged then continued. "Our doctors have repaired what damage they could, but several people have been permanently maimed by the torture they endured."

He saw Jared close his eyes, the only sign that what he heard affected him. "While I'm here, the general wishes me to pick up the assessments. They want to have a feel for the stability of the community as a whole before we open up the Sandpoint complex. They were also hoping that you would consent to send copies of your medical files. Maybe there's something one of them can find to help some of these people's physical damage."

"I'll talk to Beth. I can't guarantee that she will be willing to turn them over."

Jared's expression remained neutral, then he asked, "So, have they decided? Who's going to be accompanying Nickolas?"

Part of the uncertainty that had driven Marcus to seek the solitude of the cliffs came rushing back. In some ways, the possibility of losing Robin was worse than his own blood sons. He didn't have the heart to influence Robin's decision though. "The final count isn't in, but it looks like most of the Facility Valkyries will stay with Nickolas. A few of my people are drawn to the Alpha pair and have approached me with the desire to join them as well. None of the newly freed are willing to even get close to something resembling a facility situation. They wish to remain here."

"What are we looking at? A couple hundred?"

"Closer to seventy-five, if you're lucky."

"Out of seven hundred."

"What do you people expect? None of us are thrilled at the idea of being controlled by you. No matter the type of leash."

Marcus watched Jared take a breath and relax his shoulders. "The numbers are fine. So long as Nickolas, Jessica, Kieran, and Jays are among them. And the invitation is still open for all of you. General Faulk hopes to maintain open relations with Aurora. He's hoping you will feel free to come and utilize the space he has set up, allowing all of you an opportunity to reintegrate into society."

Pursing his lips, Marcus shook his head slowly. "It's tempting, Jared, but I'm not sure. We've been out of the world for a long time. There will be some level of communication between us, that's certain; but how much? I don't know yet. We can't change the fact that we've been found. Luther knows the location of our valley. And now, so does Gabriel. But what about the others in the Facility? We've lived in secrecy for so many years to protect our safety that it might just be a habit. Then again, it might still be necessary. What is there to stop one of them from attacking us on their own? There are too many heads and arms to the Facility for me to completely trust Luther's protection. Aurora's location may have been exposed, but we still have more defenses here than we would there. I won't stop protecting my people."

"Well, you will be welcome, Marcus."

"Thank you." He turned back to the hustle and bustle down below and smiled. "We have a wedding in a couple of hours. We should probably head down and help get ready."

Jays prepped the slide then set it aside to dry and started on the second one. "We have plenty of time, Beth. They don't need our hands, and what we're doing is important. So don't stress so much."

She blew her hair out of her eyes and continued rolling the bandages she was preparing. "I should feel old, Jays. My eldest son is getting married today. Yet, I don't feel the age. My body still feels like it did twenty years ago."

The statement caught his attention, and he stopped what he was doing to look up at Beth. "What do you mean?"

She tucked the neatly rolled strips of cloth into a drawer then pulled out the next and started going through its contents. "I don't know, Jays. Just that I don't feel old. Shouldn't I at least be feeling a little creaky or something? I'm fifty-six years old. But I still feel thirty."

He cocked his head as he studied her. "Your and Marcus's group are the oldest living Valkyries besides Gabriel. It might be good to do a full work-up on your group if we can. Just to see how the mutation has handled the passage of time."

Beth looked up and met his eyes. He could see curiosity and something else in their depths. "We'll see. After everyone is settled, we can talk about it, Jays."

He held her eyes for a moment then turned back to his slides. "Ok."

They worked in silence for a few minutes, then Beth said, "It is strange for it to be so quiet in here now."

"It was a full house for quite a while, wasn't it? I'm glad we were able to help as many as we did."

"It still wasn't enough."

"Maybe not, but it was better than none of them." Jays took one of his slides and placed it into the microscope.

"I'm just still so frustrated to not be able to do anything for Edana. Why can't we get her to wake up? All physical injuries have healed. All residual drugs have worn out of her system. What is keeping her locked up? I don't know how long we'll be able to keep her alive in the coma she's in now. We don't have all of the equipment we need for this type of situation. We need Kieran."

Placing his eye to the scope, Jays adjusted the dials, bringing it into focus. "He's not ready, Beth. You know that."

"I know. And that's another thing I'm worried about. Kieran's got some problems, Jays, and no one has had any time to help him because he's not physically bleeding. But his emotional wounds aren't healing."

"I am very aware of that, Beth. Nick told me some of what happened during the rescue. Donald has always been an emotional anchor for Kieran. He got Kieran through his isolation. Kept him alive and sane when Ian didn't think he'd make it. Of course Kieran isn't going to respond well to his death. And now he's not only grieving but dealing with the consequences of using his talent to kill. I don't think he trusts himself anymore. And I have no clue how to go about getting him back in the saddle again."

Beth slammed the drawer shut and sighed. "Me either. And until we figure it out, Edana is going to stay in limbo, I think. I've tried everything I can think of so far."

"We just need to keep working on him. Get him to..." Jays trailed off and adjusted the scope again. Hissing, he quickly grabbed the second sample and replaced the first one. "No way," he breathed.

Beth had come up next to him, alerted by his response. "What is it?"

"I know what's wrong with Jess now."

"What? I checked for everything, but it all came back negative. I couldn't find anything to explain her lethargy."

"I need Jessica and Nick here now." *Nickolas. I need to see both you and Jessica in sick bay, please. Right away.*

"What is it, Jays?"

"I'm not surprised you didn't think to check for this, Beth. You haven't spent as much time with them as I have."

Jays we're a little busy right now, can't this wait?

No, Nick. I want both of you here now.

All right, we're coming.

"Jays..." Beth said, irritated.

"They'll be here in a minute." He looked back into the microscope to double check what he had seen then pushed his chair away. "Here, what do you think?"

She gave him a strange look but took his seat, placing her eye to the scope. Adjusting the dials, she froze. "Is that..."

"Yes." The door to the outside opened and a waft of warm air drifted in.

"Ok, Jays, we're here. What was so important that you had to stop our rehearsal?"

He exchanged a look with Beth before he turned to face the pair. "Um." He ran his hand through his hair as he stared at them both for a second. "I...ah..." He cleared his throat and tried again. "I've figured out why you haven't been feeling so well lately, Jess. You're pregnant."

Silence.

Then Jessica blindly groped for a chair and sank into it. Nickolas knelt down in front of her, and Jays heard him softly say, "He did say it would happen."

Her eyes blank, she nodded. "I know, but it's still a shock."

Beth's hand rested on Jays's arm. "You're right, I wasn't remembering their caste, that was not something I thought to check for. We're going to need to get an ultrasound device."

"Jays," Nickolas said. "Let's keep this quiet. I don't want Jared to know and tell Luther. Obviously, we won't be able to keep it a secret forever, but the longer we do, the better."

"Right, Nick." He pulled a chair up then sat down in front of them. "We have no idea what to expect. You've been extremely tired lately, and this definitely accounts for your diet change. It looks like you're going to need and want red meat even more than during your isolation. The best we can do is treat your pregnancy like a normal woman's until we know more."

"What do I do now?"

"For today, just try to forget about it and enjoy your party. We can talk about it in more detail over the next couple of days, ok?"

"Sure." She rose from the chair and shook her wings out. "How far along am I?"

"About six weeks, it looks like. That's my best guess at the moment."

"Wow. I can barely take this in."

Nickolas stood behind her and kneaded her shoulders. "Don't worry, Jess." He leaned down, brushing a kiss on her neck. "One step at a time. We'll take it one step at a time." Nickolas wrapped his arms around her. "On a different subject, have you been able to find out what's wrong with Chris? He's avoiding everyone and neither of us can reach him through the link."

He turned to look at Beth. She shook her head. "His physical injuries have healed," she said. "He was deemed flight worthy a week ago, but the trauma of watching his Second killed is still with him. I can heal his body but not his mind. The only mind healer we have is too injured himself to be of use right now."

"Kieran isn't showing any improvement?" Nickolas asked.

"Not yet. He's still withdrawn."

Nick closed his eyes and rested his chin on Jessica's shoulder. "We'll have to deal with it after things have settled down. Today, we have a celebration to attend."

"And they're waiting for us, Nick." Jessica patted his hands resting on her waist. "We'd better get back."

"Thank you for letting us know, Jays."

"No problem, Nick. We'll see you at the ceremony."

His muscles straining, Christoff pitched the forkful of manure out of the stall. Wiping the sweat out of his eyes, he scraped up the last forkful and dumped it in the wheel barrow then pushed the barrow out of the barn and made his way to the compost heap to dump the contents.

He left the wheel barrow in the doorway of the barn, hefted a bale of straw over to the empty stall, and split it open. After the stall was bedded, Chris retrieved the wheel barrow and started on the next stall.

Solitude.

He couldn't work in the ring anymore. This way he could exhaust his body and try to outrun his nightmares. But the others were noticing.

He knew what they thought. That he was damaged. Still hurt by his experiences at Gabriel's hands. And they would be right. But not in the way they all thought.

And he couldn't tell them why.

Oh, he had tried. Every waking moment, he tried. But the insidious voice slithered through his brain, and he couldn't defy it.

His muscles burned, and the sweat trickled down his back. Shivering his wings, he felt a cold draft across his skin. Stab the fork, lift, and pitch.

Stab the fork, lift, and pitch.

"Christoff," a voice called from the doorway of the barn. "Are you still in there?"

He ran his forearm across his forehead and called back, his voice rough. "Yeah."

The other Hunter stopped next to the full wheel barrow. "You're going to be late at this rate. You should go get cleaned up."

He turned back to his stall and replied, "I'll finish this one, then I'll go."

"That's what you said on the last stall," the Hunter muttered as he left.

Closing his eyes, Christoff took a deep breath. Phantom pain skittered through his body, and he pushed the memory away. He couldn't think about that. He especially couldn't think about Donald. Anger, pain, and confusion all raged around one thought. He knew it wasn't fair, wasn't right. Be he couldn't stop thinking it. *You got to escape, Donald. You got to escape.*

He snarled and threw the pitch fork then took the wheel barrow out to dump it again.

The Hunter was right, he would miss the wedding. He was glad for his brother and Jessica. Their happiness was the most important thing in his life. He wished he could share in it. He should have been able to share it.

He dropped the wheel barrow with a clang back in front of the stall then resumed his cleaning.

The sound of wings rustling a few minutes later made him aware of a new watcher. He pitched another forkful while he waited for his brother to make the first overture.

"You ok, Chris?" Nickolas asked softly.

No, Nicky, I'm not. Please help me, he pleaded silently. Scraping the bedding into a pile, he fought himself, trying to make his voice say the words. The twisting snake coiled, strangling his free will. "Sure, Nick, I'm fine."

Out of the corner of his eye, Christoff saw Nick fold his arms on the top of the stall wall and study him. "I'm not sure I believe you, Chris. You've been avoiding practices since you were declared recovered enough to work again. What's up?"

"I'm just not ready yet, ok?" He stabbed the fork into the floor and turned to look at his brother. "I'm trying, Nickolas."

"If there's anything you need, just ask. When you're ready to talk, I'm here."

Chris lowered his head and looked at the ground, hiding the spasm of pain.

"Are you up to being in the wedding, Chris? Jessica and I both want you there, but if you can't, we understand."

"I want to do it."

"Good. I'm glad to hear it."

They were silent for a moment, and Chris pulled the fork out of the ground.

"I have some good news, Chris. We don't want to tell anyone yet. We want to keep it from Luther and the rest of the Facility as long as possible. Jays just discovered that Jessica is pregnant."

Jerking his head up, he met Nickolas's eyes. "No," he whispered. His mind skittered in disbelief and fear. *Don't tell me, Nicky. Don't!*

"Yes." His brother's eyes shone with happiness. It was a happiness unshadowed by the pain that had been haunting Nickolas for so long now. "We haven't told anyone else, but you're my brother, and I wanted to share it with you. I thought maybe it would help perk you up."

Feeling a smile stretch his mouth, Chris heard himself say, "That's wonderful news, Nick, congratulations." But inside, he was howling. The well of despair deepened.

"I'm glad I could make you smile again, Chris." Nickolas straightened away from the wall and stretched his wings. "We have an hour before the start of the ceremony. You should probably go get a shower."

Nodding his head, Chris replied, "Let me finish this stall first."

"Ok, see you in the field." He waved on his way out of the barn.

Christoff took a deep breath. Unfortunately, it didn't suppress the self-loathing or pain. *Damn you, Donald. I hate you. This is your fault. How could you leave me to do this? If you had stayed home, this never would have happened to me. If you had stayed home, you'd still be alive.* Tears burned in his eyes. Christoff bent down and slowly pulled the knife out of his boot. *Why did you have to tell me, Nicky? Why? Now I'll have to tell Gabriel. It's just a little baby. A little baby.*

He placed the knife hilt against the wooden stall wall and pressed his bare chest against it. A tiny pinprick of blood welled up, and that was where his muscles froze.

Do it! Just do it! he screamed to himself. But, like all of the other times since his rescue, he couldn't force his body to his command. Dropping the knife, it fell with a dull thud to the dirt, and he followed it down, his head resting in his hands.

"I hate you," he whispered, not sure if he was referring to Donald, himself, or Gabriel. "I hate you."

The sight and scent of flowers surrounded Jessica. Breathing in, she let happiness fill her and made an effort to push the troubles and uncertainty away. She carried new life. The realization stunned her. A new life. Along with a new hope for their future.

It was still an uncertainty, but this one was nice at least. *I have no idea what to do with a baby.* She shook her head and refocused on the flowers. They were beautiful. Someone must have told Jared how much she had wanted flowers.

The little sneak. If he thinks that this will change my opinion of him, he can think again. But she still felt a softening of her attitude toward him. With a sigh, she bent down, and cupping a soft white rose in her hand, she inhaled its sweet scent. More types of flowers than she could name filled the arrangements on the buffet tables. More were tied as garlands to decorate the arbor that had been erected.

All of the arrangements had been taken out of her hands. She laughed to herself. She was just the entertainment, a doll to be dressed and posed. And really, she was just as glad that she hadn't needed to do anything. As the first Valkyries to form this type of bond, the ceremony had become a symbol for everyone, not just her and Nick.

They'd at least run some of the ideas by her so she wouldn't find herself abhorring their choices. So she found herself wearing a lovely skirt that swished around her ankles in a soft shade of yellow. The top draped around her wings and fluttered in the breeze. Nickolas wore a complementing outfit, both embroidered with beautiful designs done in green, blue, and red. More of the flowers formed a circlet in her hair.

Well, let them have their fun. I can enjoy today knowing I have the greatest surprise of all. She smiled and wandered around, looking at all of the arrangements. It really was how she'd dreamed it would look like as a girl. The cake was covered in fresh fruit and yet more flowers.

The septs in charge of taking care of the food had just started carrying it out, arranging it beautifully on the tables. Nerves jittered along her spine. It was almost time. The field had been nearly empty when she came out to look at the display, but now it was filling up fast.

"You look beautiful."

She suppressed a squeak of surprise, and Robin laughed behind her as he rested his hands on her shoulders.

"Mom and Dad would be proud," he whispered in her ear. "And so am I."

Swallowing the lump in her throat, she turned in his arms and laid her head against his chest. "I'm scared, Robin."

"What?" he said teasingly. "You can't be getting cold feet."

She shook her head. "No, of course not. It's just that I...I don't want to go to Seattle." His arms tightened around her, and she closed her eyes, forcing the tears back.

"I wish you didn't have to either." He was silent a moment. "I won't be going, Jessica."

Not surprised, she nodded her head. He raised her chin with his hand. "I'm sorry. I just don't belong with you guys. I belong to Marcus."

"And I never did."

He smiled slightly. "No. You never did." He kissed her forehead. "You'll still be seeing me, though. I plan to make regular visits. And you had better make trips out here, or I'll come take a piece out of your hide."

Sniffing, she agreed.

"Come on, Marcus sent me to collect you. They are ready to get started."

Her nerves coming back with a vengeance, she followed her brother as he led her through the gathering crowd of people. Almost every known Valkyrie on the planet was present here in the valley, standing witness. The guests also included the grounded who had come with them after the rescue.

And Jared Roberts.

That last came with strings she really didn't like. *He's as bad as one of the Hunters.* She thought of his dominance and "I'm right" attitude.

They wove through the throng, and Robin led her to the arbor where Marcus stood. Behind the Auroran Alpha, arrayed in a half circle, were the Primes and their Seconds. Kelley stood in Robin's place with Leslie as her Second. Jess stopped in front of Marcus, and Robin took a place on her left, a step behind her. Nickolas arrived from a different direction and took his place next to her with Chris flanking him on his right. All rumble of conversation ceased.

Marcus smiled at both of them then spread his wings, raising his hands in the air. "Welcome, everyone," he called. "Today the clans have gathered to witness the bond between Nickolas Sinclair and Jessica Reuther. This is a starting point for our species. Over time we will build traditions and ceremonies that are uniquely our own. I am honored as Alpha of Aurora Valley to preside over them today. The first mated pair of Valkyries to emerge. May there be many more in our future." He lowered his arms and folded his wings. "Today's honor should have belonged to Ian, as Nickolas's Alpha, may he rest in peace." A moment of silence followed his statement.

Beside her, Nickolas chuckled, and Marcus shot him a glance to silence him. Jess caught her mate's eye and smirked. *I'll need to remember to ask what Ian said.*

Clearing his throat, Marcus continued. "In his stead, I ask, who stands for each? So that the family and clans may know this is a bond freely given."

Robin stepped forward. "I stand as Jessica's brother; this is a bond freely given and freely taken."

Christoff stepped forward. "As Nickolas's brother and Second, I stand; this is a bond freely given and freely taken."

"Who wishes to join with the nucleus of the new clan and stand as witness?"

Several Valkyries stepped forward, Kieran in the lead. "I stand as Seer Prime," he said. "With Jays as Second." They took places behind her, mirroring the Primes from Aurora.

Dev and Aiden came next. "I stand as Caster Prime," Dev stated, "with Aiden as Second."

"I stand as Hunter Prime," Dylan said, "with Chelsea as Second."

After they were all arrayed behind Nick and Jessica, Marcus turned and accepted a knife from Kelley. He held it out across his palms as he turned back to them. Jessica watched the sun glint off the steel. "With the drawing of our blood, our power can combine, entwining together to form one entity where there had been two, each stronger than they were singly. The purpose to form a nucleus and a new clan is formed."

He took the knife by the hilt and stepped forward. Nickolas held out his right arm. Marcus used the sharp tip of the blade and flicked a cut in the join where Nick's wrist and palm met. The blood quickly welled up.

Marcus turned to her, and she looked into the Alpha's eyes and held out her wrist. The stinging pain burned her wrist, and she drew in her breath. At a nudge from Robin, she turned to Nick, who was already raising his wrist to her mouth. She pressed her own to Nick's mouth and closed her eyes as his power flowed through her.

It wasn't nearly as intense as their true binding. More of a reaffirmation of sorts. She lowered her arm, and Nickolas gave her an encouraging smile. *Almost done, love.*

She sighed then turned with Nickolas to face their Primes and the crowd of watchers. Christoff stepped in front of them to kneel on the ground. First, Nickolas presented his wrist. After Chris took a token amount, she presented hers.

Kelley stepped forward with the knife and cut a nick in Christoff's wrist. After the offering, she pulled a green strip of cloth from her belt and bound Chris's cut, then he returned to his place at Nickolas's side.

Nathan stepped forward, accepting the knife from Kelley, and he in turn nicked both Kieran and Jays, binding each of them with a blue strip of cloth when the exchange was complete.

Kevin did the honors for Dev and Aiden, binding them with red.

Kelley took back the knife and sliced Dylan and Chelsea, binding them with green for the Hunters.

Starting to feel a little woozy after all of the people who had just invaded her mind, Jessica almost didn't notice Robin gently wrapping her dripping wrist with a white cloth to staunch the flow. She shook her head and looked at the people gathered before her. Her new clan. Her friends. They looked back, their eyes glazed from the binding. She knew they would all stand before her if there was ever danger. She hoped it would never come to that.

She smiled at Robin as he finished tying off the cloth then looked at it and saw that it wasn't just white. It had a weaving down the center, a braid of all the other colors used.

Chris moved to stand next to Kieran, and Robin stepped back with the Primes of his clan. The wind as Marcus opened his wings behind them stirred her hair.

"Who stands as witness to the bonding of Nickolas and Jessica?" he called out.

The deafening thunder of nearly eight hundred voices echoed across the valley. "Witnessed!"

Jessica caught the shock flash through Jared's eyes as the Valkyries' response caught him off guard. He saw her studying him and smoothed his expression.

After the reverberations died down, Marcus declared, "May I now present to you the newly mated Alpha pair, Nickolas and Jessica. You can now kiss the bride, Nicky."

Laughter and cheers circled around the valley, and Nickolas brushed his fingers across her cheek before he lifted her chin. He lowered his mouth to hers, and she closed her eyes when she felt his tongue lightly trace her lips. Losing herself in the kiss, the sounds of bawdy encouragement disappeared and all she could feel was Nickolas surrounding her, the pathways in their minds open, their power twining together.

"Enough already. Or do you need to get a room this early in the day?"

Blushing, she pulled away from Nickolas to glare at Robin. Her brother kissed her on the cheek then clapped a laughing Nickolas on the shoulder. She narrowed her eyes at her mate.

Just when she'd decided he deserved her elbow in the gut, he stepped away, a knowing glint in his eye. A grin broke free, acknowledging his tactical maneuver, and she turned to the other well-wishers that were coming up to her. She accepted a hug and kiss from both Beth and Marcus.

"Thank you, Marcus. It was a lovely ceremony."

He ran a hand down her hair, a wistful smile in his eyes. "I just hope that Jennifer and Andrew were able to see, Jess."

She swallowed the unexpected lump in her throat and nodded, and they stepped away, making room for Kieran.

"It wasn't so hard the second time around." Kieran smiled, though Jess noticed that it didn't reach his eyes. "Your blood is potent." He took her hands and looked down at them. "I'm happy for you, Jess. Promise me you will stay safe, all right?"

Tugging her hands, she drew him into a hug. He clung to her, and she stroked his hair. She quickly thought back over the last several weeks and realized that this was the first time she had seen Kieran allow anyone to touch him. Concerned, she made a mental note to bring it up with Nick later. "You're stuck with me now, Kieran, so you had better get used to it. I don't plan on going anywhere."

His shoulders relaxed and he pulled away. This time a small smile reached his eyes. "Good."

"Hey, out of the way, no hogging the Alpha female," a voice bantered.

Raising his hands, he backed away before Dev had a chance to touch him. "She's all yours."

Dev cast a quizzical look at Kieran as he left, and Jessica shook her head, silently telling him to let Kieran be for now. He and Aiden each gave her a peck on the cheek.

"Did you like our wedding present?" Aiden asked.

His hopeful tone made her glance at Dev for clarification.

"The weather. We made sure you would have sun."

Understanding dawned and she beamed at Aiden. "It was wonderful, thank you."

At a light touch to her shoulder, she turned around. Chris stood behind her, his face strained, though she could tell that he tried to hide it.

"I need to go, Jess." He picked her up off the ground in a big hug. "Congratulations," he whispered in her ear.

She pulled back and looked into his face, certain that he wasn't referring to her wedding. The sadness deep down in his eyes made her heart ache for him.

Reaching up, she kissed him on the cheek. "It's all right, Chris. If you have to go, go. But put me down first."

He smiled slightly as he set her down. "Thanks, Jess."

Watching him walk through the crowd, her spirits dipped. Nickolas slipped up behind her, wrapping her in his arms and resting his head on her shoulder. "I don't know how to help him, Jess."

"Me neither."

Before they could get too depressed, the next well-wisher paused before them. She looked up into Jared's tan face, and Jessica felt Nick tense ever so slightly against her back.

Jared acknowledged their wariness with a nod. "Did you like the flowers, Jessica?"

Annoyed that he had figured out how to get on her good side, she wrinkled her nose at him. "Yes, thank you. They are lovely." He studied her, and she could see his uncertainty in the depths of his eyes. "I do mean it. They were exactly what I always dreamed of."

Relief passed through his eyes, but he quickly suppressed it. "You're welcome."

Then he smoothed his face completely as he reached into his pocket. "General Faulk gave me a present for you."

She held out her hand so Jared could drop something into it. It was a skeleton key tied with a scarlet ribbon. Hissing, she tried to drop it, but Nick stayed her hand, closing her fingers over it.

"The base in Seattle will be completed enough for you to take residency by the end of the week. Do you wish to fly out, or would you like me to arrange transport?"

Irritation swarmed through her veins, but Nick squeezed her hand. "Settle, Jess. It's just Luther's way of trying to remind us that he thinks he's in control." Every sharp edge on the key dug into her skin, but Nickolas didn't let up as he addressed Jared. "I'll get in touch and let you know. I need to talk to the others and see what they want."

"Fair enough. We'll wait for your call."

A buzzing sound filled the air, and they all looked up. Jessica felt Nick tense, and suddenly all of the Facility Valkyries who had just bonded to them circled around. The mechanical sound grew louder, and Jess saw Robin lead a Wing t of Hunters into the air. A funny little plane crested the treetops rimming the valley.

"Is that an ultralight?" Dev asked.

"It sure looks like one," Marcus replied.

Robin and his Wing intercepted the aircraft and circled around it. Almost immediately, Robin broke off from the Wing and dropped down to land, a huge smile on his face.

Jessica watched the little craft as it was escorted down to a bumpy landing in the field a little ways away from the reception and whirred to a stop. Jessica caught her breath. A diminutive figure wearing a flight hat and goggles from a century ago unstrapped from the craft. Getting out, the pilot pulled the close-fitting leather cap off, stowing it in a bag strapped to the tube struts, and arranged a big floppy sun hat that matched her rainbow hued skirt in its place.

"May!" Jessica yelled, breaking away from Nickolas's hold. Behind her, she heard Marcus groan and her Valkyries shout at her to stop. Not heeding either, she raced through the grass to her guardian. May had waved at her call but had moved to the other side of the craft. She heard the sound of a happy dog bark, then Byron's body shot into view as he stretched his legs in a quick run.

"May! How did you get here?" she asked breathlessly.

Cocking her head, the little old woman turned to look at the machine then back at her.

Jessica shook her head, groaning, then clarified. "How did you know where we were?"

Her eyes twinkling, May pulled Jessica into a hug. "I know what you meant, dear. I've always known the way here." May kissed her cheek then pushed back and held her at arm's length to study her. "There, my dear, look at those beautiful wings. And your face looks happy again."

Byron, tongue lolling, came up to her, pressing against her leg. Absent-mindedly she reached down to pet the German Shepard's head. "I wasn't unhappy, May," she said, confused.

"Sure you were, girl. You just didn't realize it."

Not sure what to say to that, Jessica was relieved when Nick and all of the rest arrived. Pulling Nick forward, she introduced him to May.

With a smile, she patted his cheek. "You look even better in person. And you managed to catch my girl, so you're doing all right so far."

Robin pushed through and caught May up in a big hug, lifting her off the ground. "Put me down, you brute." She laughed, then kissed him on the cheek also. "You look good, Robin."

"Thank you, ma'am."

"Oh would you listen to those manners. Must be Beth's doing. Marcus wouldn't recognize good manners if they hit him upside the head."

"What?" The man in question spluttered. "May! What do you think you're doing arriving here like this? Alone?"

Firmly fixing a glare on her face, May pulled herself up to her full height, which barely brought her to Marcus's breast bone, and still the man shrank back a step. "Well, if you'd come and gotten me like I requested, I wouldn't have gotten tired of waiting, now would I? Calm your arse down, Marcus, I'm a fully qualified pilot, and you know it."

Surprised at the byplay between May and Marcus, Jessica looked at the crowd that had gathered around the ultralight. Beth was smiling, and her brother was trying somewhat unsuccessfully not to laugh, but the one who caught her attention was Jared.

His eyes were wide enough that they looked like they might just fall out of his head.

May turned in his direction and he glanced behind himself as if in disbelief that she was truly looking at him. He pulled himself to attention. Confused by his response, Jessica watched May step toward him. Silently, May looked him up and down.

"You'll do, lad. Tell Remy yes, but I'll let him know when."

Choking briefly, Jared finally got out a soft, "Yes, sir."

"May?" Marcus said in disbelief.

She turned away from the Facility agent, hooked her arm with Jessica's, and started leading her back toward the food at the reception. "Oh hush, Marcus. You don't know the half of it." Everyone fell in behind them.

They walked silently for a moment, then Jess asked softly, "Why did you turn me in?"

May glanced at her out of the corner of her eye. "How'd you figure it out?"

Jessica looked ahead. "The phone call. You knew where I was, and it was just too coincidental that you left suddenly the night the recovery team came for me."

Pain flashed across May's face. "It was necessary. Your mother and I discussed this. She was positive there was no other way to make everything else fall out in the best possible manner. You had to meet Nickolas, and the only way for that to happen was if you ended up in the Facility. If you had come here to change, none of the Facility Valkyries or the poor souls Kratz had in Eastern Washington would now be free."

Jess stumbled to a stop and thought about everything she'd gone through. Ian, Donald, those maimed and trying to learn to live again.

She looked at the woman who had raised her after her mother had died. The rest of the Valkyries except for Nickolas quietly skirted past the two of them. Nickolas placed a comforting hand on her shoulder.

"Jessica, you are where you need to be now, are you not?" May asked.

Nickolas squeezed her shoulder, and she remembered the lies, everything that had happened over the last six months. A lot of it had been bad, but there was also a lot of good in there too.

And now she carried new life.

The realization blossomed in her again.

May smiled as if she understood. "The old adage 'home is where the heart is' is a proverb for a reason, Jessica. There is usually a grain of truth in any saying. Just remember it doesn't matter where you live so long as you have your heart there. Then it's home." Byron walked up and sat at his mistress's feet.

Nick leaned in and said, "You are my heart."

Smiling, May held out her hand to both of them. "You'll do, lad, you'll do."

ABOUT THE AUTHOR

Siana Wineland lives in the beautiful, but soggy, Olympic Peninsula of Washington State. When she is not writing urban fantasy or paranormal romance she is spending her time shepherding her young children, or the goats and sheep she raises on their little farm. For updates on her writing, please visit her website at sianawineland.com or follow her on Twitter at twitter.com/sianawineland.